THE SON'S SECRET

Praise for Daryl Wood Gerber

"Readers will be shocked by this exciting,
fast-paced thriller's twists and turns"
Kirkus Reviews on *Girl on the Run*

"A savvy and energetic whodunit"
Kirkus Reviews on *Day of Secrets*

"Nonstop action and a surprise around every corner!
Will have you turning pages as fast as you can"
Hank Phillippi Ryan, award-winning author of
Her Perfect Life, on *Girl on the Run*

"Guaranteed to keep you on the edge of your seat"
Hilary Davidson, award-winning author of
Her Last Breath, on *Girl on the Run*

"A twisting tale of family secrets with a
shocking murder at its core"
Jamie Freveletti, bestselling author of the Emma
Caldridge series, on *Girl on the Run*

About the author

Daryl Wood Gerber is the Agatha Award-winning, nationally bestselling author of the Aspen Adams novels of suspense and standalones, as well as the Fairy Garden mysteries, the French Bistro mysteries, and the Cookbook Nook mysteries. Under the pen name Avery Aames, Daryl writes the Cheese Shop mysteries. Daryl loves to cook, read, golf, swim, and garden. She also likes adventure and has been known to jump out of a perfectly good airplane.

www.darylwoodgerber.com

To my son for bringing me such joy.

'Energy and persistence conquer all things'
—Benjamin Franklin

ONE

The alarm on my cell phone jolted me from my nightmare. I grabbed the phone from the bedstand. Reviewed the texts I'd sent my son a week ago. Tried not to panic. *Silence for a few days is normal, Maggie*, I reminded myself. *Normal.* Aiden was a senior in college. Independent. Forging his own path.

> April 1:
> Me: *How are classes going?*
> Aiden: *Fine. TTYL XO*

> April 2:
> Me: *How is the internship going?*
> Aiden: *OK. XO*

> April 3:
> Me: *How is Celine?*
> Aiden: *Mom, stop trying so hard. You made your decision. Talk soon. XO*

That one had caught me up short. Aiden could be succinct but never curt.

> April 5:
> Me: *Touching base.*
> Aiden:

> April 7:
> Me: *Knock, knock, you there?*
> Aiden:

Up until the last few days, all had seemed OK. What was going on? Throughout his life, we'd been able to talk about issues. See the reasoning behind things. He was nothing if not pragmatic.

I wrote him one more time. Willed him to reply even though it was early.

Me: *Hello? Everything OK?*

And then it came.

Aiden: *Taking off for a bit. Getting my head on straight.*

Taking off? Getting his head on straight?
'Crap.' I tossed my cell phone aside.
Chill, Maggie. Inhale, exhale, let go. He's young. Probably thinking about graduation.
The drone of the industrial fans on the ground floor of my late-Victorian period home shifted my angst to my other major concern – the overpowering smell of mildew that was pervading my senses. The remediation people said they'd sopped up every last lick of water from when the main plumbing line burst last week, but I was certain they hadn't. I'd have to contact them later. Tell them they needed to come back.

I lumbered out of bed, donned blue leggings, tank top, and zippered hoodie, and slipped on my favorite tennis shoes. I needed a cleansing run to kick my focus into gear before heading to my job at Pelican University. A run to rid me of the nightmare that had, yet again, invaded my sleep. The young student dead by his own hand. His tortured face. The crowd of sweaty college-aged football players watching on as they cheered *Bravo*.

Just as I reached for the front doorknob, my cell phone jangled. A frisson of dread spiraled down my spine. Was it Aiden? No. He only texted. Was it Provost Southington? Or our biggest donor, Gregory Watley? It wasn't my assistant. She knew not to disturb me before my first cup of coffee.

I hurried to the bedside table and scanned the display. *Josh*. The dread turned to irritation. When he moved out, all of the fond memories from our marriage – painting the rooms of our house, welcoming Aiden into the world, hiking trips, and more – evaporated. I stabbed Accept. 'Do you know what time it is?' I demanded. No preamble. No warmth.

'Maggie,' a woman said. Not Josh. 'I'm sorry to bother you. It's Tess Toussant.'

Tess. Josh's fiancée. The news about their engagement had stung more than I'd cared to admit. When Josh left me five years ago, it wasn't simply because he'd hated how much time I gave to my job – he dedicated himself to his career, too. No, it was because he'd found someone new. A woman who adored him and made him feel special. Not Tess. The first one's name was Allie. A year later, he dumped her and hooked up with Marianna. Now he was with Tess, twenty years his junior, like the others. But he hadn't asked the others to marry him.

'Joshua—' Tess stopped abruptly. Was she crying? 'Joshua . . .' she tried again.

During my last conversation with Josh a couple of months ago, he said he preferred to be called Joshua because it was hipper and classier. I didn't mention that my older brother Benjie, in his freshman year of high school, had told everyone to start calling him Benjamin, believing it would earn him more respect. It hadn't.

'What about him, Tess?'

'He's been shot,' she blurted. 'He's in the hospital.'

My breath snagged. 'Is it serious?'

'Yes, but the doctor said it was noncardiac penetrating. That means—'

'I know what it means.' The bullet hadn't hit his heart, but that didn't guarantee things couldn't go south. 'How did it happen?'

'He was ambushed.'

'Do the police know who did it?'

'Not yet. He's been investigating a case of corruption, but . . .' Tess sucked back tears.

Despite our break-up, I had always respected Josh's ability to hunt down the truth. He was fearless when it came to the consequences. His father, who'd also been a reporter until he died, had been equally intrepid.

'I want Aiden to see him,' Tess said, 'but he isn't answering his phone. I've left messages, but he hasn't responded.'

He'd just texted me. Why wasn't he answering his phone now? Had I been wrong not to worry about him? Wrong not to be the smothering mother he hated? Wrong to untether myself from the helicopter?

Maggie, get a grip.

I knew why I was overreacting. After my brother committed suicide, my mother checked out, and I'd made a pact with myself that when I became a mother, I wouldn't be like her. I would be in control. I would be present. My child would feel safe and loved.

Maybe Aiden went back to sleep after his acerbic reply to me, I told myself. The simplest explanation was usually the best one.

'It's early, Tess,' I said. 'School doesn't start for a while. His phone is probably on mute.'

'Could you follow up and have him call me? Please. I know you and Joshua don't get along—'

Don't get along? Understatement of the year. Two years after Josh and I married, I'd been an English professor at Tulane when I was offered the position of chair of the English department. Four years after that, Pelican came knocking. I'd told Josh it was an honor to be selected as the first female dean at the boutique college. He'd agreed. He didn't start taking potshots until a year later. When he did, they were doozies. And when I started to have less time for him, and when Aiden, who had become so involved with high school and his girlfriend, could no longer act as our buffer, Josh snapped. He was done. With me. With the marriage.

'The doctor is keeping him sedated,' Tess said. 'He says it'll help with the healing process.'

Josh. Devil-may-care, yang to my yin. Before Aiden came along, Josh and I had strolled to dinner holding hands. We'd sat on the porch every evening to discuss the problems of the world. We'd even solved a few. Once Aiden was born, we did everything as a family. Mardi Gras parades, graveyard tours, voodoo doll crafts. We had embraced every aspect of New Orleans' steeped-in-history culture. We'd laughed. We'd loved. Oh, how we'd loved.

I ran my fingers through my short hair and sighed. The day Josh left, I'd cut it.

'Aiden always returns Joshua's phone calls,' Tess said.

Of course he did. He adored his father.

'Do you think he's OK?' Tess asked.

'I'm sure he's fine,' I said, more to convince myself than her. His text said he was going to get his head on straight. Why? Not just graduation. What had set him off? I shuffled into the kitchen. Caught sight of a half-drunk bottle of wine on the counter. No, I would not pour myself a glass at six in the morning. Unlike my father, I had a modicum of restraint. 'Which hospital is Josh . . . *Joshua* in?'

'University Medical Center. A policeman has been assigned to protect him.'

I agreed to track down Aiden and ended the call.

'Coffee,' I said, under my breath. 'Must have caffeine.' I put a pod into the Keurig and set it to brew, then dialed Aiden's number.

His phone rang three times before going to voicemail. I listened through his brief message. 'Yo, it's Aiden. Be your creative self. Beep!' He chuckled after saying *beep*, so like my brother. How I wished they'd met.

'Aiden, it's me. Mom.' I clicked my tongue. 'Yeah, you probably know that. My name popped up on your screen. It's about . . .'

My throat went dry. Why were my nerves jangling? Because I didn't want to burn bridges. Because bad news needed to be said person to person, not left as a message.

Speak, Mags. 'Call me.'

I stabbed End, clapped the cell phone on the counter, and muttered, 'Where are you, my sweet, emotionally overwhelmed, artistic son?' Single-minded creativity was his go-to default response, not anger. Granted, he'd changed since he'd met Celine Boudreaux and married her. He hadn't exactly become distant, per se, but he wasn't as willing to confide in me as he'd been in the past. Sure, I'd expected us to grow apart as he aged. Many of my students experienced a deep-seated need for parental separation. Lately, whenever I asked Aiden if he needed to talk, his answer was *Yeah, sure, soon.*

I reread the last text exchange. No *XO*. Aiden always signed off with a kiss and hug. Was omitting the letters his way of being defiant?

Sure, he was upset with me for cutting off his funds. Got that. Money issues could be prickly, I told him. I tried to explain the perfect storm. The rising cost of my mother's living facility. My ten-year-old car biting the dust. The main plumbing line bursting in the house. The lapsed insurance because my business manager – my now fired business manager – had forgotten to pay the premium. The cash-out-of-pocket cost to repair the damage had literally put me under water. He said he understood, although he'd added that he thought I was doing it on purpose to prove a point. I wasn't.

I removed the mug of coffee from the Keurig and took a sip. And then I eyed the cell phone. Aiden was fine, I assured myself. After I'd informed him that, with all my other obligations, I was tapped out, I'd reminded him that he was married. He had a wife who'd graduated and had a good paying job. Plus he was weeks away from graduating himself, with a viable position in the works. It was time for them to start supporting themselves.

To be fair, up until then, I had paid for everything. Tuition. Housing. Books. Extra cash for fun. I'd never been good at saying *no*. His father had been quite deft at saying *no*, claiming his own father, Aiden's grandpa, hadn't helped him a whit. But I was a hoverer. A nurturer. OK, yes, dammit, a smotherer.

I studied his last text again, and unease scudded through me. *Why no XO?*

TWO

The lack of Aiden's signature sign-off felt passive-aggressive. He wasn't that way. He was candid. A communicator. Since birth, he'd been able to talk to me. About anything. His art, his projects, his dreams for the future.

Wrong, Mags. Not about anything. He'd kept his relationships private. And rightly so. A mother shouldn't know everything there was to know about a son, my best friend Gina advised. What mattered was if they were happy. Aiden told me he and Celine were blissful. I replied that, if that was the case, I was pleased for them.

Money. Why did so many friendships, marriages, or families struggle over money?

Cursing, I started typing a message to Aiden. Halfway in, I paused. I certainly couldn't text that his father had been shot. But I wasn't going to dial him a second time, either. I erased what I'd written and revised.

Me: *Call me. Urgent.*

Cup of coffee in hand, nostalgic for happier times, I opened the camera roll on my iPhone and viewed pictures of my recent weekend getaway at my friend's cabin, offered to me free of charge. A squirrel. A deer. Flowers with the most beautiful purple stripes. My chocolate donut impulse buy, up close and personal. No doubt about it, I was an amateur photographer, but I'd always had an eye for framing a subject. I caught a glimpse of the last picture of Aiden I'd taken, and against better judgment, typed his name into the search bar. Two months ago, while bored on a flight to a convention of deans overseeing southeastern and southern schools, I'd tagged all of my photographs.

Dozens of pictures of my son emerged. Aiden at ten, posing goofily in a painter's smock and beret. At fourteen, holding up an award for the Congressional Art Competition for high schoolers. At sixteen, with an award for the Scholastic Art and Writing award. Remembering how students in high school and earlier had bullied him for being an artist made my heart ache. They'd chided him for being too sensitive, like Benjie. I'd assured him that he'd forget their cruelty when he grew up because what he could do with pen and ink was incredible, as was the way he could manipulate digital images. He would be a huge success. They'd see.

I tapped the photo of him in his high school graduation gown, his mortarboard tilted jauntily to one side, his curly blond hair peeking from beneath. His girlfriend Keira stood beside him grinning. Keira, gone too soon from this world after being struck dead at a crosswalk toward the end of her sophomore year in college.

Emotions clogging my throat, I switched on the television to distract me. I selected the local news, muted the sound, and watched the scrolling highlights. Josh used to accuse me of being deaf because I played the TV too loudly. Maybe I had back then, to drown out the negative thoughts riding roughshod in my head.

I poured a dollop of cream into my coffee and added a teaspoon of sugar, anything to ease the sourness in my gut. Then I lifted my cell phone and typed an additional text to my son.

> Me: *Your father needs to talk to you. ASAP. You can ghost me but not him. Call him back.*

In the fall of his senior year in high school, Aiden announced that Keira wanted to go to Tulane, so he got it stuck in his craw that he wanted to, too. I said no, arguing that he'd received a preemptive offer from Pelican University with a partial scholarship. They had an excellent art program. But he pleaded. Tulane was better on the digital front, he said. With that kind of education, he would rock the digital world. And Keira wanted to go into politics. Tulane's poli-sci division won a comparison with Pelican hands down. Ultimately, I caved, knowing the only way he would find his confidence – find *himself* – was to let him do as he pleased. *He loves Keira*, Gina advised me. *Cut him some slack. Don't smother.*

Why hadn't my pal, a well-respected therapist, sensed the danger and warned me that Aiden might be so distraught after Keira's untimely death that he'd do something as impulsive as elope with another woman? OK, Celine, a graduate student and older than Aiden by a few years, wasn't just any other woman. She'd been one of Keira's best friends. Everyone knew that two grieving people who lost a loved one could bond after a great tragedy. Aiden fell for Celine. Hard. With concerted effort, I'd held my tongue, all the while wishing my son would slow down and see a therapist. Had he yet? Would he?

Run, Maggie. Shake it off.

I dumped my half-drunk coffee in the sink and headed out. My route rarely varied. I jogged to the end of my street. Veered right on the shopping corridor known as Magazine Street. Right on Harmony and right again on Prytania. Past Brix, my favorite gourmet grocery store. Past the gym that everyone and his brother went to in New Orleans. Past the bookstore that delivered. Past my neighbor who walked her Rottweiler daily, rain or shine. Past Lafayette Cemetery, trying to hold my breath as I always did when going by it – a silly habit made even loonier by living in a place like New Orleans, which was rife with superstitions.

When I arrived home, my irritation was at a minimum. A steaming hot shower erased it completely. However, after studying myself in the bathroom mirror, I realized no amount of make-up would help me today. I could no longer claim to be in my early forties. I was forty-nine and had plenty of wrinkles to show for it.

I put on a charcoal-gray suit with cream silk blouse and heels and viewed my text messages again. Nothing. Maybe Aiden had gone back to sleep, as I'd reasoned earlier to Tess. Should I drive over and check? No, that would be too intrusive. His father wasn't dead. He was injured.

Josh.

The first time we met, I was a crime beat reporter for *The Advocate*, Louisiana's largest newspaper, and he was a bigshot investigative journalist. I didn't pay an ounce of attention to him, however, because the coworker he was with was super intelligent and as glib as all get-out. A couple of years later when I ran into

Josh again – I'd quit the reporter gig and had gone back to Tulane
to earn my PhD so I could teach English at college level like my
mother had – I saw him in a different light. He was dedicated and
driven, not to mention handsome, with dark curly hair that I ached
to run my fingers through. We connected when he wanted to interview me about a woman I socialized with. She worked in the
administration department. Embezzlement was the issue. It didn't
hurt that he'd done his homework and brought me coffee just the
way I liked it. A week later, he invited me to a candlelit dinner.
During the meal, he questioned my unusual career path, from
wannabe cop to crime beat reporter to professor. I explained how,
after my brother's suicide, I'd thrown myself into everything – sports,
school, and extracurricular activities. Eager to prove my worth, I'd
excelled. Especially at track. After graduation, I'd followed in my
father's footsteps, determined to master every aspect of the law so
that the next time anyone bullied someone I loved, I could drag that
person's sorry ass to prison and watch them rot in hell. However,
halfway through the first term at the Los Angeles Police Academy,
with my father's nonstop drinking and my mother's endless crying,
I gave up on becoming a police officer. Gave up on Los Angeles.
Craving normalcy, longing for sanity, I applied to Tulane University
to get as far away from the sad memories as possible, wondering
if it would ever be far enough. Becoming a crime beat reporter had
seemed like a natural progression. I could dig up the truth. Could
right wrongs. Could out bullies. It seemed a perfect fit, until it
wasn't. I'd been good at it, but not nearly as dogged as Josh. In the
end, the work didn't suit me. It left me angry and bitter and feeling
dirty.

Josh and I talked for three hours straight that night. How I'd
adored the way his brow would crinkle when he was weighing his
next question. Our son's did the same thing.

Aiden. Why haven't you responded?

Standing at the kitchen counter, I ate two scrambled eggs and a
piece of wholewheat toast slathered with blackberry jam; the flavor
of berries came a close second to chocolate for me. When the dishes
were washed, I reached for my cell phone. Twirled it with my index
finger. Once. Twice.

Finally, I lifted it and tapped in Aiden's telephone number. As
before, it went to voicemail. I listened through his brief message.

'Aiden, it's me, Mom,' I said, starting as I had earlier. 'Listen, your father is trying to get hold of you.' *Keep it light. Don't let him think it's life or death.* 'You know how cranky he can get if you make him wait.'

Cranky was a code word Aiden and I had used whenever Josh would come home from work in a bear-like mood. When Josh was calm and supportive, he could sit beside Aiden and watch him create designs on the computer for hours. I hadn't been able to do that. I liked seeing the end product, not the process.

'After you've spoken to him . . .' *Spoken to Tess,* I thought, but didn't revise. 'After that, will you please, you know . . .'

Stop. You're prattling.

'Text me.'

THREE

On the drive to school, I replayed the showdown I'd had with Gregory Watley on Friday before I left for my mini vacay. *Bantamweight wrestlers are weaklings, Dean Lawson*, he intoned after a five-minute tirade about the lack of *real* sports at the college – real sports being code for Division I sports. He'd ranted about the very same thing three times since January. As I had on prior occasions, I needed all of my reserve not to shout that my brother had wrestled bantamweight, and he had been anything but a weakling. In his category, Benjie had won more matches than any other wrestler in the history of Van Nuys High School. Without a rebuttal from me, however, Watley had continued his familiar diatribe: *Build up the basketball program.* Except on Friday he'd added *Or else.* I seethed. I gritted my teeth. I wanted to tell him I felt sorry for him because he'd become mean since his wife passed away last year. Ultimately, I couldn't resist and blurted, *Or else, what?* I didn't use my inside voice. His response was terse. Or else he would demand repayment for every dime he'd donated to the college. I experienced a moment of panic. Watley Holding Corp. was a big deal in New Orleans. The corporation offered commercial and personal loans, as well as trust, insurance, and mortgage banking services to just about everyone in and around the area. Losing its backing would cost me my job.

Stop, Mags. No more thinking. Or else. The threat made me chuckle. Or else I wouldn't allow myself the chocolate donut I pictured myself buying for my mid-morning snack.

As I turned into the college, out of nowhere the nightmare I'd had last night catapulted into my head again. Why did the memory of the sophomore who'd committed suicide four years ago continue to haunt me? I couldn't have prevented his death. Maybe I had repeated dreams because the boy, a cheer squad member, had died in April. Same time of year as Benjie. Same time as now. Like Benjie, he had been bullied by fellow athletes for being slight. Did he remind me of Aiden? Was that why I was being so protective of my son?

To this day, I asked myself what more I could have done for the student. The athletic director hadn't looped me into the situation until after the young man's harrowing passing. I'd never forget when his mother, a slight woman with gray eyes, came into my office dressed in an ill-fitting suit, her hat squished on to her honey-brown hair. Directly after her, the boy's sister, who dwarfed the mother, stomped in. She was a slim, dark-haired young woman in her late teens wearing thick-rimmed black glasses and steampunk, military-style clothing. The mother spoke softly. The sister swore like a sailor. She said they were going to sue the university. I fetched them tea. Listened to the girl screech and keen. Watched her uncross and cross her legs or scratch the exotic tattoos on her neck. The mother sat stoically, wringing her hands. When the girl calmed, the mother apologized for their visit and left. Neither of them sued the college.

As I pulled into my parking spot, I urged myself to refocus and think of something nice. Like the relaxing weekend I'd had. Reading and hiking. Eating good food. Antiquing.

When I regained my equilibrium, I climbed out of my Prius and strode to my office, a tranquil environment with peacock-blue walls, blond furniture, and potted ferns.

My assistant, Yvonne, a mahogany-haired thirty-something with a penchant for colorful sheath dresses, followed me in. 'How was your weekend?'

'Too short.' I didn't tell her about Josh being shot or Aiden not returning my messages. I wouldn't bother her with the drama of my life.

'Busy day,' she said, handing me my schedule. 'Want coffee?'

'Water, thanks. Any messages?'

She shook her head. I set my cell phone on my desk face up –
still nothing from Aiden – and picked up a pen to make notes on
the itinerary. I had a lot of duties to attend to, including overseeing
a budget meeting via Zoom at nine. I wasn't looking forward to it.
Gregory Watley had muscled his way into the forum. I hoped he
would represent himself using his avatar so I wouldn't have to look
at his tiny, critical eyes. After the meeting, I would attend to the
Coach Tuttle sexual harassment suit instigated by a few female
students.

'Dean Lawson,' a man said.

Gregory Watley appeared in the doorway, his meaty face beet
red, his gray-brown combover tousled. I felt my blood pressure rise.
Behind him, Yvonne was making an *I couldn't stop him* gesture.

'Thank you, Yvonne. Mr Watley,' I said solicitously.

Again the meeting with him on Friday steamrolled to the front
of my brain with me explaining that moving from Division III to
Division I could take a year or longer. Telling him Pelican didn't
have the resources. Making it clear that all the university could
afford were smaller sports programs: rowing, wrestling, archery,
and yes, Division III basketball, which didn't necessitate scholarships. But Watley wouldn't back down. His grandson – his pride
and joy – the boy that he and his wife had raised for the past ten
years, was considering colleges. The kid was a star basketball player.

'I need to talk to you, Dean Lawson.' Watley tugged the hem of
his too-tight jacket.

I looked pointedly at my watch. 'You have two minutes.'

'Have you resolved the issue as I proposed?'

'Sir, what did you expect me to do over the weekend?' My smile
felt strained.

'Your job. But no-o-o.' His sarcastic tone was biting. 'Instead,
you went out of town. Why couldn't you wait until spring break to
take a vacation? It starts Friday.'

'Sir—' I rose to my feet, working hard to keep my hands from
balling into fists. 'I'll have you know that my home is recovering
from a flood, thanks to a plumbing issue. I had to leave—'

'I don't give a rat's tail about your problems. I expect results.'
He jabbed a pudgy finger at me.

If only I could launch myself over the desk and lop it off. Not only
had I been a good sprinter in college, I'd also been a good hurdler.

'Mr Watley, listen up. I will not be browbeaten into compliance.

However, you'll be pleased to know that I have put in calls to set the ball in motion. When I know more, you'll know more.' *Liar.* I hadn't contacted anyone. I wanted to ignore the problem, but I knew he would press, so I'd have to make good on my word. Soon. 'In the meantime, you might want to make sure your grandson gets his grades up if he wants to be accepted at Pelican.'

Watley fumed. 'I take umbrage at that, Dean Lawson.'

'Take all the umbrage you want.'

On Friday, when I'd suggested *the kid* apply to other colleges with established programs, Watley had revealed his underbelly. Other colleges' athletic departments weren't considering his grandson because he was too short. *Is that the primary reason?* I'd asked. He hadn't answered, so I'd done some digging on my vacation and learned that not only was his grandson a middling student, but that he, Watley, had attended Harvard Business School. It was then that I realized if Watley wanted his grandson to follow the same path, he would need to get him enrolled in a school that Watley believed he could pressure into giving the kid straight A's – i.e. Pelican.

'Your two minutes are up, sir. See you on Zoom.' I sat down and swiveled in my chair, dismissing him.

Watley stomped out of the office and barked an order at Yvonne. She told him to have a nice day.

The Zoom meeting went as expected. Each division's dean requested a bigger budget come the fall semester. Watley questioned the university's fiscal health. I rallied and quelled doubts, but I knew there would be repercussions.

When the meeting ended an hour later, I checked my cell phone – nothing from Aiden. Exasperated but somewhat concerned because not responding simply wasn't like my son, I locked my office, a habit I'd taken up three years ago following the theft of my grandmother's cameo necklace. I'd set it on the blotter to remind myself to get the clasp fixed. When I'd returned from a meeting across campus, it was gone. Yvonne hadn't allowed anyone in, although, when pressed, she admitted she'd taken a two-minute bathroom break. The thief must have been watching. That day, I found enough in the school's reserve funds to have security cameras installed. No future incidents had ensued.

'I'm going to the café to grab a coffee and donut,' I said to Yvonne. Pelican had a commissary, a café, and a number of food carts on campus.

'Will you write more of your novel?' She eyed the journal that was poking from my tote.

More? Ha! I hadn't started it. I'd wanted to in high school, but Benjie's death had shaken my resolve. I'd tried again after having Aiden. Nothing had clicked. I'd vowed to start it on my recent vacation but hadn't, although an idea had started brewing. 'Maybe,' I said. 'Want anything?'

'I'm good.'

Stepping into the hall, I veered right. The café was across the quad.

'Dean Lawson, a moment!'

I tensed. It wasn't Watley, ready to accost me again. This time it was Provost Southington, a stuffed shirt who liked his T's crossed and I's dotted. The man was known for his expertise in empirical decision-making. And sound fiscal management. And orderliness. To anyone who mattered, he was gracious and congenial. To me, he was a hard-nosed boss.

I forced a smile. 'Provost Southington.'

He smoothed the lapel of his Armani suit and straightened his geometric-patterned bowtie. 'Have you spoken with the attorney for the prosecution handling the Tuttle case?' His deep bass timbre never failed to unnerve me. The first time I'd spoken to him on the telephone about the position, I'd flashed on Darth Vader. And shuddered.

'Not yet, sir.'

'She needs to see you.' He polished his gleaming bald brown pate with his palm.

'Yes, sir. It's on my agenda for this afternoon.'

'I've met with her.'

'And . . .' I tilted my head, waiting.

'I didn't have much to say. I barely know Coach Tuttle.'

'Nor do I, other than he's married to a nursery-school teacher, he placed tenth in the rings in the Olympics in the nineties, and he has coached his female gymnasts to two division titles.' How I wished I could bury my head in the sand about the matter. 'He reports to the new AD.' The previous athletic director quit.

'Well?' Southington shoved a hand into his pocket.

'Well, what?'

'What are you going to say?'

'It's not like I have first-hand knowledge of anything untoward having occurred.'

'You can speak to the man's character. You can talk up his honor and trustworthiness. You have eyes. You've seen him in action.'

What I'd seen were platonic hugs here and there. Modest kisses to the cheek. However, I'd never been behind closed doors with Tuttle. Sadly, a few coeds had, and their stories concurred. He'd made unwanted advances. Last week, when the man marched into my office upset that I'd agreed to escalate the complaint, he hadn't threatened me, but he'd implied that if I did speak against him, I would bear the consequences. These young women, he claimed, were out to get him because he'd benched them. As in all our previous meetings about his salary, commendations, or attentiveness to the women's athletic program, the door remained open. Yvonne heard the entire conversation.

'I don't know, sir,' I said. Frankly, I understood Tuttle's distress. If he was declared guilty, his career was over. And I had to admit that his righteous indignation did make me question the students' accounts. On the other hand, if what they were claiming was true, that kind of behavior was unacceptable, pure and simple. 'Rest assured, I'm taking this seriously. I will provide every detail I can, given the gravity of the situation and the propriety of my position.'

What else could I say until the attorney for the prosecution laid out her case?

I headed to the café and bought a black coffee. Sadly, they were out of donuts. I returned to my desk and plopped into my chair. I didn't flip through my journal. I didn't write.

At noon, I took a walk on the quad, an arbor-lined brick expanse between the main educational buildings – Boles Hall, Watley Science and Math, and Thomason English. There was still no response from Aiden on my cell phone. No voicemail message. No text. Knowing how unforthcoming teens could be, I had been grateful for our communications through texts. Now? His silence annoyed me. No, to be frank, it angered me. It also made me nervous. Edgy. I was doing my best not to panic and I was failing. Was he OK? Radio silence was not like him.

'Dammit,' I muttered, barely drinking in the cool morning air or taking in the threatening mass of grayish clouds scudding overhead. 'Why are you being so stubborn, Aiden? What did I do to deserve—'

Stop, Mags. Just stop. Inhale, exhale, let go.

'He still loves you,' I muttered. 'You're overreacting.'

Maybe after falling back to sleep, he'd awakened late and rushed to school. His independent projects were, in his words, extremely time-consuming. The results could impact the possibility of full-time employment as a digital artist with Le Gran Palais, his dream job, the one he'd hoped all his life to nail. According to him, the design firm, which a pair of geniuses created, produced captivating design solutions with painstaking attention to detail and innovation. They catered to big clients like BiblioTech, UMI music, and world-wide volunteer organizations. In a few years, they hoped to break into the sports market – Aiden's specialty. He wasn't an athlete like me or his uncle, but he had a natural talent for knowing how the body moved. He got a kick out of sketching torsos, hands, and feet. How excited he'd been when he'd told me that Le Gran Palais, aka LGP, had served on the jury for the Design and Digital Awards.

Rounding a bend, I spotted Coach Tuttle talking to a colleague by the sports complex. New Orleans was a small town where you could run into anyone you knew at any time. Pelican U was an even smaller microcosm where I repeatedly ran into professors and students I was acquainted with. In his fifties, Tuttle was tall for a former gymnast, with thinning brown hair and a prominent forehead. His muscular biceps pressed at the seams of his shirt. He spotted me and beckoned me over. I shook my head, signaling I didn't have time to engage with him now. His gaze grew hard.

Pretending I forgot something, I made a U-turn and headed back in the direction I'd come. At the same time, I eyed my cell phone again. The darned thing was like a magnet. Worse, an addiction. Still zilch from Aiden.

I tapped in Josh's cell phone number. Tess answered. 'Have you heard from Aiden yet?' I asked.

'No.'

OK, I understood his demanding schedule, but getting no response from him – especially after the message I'd left regarding his father – sent a shiver through me. 'Any change in Josh . . . *Joshua's* condition?'

'He's stable and sleeping.'

'I'll check in again soon.'

Lightning pierced the sky. Seconds later, thunder rumbled. Then rain fell from the clouds.

I stood frozen in my spot as a memory of one of New Orleans' many hurricanes roared into my mind. Josh was upstairs working on a story. Aiden, not yet five, was in the kitchen with me. Shutters flew off and banged the house. Aiden rushed to me and hugged my legs.

'Mommy, when I die, will you remember me?'

The words caught me off guard, the fear in his voice so poignant.

'Sweetie,' I said in the most soothing tone I could, 'you won't die before me or your dad.'

'The rain is scary,' he mewled.

'Yes, it is, but I'm here to protect you.' I ruffled his hair and pulled him closer.

At that moment, Josh raced into the kitchen and threw his arms around Aiden and me. His calm assuredness steadied me. Steadied us.

'Shh,' he said. 'Everything will be OK. Shh.'

Thunder clapped again, jerking me back to the present. Rain sluiced my face. Stupidly, I'd left the administration building without an umbrella. I raced toward Chavert Hall, which housed International Studies and History, fields for which Pelican University was best known. Beneath the overhang a small group of students was huddled with adults. Parents, I presumed. On a pre-college tour. Most high-school juniors weighed their options in the spring so they could apply speedily in the fall. Seeing all of them, sans umbrellas, made me feel better. I wasn't the only unprepared soul.

I stopped dead in my tracks when I recognized a man in the mix. Carl Underhill, a Texas plastics billionaire. To anyone not in the know, he looked like a respectable guy. His roots were in money management. Like Watley, he'd earned his MBA at Harvard. But ten years ago, Josh had uncovered Underhill's main source of income – illegal pharmaceuticals marketed to college students. Distributing narcotics was a felony earning three to five-plus years. Underhill's product had included painkillers like Norco, Oxycodone, and Fentanyl. There had been eight defendants, with Underhill as the kingpin. When Josh's story broke and led to the man's arrest, Underhill vowed revenge. Death threats to Josh as well as to our family ensued right up until the trial. In the long run, Josh's reporting had given the Feds enough to seal Underhill's fate. He went away for seven years. But he was free now. Was he or someone who worked for him the person who'd shot Josh?

Underhill pivoted, as if sensing I was watching him, and tipped the brim of an imaginary hat. Broad-chested with thick dark hair and a dashing smile, he was a real charmer. The running back-sized teenager next to him was his son. I'd seen photos of the whole family in the news.

Separating himself from the pack, Underhill approached me with the boy. Both had long loping gates. 'Dean Lawson, how nice to see you.'

Bumping into me was coincidental, I assured myself. Underhill couldn't have known I'd be on a break at the same time he and his son were taking the parent–student tour. On the other hand, if he'd specifically set up the chance meeting so he could gloat about the attack on Josh . . .

'Mr Underhill,' I said flatly. 'Nice to see you, too.'

'I'd loan you my umbrella if I'd thought to bring one.'

'Yes, rainstorms can take us by surprise.'

'My youngest, Caleb, is considering Pelican.'

I forced a smile. 'Welcome. I hope you like what you see.'

'Son, say hello to Dean Lawson.' Underhill nudged the boy's shoulder.

'Hello, ma'am.'

'He wants nothing to do with Rice University, my alma mater,' Underhill went on, his Texas accent bold and unvarnished. 'I've heard great things about your college from an old friend. He tells me the academics are on par with Tulane.' He smiled, but his gaze was shrewd. 'My son wants a small college experience. We parents do all we can for our children, don't we?'

'I'd like to think so.' I nodded to Caleb. He looked tentative, unsure, like many other students his age.

'Caleb is a history buff. He's like an elephant.' Underhill tapped his temple. 'He never forgets.'

I flinched. Was the man issuing a veiled threat? Was he warning me that *he* wouldn't forget the incarceration foisted upon him by Josh and, therefore by association, me? Unwilling to let him sense my unease, I wished them well and hurried through the rain to the shelter of my building.

In the privacy of my office bathroom, I dried my face and clothes. After using a tissue to remove the mascara that had leaked down my cheeks, I assessed my face again. The parallel lines between my eyebrows had deepened. To ward off what I knew would be an impending tension headache, I swallowed two Tylenol dry and returned to my desk.

I straightened the blotter on the desktop and peered out the window. Rain drizzling down the pane reminded me of a favorite poem by A.A. Milne, 'Waiting at the Window.' It was about a child whiling away the time, watching the race of two raindrops named James and John. My mother had loved to recite the poem to her University of California sophomore English class. She would ask each of the students to create a poem with the same *aa*, *bb*, *cc* rhyming pattern. Twenty-six lines in all. Knowing it was a brilliant and challenging assignment, I'd given the same exercise to my creative writing students at Tulane. Only one had written something extraordinary in the three years I'd taught there.

For a moment, I leaned my head against the back of my chair, closed my eyes, and thought about the starting place for my novel. I'd decided it was going to be about a woman living on an island looking for redemption as a hurricane threatens to wipe out everything around her. What an appropriate metaphor for how I was feeling at the moment, with a powerful emotional storm on the horizon.

The wind began kicking up outside. My eyes popped open. The rain had stopped – a spring storm could be fleeting – but the young sycamores the university had planted last year were bending and near to cracking.

Just like you, Mags. Aiden incommunicado. Josh shot. Underhill out of jail. How much could I take before I snapped?

I glanced at my cell phone. Still nothing from Aiden. Should I reach out to Celine?

After Keira's death, Celine became a fixture in Aiden's life. Three months later, she moved in with him. The timing felt too soon, but I bit my tongue. I hadn't yet met Celine at that point. For all I knew she could be the best thing that had ever happened to him. A few weeks after that was when I started to notice a change in Aiden. His texts to me became shorter. Rarely did he ask how I was doing. So I concluded that I had to meet Celine. I invited them to dinner at Emeril's, a legendary restaurant in the Warehouse District. The moment Celine entered through the restaurant's front door, warning bells clanged in my mind. Curvy and broad-shouldered, she carried herself like an Amazon goddess. Power oozed out of every pore. The skirt of her white lace dress swirled as she sashayed to the table, her ice-white long hair wafting in syncopated rhythm. She had natural grace and the potent predatory pheromones of a panther, and I could see why my son had fallen for her. She smiled as her strikingly blue eyes sized me up. Did she mistrust me instantly because I was his mother? Did she worry that I would infringe on their relationship?

Would she think the same of me now if I reached out? No, I would not – could not – call her. I wouldn't be able to bear it if she thought I was intruding. Hovering.

'Yvonne,' I called to my assistant, 'do you have chocolate?'

She came running in with a two-pack of Reese's peanut butter cups.

'Bless you.'

'Would you also like a sandwich? A little protein?'

'No, thanks.'

After satisfying my sweet tooth, I tackled the next hour with gusto. Between one and one thirty, I met with two track stars who had come to beg for, at the very least, a modest grade boost so their D-plus grades would become C-minuses – anything denoting a passing grade which they needed to protect their partial scholarships. Between one thirty and two, I met with the attorney for the prosecution in the Tuttle case. She prepped me for the deposition that would take place after spring break. Every question made me want to tell her to jump in a lake, but I answered as best as I could. If only I knew what had really happened.

At two fifteen, I wondered how many challenging meetings I had endured since taking the job. Had losing Josh been worth it? Yes, I assured myself. Seven times over, because I had guided dozens – no, hundreds – of students to a prosperous and more fulfilling future. I had felt strangled creatively as dean of the English department at Tulane. At Pelican U, I had been granted free rein to introduce any program I'd wanted.

True, there had been multiple dropouts during my tenure, but they would have quit whether I had been the dean or not. Not everyone was college material. *If you give them a trade, you give them a career for life*, I'd told Josh. *If you give them confidence, they'll figure it out*. Back then, he'd praised me for my passion. Back then . . .

A text message pinged on my phone. Not Aiden.

Gina: *Got time for a late lunch? 2:30? Bobby Sox?*
Client canceled. Can't wait to hear about your vacay.

Me: *Yes!*
Gina: *Great. BTW, is everything on schedule at your
house?*
Me: *Yes, but not resolved. It stinks.*

When I'd left for the weekend, I'd given my friend the keys to
my Victorian in case anything went awry with the remediation people
getting access.

Me: *FYI, you were right. I needed the time away. I am
no longer wearing my shoulders for earrings.*

It was a lie. Worrying about Aiden had ruined any of the restful
benefits from the weekend.

Gina: *[Smiley faced emoji with tears.] See you soon.*

Peeved or, more to the point, crazed to distraction, I swiped the
cell phone screen and typed a new text to my son.

Me: *Look, I don't know what's going on, but your
silence is unacceptable. Your last text was curt at best.
Are you alive? Breathing? Your father needs you. He's
been hurt. So call him. And while you're at it,
FaceTime me. I need to see you and hear your voice. I
want to make sure you're all right.*

I'd never sent him such a sharp-toned text, but before I could
talk myself out of it, I stabbed Send. The thrust of the motion sent
a thunderbolt of pain up my arm.

FOUR

B obby Sox, a turquoise-blue and pink, fifties-themed diner,
was packed. I scanned the crowd and spotted Gina seated at
the counter. How could I miss her? She was wearing neon
yellow like she had the first time I'd met her at a Tulane alumni

mixer. Yellow, she said, was associated with happiness, laughter, and optimism and boosted one's serotonin levels. Despite the fact that she liked to wax rhapsodic about psychology and the complexities of the human brain, we'd become fast friends. She wasn't my therapist – I'd given up on therapy years ago – but she was the one who'd taught me the *inhale, exhale, let go* mantra.

I tapped her shoulder. 'Sorry I'm a few minutes late,' I said over the blare of Elvis's 'All Shook Up' playing from the jukebox.

'Sit!' She removed her oversized Prada tote from the stool to her left, set it on the counter, and met my gaze. 'Look at you,' she said with a tinge of sass, her New Orleans accent as strong as ever. 'All relaxed from a short vacation.'

Relaxed. Ha! I forced a smile. 'Yes, it's oh so relaxing coming home to a house under water. The odor. The fans. And then Aiden . . .' I began to cough uncontrollably.

Gina hopped to her feet. Patted my back. 'What's wrong with Aiden?'

'Nothing. At least I don't think so. I don't know. But Josh has been shot.'

'Shot?'

'Tess contacted me because they can't reach Aiden. And he's not calling me back. And . . . and . . .'

'Deep breath.'

I tried.

'C'mon. Try harder. He's not touching base? Big deal. He's a kid.'

When I was breathing normally again, Gina straightened my lapels. 'How many times have I told you to wear something red when you're struggling? Red is' – she flicked her fingers – 'magical. Powerful. It infuses confidence.' She rummaged in her tote bag and withdrew a red chiffon scarf. 'Even a splash of red can do the trick.' She wrapped the scarf around my neck with flair. 'There. It looks lovely. It's yours. I bought it online at Neiman's. It was a steal.'

No color could fix the anxiety swirling inside me. Even so, I thanked her, and we both sat. A counter waitress sporting a turquoise-blue dress, pink apron, and pink soda jerk hat asked for our beverage orders. Gina and I both requested sweet tea. The moment I did, though, I wondered whether I should cut sugar from my diet altogether. Go cold turkey. No chocolate. No sweets. I was antsy enough already. Maybe sugar was making me jumpier.

'Talk to me.' Gina fastened her tote. 'Which is bothering you more, Josh being hurt or your son snubbing you?'

'Joshua,' I groused. 'He likes to be called Joshua now.'

'What a crock! Go on.' Gina waved a hand. 'Josh has been shot. Is it bad?'

'Not fatal. Tess has been trying to reach Aiden, but he's not responding. She asked me to do so. It had been quite a while since he last texted me. Due to the money issue.' Gina knew all about me being financially under water. 'Actually, that's not true. He sent a terse one early this morning in response to one from me. But by that point I was starting to worry because you know Aiden. He's not snippy. So I did what Tess asked, sent another text, and when he didn't respond, I called. He didn't pick up so I texted again, and . . .' No, I would not cry. Not over a stupid text exchange or lack thereof. If only I hadn't sent the last one. 'Mine was pretty snarky. He didn't respond.'

'He's ghosting you?'

'I wouldn't go that far.'

Or maybe I should. Was my son truly snubbing me because I'd stopped giving him money? Had he suddenly become petty, which was totally against his character? Or was it something more? I'd never told him that I was miffed that he'd gotten married without consulting me, not that weighing in with my decision would have changed their plans, but a heads up would've been nice. Had he sensed my displeasure? Yeah, probably. I wasn't a good liar. In high school, I'd worked crew in theater, but I'd never acted on stage. After Benjie's death, faking it hadn't worked for me.

I shuddered. *Aiden is fine.*

'Maggie, why would he ghost you?' Gina asked in her modulated therapist voice. She couldn't help herself. Both of her parents had been therapists. She once told me dinners at her house during high school had been grueling. Every iota of her life had been picked over and dissected for *intention*.

'Because I'm smothering him,' I said.

'You don't smother. You nurture. You care.'

'I care too much.'

'There is no such thing as too much.'

'Sure there is. If you plant a flower and suffocate it with dirt, it can't thrive. That's what I've been doing to Aiden. That's—'

'Listen up. Do not interrupt me.' She tapped the counter with her index finger. 'You, my friend, have the ability to convince people

to see things your way. You talk. But you also listen. You balance
reality and fiction as very few can. It's why you're an excellent
dean. It's why you're a superb mother.'

'A suffocating mother,' I said, wallowing in self-pity.

'OK, you've been working on cutting ties. Stepping back.
Allowing Aiden to become his own man. But now is not the time
for you to take his silence as normal. His father is hurt and Aiden
isn't reaching out? To either of you? That's not like him.'

That was what was eating at me. Aiden wasn't insensitive and
callous. He saved birds with broken wings. He carried spiders
outdoors to release them into the wild. After Keira died, he started
doing annual bike-a-thons for MADD because he was convinced
that whoever killed her had to have been drunk. That was the only
reason he could fathom that would make the driver speed away and
not face up to what he'd done. That notion rekindled a memory of
Aiden coming over for dinner after the last fundraiser. He'd needed
to talk. To process the tragic effects of alcoholism. When we'd
determined that we couldn't solve the world's problems, we'd dug
into two pints of chocolate swirl ice cream and watched three
Twilight Zone reruns. When he left, I stumbled into bed, treasuring
the bonding moment with my son.

The waitress set our drinks on the counter and asked for our
lunch orders. Burger, no bun for Gina. An open-faced tuna melt
sandwich for me.

After we'd ordered, Gina said, 'Let me see your text
conversation.'

I swiped the app on my cell phone and showed it to her.

She *tsk*ed. 'He needs to get his head on straight about what?'

'I don't know. His future? How to make ends meet now that I'm
not providing funding for everything?'

'C'mon. The stupid kid doesn't understand what *under water*
means?'

'He'd better not neglect his studies,' I groused. 'If he does . . .'
I flicked the air. 'No. It's not up to me. He's on his own. Let him
work it out. It's not my problem, right? I can't fix it.'

But it *was* my problem. A mother worried. Or she should if she
was worth her salt. A mother was supposed to be there to pick up
the pieces. When Keira died, I'd listened to lord knew how many
late-night phone calls from Aiden. The tears. The agony. And then
Celine entered his life.

'Have you reached out to Celine?' Gina asked, as if reading my mind.

'I don't think I should. She might feel I'm intruding.'

A few months ago, I'd spared no details about Celine to Gina. When Celine and Keira met, Celine was earning her master's degree in political science and became a mentor to Keira, a sophomore. Keira had held dreams of becoming a politician. She'd wanted to right the wrongs of the world. Often she invited Celine to dinner at the duplex that she and Aiden rented off campus – the unit that I, at the time, was paying for because I'd agreed to help him financially through all four years of undergrad school. In May, when the car struck and killed Keira, Celine was there to comfort Aiden. Miraculously, *if one believed in miracles*, I'd carped to Gina, Celine liked everything Aiden did – the same music, books, and movies. They even liked the same kind of cat. Gina had replied sarcastically that no two people liked all of the same things. She'd hated her ex-boyfriend's model car hobby, and I'd loathed Josh's love of Zydeco music. Loathed was too strong a word. It was fun but too erratic for my taste.

'She won't think you're intruding,' Gina said firmly.

'No. I can't call her. We don't know each other well. Honestly, sometimes I feel like I'm walking on eggshells with her. Like she doesn't trust me.' I sighed. 'Do all mothers feel like that about their daughter-in-law?'

'You're asking the wrong person.'

When the waitress returned with our lunches, Gina and I moved our totes to our laps. The woman refilled our teas and asked, 'Anything else I can get you?'

'We're good.' I cut my open-faced sandwich into bites as my mind cycled back to the night I'd taken Aiden and Celine to dinner.

Throughout the meal, I was intrigued by the way she treated him. Over appetizers, she cooed to him, as a lover would, but once the entrée was delivered, her cooing morphed into commands. *Hand me that. Don't eat those. Let me tell the story.* I reasoned silently that Aiden was easy-going. Celine was assertive. Opposites attract. By the end of the meal, I let out the breath I was holding. She and Aiden seemed happy. A month after Aiden finished his junior year, when I learned that he and she had eloped, however, it took all of my reserve not to tell him it was a huge mistake.

'When was the last time you saw Aiden?' Gina asked around a mouthful of her burger.

'Two weeks ago.'

Aiden invited me out for coffee. I was disturbed by his weight loss and asked if there was something troubling him. He looked as if he was going to say yes, then shrugged and muttered, *Nothing I can't handle.* I imagined he was missing Keira but couldn't give in to the feelings. In the end, he claimed he'd lost a few pounds because he'd switched to a Keto diet to help with his creativity. *Artists, even digital artists, need to stoke the flame*, he joked.

'Yoo-hoo.' Gina waved a hand in front of my face. 'Where'd you go?'

'Did you see my last text?' I displayed the thread again. 'I couldn't help myself. My son is going to hate me. For whining. For hovering. For—'

'No, he won't.'

'What if he never calls again? What if he cuts me off completely?' I pushed my plate away.

'OK, we need more than a lunch to calm the frenzy you're working yourself into. But for now' – Gina swiveled on her stool – 'confront him in person.'

'What? No. How can you of all people suggest that? You've been warning me to keep my distance.' I held up my palm. '*Stay away*, you said imperiously last week.'

'I did not.'

'You said, "Listen to me. You know I'm right."'

Over the past couple of years, Gina – as a friend – had helped me dissect my messed-up relationships. The abandonment I felt from my parents. The feeling of failure that plagued me after the divorce from Josh. She'd taught me to value my strengths. Most importantly, she'd urged me to stop raking myself over the coals. I was human. And, yes, flawed. But worthy of love. Was I now suffering a new kind of angst? My relationship with Aiden had always been on such solid ground. He was my little buddy. I was his Super Mom. Way back when, that was what he'd dubbed me. I couldn't bear to lose what we had. Was I being ridiculously naïve?

Gina seized my wrist. 'You deserve to hear what's going on from him. Face to face.'

'I can't. No.'

'If it's about money, so be it. If it's something else, you'll meet up with me for a glass of wine, and we'll do the deep dive.'

'Deep dive? Uh, no.' I glimpsed my watch and realized it was getting late. I pulled a couple of twenties from my tote and set them on the counter.

Gina rose. 'You're not paying.'

'You just gave me solid advice, doc.'

'I am not your doctor and never will be.'

'I owe you.'

'Fine.' She polished off her burger and led the way to the street.

On the sidewalk, we hugged goodbye, and then I pushed apart to wipe a tear. 'I'm going to swing by the medical center and see Josh. Maybe he's heard from Aiden by now. Maybe Aiden's there. Visiting.'

She frowned.

I said, 'A mother can dream.'

FIVE

Striding from the University Medical Center parking lot into the hospital, I rang Yvonne and told her what I was up to. She understood and would reschedule my appointments. Once inside the building, I went to the reception to find out which room Joshua was in.

Minutes later, I exited an elevator and drew up short. A burly security guard was avidly questioning a young nurse outside Josh's room.

'What's going on?' I asked, drawing near, pulse skyrocketing. 'I'm Joshua's wife. I mean ex-wife. We're friendly. Is he OK?'

'He is,' the nurse said.

'Where's the officer that the police assigned?' I asked.

'He must be taking a leak,' the guard said. 'Relax, ma'am, Mr Lawson's fine. Her and me' – he gestured between himself and the fresh-faced nurse – 'are just having a friendly chat.'

Friendly. Of course. He was probably asking her on a date. Suppressing my panic, I stepped into the room.

'Ma'am,' the nurse said, following me in, 'Mr Lawson needs his rest.'

'It's still visiting hours, isn't it?'

'Yes, ma'am.'

'Then I'll stay.'

She gave a nod and retreated into the hall.

Both of Josh's muscular arms lay above the covers. Tubes for meds were attached to his left arm. His face was ashen. His light brown hair was shorter than it was the last time I'd seen him. A large wound dressing over his right shoulder peeked from beneath the neckline of his blue gown. I could only imagine how extensive the bandaging was around his chest. I'd questioned a few gunshot victims during my stint on the crime beat. Each had said how difficult it was to breathe.

'What are you investigating, Josh?' I asked.

He didn't stir.

A different nurse poked her head in and informed me that Miss Toussant, the fiancée, had stepped out to have a bite with her sister.

I thanked her, glad Tess wasn't there. I didn't have it in me for small talk. I sat in the chair beside the bed and took hold of Josh's hand. It was cold. 'Josh,' I murmured, 'are you digging up dirt on Underhill again?' Tess had said he was investigating corruption. Dealing in illegal pharmaceuticals could be deemed corruption. I shivered as another thought occurred to me. Had Underhill kidnapped Aiden to leverage Josh? To make him quash whatever new story he was working on? Had he taken control of Aiden's cell phone and typed all of the responses? A kidnapper wouldn't know about Aiden's *XO* sign-off.

'Josh,' I repeated, my voice small and brittle. 'I'm worried about our son.' I wanted to lay out my theory about Underhill but held back, knowing Josh would chide me. *Don't be ridiculous, Mags*, he'd say. *Kidnap Aiden? Get real.*

'What are you digging into, dammit?' I hissed. 'It must be bad if someone wants you dead. Did you consider that? Did you even once consider—'

I ground my teeth together. Madness didn't become me. But *what ifs* were cycling through my brain at breakneck speed. Of course Josh had weighed every angle. He was a good reporter. No, he was a great reporter, particularly when his story involved drug-related crimes. His sister had accidentally overdosed in college. Until the end of our marriage, I'd held him in high regard for his dogged moral compass.

For an hour, I sat with him. Stroked his long fingers. Talked nonsense. About the flood at the house. About Gregory Watley hounding me. I didn't want to mention Aiden. I didn't want to put words to my concern. He was fine. *Fine.*

Late afternoon, I returned to Pelican and doused a few fires – none with Watley, thank goodness.

At five p.m., the attorney for the investigation wanted another word with me. In the middle of the meeting, the armpits of my silk blouse and jacket soaked through, I wondered how many ways I could tell her that I hadn't been in the room where it happened. She repeatedly pressed me to vouch for the students, but I kept hashing over whether I could without knowing the full story. Tuttle was a good coach, I told her. He had an outstanding record. Would he find some way to hold me personally responsible if I took the students' side? My allegiances felt so divided – to the students, to the staff, to the university.

At six, exhausted to the point of breaking, I drove home. I parked in the driveway, trudged up the steps, and slogged inside. Because parts of New Orleans are below sea level, homes in the city don't typically have true basements. The ground floor served as one. I entered on the second. Switched on a light. It flickered, crackled, and fizzled. I recoiled and let out a gasp. I hated the dark. After Benjie died, my mother had taken to living in gloom. My father hadn't coaxed her to snap out of it.

I switched on another light at the far end of the foyer. *Pop!*

Cursing, blaming my pent-up energy for the shortage, I opened the flashlight on my cell phone to get my bearings. I still hadn't received a text response from Aiden, which gave me pause. Should I go to his duplex like Gina had suggested? Pound on the door and demand we have an adult conversation?

I set my briefcase and tote on the hardwood floor and inhaled. The house smelled like vanilla from all the scent infusers I'd plugged into the walls before leaving this morning. But it also smelled dank. I'd spoken with the remediation people right before I left campus. They'd assured me that the water damage hadn't created a mold issue, and they doubted it would because they'd sucked out the majority of water in record time. The perky female I'd spoken to quipped that I was lucky the days were cool.

Lucky, indeed.

My cell phone jangled. I scanned the display: *Spam risk.* I grumbled. How did so many robocallers find my number?

I headed to the kitchen to fetch some matches and candles but stopped when I glimpsed a family picture beyond the pitted brass coat hooks. I turned the flashlight toward it. My mother, father, and Benjie stared back at me. We'd gone on vacation to Breaux Bridge, a Louisianan resort area that my mother, having grown up in the state, had frequented as a girl. I sighed, drinking in Benjie's sunburned, smiling face as the memory of finding him dead that morning in April close to the end of my freshman year in high school – his sophomore year – flew into my mind. I raced into his room at seven a.m., ready to taunt him about his whack-a-job science project and eager to show off the first chapter of the novel I was writing.

'*No!' I gasped for air. 'Benjie, no!' The rope looped around his neck and attached to the ceiling fan rod was taut. Unforgiving. 'Mom!' The word popped out of me.*

'*In a minute,' she called from the kitchen.*

'*No, Mom, now!'*

Adrenaline zipped through me as I righted the chair. Slid the seat under my brother's feet. Tried to climb on to the chair alongside him. Not enough room. I stumbled to the floor. Always slight and thin, Benjie looked even skinnier in nothing but his wrestling shorts, his head lolling to one side, his face a ghastly blue.

I remounted the chair. Shuddering, I grabbed his wrist. No pulse. I tried to loosen the knots. When I'd awakened to get ready for school, I'd felt a tug at the pit of my stomach. I'd thought it was nerves. Had I sensed he needed me? We were born eleven months apart. We were close.

'*Mom!' I leaped off the chair. Screamed down the stairs. 'Get up here now! Benjie . . . He's . . . I think he's . . .' I couldn't say the word. Wouldn't.*

I sprinted back to Benjie. Touched his bare foot. Cold as ice. It wasn't cold outside. It rarely was in Los Angeles. Certainly not in April.

'*Benjie. You creep. You idiot. Why?' I sucked in air. 'I wanted to run my first chapter by you. I have to read it aloud in class. You promised . . . You—'*

'*What's wrong, Maggie?' My mother raced into the room, tying the belt of her pink robe. When she saw Benjie, she launched forward. 'Maggie, help me.'*

'*He's dead, Mom.'*

'*No, he's not.' My mother climbed on to the chair like I had.*

'Keep me from falling.' I braced her hips so she wouldn't tilt backward. She kissed Benjie's cheek over and over as she worked furiously to undo the knots. 'Benjie, sweetie, Mommy's here. Hold on, baby.' She glowered over her shoulder at me. 'Why would he do this?'

'I don't know.'

A tear trickled down my cheek as I studied my brother's features in the photograph. We'd had the same green eyes, the same blond hair. Unlike me, he'd been a gentle soul; I'd been a wiseacre, taking people on to prove I was smarter and tougher. Earlier in the school year, three boys had trapped me near the boys' restroom. They'd planned to shove me inside and have their way with me, but thanks to Benjie, who'd taught me some of his primo wrestling moves, I'd fought them off. No boy in high school ever came near me again. At five foot six, I hadn't been daunting, but I'd had attitude. Attitude that had helped carry me through life, even after everyone I loved left me to flounder.

'If only you'd had some 'tude, bro,' I murmured.

We found his suicide note later that day buried beneath his pillow. He said he couldn't cope. He'd never be big enough. Never be respected. I remembered my mother crumpling the note into a tight ball and hurling it at the wall. How dare his jerk teammates tease him about being a bantamweight, she'd yelled. He'd been a fierce wrestler. The best. She said picking on a person's size was nonsense. An athlete was an athlete. Would they bully a jockey or a gymnast?

I touched the rim of the picture frame. *May you rest in peace, my sweet brother. And Mom –* I blinked back tears *– I'm glad you didn't have to witness Dad's downfall.*

Pity party over, I shrugged out of my wool coat and blazer. Hung them on the coat hooks. Urged my jaw to relax.

Turning left, I entered the kitchen and crossed to a drawer. I pulled out a long match from a tube and lit the pillars of vanilla candles I'd placed on the counters. In the comfort of the warm glow, I opened the broom closet and aimed my cell-phone flashlight at the breaker panel. Two switches had flipped. I fixed them, and the lights in the foyer went on. I breathed easier.

Though the cost of homeownership was a burden, I loved living in the Garden District, a luxury suburb created from the Livaudais plantation in the 1800s. Josh and I had purchased the house when I'd taught at Tulane, and we hadn't needed to move when Pelican offered me the job. The house spoke to me in myriad ways. The garden overflowed with perennials. The remodel of the kitchen, with state-of-the-art appliances, Kashmir white granite counters, and massive island, was perfect for someone who enjoyed cooking. I used to love it. Now, cooking for one? Not so much. The rich burgundy walls of the living room, repainted the same color for over a century, filled me with curiosity about the history of the families that had lived here before me. What customs had they followed? What superstitions had they bought into? If only we'd thought to have a trustworthy plumber check out the ancient pipes before we'd bought the place.

I set my cell phone on the counter, poured a glass of pinot grigio, and thought again of Benjie. He'd been a happy child and a joyful teen until the second year of high school. That was when things went south. Star wrestlers started to pick on him, calling him puny and worthless. Everyone thought that Benjie, being an athlete himself, could weather the taunts. It was stupid locker room chatter, our father told him, and advised him to raise his chin proudly and to laugh in their faces. But clearly he hadn't been able to.

Even to this day, I blamed myself for not realizing Benjie had been at the edge of a precipice. Dad said I couldn't have known; I was a child. He was the parent. He was the one who should've been held accountable.

Dad. So strong, so brave. So broken. And my mother? How she had loved Benjie and then Aiden, even though she'd never been able to separate the two in her jagged mind.

I shuddered, wondering whether I was missing a big clue in the puzzle regarding my son. He was so similar to Benjie, in stature, in nature. Had he been suffering more than I realized since Keira died and hiding his hurt with a brave smile? Was his marriage simply a bandage to cover the wound his heart had suffered? When we had coffee, should I have pressed him harder to unburden himself? Did I fail him?

Aiden. Where are you?

Craving fresh air, not indoor crud stagnant with creeping mold and mildew, I fetched a parka and moved to the back porch with my wine glass. The door creaked, reminding me I needed to pick up WD-40 at the store. The air was chilly, but I didn't mind. I ignited the multi-purpose lighter I kept on the table and lit the citronella candle. The candlelight danced on my glass. Neither of the neighbors on either side of me were home yet, though their exterior lights, like mine, had already switched on. Incapable of settling into the rocker, unpent energy zinging up, down, and sideways through my body, I paced from one end of the porch to the other. I didn't want to dwell on Aiden, so I worked through theories about Josh.

What if the mark for one of his other investigative stories – not Underhill – shot Josh? What else constituted corruption? Monetary fraud spurred by a person or an organization was prevalent all over the world. Kleptocracies. Oligarchies. Narco-states. Mafia states. The list was endless, and without Josh's input as to what he'd been delving into, I wouldn't be able to pin it down.

My thoughts returned to Underhill and suddenly took a left turn. What if he went after Aiden, but Aiden eluded him and was lying low? Was that feasible? Why wouldn't Aiden tell me if that was the case? Did he worry that using his phone could get him killed? Maybe Gina was right. At the very least I should reach out to Celine. If everything was fine, I would suffer the rebuke in person.

I took a sip of wine. Emotions fueled by fatigue caused my hand to shake. The wine sloshed and dripped down my chin. I tried to catch it with my upper lip. The motion made me think of Gregory Watley and how he'd smacked his lips not once but twice during the Zoom call. What if I was wrong about his peeve with me being just that – a peeve? Did his threat of *or else* mean more than pulling his funds from the university? Had he done something to my son to make me fall in line? No. If he had, he'd have lorded it over me by now. *I've got him, Dean Lawson. You will do as I say.* Watley lusted for power and longed for my submission. Bragging was his default setting.

Another thought nearly crippled me. What if Aiden, upset about my having cut off his funds, had done something foolish to raise cash? All his life, he'd talked about becoming wealthy beyond his wildest imagination. I'd considered it the stuff and nonsense of a kid dreaming big. It wasn't like he'd grown up poor. We'd had plenty of money. He'd earned a good allowance. But what if my cutting him off had left him wanting? What if he'd decided to do something illegal to make his bigger-than-life dream come true? Was doing something unlawful even in his DNA?

No. It wasn't. I recalled the essay he'd written to get into Tulane.

The theme had surprised me. Aiden proposed that there needed to be a better criminal justice system in America. His argument had been solid. Right was right and wrong was wrong. Looking back, I had to wonder if Keira had helped him craft it.

I thought again of his earlier text saying he needed to get his head on straight. Did he go somewhere alone to do so? Would Celine know where he was? If she did, would she tell me? Or would she keep his whereabouts private, as a supportive spouse might? I could ask, but again worried that she would see me as a meddling mother-in-law. I didn't want to wear that label. I wanted her to trust me. To like me.

Unwilling to berate myself any longer, I extinguished the candle and returned inside. I microwaved a frozen chicken breast meal and ate all of it. Something for sustenance, not for taste.

Sleep didn't come easily.

When I woke Tuesday morning, I felt parched and groggy but eager to hit the ground running because, around three a.m., I'd decided Gina was right. I was wrong. If Aiden chastised me for being a helicopter mother, so be it. I had to face the problem head on. No more dallying. No more waiting for a text that might not come just to make me look like I was a grown-up. And no more allowing Aiden to diss his father, dammit. That was plain rude and spoiled, and Aiden was neither of those things.

I ate a quick breakfast, slipped into jeans, a black sweater, and Keds, and drove to his duplex. On the way, I let Yvonne know I was taking a sick day. It wasn't a lie. I felt nauseous.

SIX

I'd visited Aiden's place a couple of times when he and Keira had lived there, but not since her death. Aiden and Celine had never invited me over. Gina joked that Celine worried I would criticize her housekeeping. *As if.* But a cliched reality was that daughters-in-law often felt judged by their mothers-in-law. I got it.

I parked near the white-and-gray duplex and took the stairs to the porch two at a time. Beside the rocking chair stood a pot with a dead plant, the remnants of the chrysanthemum I'd given Aiden and Celine in October as a housewarming present. A goodwill gesture.

I heard talking inside. A man and a woman. Aiden was home. Though my nerves were jittery with worry about how he would respond to my visit, I knocked. No one came to the door. I knocked again. Celine peeked past the lacy drapes that covered the front window. She had wax on her upper lip. Her hand flew to her face. Her eyes went wide.

Seconds later, the door opened a crack. Celine's upper lip was pink from the distress of having stripped off the wax. 'What are you doing here?' Dressed in a cleavage-revealing negligee and pink floral robe, she reminded me of a character right out of *A Streetcar Named Desire*. She fussed with the tendrils of ice-white hair spilling from her messy bun. 'Maggie, what are you doing here?' Usually she spoke with a genteel accent, as if she'd practiced how to sound cultured for years, but today, graciousness failed her.

Her brusqueness made perfect sense. I'd surprised her and intruded on her at a vulnerable moment. I smiled to ease the tension. 'Is my son home?' I tried to peer past her but failed. Her scent reminded me of the vanilla candles in my house.

'No.'

'I hear a man's voice.'

'I'm listening to talk radio while I dress for work.' She glanced over her shoulder.

'Where's Aiden? His first class doesn't start for another hour.' Before pulling the funds, I had been privy to Aiden's schedule.

'He's not here.'

'So you said. May I come in?'

'Don't you believe me?'

'Of course I do.' I didn't, but I bit my tongue. 'Except it's chilly and I forgot my jacket.' I'd left it deliberately on the floor of the car. I shuffled my feet to demonstrate I was cold.

After a long moment, Celine opened the door. She motioned for me to enter. Spirit, the Persian cat with hair as white as Celine's – they had acquired the cat five months ago; I'd only seen photos of it – sprang off the sofa and padded to her. He was a gorgeous cat and clearly loved. He butted Celine's calf with his head.

'It's OK, boy.' She bent to pet him and gently nudged him with her toe. 'Go back to sleep.' He returned to his pillow. 'Don't mind the mess,' she said to me. 'I've been meaning to clean, but work has been demanding.'

There it was. The apology to the mother-in-law. I stepped inside. 'I think your place looks lovely.' *You catch more bees with honey,* I mused. 'You have a nice eye for color.'

'Thanks.'

'Are you enjoying work?'

'Yes.' After getting her master's, Celine had won the plum position of constituent advocate in the office of the representative for Louisiana's 2nd congressional district. The job required monitoring local issues and updating the congressman as necessary. It was a position that Keira would have coveted.

'So where did Aiden go?'

She closed the door. 'Out.'

Could she be more cryptic? I surveyed the living room. It wasn't messy at all. In fact, everything was in its place. Pillows on the deep blue couch were neatly propped against the arms and back. The bookshelves were filled with books and LPs – not CDs. Aiden told me they'd started collecting records, preferring the sound of authentic vinyl records to that of CDs. The items seemed carefully positioned, as if for a photospread in *Architectural Digest*. A selection of popular magazines were neatly arrayed on the coffee table. Photographs and Aiden's sketches, primarily torso drawings all framed in silver, adorned the walls. The dual altars that Aiden and Celine had set on the burlwood buffet table – creating ritual spaces in homes was common in New Orleans – were cluttered with trinkets, crystals, candles, and photographs, yet tidy.

When I'd first moved to the city, it had unnerved me that there was an omnipresent belief in something existing beyond the here and now, like ghosts. My mother, being from Louisiana, had had similar beliefs, though my father had wholeheartedly dismissed them, and after Benjie died, I'd given up believing in anything. But a year or two after graduating Tulane, I embraced the woo-woo New Orleans spirit. In fact, I found it quirky yet comforting. What I enjoyed most about the altars that I'd come across was the importance of family, evident by the placement of photos near or on the altars.

Out of nowhere, I flashed on the altar in the room of the Pelican student who'd hung himself. Like Celine and Aiden and so many others in New Orleans, he too had displayed his altar prominently on a chest of drawers. That was where we'd found the note he'd left saying he couldn't cope.

I shook my head to clear it of the past and refocused on the present.

A two-inch-square, silver-framed picture of Aiden and Celine's wedding day stood on each altar – Aiden with his wavy layered hair, like mine, and tan face like his father, and Celine pristine in a form-fitting, off-the-shoulder white lace gown. I leaned toward it to get a better look.

'We should've invited you,' Celine murmured. 'It was wrong of us not to.'

I was hurt that they hadn't, but I was more miffed that Aiden waited a week before telling me what they'd done, like he was worried I'd have tried to dissuade him. I glanced at her. 'You're simply beautiful.'

'Thank you.'

Out of the corner of my eye, I caught sight of Aiden's Cannondale bicycle leaning against the far wall. I'd given it to him on his eighteenth birthday. A sleek silver helmet hung from the handlebar.

'Are you all right, Maggie?' Celine asked. 'You seem transfixed.'

'I'm fine.'

Celine crossed the living room and switched off the radio that was sitting on the counter dividing the room from the kitchen. 'Coffee?'

'No, thanks.' Normally, I would accept, but my stomach was queasy.

'I'd offer you something to eat, but I just burned the last piece of bread.'

That was the charred smell that hung in the air.

'That's all right.' I spun in place, taking in the rest of the unit. It wasn't large. The bedroom door at the far end of a narrow hall was ajar. Thanks to the full-length mirror standing in the corner, I could view the entire room. The bed was made. Women's navy-blue slacks and matching jacket lay on the blue comforter.

Celine tightened the belt of her robe. 'As you can plainly see, he's not here.'

I faced her. 'When will he get home?'

'What's this about?' Her forehead pinched in the center. 'Why did you really come here?'

I couldn't blame her for being irritated. I was coming on too strong. My go-to defense mechanism. It worked as a dean, not as someone who wanted to earn another person's trust. 'Aiden wrote me a text yesterday saying he was taking off for a bit. To get his head straight.'

'He's been feeling pressured.'

'Because I cut off his funds?'

'That, as well as other things.'

'What other things?'

'His final project. It's not going the way he liked.'

Aiden had told me about the project. The time he'd put in. How he hoped it would lead to a grant so he could pursue his master's degree while working at LGP.

'Plus my work has been stressful,' she said, her gaze softening. 'I've got a lot of responsibilities. I haven't been as supportive as I should.'

'He says you're good at your job. Not just good. Excellent.'

She looked pleased by the compliment. 'I do my best.' She toyed with a strand of hair at the nape of her neck.

'Celine, I'm sorry I barged in, but I need to find Aiden. His father is in the hospital. He's been shot. He wants to see Aiden. I've phoned and texted, but Aiden isn't—'

'Oh, my! I had no idea about Joshua.'

Swell. She called him Joshua, too. I pushed aside the prickly sensation.

'Is he going to be OK?' She laid a hand on her chest.

'Yes,' I said, my insides contracting because honestly I didn't know. I hadn't been able to chat with his doctor. Would he be all right? He had to be. I might feel angry because he abandoned me. But I still loved him. If someone was out to get him . . .

No, I refused to go there. 'I repeat, when will Aiden be—'

'He . . . He won't be.' She pressed her lips together. 'He . . . He left me, Maggie.'

'What?'

'He was embarrassed about not being able to offer more to our marriage financially when you . . .' She didn't finish.

Cut him off. Yeah, drive the point home, why don't you. Crap. What had I done?

'He said I would be better off without him,' she went on.

Her chin began to quiver. I took a step toward her, but she

retreated. I held up my hands, palms forward, placating. I wouldn't touch her. Wouldn't comfort her. Wouldn't *smother* her.

'I'm sorry,' I said gently. Granted, she and I weren't warm to one another. How could we be? We'd barely had more than a few conversations. I wasn't sure how I felt about her. But Aiden was happy with her. I hadn't thought that by cutting off his finances, he would abandon her. What did he not understand about keeping wedding vows? In sickness and in health, for richer or poorer?

Until divorce, that is.

Stop, Maggie, this is not about you.

'He's done it before,' she said demurely.

'Done what?'

'Left. To clear his head.' She twirled a polished fingernail beside her ear. 'He says it opens up his creativity. I keep telling him that if he would just cleanse his chakras . . .' She wiggled a finger in front of her solar plexus. 'But this time, I don't know. He might have left me for good.'

'He's still attending classes, isn't he?' I asked.

'Maybe. I don't know. As I said, he's done this before, like when he didn't get—'

'You have no idea where he's gone?'

'No. He doesn't . . . I . . .' Celine wrapped an arm across her waist, propped the other arm on it, and cupped her face with her hand. Her pinky finger caressed her lips in a restless rhythm. She fought tears.

'How did he leave?' I asked. 'His bike is here. Your VW Rabbit is parked on the street.'

'On foot.'

Had he hitchhiked? Caught a bus? 'When? Today?'

'Sunday.'

So he'd texted from someplace else yesterday morning. Where? If he'd been kidnapped, he wouldn't have been able to text, would he? Unless, like I'd theorized, his captor was sending the messages and posing as Aiden.

'Celine.' I didn't hold back this time; I clasped her shoulders. 'I told him why I needed to stop paying for everything. He said he understood.'

'Yes, ma'am, he said that, but he didn't. He told me you were being spiteful because you didn't approve of us getting married. He said you were afraid when he graduated that I'd think it was time to get pregnant, which by the way, I can't as it turns out, and he said you were worried I'd stop working, and it would all fall on you.'

I'd never said anything of the sort to Aiden. I'd never uttered a word about them having or not having children or being worried that things would *fall on me*. He'd lied to her. Why? To pit her against me? Or was I right in assuming something bigger was weighing on him? He wasn't a liar by nature. His father was. But Aiden, not a chance. In fact, when he'd learned his father had been unfaithful to me, he'd taken my side. He said liars had no place in this world. If he'd lied, he had a reason. A good reason.

'Were you?' Celine raised an eyebrow. 'Being spiteful?'

'No!' I released her. 'No, I . . . the timing of the flood was unfortunate. I'd meant to help until he finished college and got his new job, but it just turned out this way. The insurance lapsed. It was a huge oversight. A costly oversight. But I didn't do it on purpose.'

I worked through the timing in my head. Was I supposed to have reminded my business manager to pay the policy? Had I subconsciously not done so in order to have an excuse to stop supporting my son and his bride? *Sink or swim, kids. I'm giving up being a helicopter mom. No more whoosh, whoosh.*

No. No way. I was not vindictive. Josh used to say I was one of the least vengeful people on the planet even though I had every right to hold a grudge. Aiden knew that.

'I'm sorry about you not being able to get pregnant,' I murmured.

'It's OK. We talked about it and decided when we're ready, we'll adopt. I guess . . . I guess that could be moot.' After a long moment, she said, 'Aiden said maybe you could have gotten a loan.'

I bridled. 'No, I couldn't have.' I'd already done so to cover my mother's assisted living bills. I was tapped out. He knew that, too. 'When was the last time you talked to him?'

'Sunday night. He said he's OK,' she assured me. 'Don't worry. At least he's responding to my texts.'

'He is?' I breathed easier. She didn't know where he was, but he was in communication with her. He was fine. He just needed to sort some things out. He'd come back to her.

'If you don't mind, I need to dress for work.' She pointed to the door.

'Would you please text him and tell him to contact his father?

He can call Josh's cell phone. Tess will answer. Or better yet, he could go to University Medical Center.'

Celine nodded. 'Who shot Joshua? Did the police catch the guy?'

'Not yet. They think it was someone he was investigating.' Or maybe by now they had arrested whoever did it. I'd have to ask Tess.

Celine opened the front door for me and stopped me with a hand on my arm. 'I'm worried about Aiden. He seemed . . . Unstable isn't the right word. He's just . . . I hope he won't . . .' She licked her lips, hesitant to voice what must be going through her mind because it was going through mine.

'He's not suicidal.'

'Right. He's not crazy like your broth— No, wait. *Crazy* isn't the word I meant to use,' she added quickly. 'I should have said tormented.'

'Because he was bullied.'

Her pretty mouth turned down in a frown. 'There are too many bullies in this world.'

No kidding. I knew dozens.

'All I'm saying is Aiden's not . . . he wasn't bullied. He won't . . . you know . . .' Celine removed her hand from my arm.

SEVEN

I climbed into my Prius, every nerve ending jangling. Celine's parting comment had rocked me to my core. Was I wrong? Was Aiden suffering in a way I'd never imagined? Was he contemplating ending his life? Was my mother's intuition failing me?

No. Not possible.

When he was five, I'd sensed he was hurt. I went in search and discovered he'd fallen off the wall between the neighbor's house and ours and was lying on the ground, the wind knocked out of him, unable to make a sound. When he'd gone to a party in junior high, I'd had the feeling he was being ganged up on. As it turned out, two boys had given him a Gatorade shower with a cooler full of the sugary juice to humiliate him.

Maggie, he might be in trouble. Act. Now. I couldn't wait for my son to text me, and I sure as heck wasn't going to hang around until I heard from the police that they'd found my son's body. I'd worked the crime beat, for Pete's sake. I knew how to chase down a story.

I tapped the Internet icon on my cell phone and pulled up the address for Le Gran Palais, the digital design company where Aiden was interning. Maybe everything was fine. Celine could be right. Maybe he'd opted to take a break from his marriage so he could focus on his art. On his future. To make a good impression so LGP would hire him full time.

The French Quarter was the most famous area in New Orleans. Known for its lacy, cast-iron balconies. Popular for its night life. Home to many restaurants. I'd dined in nearly every one and had shopped at many of the clothing stores. LGP was set in a brick-red building, its balconies painted white. Pots of flowers lined the balconies. Ivy grew up the trellises.

I stepped inside the building and was taken aback by the ultra-modern décor. What a contrast to the exterior. The reception desk and chairs were black-and-gold and sharp-edged. Glass partitions allowed a view of all adjoining rooms. The wall behind the receptionist was solid, painted with a geometric pattern, and featuring framed posters of some of LGP's biggest accounts. In an office to the right, a gaunt woman in her forties was consulting with an equally bony man in front of a wall decorated with architectural blueprints. In the office to my left, a thickset man in his thirties sat at a sleek black desk. He was leaning forward talking toward a telephone. On speaker, I presumed.

Another room featured numerous workstations with iMacs, iPads with Apple Pencils, art supplies, mood boards, and four young artists – none of them Aiden – hard at work. On the walls behind the artists were images by some of Aiden's heroes, like Andy Warhol, Deborah Kass, and Bill Claps.

A young redheaded receptionist – Rosalie, her nameplate read – sat at a desk fitted with angled legs and drawers suspended by metal cords. She had deep-set hypnotic eyes and a pouty mouth. Her black-and-gold sheath matched the office's décor. Had she dressed that way on purpose?

'Help you?' Rosalie asked in a rich New Orleans accent.

'I'm Aiden Lawson's mother.'

'I see the resemblance. You look like him.' She twirled a finger. 'Your hair. The line of your jaw. I don't look anything like my mother. And that's a blessing, I assure you. Mama doesn't know how to say no to bacon.'

I didn't want to engage in small talk. 'Is Aiden here?'

'No, ma'am.'

'Seen him lately?'

'He hasn't been here in a couple of days.' She stroked her long neck languidly.

'He reports to a man named Stan Studebaker, doesn't he?'

She nodded. 'Sure does. And sometimes to me if I have a task to dole out.' The corners of her mouth curved up mischievously.

'Is Mr Studebaker here?'

'Yes.'

'I'd like to speak with him.'

'Sure thing.' Rosalie swept her long curls over her shoulders and flounced in her high-heeled gold sandals to the office where the thickset man was conversing. She rapped on the door, opened it, and poked her head in. 'Hey, Stan, sorry to interrupt. Aiden Lawson's mom would like to see you, if you got a moment.'

The man squinted in my direction and ended his call. He lumbered to his feet, smoothed his hair with his palms, and fingered the buttons of his black linen shirt, to make sure none of his buttons had popped open. He moved into the foyer. 'Mrs Lawson, or rather, Dean Lawson. Stan Studebaker. Call me Stan.' He extended his hand, his gaze warm. We shook. 'A pleasure to meet you. I've heard a lot about you.'

'Good things, I hope.'

'Good enough.' Stan laughed at his own wit.

I flinched. Aiden wouldn't have talked to his boss about me cutting him off, would he? *Chill, Maggie. Don't go all paranoid. Aiden is a total professional.*

'What can I do for you?' Stan smiled broadly.

'My son—' I hesitated. Did I really want to say Aiden was ghosting me? 'Have you seen him? His father had an accident.' That seemed the easiest way to put it.

Rosalie gasped. 'I'm so sorry. Is he OK?'

'He's in the hospital. He'd like to see Aiden.'

Stan said, 'He was due in yesterday but didn't show. He texted. Said he needed a break. Isn't that right?' He looked over at Rosalie.

'Yep,' she said. 'I texted back that Stan said it was fine.'

Stan nodded. 'We haven't been under the gun on any projects.'

'Did he say why he needed a break?' I asked.

'I figured it was a school thing,' Stan said. 'I remember how rough it was during my last semester at Tulane. The pressure.'

'But he didn't specify the reason?' I pressed.

Stan looked at Rosalie, who shrugged. I cocked my head, wondering if they were being purposely evasive.

'By the way, Aiden is quite a talent,' Stan said. 'He has a bright future in the digital world.'

Rosalie peeked at her iWatch. 'You've got that meeting in a few, Stan.'

He glanced at the clock hanging on the wall. 'Right.'

Wanting to keep them talking a tad longer, hoping Aiden might contact them while I did, or better yet, walk in, I said, 'How does one make a living as a digital artist? There have to be millions of them around the world, all working from home.'

Stan offered an indulgent smile. 'First of all, yes, there are millions, but they aren't vetted. Our company is vetted. We have a stellar reputation. So working for us is a super way to start.'

'You've won awards.'

'Yes. That gives us traction.'

'How will Aiden earn his keep?' I asked.

'Mostly he'll be getting commissions on work he does for us. In addition, we're opening our facility to more interns, artists younger than Aiden, so we've offered to pay him a salary to teach them the ropes.'

'He's a good little teacher,' Rosalie chirped.

Aiden was a good little teacher. When he was eleven, he entered the school talent show so he could give a step-by-step chat of how his art came to life. I'd never forget how much he was shaking as he took to the stage, his portable easel in hand. But he propped up his sketch and then, like a seasoned professor, described each brush-stroke, each technique. The children taunted. They pointed. He didn't falter. He accepted their slings and arrows with courage. Later that night, I perched on his bed and answered the question I knew he'd ask some day. What had driven Benjie to such despair that he would kill himself? I tried to explain my brother's mental state, that the torment of his fellow athletes had hurt him so deeply he couldn't rally. Aiden kept shaking his head. *Death doesn't solve anything. You can't fight back if you're dead.* I knew my son would never take his own life. He simply wouldn't.

I said, 'The last time Aiden and I spoke, he mentioned NFTs.' In fact, a couple of months ago, he'd done his best to explain the concept to me, and I hadn't understood, so I had done a deep dive. Like my ex-husband, I liked to have a thorough knowledge of a subject. 'What are those exactly?' I asked, playing dumb.

Stan frowned. 'Non-fungible tokens, otherwise known as units of data, are stored on what we call digital ledgers.'

'Blockchains,' Rosalie said.

'Yes, blockchains' – Stan bobbed his head – 'which certify that the digital asset, in Aiden's case his particular piece of art, is unique and, therefore, not interchangeable. Ergo, NFTs can be used as currency.'

'Cryptocurrency,' Rosalie cut in. 'Think of 'em like casino chips. You use 'em to trade for something else.'

'Without taxation?' I addressed Stan.

'No, there are taxes involved,' he said, 'but not everyone reports the transactions properly. And there are some scams. Like this guy who boasted that he'd created an NFT and then sold it back and forth to himself until he'd run the price up by four.'

'Real sketchy,' Rosalie said. 'In any other market, that'd be totally illegal.'

'Are there fake NFTs?' I asked.

'Good question,' Stan said like I was his prized student. 'Yes. That's when someone copies an artist's digital work, places it on the blockchain, and sells it in the artist's name.'

'This is a significant problem,' Rosalie said.

'One of our artists woke up last March to find emails and tweets asking him if his NFTs were for sale on a couple of sites.' Stan shook his head. 'They most definitely were not.'

'So it's a form of corruption,' I stated, having arrived at the conclusion I'd aimed for.

Stan and Rosalie exchanged an uncomfortable look.

I said, 'The NFTs are tracked on blockchains so that the owner, or rather the artist, can claim ownership and, therefore, copyright.'

'Uh-huh,' Rosalie murmured.

'Can Aiden make money this way?'

'He can earn a very good living,' Stan said.

'An artist just sold the NFT for his game character for over a million bucks,' Rosalie said. 'Even blue-chip artists like Damien

Hirst are jumping on the bandwagon. You know who he is?' She
didn't wait for a response. 'He's brilliant. He does laminated *giclée*
work on aluminum composite panels.'

I whistled, acting impressed. 'Will you own control over my son's
NFTs, Stan?'

He pursed his lips, weighing his answer. 'Is that why you're
really here? To negotiate on his behalf?'

'No.' I drew in a long breath and released it. 'I'm here because
Aiden is not returning my text messages or phone calls.'

'Aah.' Rosalie bobbed her head. 'My guess is he hasn't answered
you because things have been edgy between you two. You're sort
of estranged, aren't you?'

'We're not estranged,' I said, emphasizing the word. 'Where did
you get that idea?'

'Aiden said you were at odds. You know, off.'

Estranged was harsh and not a word Aiden typically would use,
but perhaps he'd considered Rosalie, who worked in the same field,
a confidante. He might have asked her if she and her parents were
ever *at odds* about finances, and that kind of intimate exchange
made Rosalie come up with the word *estranged*. I assessed her with
a keener eye. She seemed to know a lot about my son. Had she
made a play for him? Had he left his wife for her? No, he loved
Celine. Adored her.

I said, 'Off or not is beside the point. He can ghost me, but not
his father. I'm worried—'

'I'm sorry to hear about his dad,' Rosalie cut in. 'Truly. But don't
fret about Aiden.' She tapped her sparkly gold cell phone. 'He's
fine.'

EIGHT

I left the building and marched to my car. Red-faced for even
thinking I could wheedle information from LGP, I sat in the
driver's seat but didn't switch on the car as apprehension swelled
within me again. Despite Rosalie's assurance, I wasn't confident
that my son was, indeed, *fine*.

A bicyclist whizzed past the car. I flashed on Aiden, passionate about bicycling. He wouldn't have walked out on Celine without taking his Cannondale. He prided himself on getting in a ten-mile ride every day. Often, he rode with a buddy from high school, Zach. I tattooed the steering wheel trying to come up with his last name. Then it dawned on me.

I searched for Zach Iles online and found him on Facebook. He was an ecology and evolutionary biology major at Tulane. No personal information. No email. I tried a new search, adding the words *telephone number*. Nothing new came up for him. Then I remembered his father's name, Zebadiah. A single dad, he'd served on the PTA with me. He owned a funeral and cemetery services company, quaintly referred to as *hospitality* in New Orleans. I located the company listing and dialed. Mr Iles wasn't in. To my good fortune, his assistant turned out to be his daughter. When I told her I was looking for Aiden and hoped Zach might have a clue as to his whereabouts, she was more than happy to share her brother's info. She liked Aiden.

I phoned Zach. He had a break in classes and agreed to meet at a nearby café.

Beignet Bistro was fitted with a mish-mash of antique furniture. According to posters on the walls, their beignets were every bit as good as the ones at Café Beignet on Royal and Café du Monde on Decatur. I wondered if a business could boast such a thing without receiving some kind of backlash, but if the size of the crowd was any indication, the café wasn't lying. The place was packed. Zach, dressed in black-and-yellow bicycle gear, was sitting at a corner table. The straps of his fanny pack and helmet were slung over the prong of his ladder-back chair. A hands-free hydroflask, the kind I'd seen many bicyclists strap on for hydration, sat on the table. He rose when I approached and gestured to a cup of coffee and beignet he'd purchased for me.

'Figured you'd be hungry, Mrs L,' he said as if no time had passed between now and the last time I'd seen him. He was nice-looking in a boyish way. Shorter and slenderer than Aiden. A thatch of hay-colored hair fell on his forehead. His face, like Aiden's, was burnished by the sun. He took a bite of his treat, wiped the powdered sugar off his mouth with the back of his hand, and sipped his coffee. 'You said Aiden's missing. You're sure? I mean, knowing him, he's, like, probably gone on a super-long bike ride to prepare for finals and such.'

'Except his bike is in his duplex.'

That puzzled him.

I said, 'Celine told me he left her.'

'Nah. He wouldn't. He's committed to the relationship.'

Quickly I summed up the situation – my house, the flood, cutting Aiden off financially, the text saying he needed to get his head on straight, Josh in the hospital. 'I think something's wrong. I can't explain it.'

'Mother's intuition?' Zach grinned.

'The news about his father should have made him call. You'd phone your mother if you heard something had happened to your father, right?'

'Sure would.'

'Maybe I'm being overly concerned.' *Whoosh, whoosh* zipped through my mind. I took a sip of the coffee. Hickory. It was bitter but good. I eyeballed the beignet but didn't eat it. My stomach was getting sourer by the minute. 'What if he's in trouble, Zach?'

'C'mon.' He pushed his coffee away, folded his arms on the table, and leaned forward. His mouth twitched with good humor. 'Is this your Spidey-sense talking, Mrs L?'

'No. I rely on cold hard facts. But let's face it, I've known my son the longest, so I know him better than anybody, and being incommunicado isn't like him.'

'My mom says the same about me.' Zach's expression grew grave. He lowered his hands to his lap. 'You know, I've been sort of curious why he hasn't touched base with me, too. I mean, we go riding every couple of days. If I'm being straight, something's been different with him for a couple of weeks.'

'A couple.'

'Yeah. We came here for a bite, and I told him to spill, but he pretended to be out of breath and said he couldn't respond. FYI, Aiden is never out of breath. He has the lungs of a sea turtle.'

'The lungs of a—'

'Sea turtles can hold their breath for nearly ninety minutes.'

I ran a finger along the rim of my coffee cup, waiting.

'I knew it was a hedge.' Zach scanned the restaurant, as if picturing their last meeting. 'I pressed him harder. Asked if he was mooning about Keira. I happened to know it was her birthday. He said to leave it alone.'

'Leave it alone?'

'Yeah, like, he even hissed.'

OK, that was not Aiden at all. 'He didn't apologize immediately?'

'Nope. Hey' – he propped his hands on the table – 'maybe this could mean something. Later, when I was coming back from the restroom, I saw him writing something. I thought he was crossing off a debt he'd paid in his ledger.'

'A debt?'

'Yeah, me and him, occasionally, we borrow a couple of bills from a guy. No big deal. We both record everything. Nothing's ever left hanging in the wind, you know?' He fanned the air as if to emphasize the casualness of the arrangement before leaning forward on his elbows. 'But then I realized he wasn't writing in his ledger. He was jotting something in his journal.'

In high school, an art teacher had suggested Aiden record his thoughts whenever someone bullied him about his gift. She said it would help him make the words his tormentors used less hurtful. He told me after graduation that his journal had helped him process everything and gave him perspective. As far as I knew, he'd continued the practice because he'd mentioned how much journaling had helped him after Keira's death, too.

'Seeing me approaching,' Zach continued, 'he shoved the journal into his CamelBak.'

'Is that his fanny pack?'

'Yup. Hey, maybe if he left the Cannondale behind, he left the journal behind, too. Maybe he wrote down where he planned to go to work things out in his head. My two cents?' Zach rose to his feet and grabbed his fanny pack and helmet. 'I don't believe he'd leave Celine. Not for good. I mean, yeah, he misses Keira and everything, but he's, like, madly in love with Celine. He's probably just on a walkabout. Thinking things through. Give him time.'

I wasn't sure I had time.

NINE

I drove home and poured myself a tall glass of ice water. Downed it in one long pull. Then lurched to the porch, my brain aching with information that led nowhere. Where was my son? American kids didn't do walkabouts. They didn't live in the wilderness for six months to make the spiritual transition into manhood. They were softer. Needier.

A thought occurred to me. I set my glass down on the table with a *clack*. Was Aiden ghosting me while staying in communication with Celine? Had Rosalie tapped her cell phone to intimate that she, too, was receiving regular texts? If that was the case, why wasn't he reaching out to his father? And why wouldn't he, at the very least, contact Zach, his riding buddy?

'Dammit,' I grumbled. If only I really did have Spidey-senses and could suss out the truth.

I returned inside for a glass of chardonnay. As I poured, I dialed Yvonne. She ran through a list of messages. The attorney for the prosecution in the Tuttle case wanted to chat with me. Again. Provost Southington needed an updated list of professorial prospects. Gregory Watley wanted yet another in-person meeting.

'He'll have to wait,' I said. 'Anything else that's actually urgent?'

'No fires.'

'Thanks. I'll see you tomorrow.'

I hung up, took a sip of wine, and tried Josh's cell phone.

Tess answered. 'Hi, Maggie.' She sounded stuffed up. She blew her nose.

'Hi,' I said. 'Any change with Josh?' I was over trying to say *Joshua*. It didn't fit him. He wasn't fussy.

'He woke up, but he's sleeping now.' She sniffed. 'I wish I'd run into you when you came by to see him.'

'Me, too,' I lied. I had no desire to see her. I wasn't her enemy, but I wasn't her big sister, either.

'Aiden still hasn't touched base.'

'Not even a text?'

'No.'

'Do the police know who shot Josh yet?'

'They're investigating. How long does it take? Will they—' She cut herself off. Blew her nose again.

'Investigations take time.' *Too much time*, I thought. 'You mentioned Josh was looking into a case of corruption. Do you know who the mark was?'

'The mark?'

'The person he was tailing. Was it Carl Underhill?'

'Who?'

'A Texas businessman who deals in illegal pharmaceuticals, or used to.'

'I don't know. Joshua didn't—' She faltered. '*Doesn't*. He doesn't ever mention names. You could talk to his editor at *The Advocate*, I suppose.'

'Did Josh have notes or a recording on his cell phone or other device?'

'I didn't check. I've never peeked at his work. The police didn't ask, either. Maybe I . . .' She made a grunting sound. 'No, I couldn't. That would be overstepping. He's . . . He's not open about his work. You probably know that.'

Actually, when we were married, Josh was eager to discuss his investigations with me. Maybe because I, too, having been a crime reporter, understood the nuances. I could pinpoint holes in his discovery. He'd liked the way my mind worked. I'd felt the same about him.

'Yes,' I murmured to appease her. 'Reporters can be tight-lipped.' She didn't need to feel *less than* at this moment. 'If he wakes, will you text me?'

'Sure.'

'And when Aiden touches base, let me know.'

'OK.'

I ended the call and fingered the wineglass. *Oh, Josh. What were you working on?* I'd never insisted he change his career. He was smart. Cautious. Always on the alert. But this time it was clear that he'd stepped into something bad. Had he poked a hornets' nest? I remembered the day Underhill was released from prison two years ago. He'd paraded his wife and five boys in front of the TV cameras and claimed he was a changed man. A law-abiding family man. He vowed he was going straight from that moment on. He'd learned his lesson. He held no grudge. Was that all a crock of bull?

Did you catch him in a new scheme, Josh?

Crash! Thud! Glass shattered. And something else.

My pulse skyrocketed. I pulled a carving knife from the knife block. Stole to the archway between the kitchen and living room. Sneaked a peek. Ducked back to process what I'd seen. Nothing. No prowler.

Heart jackhammering my ribcage, I looked again and realized the painting over the mantle had fallen to the floor. It had taken part of the wall and a ceramic vase with it. The picture hanger hook that had held it in place dangled precariously. The plaster had given way.

Chill, Maggie.

I was not being invaded. So why did I suddenly feel as if I was being watched? I crossed the living room and peered out the glass windows. Into the darkness. I didn't detect any shadowy movement in the yard other than from the branches of the sycamore, which was an eerily shaped tree even in daylight.

Fear prickled the nape of my neck as I returned to the kitchen. I focused on the synchronicity of the crash and my thoughts about Josh and Underhill. I wondered again about my misgivings at the hospital. Was it possible Underhill or one of his minions had kidnapped Aiden to wield power over Josh?

No, Mags. Stop! Aiden texted Celine and his workplace. He's fine.

But if he was all right, then why wasn't he reaching out to Josh? Why not at least let me know he was following up on that?

'Poor Celine,' I whispered.

Had I, with my money troubles, inadvertently driven a wedge between her and Aiden? That hadn't been my intention, but I really did believe they could make ends meet on her salary. If only I could tell Aiden that in person. Ask forgiveness. Make things right.

I took a sip of wine, shrugged into a peacoat, and carried my cell phone back to the porch. I needed a voice of reason to talk me down from the ledge. I dialed Gina.

She answered after one ring. 'Hey. How did it go with Josh?'

'He'll survive.'

'And Aiden?'

'He hasn't touched base with me, and he still hasn't reached out to Josh. I went to see Celine.'

'Spill,' she ordered.

I recapped my day. The interaction with my son's wife and the people at his workplace. Coming away from the meeting with Zach feeling that I was missing something.

'The journal. If I could find the journal, maybe that would give me a clue.'

'Maybe.'

'Last but not least,' I said, 'I've got to wonder why I'm so worried. This is not me. It's not at all me.'

'Because your son is being a jerk, which is definitely not *him*. I'm not a mother, Maggie, nor do I ever wish to be one, but it's got to be hard carrying a child for nine-plus months, raising him to be an upstanding citizen, and then getting the cold shoulder for no reason.'

'But there was a reason,' I moaned.

'No. Stop that. Cutting off his funds does not warrant his silence. He knows banks have limits on how much they'll lend.'

'Unless he's ticked off that it caused friction between him and the woman he loves.' I sighed. 'She's bereft, Gina, and it's all my fault.'

She waited a moment to allow me my pity party, then said, 'Maggie, let's talk about what's really going on with you.'

I knew by her solemn tone where she was headed. 'You mean my abandonment issues?' We'd talked about them ad nauseum.

"Sweetie, everyone you've ever loved—'

'Has left me. My brother killed himself. Days later, Mom and Dad checked out. Got it.'

'And Josh. Don't forget Josh.'

'Don't sugar coat it,' I jibed.

'Not only with the divorce, but right now he's threatening to leave you in a whole different way.'

'No, Gina. He's not dying. He's stable.'

'As for Aiden—'

'He's missing in action.'

'His disappearance feeds right into your lack of self-worth.'

'I don't have a lack of self-worth.'

'Um, I beg to differ.' Her singsong lilt lent a moment of levity to the conversation. 'So let me remind you as I have before, you are a good mother. A loving mother. A mother who nurtured a kind and caring son.'

'Exactly.'

'A son who is acting totally out of character. You don't deserve this kind of behavior.'

'He thinks I cut him off on purpose. Because he got married without my permission.' I moaned. 'Did you hear what I just said? My *permission*? As if I needed to grant it. He's over eighteen.'

'But he was on your dole.'

'Yes.'

'So he equated the two.'

'He told Celine I was afraid when he graduated that she would think it was time to get pregnant.'

'That's bull. You never once expressed those sentiments to me.'

'I know. Never!'

'Now, listen up . . .'

For the next half-hour, she asked me about my feelings and suspicions. She wasn't my doctor, she said, but she couldn't help herself. When I was so tired I could barely see straight, I told her I needed sleep. She made me promise I would meet her for drinks at seven tomorrow night. I vowed I would.

But when I ended the call, I didn't just swear. I cursed like a sailor.

TEN

Wednesday morning hit me upside the head. After dreaming of Gregory Watley working in cahoots with Carl Underhill, and Le Gran Palais stealing all of Aiden's creations, and Celine's cat scratching my eyes out, and Aiden gasping for breath while pleading for help, I realized I couldn't wait around all day on the off-chance I'd hear from my son. What if I was right about him being kidnapped? What if my theory that his captor was sending the messages was true? What if . . .

I needed to know what Josh had been up to and who he might've angered. I called *The Advocate*. The woman I spoke to had no idea what Josh was investigating.

Back when I'd worked the crime beat, I'd gone to NOPD's Second District Station to pick up news bites. Officer Frank Filuzzi had been my first contact. Filuzzi had followed in his father's footsteps and entered the department bursting with optimism. He'd made it his mission to right the world's wrongs. He and he alone would make New Orleans a safe place. Given my father's history at LAPD and the fact that I'd attended the police academy, albeit leaving before graduation, Filuzzi had taken me seriously. Enough. He gave me a couple of scoops. He flirted. We ended up dating for a New Orleans minute but agreed we had no future. He hated writers and, after my father's downfall, I hadn't been keen on cops. I remembered Filuzzi being a good kisser. He'd been an even better listener.

Nowadays, Filuzzi was a big deal. After working in the Fourth District as an investigator and the Fifth as a supervisor, he was promoted to District Investigative Unit Sergeant in the Crime Investigations Division. Last I'd checked, he was married with two children, a boy and a girl.

I left a message for Yvonne to tell her what I was up to and went to the precinct on Broad Street. The building was impressive from the outside. Inside the precinct, I felt like I'd walked on to the set of a television cop show. The bored clerk at the security desk had me sign in. I needed a badge to enter.

The main squad room was abuzz with activity. Cops were dealing with perps or hanging with colleagues, catching up. Filuzzi was in the middle of a gab session with three other guys. He spotted me and approached.

'Well, well, Dean Maggie Lawson,' he said. 'As I live and breathe. What a surprise.' He was tall and muscular with a flat nose that had received a beating or two. His hazel eyes could be cold or warm, depending on his mood. For the moment, they were warm. He buttoned a single button on his blazer and motioned me to follow him to his desk. 'You look nice in blue. You always do.'

'Thank you.' My cheeks warmed. I hadn't received a compliment from a man in a long time. I'd donned a peacock-blue sheath dress, matching sweater jacket with soft lapels, ballet slippers, and a silver heart charm necklace – the one I'd bought to replace my grandmother's missing cameo necklace. I'd wanted something to hand down to a grandchild, should I ever have one.

'To what do I owe the pleasure?' He sat and gestured to the chair at one side of his desk. 'Did you come to donate to the police fund?' He nudged a pencil holder to one side. Righted the edges of the blotter. Leaned forward on his elbows, hands folded. 'We're accepting donations of any denomination.'

I sat and tucked a loose strand of hair behind my ear. 'My son Aiden is sort of missing.'

'Sort of?'

I knew the words sounded idiotic the moment they'd escaped my mouth, but I couldn't retract them. 'I've texted him, but he's not responding. To me or his father. And Josh has been shot!'

'Woah. Wait. Josh took a bullet?'

'In the shoulder.'

Filuzzi had met Josh during an investigation. He'd never liked him. He'd thought he was cocky and told him so to his face. After their encounter, Josh had ranted at me about what a jerk Filuzzi was. *Men.*

'I'm not sure who shot him,' I went on, 'but ten years ago he investigated a drug lord masquerading as a Texas businessman, Carl Underhill. The man went to prison and vowed revenge.'

'I'm familiar with the case. He's out now and has cleaned up his act.'

'Has he?' I arched an eyebrow. 'What if he kidnapped my son to punish Josh or to keep him from investigating something new?'

'Kidnapped? That's a leap.' He motioned with a hand. 'Go back. From the beginning. Your son is ghosting you and your husband.'

'My ex. He's engaged now.'

'Bully for him.'

'I've texted and left messages for Aiden about how vital it is to see his dad, but I get zip.'

Filuzzi leaned back in his chair. 'What's new? My kids don't want anything to do with me unless it's about baseball. How old is he?'

'Twenty-one.'

'Yeah, once they can drive, they want total independence. Mine are seventeen and eighteen and champing at the bit. Their mother is climbing the walls with their attitude. Is your son in college?'

I nodded. 'At Tulane.'

Filuzzi whistled. 'He's smart. Good for him. Ours are so-so students and will do community college for two years, then we'll see where it goes.'

'Aiden is smart enough. But that's the thing. He's in his last semester and should know not to go off and miss classes and . . .'

I sighed. 'Truth? He's mad at me.' I quickly filled him in on the situation. The flood. The money issue.

'So he's ticked off because you pulled the plug on the ATM.'

'Yes, but the fact that he should've contacted his father by now and hasn't done so eats at me. He adores his father. I visited Aiden's wife—'

'He's married?'

'Yes.'

'Is she PG?'

'No.'

Filuzzi arched an eyebrow. 'Why'd they get married so young?'

'They fell in love,' I said matter-of-factly. In bullet points, I briefed him on Aiden's history with Keira, the accident, and Celine consoling Aiden.

'Has the wife heard from him?'

'Yes. Sunday night.'

'You saw the text?'

'Well, no. I didn't ask. He also texted his workplace where he's been interning.'

'Just not you. C'mon, Maggie—'

'Or his father,' I retorted. Anxiety radiated through me. 'Celine, his wife, says he was upset because he couldn't offer anything financially to the marriage, so he left her. On foot.'

'Why does mode of transportation matter?'

'He has a bike. He rides every day. He left it behind.'

'Oka-ay.' He dragged out the word, his expression stoic.

'Celine claims he's done this before.'

'Has he?'

'He's never mentioned it to me. But boys have secrets.' The word rattled me. Boys had secrets. Husbands had secrets. My brother had held on to the biggest secret of all.

'So do girls. My youngest?' Filuzzi's mouth turned up on one side. 'Man, she's like an emotional tornado sometimes, but when I ask what's wrong, it's always' – he mimed air quotes – 'nothing.'

'Aiden's bicycle buddy Zach Iles hasn't heard from him. That's bugging me, too. Why communicate with his wife and this other woman' – if he was communicating with Rosalie – 'but not Zach or his father?'

'One is his main squeeze and the other – let me make a wild guess – is his dream girl. He knows his buddy Zach will be *chill*.

As for his dad, Aiden probably thinks you're blowing what happened to him out of proportion, and he'll touch base in a while. Time is relative.'

'It's not just me. Josh's fiancée has left messages, too.'

Filuzzi folded his arms across his chest. 'Look, Maggie, I'm sorry to say it, but your son is an adult and has a right to privacy. Your mother's intuition that something's wrong' – he twirled a finger at my face – 'holds no water in our hallowed halls.'

'What if he's hurt?'

'There're no sign saying he's come to harm, is there? Blood? Torn clothing?'

I shook my head.

'Didn't think so.' Filuzzi rose and laid a warm hand on my shoulder.

I bolted to my feet and shimmied away. 'Don't, Frank. Just don't. I don't need you to patronize me. You know me better than that. I'm levelheaded. I don't get flustered.' If anything, I could be cool, calm, and collected to a fault. At least I used to be. 'And not calling his dad? He's not like that. Aiden is a compassionate soul.' Like Benjie, I thought. Angrily, I spanked one hand against the other. 'Please, Frank, if we'd taken the other path, this could be our son. *Ours*.' I'd hooked up with Josh six months after Filuzzi and I ended things.

'Hey! I get it. He's your kid. You want answers. And, Maggie, if I could do something to help, I would, but for now, I can't. No probable cause.'

'What about looking at closed-circuit TV footage? Maybe he was seen getting on a bus. Or climbing into a stranger's car.' The latter thought nauseated me. I whipped a photograph of Aiden out of my wallet. 'This is him. Aiden Lawson. Blond hair. About five-ten. One hundred and seventy pounds.'

'Nice looking kid. Looks like you and—' He balked.

'And my brother.'

I knew the connection Filuzzi was making. During our courtship, I'd invited him over for a homecooked meal. He'd seen the family photos. Heard the saga. Yet again, a wave of anxiety scudded through me. Yes, Aiden looked like Benjie, but he was not *like* him. Not in that way. He'd handled the bullying. His art had given him confidence. He was not suicidal. *Not*.

'Don't go there, Frank.'

'OK.' He didn't sound convinced.

'About Carl Underhill,' I said, stowing the photo. 'He showed up on campus out of the blue.' I paused. 'No, not out of the blue. For a parent-student tour. But he made a point to chat with me, and running into him like that felt more than coincidental. It felt purposeful, like he—'

'Has Underhill dunned you or Josh for ransom?'

'No.'

'Has he made threatening phone calls? Or made any demands through other sources?'

'No.'

Filuzzi's face remained passive. 'Maggie, my hands are tied. There's nothing we can do for at least forty-eight hours, and even if we could, there's no smoking gun. No foul play. No body. Nothing to link your son to Carl Underhill or anyone else. My advice? Go home. Send Aiden another text. Tell him how seriously you're taking this. Tell him to give you a sign that he's OK.'

I flashed on the handful of parents I'd blown off when they'd come into my office complaining about lack of communication with their children. *How does it feel now that the shoe is on the other foot, Mags?*

'Fine, Frank.' I huffed. 'Thanks for nothing. I'll find him myself.'

'If he wants to be found.'

ELEVEN

On my way to Pelican, I thought of something Filuzzi asked. Had I seen the text Aiden sent Celine? I sure hadn't viewed the texts Rosalie and Aiden's boss Stan Studebaker said they'd received. Could they all be lying? Why? To drive me insane? The lyric *Paranoia my old friend* ran through my head to the tune of 'The Sound of Silence.'

Determined to get answers, I changed course and zoomed to Celine's place of business, the local office of the representative for Louisiana's Second Congressional District. Though the congressman primarily worked in Washington DC, he needed a place to call home whenever he came to New Orleans. The space was small but efficient with six employees, each at his or her own desk, each of the desks facing inward so employees could communicate freely. Celine was at the desk nearest the window. The view of Canal Street, the upriver boundary of the French Quarter, was behind her. She rose when I entered, looking chic in a trim red suit and white blouse, her hair swept into a chignon.

I strode to her desk. 'I'd like you to contact Aiden. Now.'

She gawked at me. 'Good morning to you, too.'

'I want to see his response.'

'I'm sorry, Maggie.' She clipped off each word. 'We're not allowed to make private calls during work hours.'

'Text him, then.'

'Maggie.'

'Do it!'

A gentleman in a blue suit lurched to a stand. The other employees sat taller.

'Calm down, Maggie. Take a deep breath. After your visit, I wrote him. Here's his response. He's fine. He'll be coming back to me. I overreacted. Look.' Celine flashed her cell phone at me.

> Celine: *How are you?*
> Aiden: *Doing fine. Wrapping my head around things.*
> *CU soon.*

'Not good enough,' I said, wound too tight to be civil. 'Text him that his father has been shot. He needs to call Josh now. And he needs to text you back that he has. Do it!'

'Fine.' Celine waved for her colleagues to relax and followed my directive.

Within seconds of her pressing Send, I heard a muted buzz. Three of her coworkers lifted their cell phones and scanned the display. None acted, I presumed because of the office policy.

Celine stared at hers. Waiting. I peeked at it, too. No three texting bubbles appeared signifying Aiden was typing. 'He might be in class,' she suggested.

'I'll hang out and wait. Go back to what you were doing.'

Her nose twitched. 'Maggie, I know how upset you are. I am too.'

'I'm sorry.' I breathed in and exhaled. 'I'm . . . I'm really worked up by . . .' I stopped short of revealing the horrific possibilities cycling through my mind, like Aiden being kidnapped.

'Want some coffee?'

'No, thanks.' Caffeine was the last thing I needed. I slipped my hands into my pockets and tried to temper the erratic energy surging through me.

Ten minutes passed. Fifteen. Nothing.

Telephones jangled repeatedly. Celine and her coworkers manned them, answering questions and putting out fires. Even from a distance, I could hear some of the foul language constituents were hurling – community outreach was not for the faint of heart – but Celine was coping. She was good at her job. Calm in a storm. Aiden had often praised her ability. Seeing her in action, I understood why.

When an hour passed, Celine picked up her cell phone. She scanned the screen. Wrinkled her nose. She pressed a button to reboot the phone. Once it refreshed, she swiped the message app. Nothing from Aiden. No three texting bubbles as if he was typing a response.

'If he went to class, he'd be out by now,' I stated.

Celine's jaw started to tremble. Was she finally accepting that my concern was warranted? Voice quavering, she said to her coworkers, 'Hey, you guys, I'm getting some fresh air with my mother-in-law.'

One of the women waved. 'Take your time. We've got this.'

Celine fetched a wool coat off a hat rack by the door. Outside, the air had become crisp. I drew the folds of my sweater jacket tightly around my torso and held them there.

'Usually he considers responding to texts a professional courtesy,' Celine said softly. 'This isn't like him, Maggie.'

'No, it's not,' I said, pleased that she could admit that.

'I'm worried.' Her voice was childlike. Vulnerable. So out of character from the woman I'd just witnessed manning the phones. More like the woman I'd seen struggling to hold it together at their duplex when she'd said Aiden had left her. 'Aiden wouldn't . . .' Using her pinkies, she blotted the tears that had pooled in the corners of her eyes and shook her head.

'Wouldn't what?' I realized where she was going and said, 'No. He wouldn't!'

'Is it genetic?'

'Is what genetic? Suicide? No!' I couldn't accept that. Aiden has always been healthy. Focused. Dedicated to his future. Something knocked him off track. That was all. Not my cutting off his funds. Not my smothering. Something else. But what?

'Lately, he's been withdrawn. He won't tell me what's going on,' Celine said. 'It's because my work occupies all my time. I can be hyper-focused.'

'I can, too. Men aren't the only ones.'

She smiled weakly. 'Aiden has always said he understood my one-track mind. He's come to my office parties to be supportive. He chats with everyone. He's got an easy way about him. He's good at telling stories.'

Josh was, too.

'Me? I'm not nearly so nice,' she went on. 'I don't go to his art school parties. His friends – not friends, colleagues – are always a bit much for me. I'm not an art kind of person. Are you?' She was doing her best to connect with me.

I brushed her arm. 'I like art, but I don't know anything about it. Monet versus Manet? Forget about it.'

'So I'm not the only one?'

'Nope.'

A companionable silence fell between us.

After a long moment, Celine said, 'The money situation. Maybe . . .' She paused.

'Maybe what?' I asked, hoping she wasn't going to ride me about my predicament.

'One time, Aiden borrowed money from a friend. To buy a new computer.'

I thought about what Zach had said, how Aiden wrote down any debts he incurred in a ledger.

'To pay the friend back, he gave him some marijuana,' Celine added. 'You know Aiden smokes, right?'

I didn't, but I wasn't a prude. Marijuana might seem like a gateway for some to more reckless drug use, but I knew plenty of people who smoked that weren't hooked.

Celine picked at a cuticle. 'And there was this other guy Aiden got a loan from. A real lender. He'd only accept cash as repayment.'

Had Aiden really been so strapped that he'd needed to borrow from more than one person?

'You don't think Aiden would have gone back to the real lender to, like, help us over the hump, do you?' she asked. 'We were living off everything you provided and then some. So, yes, when you cut us off . . . I mean, cut Aiden off . . . I mean, when you went under water . . .' She heaved a sigh. 'We've been trying to stick to our budget, but it's been hard. I needed clothes for work. He had to buy some art supplies and a couple of digital art programs to stay current. It adds up.'

I kept mum. Now was not the time to dig into the details of their budget.

'I heard this lender could be pretty tough,' she went on. 'What if he—'

'What's his name?'

'Something LeBlanc. His office is on Royal.'

'Would his name be in Aiden's contacts?'

'It might be, but he took his computer.'

Of course he did. He'd need it for work. And for classes, if he was still going to them. Was he? Would his counselor tell me if he wasn't?

'And the other guy?' I asked.

'A fellow student. I don't know who.'

'What about Aiden's marijuana supplier? Do you know his name?'

'It's a *she*. Mirlande something.'

I was stunned by how little Celine knew about her husband. When Josh and I were married—

No, don't go there, Mags. You didn't know everything about Josh, either. Secrets suck.

I thought of something else Zach said, that Aiden had attempted to hide whatever he was writing when they'd met for coffee. The ledger might hold transactions, but like Zach suggested, Aiden's journal might reveal what his plans were. 'Do you know where Aiden's journal is?' I asked.

'I keep a diary, but I've never seen him write in a journal.'

'Zach said he had one.'

'You spoke to Zach?' Her gaze narrowed.

I bristled at her presumption that only she had access to Aiden's friends. In the past, whenever Aiden and I caught up, I'd inquired about his social life. He'd shared information freely. 'Aiden and Zach were friends in high school.'

'Yes, of course. He had lots of friends.' She lowered her gaze, mollified. 'I only had one back then.'

I chided myself for not having been more interested in Celine or her past. Aiden told me her mother died. She had no siblings. He hadn't mentioned her father. 'I'm sorry.'

'It wasn't your fault. I was shy as a teen.'

Her candidness caught me off guard. Again, I felt the impulse to hug her but held back. She was a grown woman. She didn't need me crowding her.

I allowed silence to fall between us for a respectful moment before saying, 'Are you sure Aiden didn't have a journal?'

'I'm not sure about anything these days.'

I didn't think Zach was lying, which meant Aiden had kept his writing private from his wife. Interesting. Was he protective of what he'd written for a reason? Was he worried about her reaction to what she might read? Had he written about his feelings for Keira?

'I hope you know I wasn't going behind your back by meeting Zach, Celine.' I groped for the right words to convince her but drew a blank.

She lifted her chin. 'I get it. You thought I was lying about the text messages Aiden sent.'

'No, not lying. That's not the right word. I . . . I didn't know what to think, and I was worried.' I couldn't quiet the quaking in my voice. 'Admit it. You're concerned now, too.'

'Yes,' she said meekly. Her shoulders slumped. A tear trickled down her cheek. 'What are you going to do?'

'What I used to do before I ventured into academia. Investigate.'

TWELVE

D espite the sparse information Celine had provided, with Zach's help – I reached out and point-blank asked him about the guy he and Aiden had borrowed *a couple of bills* from; by now I'd figured out that meant hundreds – I was able to track down Leonard LeBlanc's place of business, Cash Quick. The building was dilapidated, the balcony close to falling off. The surrounding buildings were in equal disrepair. How had Aiden and Zach found this guy? Someone must have referred them.

The front door was ajar, one of its hinges worn down to nothing. I stepped inside. The unit was a style seen all over New Orleans, one room beyond another, the rear exit visible from the front. The floor of the foyer was buckling from water damage. The reception desk, unmanned. A fan was humming somewhere. The aroma of stale coffee lingered in the air.

In the semi-silence, I heard a *spit-pop* and the shuffling of feet. Seconds later, a tall figure in a black hoodie tore out the rear door. It recoiled and slammed.

I juddered. My breath caught in my chest. I backed toward the exit ready to flee but halted when I heard a moan. The figure in black must have shot someone. Aiden?

No, please no.

Praying I was wrong, I crouched and stole through the unit, looking left and right. The place was empty. The acrid odor of gunpowder was cloying. In the farthest room, I saw a desk cluttered with files. A heavy safe stood against one wall, its door open an inch. Drawers in the metal file cabinet hung wide too. I spied the top of a head over the back rim of a broad leather chair. A bald head. Not Aiden.

Reluctantly, I edged to the side of the chair and gagged. The victim was flaccid and easily in his fifties and definitely dead. His mouth was agape, his right temple oozing blood. His florid face matched a picture on the wall of a man standing in front of Cash Quick. Leonard LeBlanc, I presumed.

Hands shaking, I pulled out my cell phone to call for help but stopped. How would I explain my presence? Would I draw attention to Aiden? He hadn't been the fleeing figure. That person was a good head taller than my son. I started to retreat but realized I couldn't just do nothing. With a tip, the police might be able to catch the killer. No matter what kind of man LeBlanc might have been, he deserved justice.

Tugging the sleeve of my sweater over my hand, I lifted the landline receiver from the desk and tapped in 911. My teeth were chattering as I stated the emergency. The responder told me to wait for a team to arrive.

Not on a bet.

I was ready to beat a path out the front when my gaze landed on the opened filing cabinet. What had the killer been searching for? Money? Dirt on one of LeBlanc's clients? Did he want to retrieve his own IOU marker?

It dawned on me that there might be one of those with Aiden's or Zach's name on it, too. If there was and the police discovered the markers, would the two of them be considered suspects in LeBlanc's murder?

I broke into a sweat, fearful that by overstaying my welcome, the killer might return. But I had to check. Repeating the sweater-over-hand trick, I scoured the drawers, starting with the topmost. In the second, I landed on a manila folder marked *Iles, Zach*. Inside was a ledger sheet showing Zach had borrowed three hundred dollars. At the bottom in bold red letters it read *Debt Repaid*. In the next drawer, I found a folder with the tab *Lawson, Aiden*. He'd borrowed one thousand dollars. At the bottom of the ledger sheet it, too, read *Debt Repaid*.

Breathing easier, I left the IOU's in place and raced out of the building. I spied a police vehicle approaching as I rounded the corner.

Blocks from Cash Quick, I touched base with Zach again and told him what had happened to LeBlanc – he gasped – and I asked him about the marijuana dealer. He knew her. He, like Aiden, smoked occasionally. Neither of them, he assured me, was a pothead. Mirlande the Haitian – that was how she preferred to be addressed, he said; her name matched the one Celine had given me – worked days at Marie Laveau's House of Voodoo, situated between Preservation Hall and Lafitte's Blacksmith Shop on Bourbon Street.

The shop was small and offered a variety of talismans, spell kits, and voodoo dolls – for both good and bad luck. Studying the dolls on a rack to my left, a memory of Aiden and Josh and me making voodoo dolls came rushing back to me. It was autumn. The weather had been cool, crisp.

'Despite its name,' the forty-something instructor said in a reso-nant voice, her eyes gleaming with zealous enthusiasm, 'the voodoo doll is not really part of voodoo practices.' She sat at a wooden table. Josh, Aiden, and I were on the other side, facing her. An array of felt, yarn, glue, twigs, and buttons lay between us.

A waiflike singer stood at the edge of the nearby cemetery singing a soulful rendition of U2's 'A Day Without Me.' Her audience seemed torn between listening to her and watching our craft session.

'In fact,' the instructor went on, 'its origins link back to practi-tioners of magic in Europe.'

Aiden, a sweet ten-year-old with the most gorgeous blond curls, said, 'Wow. How do you know so much?'

'I've been studying for years.' The woman traced a voodoo doll shape on a piece of felt using a marker. By the look of her weathered

skin, I deduced she slept outdoors. By choice or by necessity, I couldn't be sure. She instructed us to make the same shape on our felt. 'Now, listen up, young man.' She lifted a pair of scissors. 'You can make voodoo dolls do good and bad spells, but I prefer good spells.'

Aiden nodded. 'Me, too.'

Josh ruffled Aiden's tousled hair. 'That's my boy. Casting bad spells is for bad people.'

I watched the two men in my life and remembered a time when I was a girl. My father and Benjie and I had gone on a daytrip to make candles. Benjie had been just as curious as Aiden. It struck me, looking at my husband and son, that I'd been making the same bittersweet comparison all of Aiden's life.

'Can I make one for my friend Keira?' Aiden asked the instructor. Keira and Aiden had been inseparable since the first grade.

'You can make as many as you like. But whoever owns the doll determines its fate.'

'Well, duh,' Aiden said as if he was a voodoo doll sage. 'It's not like I could make hers do something I wanted. That's the point.'

I felt a tap on my shoulder and turned.

A caramel-skinned beauty grinned at me. In a Creole accent, she said, 'Help you?'

'I'm looking for Mirlande the Haitian.'

'That would be me.' She had the eeriest hazel eyes I'd ever seen and a tower of braids on top of her head. She was wearing a red-and-yellow plaid dress, the ruffled bodice pushed off her shoulders. 'What do you need?'

'I'm looking for someone who's missing. I'm hoping you can help me.'

'Oho, that is a new one. Do I look like a policeman?' She chortled, tickled by her witty sense of humor, then grew serious. 'Who's missing?'

'My son.'

'What does he look like?'

'My color hair. Lean, like a bicycle racer. Twenty-one years old. You know him. You sell him marijuana.'

Mirlande folded her arms. 'I know lots of people.'

'Aiden Lawson.'

'Ah.' She let the word waft in the air. 'Aiden. So handsome. So talented. So raw. He is no longer a client.'

'He's not?'

'No. A couple of weeks ago, he said he was forsaking weed forevermore.'

Aiden didn't say things like *forsaking* and *forevermore*, but OK.

'He said he needed to clear his head and save some money.' She twirled a hand by her temple. 'I told him smoking weed would not cloud his judgment, nor would spending a little cash here and there empty his savings account, but he left.' She studied my face as if determining my worthiness. 'If you're willing to do a psychic reading, I might be able to assist you. But be forewarned, I'm always candid.'

'How much?'

'Twenty dollars.'

I forked over a twenty-dollar bill.

She tucked the money into her cleavage, took hold of my right hand, and closed her eyes. She gabbled to herself for a long minute. Then she opened her eyes and met my gaze. 'He is not missing. He is hiding.'

'Hiding?'

'In a dark place. He is scared.'

'Of me?'

'Of failing. I see the eyes—'

'You see *his* eyes?'

Her nostrils flared. 'Yes. His.'

'Do you know where he is?'

'The truth is buried, but the eyes—' She stopped abruptly.

'The eyes what?'

'The eyes never lie.'

'What a load of crap,' I said. 'Eyes lie all the time.'

Mirlande released my hand. 'We are done. I have customers. Feel free to browse.'

'But—'

'The reading is over.'

THIRTEEN

I moaned, the ache in my heart so hot that it felt as if Mirlande had driven a stake through it. I apologized for being rude. Begged her forgiveness for my being an overwrought mother. I pleaded with her to continue, but she refused.

Exasperated to the point of breaking, I drove way too fast to the University Medical Center. I arrived close to dusk.

The new officer who'd been assigned to protect Josh, a fresh-faced boy no older than Aiden, cross-referenced my name against a list of approved visitors. Then he excused himself and stepped outside of the hospital room. The nurse refreshing the pitcher of water told me Josh was out of the woods, adding that his fiancée would return in an hour. Tess had needed to attend to business at her yoga studio.

'Hey, Mags,' Josh said.

I drew near to the bed. The railing was raised to keep him from falling out. The light illuminating the room was casting a green pall over everything. Josh seemed alert, but his blue eyes were slightly rheumy, and fatigue had carved gullies in his cheeks.

'You look like garbage,' I said.

'Flatterer.'

'What happened?'

'I got shot.'

'Don't be a wiseass.'

'I was careless,' he groused. 'Whoever shot me must have tailed my informant and waited at the port until the guy split. I'm lucky he was a lousy shot. Knowing the hit wasn't fatal, I dropped to the ground and played possum for almost an hour.'

'The shooter didn't check?'

'Sure he did. There was plenty of blood, enough to make him believe I'd be dead soon enough. I sure as heck didn't open my eyes. When I roused, I called nine-one-one.' He shifted in the bed, the movement making him groan in pain.

'Who did it, do you know? Was it Carl Underhill?'

'Carl? No.' His eyelids fluttered. 'Honestly, I don't know.'

'I ran into him at Pelican on Monday. He was with his son on a parent–student tour. I tried to tell myself it was a coincidence.'

'Going on a parent–student tour sounds like it was legit.'

'Sure, but was it? Or was it a veiled threat? A way to say he'd gotten to you, and he could get to me or our son. Anytime. Anywhere.'

'Look, Mags' – Josh scrubbed his chin with the back of his hand – 'I'm working three cases. For all I know, any of my marks could have shot me.'

'Is Underhill on your radar?'

'No, he's not. He hasn't been. I think he's clean. He should be. He did time. But, yeah, the man knows how to hold a grudge, so . . .' The word hung in the air.

'Where did this happen?'

'At the port. In an alley outside a warehouse.'

Port of New Orleans was the international container port in Louisiana. Cargo generated nearly half of the port's revenue.

'Who were you meeting, Josh?'

'I already said. A source.'

'Do you think he ratted you out to whoever shot you?'

Josh screwed up his mouth, not liking the prospect. 'Maybe. I don't know. Enough about me. Tell me about Aiden. Tess says he hasn't touched base. Hasn't stopped by. What's up?'

'I'm not sure. He's not responding to my texts and not returning my—'

My cell phone *pinged.* I scanned the display.

> Celine: *Maggie. Saw credit card bill online!!! Aiden rented a room.*
> Me: *Where? When?*
> Celine: *Last night.*

She texted the name of it. It was a hostel on Canal Street. Not a good neighborhood by any stretch.

> Me: *Why there?*
> Celine: *I'm not sure. But it means he's fine.*

Was he? Maybe he'd used his credit card as a cry for help. So I would track him down.

Celine: *You still there?*
Me: *Yes. Thanks for telling me. BTW, I talked to a
police detective today.*
Celine: *What did he say?*
Me: *Aiden's an adult. Nothing we can do for another
forty-eight hours.*

I didn't mention what had happened to LeBlanc. I didn't want
to upset her. His death probably had nothing to do with Aiden. And
Mirlande's prediction about Aiden hiding in the dark? Iffy at best.
I supposed a hostel could be deemed dark.

When Celine didn't respond, I wrote one more.

Me: *I'll be in touch.*

Then I recapped the text to Josh.

'Our boy is OK,' he said gently. 'You can breathe.'

I clasped the railing hard as frustration ripped through me.

Josh flicked my hand with a fingertip. 'Hey, ease up, Wonder
Woman. Don't break the merchandise. What's bugging you?'

I couldn't get rid of a niggling feeling. What if someone had
stolen Aiden's credit card and posed as him? Identity theft
happened every day. 'Why isn't he communicating with me? Or
with you?'

'Cut him some slack. I went months without talking to my mom
and dad when I was a senior in college.'

Not the same. When Josh was a senior, his parents were together,
and his little sister was still alive. He wasn't married. And he had
a scholarship to cover his college and housing expenses and a part-
time job that helped him buy beer and whatever else he needed.

'I had to cut off his funds, Josh.'

'He told me about your mother's facility raising its costs and
your car giving out and the flood, and, yeah, he's mildly annoyed.'

Mildly? So he hadn't ranted and raged to his father? Money, or
lack thereof, wasn't the reason he had gone radio silent?

'Look, I understand him not getting back to me.' I said. 'But
you? He loves you. Adores you.'

'Not necessarily. He asked if I could help, too, but I can't. I'm
strapped. I don't have any spare change.'

'Even so, there's no excuse for him not coming here to see you, and it bothers me because . . .' I toyed with the heart charm on my necklace.

'Talk to me, Mags. What is your gut telling you?'

'I'm getting this weird vibe.' I released the charm. 'Like something's wrong. Remember when I was pregnant with him? It was a week from my due date, and I knew something was off. I felt it. Right here.' I placed a hand on my abdomen.

'Of course you sensed something. He was in your womb planning to arrive feet first.'

'It was the worst feeling. Horrible. I could barely breathe. I thought the cord was wrapped around his neck. Choking him. I've got that same feeling, Josh.'

'Mags . . .'

'A mother's ties to her child never disappear!'

He rolled his eyes.

'Don't make fun of me. Do not.' *Inhale. Exhale. Let go.* I obeyed the mantra and pressed on. 'Do you think it's possible one of your targets – the one who shot you – might have done something to him?'

'Done something?'

'Like kidnapped him to coerce you to back off your investigation?' There, it was out. I'd said it to someone other than Filuzzi, who'd ridiculed me.

'Kidnapped?'

'Yes, kidnapped him, and that person is sending the texts. Your life . . . Your career . . . You live on the edge. You're always toying in the danger zone. You've never given a fig about how your investigations might impact Aiden—'

'Whoa!' Josh slapped the bed. 'Slow down. Kidnapping is a stretch, Mags.'

'Is it?'

'Look, no one has reached out to me with a ransom demand. How about you?'

Why did receiving a ransom demand make a disappearance more real to everyone? *Because it does, Maggie. Right now, all you have is an unsupported theory.*

'No,' I said.

'There's your answer.' He brandished a hand. 'And if we're playing the blame game, how about turning a microscope on your life, Dean Lawson? *Your* career. Who have you pissed off lately? Has anybody tried to muscle you into submission?'

'No one.'

He snorted out a laugh. 'Ri-ight. C'mon, Mags. You're not the friendliest authority figure in the world.'

His accusation stung.

'Being dean of an elite college comes with built-in enemies, and you know it,' he said sharply, then softened his tone. 'Look, if Aiden's been kidnapped, though I highly doubt it because some kind of demand should've been made by now, are you positive that whoever you've angered isn't the culprit? I mean, the house did flood. Have you determined that was an accident? Or could someone have set that ball in motion?'

My mouth fell open. My cheek started to twitch. Sure, Gregory Watley was angry with me about not expanding the sports program. And, yes, he would demand favors for his grandson if his kid got accepted at the university. But had he deliberately flooded my home? When that didn't break me, did he send someone to nab my son? I revisited the thoughts I'd had about Watley the other night on the porch. If he'd taken Aiden hostage, wouldn't he be flaunting it in my face? I considered Coach Tuttle. He didn't want me to escalate the complaint against him. Would he have snatched Aiden to make me bend to his will?

'Check out the motel,' Josh suggested. 'If he's there, all's right with the world. If not . . . If not' – he licked his parched lips – 'leave no stone unturned.'

The Warehouse District Hostel was seedy at best and sandwiched between a checks-cashed location and a bail bondsman. The siding was dilapidated. The threshold was rotten wood. I breathed easier when I stepped into the reception area. The lobby was clean and brightly lit. Two young men around Aiden's age, both wearing backpacks, were standing in the lounge area, studying a map. I approached the reception clerk, also around Aiden's age. He had black hair and a sparse mustache that really wanted to grow in but couldn't.

He greeted me. 'Reservation?'

'No. I'm looking for my son. Aiden Lawson. He rented a room.'

'Yeah. I remember him. He paid with Apple Pay.'

'Apple Pay?'

'You know, using the app on his cell phone. One tap. Bingo! Charges the credit card. So easy.' The clerk grinned.

I knew what it was, the convenient way to pay nowadays, though I still didn't feel comfortable using it. 'I'd like to call his room,' I said.

'Sorry. He stayed one night only. He's gone.'

'Was he alone?' I asked.

'Yeah.'

'Any luggage?'

The clerk tilted his head. 'A knapsack. Why?'

I was trying to process why Aiden would stay here. What if I was right and he'd been kidnapped and the kidnapper had posed as him? With access to Aiden's cell phone, anybody could have paid for the room. 'What did he look like? Hair color?'

'Blond. Curly.'

'Height?'

'About my height, I guess.'

'Slim? Heavy?'

'Slim enough. But who can tell, you know? He was wearing a heavy peacoat.'

'What color were his eyes?'

'C'mon, lady.'

'Please.' I couldn't tamp down the angst roiling inside me.

'Dunno. He was wearing sunglasses.'

So it could have been someone impersonating him. I spotted a document mounted on the wall. 'Why did you frame a page of your register?'

The man's mouth turned up on one side. 'Sometimes celebs come here. To be under the radar. Incognito, you know? David Bowie stayed here once.' He hitched a thumb at the document. 'His name's on there. So the boss says everyone signs the register, just in case. For bragging rights.'

'Did my son sign a register?'

'Yeah.'

'Could I see it?'

He hesitated.

I pulled a twenty from my wallet and slid it to him. He pocketed it and set a simple black register on the counter. He flipped through a few pages. Turned the register so I could read the name.

The moment I saw it my stomach lurched. Now I was certain. Whoever had pretended to be Aiden had tried but failed to capture his unique signature.

Unless Aiden deliberately mucked it up, I could hear Frank Filuzzi counter.

Nonetheless, I called the precinct. Left a message for Filuzzi. Then I texted Josh and told him about my findings at the hostel. That Aiden hadn't stayed there. That I believed somebody posed as him and forged his signature. There was no response. He was probably sleeping or Tess had commandeered his phone. I followed that text with another to Celine, providing the same update. She responded immediately.

> Celine: *You sure?*
> Me: *Positive.*
> Celine: *Will you tell the police?*
> Me: *I already left a message.*
> Celine: *Will this change things? Will they look for him now? Will they be on our side?*

Our side. Yes, she and I were a team now. We were on the same page. Aiden was in trouble. I was sure of it.

> Me: *We've got to hope so.*
> Celine: *Yes, we've got to hope. Bless you, Maggie.*

On the way back to the university, I thought again about Josh's comment about the dean of an elite college having built-in enemies. Tuttle didn't seem the type that would kidnap someone to exert power, but Watley did. He had all the trappings. He was pompous, egotistical, and demanding.

I made a quick detour.

Watley Holding Corporation was located in the middle of the Central Business District, or CBD as some called it – tongue-in-cheek cannabis reference unintentional – on the twentieth floor of the New Orleans Exchange Center, a twenty-one-story skyscraper on Gravier Street. The area was a mix of high-rise hotels, boutique hotels, lively bars, eateries, and a casino. Built in an international style, the Exchange Center had no warmth. Watley's suite was just as impersonal, despite the twinkling lights of the city visible through the myriad windows.

Mr Watley's Valkyrie-sized assistant informed me Watley was in and would see me. I followed her into his office. It was a stately room with high ceilings, oversized furniture, polished-to-a-shine hardwood floors, and dozens of goodwill-type photos on the walls. With his meaty face and lousy combover, Watley didn't photograph well. He did have fairly good teeth, but his smile never reached his beady eyes. The assistant inquired if I'd like a glass of water or coffee. I passed on both. She departed and closed the door.

'Dean Lawson, welcome.' Watley rose to his feet, his arms spread wide. In his white shirt, blue slacks, and red suspenders, he reminded me of a Bob's Big Boy statue come to life. On a bureau beyond him stood a variety of glazed works including a red snake, a twelve-inch pot with a green dragon's head, and a gigantic yellow spider.

I motioned to the art. 'Is that your handiwork?'

'My grandson's.' He beamed. Proud grandpa. 'He imagined himself a sculptor at the age of thirteen, but he gave up the illusion at fourteen when I told him how hard it was for artists to make a living.'

I narrowed my gaze. Had he made that dig for my benefit? As a slight to my son?

'Now he's into basketball,' I stated.

'And danged good at it.' Watley gestured to a brocade chair opposite his executive desk. 'I presume you've come to tell me you've arrived at a solution to our problem.'

'No, sir, I haven't.' I remained standing.

'Then why are you wasting my time?' His neck and face blazed red. 'If you know what's good for you—'

'Sir—'

'Don't *sir* me.' He seized a leather-bound book off his desk. 'See this?' He flourished it. 'This ledger outlines all of my transactions for the past twenty years. These people owe me. Pelican U owes me.'

'No, sir—'

'Yes, sir! I have steered hundreds of donors your way. Without my support, the college would be borderline broke. You will do as I say, Dean Lawson, or . . .' He let the threat hang in the air.

Every ounce of me started to vibrate. I held my anger in check. 'Sir, did you or did someone who works for you cause the flood in my house?'

'Flood? I don't know what the heck you're talking about.'

The more I thought about it, Watley causing me financial headache didn't make sense. He had to know that suffering personal monetary loss would not make me do his bidding at the university. But taking Aiden might. Josh was right.

Treading lightly, my voice laced with tension, I said, 'Sir, have you been in contact with my son?'

'I didn't know you had a son.'

'Yes, you did. In fact, we discussed him at one of our encounters. In my office. A few months ago. You pointed out his photograph on my desk.'

Watley scoffed. 'I don't remember each photograph I've seen or every discussion I've had with you.'

'My son—'

'Your son.' Watley stared at me flatly. 'What does he have to do with anything? Is he in competition with my grandson? Is he a basketball player? Is that why you're asking? Do you intend to give him special privilege?'

'No, sir, he's an artist. At Tulane. He's not—'

'I don't want to talk about your son. My time is valuable. Leave. When you have answers that suit me, contact me. We're done.'

'No, sir, we're not done,' I said, a vision of his cowardly plan playing out in my head. Take Aiden. Approach me when I was at my wits' end. Blackmail me into submission. Force me to sign a contract – a *private* contract – vowing to do whatever he asked. The idea was a stretch, sure, but it had merit. I moved toward him. 'Sit down.'

He clutched the leather-bound book to his chest as if it was a shield.

I took another step, forcing him to plop into his chair.

His thick jowls bunched beneath his neck. He propelled his chair backward with his heels. The chair struck the bureau. The snake art went flying and smashed to pieces on the hardwood floor. 'Now look what you've done!'

I towered over him. Crowded his space. 'My son is missing. I need answers. Where is he?'

'How the hell would I know?'

'Did you or someone who works for you take him?'

'Take him?'

'Kidnap him.'

Watley sputtered. 'Don't be absurd. I would never—'

'You threatened me. You told me to do what you commanded *or else*.' I lowered my face to his. 'Or else what, sir?'

He raised his chin defiantly. 'I have more direct means to make you obey me.'

'What would those be?'

'I'll sue Pelican six ways from Sunday.' He shoved me with the ledger.

My backside slammed into the desk. Pain spiraled up my spine.

'Iris!' He sprang to his feet. 'Come in here now!'

The door to his office flew open. The assistant looked as prepared to attack as a defensive linebacker.

'Get security!' Watley ordered. His spittle hit my face.

I wiped it off with the back of my hand. 'No need.' I skirted the desk, doing my best not to show fear. 'I'm leaving.'

'Don't ever come to these offices again.'

'I won't make promises.'

Pivoting toward the door, I spotted a picture I'd missed earlier. Watley was shaking hands with Carl Underhill in front of the Exchange Center. I turned back to the man. 'What dealings do you have with Mr Underhill?'

'None of your business.'

'Actually, it is. Provost Southington might want to be in the loop if Pelican University is being funded by drug money.'

'Underhill is clean. Legit.'

'Says who?'

'Says him.'

'As if a convicted felon can be trusted.' I glowered at him. 'Did you recommend that his son apply to Pelican?'

Watley's face hardened.

'Will Underhill expect the college to grant his child straight As, too, sir?'

Watley sneered. 'I never said I'd need you to—'

'The implication was there.'

'Leave now!'

I strode toward his assistant, who dodged me, a smug smile tugging the corners of her mouth – in support of me or her boss, I couldn't tell.

When I stepped into the anteroom, I heard Watley complaining to her about my intrusion. *Complain away,* I mused. I'd made my point.

The elevator to the lobby stopped on nearly every floor. By the time I exited to the street, I was as tight as an overwound clock.

The weather made me even ornerier. I hadn't been paying attention to the forecast. The skies had opened up. In seconds, I was drenched. I trotted to the corner, prepared to run to my car two blocks away. When the light changed, I stepped into the crosswalk.

Out of nowhere, a car barreled toward me.

FOURTEEN

I yelped and leaped back, knocking over an elderly man with an umbrella. Both of us fell. I landed on a knee and cursed. The man tumbled to the pavement and did a face plant.

'Are you OK?' I grabbed his elbow and helped him to his feet and on to the curb. His toupee was askew, his cheek abraded but not bleeding. While wondering whether Watley or his assistant had raced to a car in the parking lot and zoomed after me, I tried to help the man right his umbrella, which had flipped inside out.

'Forget it,' he said. 'It's hopeless.'

'I'm so sorry. That car—'

'The blue coupe.'

'Gray, I think.'

'Gray, blue, all the same in this weather.'

'Did you catch the license plate?'

'All I could make out was N2K.'

I'd seen an N or M at the end.

'Be careful where you walk, young lady.' He brushed off his trousers and tossed his ruined umbrella into a nearby garbage can. When the stoplight changed again, he hobbled to the opposite side of the street and made a left.

I limped to my car. My cell phone pinged. Gina was texting that we were still on for our date.

At home, I undressed, slipped into a terry-cloth robe, downed two Advil, and opened my laptop on the kitchen counter, curious as to who had been behind the wheel of the car that had nearly wiped me out. Using an Internet browser, I did a cross-reference check of license plates, a skillset I'd mastered during my stint as an investigative reporter. The license plate N2KN for a silver

Mercedes coupe belonged to Sherry Stitch. She owned a knitting store in the Garden District.

'Stitch.' I chuckled, bitterly. 'What a fitting name.'

I let go of my paranoia. The accident had been exactly that – an accident, pure and simple. Not Watley. Not his assistant. The driver had probably been glancing at her cell phone or had gotten distracted by the rain, as I had been.

I checked other emails and messages. Nothing from Filuzzi. I swiped the phone's screen angrily and slammed it on the desk.

Dressing for my date with Gina, I thought of my mother, an avid crafter in her younger years. What if the incident with the errant knitter was the Universe's way of saying I needed to see her in person? It had been a few weeks.

I had time before I was due to meet Gina at Arnaud's. Visiting hours at Inner Peace Assisted Living went until eight. I threw on a blue angora sweater, designer jeans, a pair of ankle boots, and my neon-yellow slicker. I accented the outfit with Gina's red floral scarf. She'd expect me to be wearing it.

The drive to the facility, which was three miles west of the Garden District, took no time at all. The rain had cleared, and traffic was at a minimum. It had been a coup to find a space for my mother at Inner Peace. Most places required repeat applications before admittance was granted. Living there wasn't cheap – one of the reasons I couldn't finagle another loan to help out Aiden – but it was the right thing to do. After my father died, I couldn't let my mother stay in Los Angeles. Occasionally she recognized me. Her attending doctor said holding my mother's hand and chatting about happier memories was the most important thing I could do. A person in her state of mind needed reassurance. Even though she'd mentally checked out when I was younger and had left me in the lurch, I couldn't abandon her. I owed her my life. And because of her and her passion for English and teaching, I had become who I was. I would do whatever I could to ease her final years on this earth.

I followed the nurse in the crisp white uniform to the rec area, a cheery circular room with lots of windows. The art on the walls – balloons, boats, flowers, and abstracts – were all done in red tones. In the past, the muted art that had hung there had bordered on boring, but Inner Peace's new administrator, a psychiatric nurse practitioner for twenty years before coming here, believed art therapy worked wonders. Maybe she, like Gina, believed red was magical and infused confidence.

The nurses and support staff did a wonderful job of providing opportunities for patients to play board games or do projects. Sadly, my mother wanted none of it. I kept hoping one day she might snap out of her doldrum. When she did speak, she reminisced, but not with stories that made sense. The doctor said there were synapses in her brain that might never reconnect due to the emotional trauma she'd suffered. I often wondered why my synapses hadn't exploded. After all, Benjie had been my best friend. My heart and soul. I would never forget him teaching me how to throw him to the mat. It had taken fifteen tries. When he was down for the count, he'd laughed so hard he'd started hiccupping.

My mother was sitting in her straight-backed chair by the window, looking intently at the night sky.

I set a chair beside her and sat down. 'Pretty night,' I said, lying. There were no stars. Though the rain had dissipated, the clouds remained.

She didn't act as if she registered my arrival. Not even a blink. She reminded me of a fragile doll that might break if I hugged it. Her hair was silver and cut short, her skin pale. She was wearing her favorite pink bathrobe and pink slippers. The blue afghan she'd made for Benjie when he was a baby – she'd knitted one for each of us – lay on her lap. My pink one was stowed in my hope chest.

'It's me, Mom. Maggie.' I petted her shoulder, wishing she would come back to me. Be present. Be her brilliant, witty self. When Benjie and I were little, she would teach us to make cookies. Cuddle us on the sofa. Read to us. All that changed when Benjie died.

Happier memories, Mags. Focus on the positive.

'Josh says hello.' I'd never told her we'd divorced. Already mentally gone by the time he and I met, she'd never grasped who he was. She had gravitated to Aiden because she had taken delight in his curly hair. She would mistakenly call him Benjie, of course, because as a toddler he had been the spitting image of his uncle. I'd never dissuaded her.

'Nice music,' I said. Back in the day, she'd love to croon with Elvis and the Beatles. *Oldies*, she'd said, *but goodies.*

I made out the instrumental strains of 'Smile' playing through the speakers. Although it was hard to smile whenever I visited her, I forced myself to.

'Benjie loved this song,' I said.

'I miss Benjie,' she murmured, not making eye contact.

'I know, Mom.'

'I wish he'd visit.'

'He would if he—' I faltered. 'If he could.' I wondered if she was thinking of him now because it was the month he died. Did she even have an understanding of days and years?

'He's such a good boy.' She nodded absently. 'So gentle. Never a bad word out of his mouth.'

Like Aiden, but unlike me. After my brother's death, I'd learned to swear. A lot. Neither my mother or father got after me for it. The principal at school had.

'He likes to wrestle,' my mother said softly.

'Yes, he does,' I said, using the present tense so as not to upset her.

She started to hum along with the music.

I allowed her singing to fill the void as I reminisced about Benjie. After he taught me to throw him and pin him, he invited buddies over to teach me more wrestling moves. A cradle. A double-leg takedown. A full Nelson. Then they taught me some underhanded moves. A shoulder thrust. A knee pop. Not used in wrestling but good in a street fight. They were gentle with me. I hadn't been so gentle with them.

After a long moment, I said, 'Mom, Aiden is—' I stopped myself. I couldn't tell her he was missing. She wouldn't understand. Besides, I wasn't sure he was. The not knowing was eating at me.

'Aiden,' she repeated.

'My son.'

'Aiden is sweet, like Benjie.'

'Yes.'

A smile graced her lips. Not for Aiden. Or for Benjie. Probably prompted by the song.

Out of nowhere, she said, 'Does Aiden call you on the telephone, Maggie?'

I jolted. She knew me? For real? She wasn't looking at me. I rose from the chair and faced her. To look into her eyes. They lacked focus. 'No. He doesn't call. I suppose he needs to feel independent.'

'Benjie is independent.' Her eyelids fluttered. '*Was*. He was independent. He's dead.' Tears beaded on her eyelashes.

The fleeting moment of clarity jarred me. I petted her knee. 'Would you like to hear a secret about Benjie?'

'Yes, please. I love secrets.'

'Once, when he was little, he wanted to jump off the rooftop. He said he wanted to learn to fly. I was against it, of course. I was the responsible one, remember?'

'You mothered him.'

'Yes I did.' As I'd mothered everyone else. Aiden. Josh. To a fault. I caressed her hand. 'Benjie took out a ladder. I told him Dad would be furious if he tried such a stupid thing. He could—' I stopped myself. The word *die* would never escape my lips.

'He could hurt himself,' she said.

'Yes.' I pressed on. 'He propped the ladder against the house and climbed. I clambered after him, scolding him. He laughed maniacally and then he—'

'That boy,' my mother said. 'That poor boy. Why did he do it? Why did he kill himself?'

'Mom, he was sad.'

'The football players bullied him.'

'Wrestlers, you mean.'

'Football,' she said crisply, and pulled her hand from beneath mine. 'You told me football.'

'Mom, don't get agitated.'

'Why did he kill himself?' she asked sharply. 'He hung himself just like Benjie. You cried when you told me.'

I gasped. She wasn't talking about my brother. She was referring to the boy at Pelican, the cheer squad member that I had recurring nightmares about. The day he died, I called on my mother to settle my nerves. To feel the warmth of her hand in mine. During the visit, she drifted off, and I relayed the story, not thinking for a moment that she had heard a word of it or would remember me crying. I'd needed to vent. To unburden my heavy heart. If only I'd known his pain. If only I could've saved him.

'That boy!' My mother raised her hands like a singer in a revivalist church choir. 'That poor, poor boy!'

'Mrs Lawson.' A nurse hurried to us. 'Calm down, ma'am. *Shh.*'

'That poor boy!' she resounded. 'You cried, Maggie. Oh, how you cried.'

'Please, ma'am, it's not good for you to be riled,' the nurse said. '*Shh, shh.*' She glared at me while petting my mother's hair. 'There you go. That's right. *Shh.*'

My mother settled down.

The nurse said to me, 'You have to leave, ma'am.'

'But I just got here.'

'Yes, I know, but you're familiar with the rules. Patients need to remain calm or the visit will be terminated.'

Terminated. What a horrid word. 'But she's peaceful now,' I countered.

'Good night, ma'am.' She left no room for argument.

FIFTEEN

When Aiden graduated high school, I treated him and eight of his friends, plus Josh and his new girlfriend and Gina to a private dining experience at Arnaud's, a famous restaurant in the French Quarter. Aiden couldn't have been more appreciative. Growing up, he'd made me promise that his first cocktail would be at French 75, a famous bar in Arnaud's, rated one of the top five in the country. Its handcrafted cocktails were made with locally sourced syrups and liqueurs. I reserved the Bourbon Suite, and we dined on Creole cuisine to our hearts' content. Though Aiden wasn't legally allowed to drink until he turned twenty-one, that night I let him enjoy his first Sazerac. It was my favorite drink, made with whiskey and bitters. After his initial sip, the gleam in his eyes told the whole story. He couldn't wait to grow up.

Located just off Bourbon Street in the French Quarter, Arnaud's was bustling when I arrived. Gina thought meeting there might help me find my center. *Fond memories settle the soul*, she'd texted.

As if on cue, a fond memory surfaced. That night, before going to the restaurant, I pulled Aiden aside.

'I'm so proud of you, my sweet son,' I said, standing in the foyer of the Victorian.

In a suit and tie, he looked so handsome, so grown-up. So much like his father.

I laid a hand on his cheek. 'I want you to know, no matter what, I will always be here for you.'

'I know, Mom.'

'You will face many challenges in the days and years ahead. There is nothing you can't weather. Do you hear me? You are strong

and talented beyond belief. You will always be able to count on your tenacity. Your courage. No one, and I mean no one, will shake your belief in yourself. Do you hear me?'

He kissed my cheek and whispered, 'Thanks for being my rock.'

I entered French 75, tears brimming in my eyes. I dabbed them away and scanned the place. The warm glow of the lamps gave the bar a golden shimmer. The clink of glasses and happy chatter between the bartenders and customers calmed me.

Gina was already sitting at the bar. She'd reserved a stool for me with the oversized fire-engine red tote that matched her dress and lipstick. 'I've ordered you a Sazerac,' she said, hanging the tote on a hook beneath the bar. 'I'm having a Bees Knees. I can never say no to a drink made with Dorothy Parker gin and honey syrup.'

I sat on the stool, shrugged off my tote bag, hung it as she had on a hook, and set my cell phone faceup on the polished-to-a-shine wood bar. The screen was idle. No text messages. Not from Aiden. Not from Filuzzi or Josh. Not from Celine. I tore my gaze from it and smiled at my friend.

'That was some storm, wasn't it? In and out in a flash.' She took a long pull of her drink and then hooked a thumb at my cell phone. 'Anything?'

'Nothing.'

'Hungry?'

My appetite had been on the wane ever since Aiden's final text to me, but I said, 'Sure.'

'The red scarf looks good on you.'

'Thanks.' I fingered the tails. 'I don't feel powerful.'

'You will.'

Gina ordered two appetizers, brie-and-jalapeño-stuffed shrimp and *gougères*, delicious Gruyere cheese puffs stuffed with fontina cheese and prosciutto.

The bartender set our drinks on napkins.

I took a sip of my cocktail, let the flavors linger on my tongue, and set the glass down. Then I recapped my day, starting with the visit to Celine, which I followed with my quest to find LeBlanc.

'You did *what*?' she squawked when I told her about not fleeing Cash Quick until I'd inspected the office.

'I wasn't sure if the killer had shot Aiden. I panicked.'

'A panicked person leaves.'

'A panicked mother doesn't.'

'The killer could have come back for you.'

'The killer was after LeBlanc.'

'And you don't think Aiden was the shooter?'

'Gina, no!' I cried, and quickly apologized to gawking customers. 'No,' I said softly. 'The figure I saw fleeing was too large and too bulky for Aiden. My son did not kill anyone. His debt has been paid in full. He won't be a suspect. Neither will his friend Zach.'

'Zach?'

I ran a finger along the tumbler as I filled her in about Aiden's bicycle, the missing journal.

Next, I told her about my chat with Josh. His thoughts about who might have shot him. 'He turned it around and suggested I check out someone who had it in for me. I thought of Gregory Watley. You know who he is. The bullheaded donor I've told you about.' I elaborated about the unpleasant exchange with Watley. 'That man irks me.'

'Because he's ugly?'

'Because he's mean. When I left his office and that car nearly hit me—'

'Hold it.' She planted her drink on the bar. 'What car nearly hit you?'

'It was nothing. A distracted knitter. It was raining.' I explained further.

'You're certain this Watley guy didn't instigate it?'

'Yes.' At least I didn't think so. 'Before I went to his office . . .' I told her about the hostel and the phony signature in the register.

'Wow, wow, wow.'

The bartender set our appetizers on the counter along with plates and silverware setups. We thanked him, and he moved on to the next customer.

I sipped my drink. Gina downed one of the shrimp and purred.

After a long moment, she patted my forearm. 'Something else is nagging you.'

'The knitting license plate made me think of my mom. I decided to visit her before coming here. The conversation left me feeling a bit shaky.' I replayed how my mother had gone on about the student who'd committed suicide. Gina remembered the story. I'd called her minutes after the boy's mother and sister departed my office. Gina had commended me for giving them the attention they'd needed.

'Why would your mother dredge up that memory?' Gina leaned forward. 'Does she think Aiden committed suicide?'

'What? No!' My pulse kicked up a notch. 'No!'

More stares from fellow customers. More apologies.

I lowered my voice. 'He didn't. He hasn't. He wouldn't.' I peered straight ahead as a horrendous image cycled through my mind. Aiden lying in a ditch somewhere because somebody – his imposter – had beaten him and left him to die. 'Gina, if he's fine, why isn't he contacting Josh or Celine?'

'You've got me.'

I lifted my cell phone. No response from Filuzzi yet. I typed a text to Celine.

Me: *Anything new?*

She responded quickly.

Celine: *Nothing. Oh, Maggie. [sad-faced emoji]*

My chest tightened. Who'd have imagined I would start to care for this woman like a daughter? Not me. I doubted she had, either. But I did. We were bonding. If only it hadn't taken Aiden's disappearance to make us warm to one another.

Celine: *If he's dead . . .*
Me: *No. Don't go there. DO NOT.*
Celine: *OK. Sorry. It's just . . .*

Three little texting bubbles emerged on the screen but no further text appeared.

Me: *Hang tough.*

My shoulders knotted with worry. No. My son was not dead. Not by his own hand, of that I was certain.

Suddenly, my neck, face, and arms flamed hot. Hotter. I needed to remove my angora sweater. I itched. Everywhere.

Gina gripped my arm. 'Maggie, inhale, exhale. C'mon.' Her voice was the epitome of calm. 'Three slow ones. You're having a panic attack.'

'Panic attack,' I echoed. 'Aiden . . .'

'Lean forward, head between your knees. Breathe.'

I obeyed with the breathing, not the head-to-the-knees move. I'd had panic attacks before. After Benjie died. Following my father's death. The night Josh walked out.

Gina requested a glass of ice water from the bartender. He brought it immediately. I gulped it down.

'Aiden . . .' I tried again, inhaling and exhaling.

A handful of young men snaked into the bar, voices heightened. If not drunk, they were well on their way. New Orleans allowed people to walk the streets, drinks in hand, as long as the drinks weren't in an opened glass container. Consequently, there were always a lot of carousers. One of the men bumped into a female customer, who snapped at him. The man raised his hands and protested his innocence. A waiter approached the man and his buddies and suggested they leave. Another waiter helped escort them out.

'Aiden,' Gina prompted.

'Aiden . . . is a responsible young man. Nothing like those bozos. You know him.'

'I do.'

I gestured to the retreating revelers. 'He's not messing with me and Celine.'

'Got it.'

'And he's not dead. He's fine.'

But he wasn't. I was lying to myself. Someone had forged his signature to make me think he was OK. Why? Where was he? The not knowing was driving me crazy.

SIXTEEN

Close to eleven, I plodded into my house and switched on the lights. Nothing burst. Nothing flickered. I inhaled. Did I smell mildew? Was I imagining it? The *wop-wop* of the fans below seemed louder than they had this morning. Even so, I needed to try to sleep. I trudged upstairs, slipped out of my clothes, put on a cotton nightgown, brushed my teeth, and climbed into bed.

My cell phone *pinged* as I set it on the nightstand. I snatched it and read the text.

> Celine: *Maggie, should I go to the police? Would that help?*

She'd probably get the same non-response I had. I typed:

> Me: *Let's talk in the morning.*
> Celine: *OK.*
> Me: *Get some sleep.*
> Celine: *You too. Thank you for helping me through this.*

Three texting bubbles appeared.

> Celine: *My mother was never supportive like you.*

I didn't know what to say. She added:

> Celine: *Night. X*

I responded in kind but still didn't tell her about LeBlanc or Mirlande's creepy psychic reading or my conversation with Josh. No need to roil the waters. Even if I couldn't sleep, she deserved a good night's rest. When we spoke tomorrow, I would fill her in.

Sleep didn't come easily. But it did come. Around four a.m.

And then I dreamed.

Of the sophomore who'd killed himself. Of going with the AD and a campus policeman to the student's dorm room. Of the three of us floating like spirits above the boy's personal effects. His altar held a picture of him with his cheer squad, a Wild Gemini concert stub, a good luck coin, a voodoo doll with cross-stitched eyes, and a *Whodat?* token – *Whodat?* being the official cheer of the New Orleans Saints.

I awoke in a sweat, moisture pooling at the base of my spine, wondering how I could remember so much from his room and feeling like I was missing something. I'd merely gone into the room once to review the incident. Had I actually seen the items I'd imagined in the dream? Maybe I'd projected seeing the token because I was a Saints fan. But I didn't understand the Wild Gemini stub. Where had that memory come from? Was there a musical group with that name?

Too restless to go back to sleep, I crawled out of bed and paced. Perhaps I was conjuring up the boy's altar because I'd seen the ones at Aiden and Celine's duplex. Maybe I was trying to process whether the journal Zach had mentioned might be sitting on Aiden's. No, it couldn't be. Celine hadn't known about it. If Aiden had left it in plain sight, she would have opened it and read it. Curiosity was human nature. During our marriage, I'd read anything Josh left out in the open, one of the reasons I'd discovered he was having an affair. He'd tossed a receipt for a bracelet I'd never received in the burlwood valet tray on the dresser. Careless? Or on purpose so he'd get caught?

The sun hadn't risen yet, but I was amped up on adrenaline. I dressed in leggings and hoodie and ran a couple of miles in the dark using a flashlight to ascertain the irregularities of the pavement. I'd given up participating in track events like hurdling and high jumping after college, but I'd been determined to maintain an exercise regime. I loved to run. Loved the instant infusion of endorphins that cleared my head.

The morning air was cool and damp and felt good on my skin. The city was just blinking awake. The bookstore and Brix Gourmet were closed, but the early gym rats were filing into the fitness center.

When I returned, I showered and slipped into jeans and a blue plaid shirt. Next I drank two cups of black coffee and downed scrambled eggs mixed with feta cheese and chives. I needed something solid to settle the roiling at the pit of my stomach.

Around eight, still with no response from Filuzzi and knowing Celine would be awake by then, I texted and asked if I could come over. She responded that it wasn't a good time. She was already at the office. She had an urgent meeting to attend to, adding that she would touch base around noon. We could have lunch.

I reviewed the text and felt sucker punched. I could barely focus on my work. My insides were bouncing around like a handball from one emotional wall to another. How could she manage? Last night's texts had made her sound so distraught. Maybe, given her job in politics, she'd learned how to compartmentalize. I used to be able to do that. I envied her that ability.

Tamping down my unease, I replied that I would see her at noon.

After ending the thread, a small voice in my head demanded I do something to answer a few questions, like find Aiden's journal.

I didn't need to be at school until at least ten. I texted Yvonne that I was running late. She responded that she'd cover for me.

Taking advantage of the window of opportunity, I hopped into my Prius and sped to Aiden's duplex. I decided not to tell Celine my intentions. I didn't want to get her hopes up. After all, she didn't believe he had a journal.

As expected, her blue VW Rabbit wasn't parked in the driveway. The drapes were drawn. I fetched the key hidden under the cushion on the rocking chair. I knew about it because, ever since Aiden was a boy, he'd notoriously misplaced his keys. And his ID. And his iPod. We'd had to label everything in the eventuality that things would be found and returned.

I let myself in. The floor creaked beneath my footsteps. I heard the neighbor's television through the thin walls. She was listening to the morning news.

Spirit bounded from the bedroom and regarded me. I bent to pet his head. He hissed. I'd never owned an animal. Not as a girl and not as an adult. I'd wanted to, but with Josh's and my haphazard work schedules, we were afraid we would neglect it. Who needed that kind of guilt trip?

'It's OK, boy,' I cooed, and tried again to pet him. Reluctantly, he accepted the attention. Then he leapt on to his pillow on the sofa and observed me.

Quietly, I tiptoed to the altars and scanned Aiden's. I wasn't surprised to see a voodoo doll. Many altars in New Orleans held one. It wasn't the one he'd made with me and Josh years ago. This one had black hair and cross-stitched blue eyes. Its neck was circled with Mardi Gras beads. Did it represent someone? Not Celine. Not Keira or Josh or me. There were no pins jabbed into it, so I doubted he'd created it to curse another person with bad juju. Had I spied it on the altar in passing yesterday? Was it the reason I'd dreamed about the voodoo doll on the Pelican student's altar? I didn't see a journal. No Wild Gemini concert stub, *Whodat?* token, or good luck coin. None of those items were on Celine's altar, either. Hers held a big-breasted fertility statue draped with numerous beads and neck-laces, the wedding picture, and a voodoo doll with blond hair. Representing herself, I supposed. There was also a guide map for NOMA, the New Orleans Museum of Art. Nothing remarkable. Despite that, I took a picture of both altars with my cell phone.

I stole to the bathroom and opened the medicine cabinet. Inside were typical toiletries, as well as contact lenses and medicine vials. I took another photograph so if I moved anything I could refer to it and return the item to the right place. Painstakingly, I peeked behind each vial. I found a prescription with Aiden's name on it for Zolpidem. Recently filled. He'd never had a problem sleeping as a boy. Perhaps the demands of college and carving out a future had interrupted his patterns.

Crouching, I inspected the cabinet below the sink, taking yet another picture for reference. More toiletries. Feminine products. Replacement contacts. Nair for the legs. Wax for facial hair removal. Bottles of nail polish. No journal.

Feeling the pressure of time in case Celine sensed my intrusion, broke free from her meeting, and found me here – let's face it, me snooping around without her permission would ruin the bond we were forming – I rushed into the bedroom. It dawned on me that, as a kid, Aiden had one special place for hiding things. I never told him I'd discovered it. He hid copies of *Playboy* there. Every boy, Josh told me, needed some privacy. I assessed the bed and determined, based on the graphic design magazines and books about *Minecraft* stacked on the lefthand nightstand, that Aiden slept on that side. I lifted up the blue comforter and fished between the mattress and box springs. It took two tries before I felt something. Two feet in from the edge. A book.

Heart hammering, I withdrew it. Air wheezed out of me. It wasn't a journal. It was a paperback of *Lord of the Flies*. I opened the cover. He hadn't hollowed it out to conceal anything. As I was putting it back, folded sheets of white paper torn from a spiral binder fell out. They had ragged edges, meaning Aiden hadn't ripped them out. He was sort of OCD about smooth edges. It was the artist in him. He would have used scissors to remove paper from notebooks, drawing pads, and the like.

I opened one of the papers. Written in block letters:

YOU ARE SUCH A DWEEB. ARTISTS DON'T MAKE MONEY. GROW UP, DUDE. OR DIE.

And another.

GET REAL, DUDE. YOU DON'T HAVE A FUTURE AS AN ARTIST. MIGHT AS WELL BRUSH UP ON MOWING LAWNS. OR DIE.

Were these notes Aiden had received in high school when kids had taunted him? Or were these fresh? Did they have something to do with his disappearance?

I flipped through the book, searching for other notes. There weren't any, but I did find a picture of Keira. Beautiful, earthy Keira with her dark brown hair and hazel eyes. She was staring directly at the camera as if challenging it to a duel. I flipped the photograph over. Aiden, like Josh, always wrote dates on keepsakes. The date written at an angle in blue ink was for Aiden and Keira's senior year in high school. Below the date, he had written in cursive, in black ink: *She knew.*

My hand trembled. She knew what? Something incriminating about him? Something damning about someone else? When Keira died, the police said it was a hit-and-run accident. There were no witnesses other than Aiden. No suspects. Could her death have been more sinister? Was Aiden's disappearance somehow linked to her? Two years seemed like a long time to wait to take action.

I took a picture with my cell phone of the notes and photograph, returned the items to the book, and slipped it back in its hiding place.

Next I attacked the closet. The drawers. Behind and beneath the dresser. Finding nothing unusual, no journal or any inkling where Aiden might be, I headed toward the front door. Passing by Aiden's altar, I caught sight of a folded piece of blue-and-white paper peeking from beneath the voodoo doll. I withdrew it. It was an origami-style triangle. When Aiden was four, I taught him how to make an origami crane. With painstakingly slow movements, he copied the steps I showed him. After that he'd become amazing at origami. Three Christmases in a row, I received origami flowers. When unfolded, the flower revealed the words *I love you, Super Mom.*

Tears pressed at the corners of my eyes. I opened the triangle and realized it was a map of a cemetery. Hyphenated digits and doodles and drawings of voodoo dolls as well as copious images of fleur-de-lys – a symbol of New Orleans from its first discovery when the French claimed the Mississippi Valley for King Louis XVI and planted a flag adorned with the flower – lined the edges of the diagram. It wasn't just any cemetery, either. It was a map of St Louis Cemetery No. 1.

Founded in 1789 and listed on the National Register of Historic Places, the cemetery housed more than seven hundred tombs and one hundred thousand bodies, including the grave of Voodoo Queen Marie Laveau. It was impossible to get in unless on a guided tour or with a permit or family member. When Aiden was five, Josh and I had taken him on the tour.

Peering at the map, a memory of Aiden at fourteen came rushing back to me. It was summer. Temperatures were soaring, the humidity factor suffocating. He'd begged to go to the cemetery to draw.

'C'mon, Mom, hurry or we'll be late,' Aiden called.

I wasn't dallying. I was tending to an email. 'I'm hurrying,' I said.

'That's work. Stop working.' Aiden prodded me. 'You promised.'

I smiled and closed the laptop. 'You're right. A promise is a promise.'

How he'd enjoyed exploring the tombs. As a teen, while taking an architecture class as an elective, he had become interested in the pyramid-shaped tomb reserved for the actor Nicolas Cage's final resting place. Pyramids, according to Aiden, were the most impossible and amazing structures in the world. Someday, he'd told me, he wanted to go to Egypt to study them. However, he soon fell in love with design, and his dream of traveling to Africa waned.

I started to fold the map when I noticed a printed command near the Marie Laveau headstone site: *Get a bead*. I smiled, determining the map was probably a memento from graduation night. Aiden and his buddies went on a scavenger hunt that took them until the wee hours of the morning to complete. He later confided that he and his friends had contemplated illegally climbing over the cemetery's eight-foot fence, but they weighed the punishment for trespassing and the possible encounter with a ghost and decided against it. To preserve the memory, I snapped a picture of the map, refolded it, and slipped it beneath the voodoo doll.

SEVENTEEN

I couldn't put off going to Pelican any longer. By this time tomorrow, many of the university offices and facilities would close for spring break, but until then, I was expected to show up. During the vacation, I could make my own hours; I didn't need to schedule any meetings. In the car, I checked in with Yvonne via cell phone. She said Southington wanted a word, adding that I also needed to attend to a half-dozen urgent messages. Of course I did. There was always something *urgent*. I didn't go home to change. My coworkers would have to accept the dressed-down me.

Minutes after I entered my office, Provost Southington burst in. 'Dean Lawson,' he boomed.

Yvonne, in a cheery lemon-yellow sheath, stood behind him, arms akimbo. She didn't like when he had the temerity to charge past her, but she kept mum.

'Good morning, sir,' I said.

'You've been out.'

'I had some personal matters to take care of.' Like locating my son, I wanted to shout, but pressed my lips together.

The scent of the man's heavily applied citrus cologne was cloying. I did my best not to wince. He marched deeper into my office and primped his polka-dot bowtie while studying a framed charcoal sketch that was hanging on my wall. One from Aiden's earlier torso phases. Smudged lines. Soft curves. Exquisite perspective.

'How can I help you?' I sat taller.

'Mr Watley's assistant phoned me.' He spun around, arms at his sides. 'You visited him in his office.'

'Yes, sir.'

'He's had a heart attack thanks to your stunt.'

'What? No, sir. No way. He was one hundred percent healthy when I left. No way he had a heart attack.'

'His assistant begs to differ.'

Traitor to womenkind, I mused, and spread my hands. 'Sir, Mr Watley has been hounding me to—'

'You'll be pleased to know he's alive and recuperating at home.'

'That's good news.'

Deep furrows formed in Southington's forehead. 'Is your son missing?'

'Yes, sir. He's been out of contact. If something has happened to him—'

'Gregory Watley said you think he's been kidnapped.' He arched an eyebrow.

'I don't know what to think.'

'Certainly Gregory Watley had no hand in his supposed disappearance.'

'He threatened me.'

'Preposterous.'

'Sir, he said—'

'Have you spoken to the police?'

'They won't search for Aiden yet. He's an adult, and he hasn't officially been missing for forty-eight hours. If you'd let me explain—'

'Did you receive a ransom note?'

'No.'

Southington smiled tightly, which irked me. 'Look, you know as well as I do, Dean Lawson, that kids take breaks from parents. Especially at this age. They go radio silent. My daughter did. My son did, too. Deal with it. Do not get wrapped around the axle. And do not accuse our donors of doing something as drastic as kidnapping. That is beneath you.'

'Sir, Mr Watley said in no uncertain terms that if I don't expand the sports program to accommodate his grandson, he would—'

'Did he threaten you with bodily harm?'

'With . . .' I faltered. Was that the provost's benchmark? Watley had to hurt me to make this real? I raised my chin. 'No, sir, he said he'd withdraw all his financial support from the university.'

'That falls way short of kidnapping.'

'Sir, he wants us to become a Division I school. Not only will this take an eon to accomplish, if it's even possible, but we don't have the funds.'

'I'll find the funds.'

I cocked my head. Regarded him with fresh eyes. 'If you do, others will come knocking expecting special treatment.'

'Let them knock. Gregory Watley is an old friend. We went to school together.'

I folded my arms defensively. 'Why did he approach me, then? Why not you?'

'Because you have the final say regarding funds. It's protocol.'

'Hold on,' I said. 'I thought you graduated from Tulane.'

'I did.'

'Watley is a Pelican alum.' Hence, the Watley Science and Math building, and more.

'Indeed. That's why he continues to fund the school. We met at Harvard Business School.'

The image of the two of them arm in arm singing the Harvard fight song flashed in my mind.

Southington patted my shoulder. 'Are we good here?'

'Yes, sir. Thank you for taking the challenge of finding the funds. I appreciate your assistance in the matter.' I forced a smile worthy of an Oscar.

Southington narrowed his gaze. 'Don't mock me. You'll regret it.' He turned on his heel and exited.

My cell phone rang. I didn't recognize the number. My breathing snagged. Was it someone calling about Aiden? Maybe Aiden was using a friend's phone because his battery had died. I answered and heard air. Nothing but air. I pulled up the Recent Calls list. Selected the top one. It rang. And rang.

'Dammit.' I ended the call and studied the number. It was a 346 area code. The code for Houston. Carl Underhill was from Texas, that is, until he'd moved his enterprise to New Orleans. Why would he be calling me? Did he have Aiden? I rounded my desk and started to dial Josh, eager to get his perspective, when Yvonne strode into the office.

'Coach Tuttle would like a word,' she said.

Not again. 'He needs to make an—'

'Dean Lawson.' Tuttle reminded me of a prize fighter ready to rumble, with a smile so tight it looked like it strained him to do so. He edged past Yvonne. 'I need to see you now.'

I stopped dialing. Instinctively my abs constricted. Benjie had taught me how to take a punch to the gut, but I hadn't been able to eat for days.

'I know you've been communicating with the prosecuting attorney regarding the disciplinary proceeding,' he said.

'Coach Tuttle, meeting like this isn't kosher.'

'Dean Lawson, how would it look if a young man came into your office and closed the door?'

'What? Whoa!' I held up a hand. Rose from my chair. 'Stop talking. Now.'

'I am not guilty. Those young women lied. I did nothing wrong.' He swept a hand along his thinning hair. 'I am deadly serious.'

The way he said *deadly* made me shiver. Was he subtly warning me to back him or else? 'Coach Tuttle, please take your case to your lawyer and tell him to mount a good defense.'

'This isn't right.' His voice broke. 'I'm a well-respected coach. A married man. I would never take liberties with young women.' His face wrenched with anguish. 'Never. I . . .' He swallowed hard, unable to finish. 'I told you before, they're angry that I benched them for poor attitude and subpar performances. They're ganging up on me to frame me. Please believe me.'

Was he telling the truth? The plaintiveness in his voice seemed heartfelt. He clearly needed one person – *me* – to be on his side. What was I supposed to do? How could I be supportive yet impartial? I couldn't.

'Please leave.' I pointed to the door.

Tuttle bridled. His face blazed red. 'This isn't over,' he warned in a hard, bitter voice and strode out of my office.

EIGHTEEN

Yvonne appeared and leaned against the door jamb. 'I need a taser to stop people from barging past me.'

'I'll add it to my next requisition form,' I quipped.

My cell phone buzzed. I viewed the display. It was a text, from Celine.

> Celine: *Can't meet for lunch. Sorry. Something came up. Nothing new at my end. Yours?*
> Me: *Nothing.*
> Celine: *[teary-faced emoji]*
> Me: *Are you getting any weird phone calls?*
> Celine: *No. Why?*
> Me: *Not sure yet.*
> Celine: *Weird how? That worries me. Are you OK?*
> Me: *Yes. Talk soon.*

I poured myself a cup of coffee in the outer office and returned to my desk to make a list of duties I needed to accomplish before spring break was over. Bored with how mundane they were, I started to doodle on a scratch pad. Realizing I was drawing pyramid after pyramid, I thought of the map on Aiden's altar. Of the cemetery. I couldn't mention to Celine that I'd seen it, of course, but I was curious about its significance. Had Aiden written the *Get the bead* note recently? What about the doodles and images he'd drawn?

Was I batty to think something at the Marie Laveau crypt might lead to a clue as to where he was? Celine might have an idea. Or she might not. She didn't know he kept a journal. She probably didn't know about the copy of *Lord of the Flies* between the mattresses, either. What other secrets might Aiden have kept from her? Had he done so on purpose? To create his own personal space or a darker reason?

I pulled up the image of the map on my cell phone and thought of Gina. One of her best friends from childhood days was a cemetery tour guide. Could she get me inside to take a peek? As if I'd psychically summoned an answer, Gina texted me.

> Gina: *How are you doing today? Better, I hope.*
> Me: *Will you ask your friend Elise if she'll give me a private cemetery tour of St Louis No. 1?*
> Gina: *I'm fine. Thanks for asking.*
> Me: *Will you? For today? Now, if possible.*
> Gina: *What's up?*
> Me: *Please. LMK.*

In less than five minutes, she responded. She'd secured a tour in an hour.

When I arrived at the cemetery, a slight breeze was stirring the air. The aroma of smoked sausage wafted to me. I sauntered past a food truck with a healthy line of customers. Past the horde of visitors trying to peek inside. Past the wizened woman selling beaded necklaces, ribbons, and more.

'Hey!' Gina waved to me.

She was standing at the entrance with her friend Elise Chenevert, a Creole with flawless copper skin, intelligent brown eyes, thick black hair highlighted with blue ombre, and a toothy infectious smile. Her spaghetti-strapped, multicolored sheath clung to her thin frame. Gina, in a double-collar skirt suit and heels, towered over her.

'So good to see you, Maggie,' Elise said. Her guttural voice was the result of many years of talking to crowds mixed with her fondness for cheroot cigars. 'When was the last time we did this?' Her gold bangles clattered as she embraced me.

'Four years ago.' I'd brought Aiden and Keira a couple of weeks before their high school graduation. They'd entertained each other with gruesome ghost stories. Headless horsemen. Mummified skeletons. Ten-feet-tall vampires. I could still hear their infectious laughter. The memory caught me up short.

'It's been too long.' Elise ran her hands along my upper arms and scrutinized my face. 'Yes, much too long.' She released me and hoisted the parasol she'd leaned against a wall. She unfurled it and offered it to me. 'Here. Your skin is fair.'

'I'm OK without it.'

'I cannot. My dermatologist makes me toe the line.' Elise held the umbrella over her head. 'What is so pressing that we need to do this today? What shall I show you? The oven vaults? The Nicolas Cage tomb? You know, they say he has ties to the Illuminati.'

'I hadn't heard that.'

'How about the grave of Homer Plessy, the man who made separate but equal a constitutional mandate? Ah, yes, he was a great and worthy man.' Elise nodded to Gina, plainly a fan of Mr Plessy's.

'I'd like to see the voodoo queen's tomb.'

'Marie Laveau. Yes, it is the best.' Elise presented her tour guide credentials at the entrance gate and waved for us to follow her.

Gina leaned in to me. 'Why Laveau?'

I told her about my foray into the duplex. About the map I'd found on Aiden's altar. About the doodles and drawings and the note regarding the bead.

'"Get a bead?" As in take aim?' She cocked her head.

'No. I don't think so.' I hadn't translated the note that way. Was she right?

'It can't mean to steal a bead,' she warned. 'It's against the law to swipe anything from the gravesites.'

'I know that.' One could take photographs and leave a token, but it was illegal to desecrate anything in the cemetery, including removing any of the gifts.

'Tell me your reasoning then.' Gina twirled a hand. 'Why are we here?'

'Aiden used to love scavenger hunts. I'm praying the map has given us a lead. A way to find him.'

'Maggie, get real. He is not so cruel that he'd send you on a wild goose chase instead of talking to you.'

She was right. He wasn't cruel, but he was clever. At times even an imp.

'Look for your birthday present, Mommy.' Aiden, six, stood at the

*foot of my bed in his cowboy pajamas clapping his hands and
chanting along with his father for me to hunt.*

*I searched high and low. In my closet. Under my bed. In bathroom
cupboards.*

'Hunt, hunt,' Aiden and Josh persisted.

*When I finally found my present – a pair of pearl earrings – Aiden
was ecstatic.*

'You did it,' he squealed. 'I knew you'd find it.'

*He'd hidden it in his sock drawer. Josh told him I'd never search
his room, but Aiden said of course I would. I was smart.*

Maybe, now, he had expected me to scrounge through his things
to find a clue.

Gina looped her hand around my elbow. 'C'mon, nervous mama.'

We arrived at the tomb, a worn gray edifice etched with *Xs*,
markers made by visitors who'd hoped the voodoo queen would
grant their wishes. At the foot of the tomb there were strands of
beads, flowers, fresh fruit, and generic garbage. Elise, Gina, and I
waited until the group before us moved on. When they did, Elise
began her spiel.

'Marie Catherine Laveau was a Louisiana Creole and practitioner
of voodoo,' she intoned. 'She practiced rootwork, also known as
hoodoo or conjure, which includes crystal spells, herb magic, and—'

I tuned her out, having heard it all before, and crouched down.
Propping my elbows on my thighs, I eyeballed everything. Searching
for something that might remind me of Aiden. Nothing stood out.
No cat's-eye marbles, his favorite. No bead-shaped crystals. I
searched for something that might have belonged to Keira – she'd
loved anything made with turquoise – but didn't see anything.

'What do you think?' Gina squatted beside me, balancing gingerly
on the toes of her shoes.

'It's a bust.'

She petted my shoulder.

As I rose, I caught a glimpse of blue stick figures drawn with
chalk to the right of the tomb. Creating any art was illegal if the
artist was caught. Whoever had drawn these had done so out of
sight of whatever guide had been leading the tour. Or they had been
drawn after hours by someone who'd sneaked in.

I inched closer to get a better look. The figures seemed to be in
conversation. One stick figure was holding an arm overhead. The
other's arms were defensive, as if they were having a fight. Had

Aiden drawn them? To represent whoever had sent the notes that I'd unearthed in his copy of *Lord of the Flies*? Had he gone into hiding until he could figure out how to confront the bully? No. I was grasping at straws.

But seeing the art gave me another idea.

NINETEEN

I touched base with Yvonne and told her I'd be taking an even longer lunch hour. Thirty minutes later, I was striding along the hall of Newcomb art department at Tulane University. I reached Helena Hebert's office and halted. Winner of the Andrew Mellon Professorship award, Helena had served as chair in digital art for over twenty years. Her written work and monographs were influential in the history of digital design. She'd also published in related fields, having focused on Creole and Cajun art and its impact on the culture of Louisiana as a whole. Per my son, she was unflagging in her dedication to her students. I hoped she hadn't left early for spring break.

No one sat in the department anteroom, but the chairwoman's office door was open. I strode to it. Helena Hebert was facing her bookshelves, slotting books into empty spaces and squaring up the various pieces of exquisite glass art – Murano, Kosta Boda, Baccarat. She was a serious collector.

I rapped on the doorframe. 'Dr Hebert?'

She whirled around. The pink orchids on her red silk caftan danced with the motion. 'Dean Lawson.'

We'd met at a couple of art department functions. At one, Aiden had received an award for Most Promising Digital Artist. Dr Hebert had always had wonderful things to say about him.

'Call me Maggie, please. May I come in?'

She beckoned me. 'If you call me Helena.' She was a full-figured woman with intelligent eyes, broad thick lips that she'd tinged dark red, and sizeable hands that appeared even larger with long, mani-cured nails. I didn't have a hint of what color her hair was because she always sported a turban, but I figured dark to match her eyebrows. 'Is this about Aiden? If so, he is excelling. One of our brightest and most gifted students.'

'Good to hear.'

She motioned to a Victoria Rose teapot sitting on a warmer on the antique credenza behind her desk. 'Would you care for some tea?'

'No, thank you.'

She sat in her desk chair and gestured for me to sit. My cell phone chimed. I scanned the number. It was the 346 area code caller again. I held up a finger to Helena and stabbed Enter. Nothing but dead air again. Crap. I pocketed the cell phone and settled into one of the peacock-themed brocade armchairs.

'Have you seen Aiden recently?' I asked impatiently.

'No.' Helena fiddled with the quartz pendant hanging on a long chain around her neck. 'Although I've been holed up the past few days. There's so much end-of-the-year business to attend to. I've merely seen a handful of students. The ones who have stopped in. Why?'

'He's . . .' I hesitated. Missing? Avoiding me? Kidnapped? 'He's been out of communication with me, and his wife Celine said . . .' I sighed. 'She said he left her.'

'Left her?' Helena's mouth curved down in a frown. 'I'm so sorry to hear that. Granted, I think marriage and college are a difficult balance, but when a young person falls in love, we often can't change the course of this decision. My son did much the same thing. No warning. Married a woman I'd never met. He was on his way to being deployed to Iraq. He didn't want to wait. He thought I would understand.'

'And did you?'

'I kept my frustration to myself.' Helena tented her hands. 'Has Aiden been in communication with Celine since leaving her?'

'He was doing so via text for a while, but now he's gone radio silent.'

'And you're worried.'

'We both are.' I sagged under the weight of my words. *We. Me and Celine.* The fact that we were a united front continued to astonish me.

Helena picked up her office phone and pressed a button. She waited. Whoever she'd dialed came on the line. 'Vera, it's Helena.' She rotated her desk chair, turning away from me. 'Talk to me about Aiden Lawson. Has he attended your lectures?' She bobbed her head. 'Mm-hm. And the last time—' She listened some more. 'Yes,

I see. Thank you.' She ended the call, spun back, placed her palms on her desk, and pushed to a stand. Her grim expression told me everything.

'She hasn't seen him, has she?' Despair colored my voice.

'Not since last week. Maybe we could find some clues in his locker.'

'I don't want to overstep—'

'Nonsense. This is not overstepping. A parent who pays tuition has the right to know.'

I didn't correct her. I had paid tuition, after all. I'd simply been unable to fund the remaining personal support.

'Each of the students signs an agreement that the school may have access at all times,' Helena said. 'We do occasional searches to make sure nothing is amiss, if you catch my drift.'

Drugs, I assumed. We had similar agreements at Pelican.

'All the students have to provide their passcodes.' She picked up her cell phone. 'Follow me.'

I trailed her out of the office.

She spoke over her shoulder as she proceeded. 'Aiden has done exceptional work this semester. I heard he's in the running for a full-time position at Le Gran Palais. That's quite an honor.'

'Do you know the owner?'

'Very well. Stan Studebaker was one of my finest students. A brilliant mind and exquisite artist. You should see some of his pen-and-ink drawings. But what he has done in the digital world is astounding. Aiden will be well tutored.'

If he's OK. If he returns to work. If, if, if . . .

Helena veered right down another hall and, using a keypad, unlocked a door. She entered and switched on a light. Banks of cube-shaped lockers with keypads, the lockers stacked five high, were secured to each of the four walls.

Referring to a file on her cell phone, she scrolled until she reached the one she was searching for. 'This way.' She led me to a locker on the back wall. 'Aiden's is two-twenty. Second row.'

Two female students entered the room, chatting. The blond one went to a locker, opened it, and inserted a sketchpad. Her friend stood inches away, checking messages on her cell phone. The young woman at the locker slammed it and jerked her head. 'Let's go.'

'Have you seen Aiden Lawson?' I blurted.

'Who?' the blond coed asked.

'Aiden. Lawson. My son.'

'Don't know him,' she said.

Her friend shook her head, concurring.

When they exited, Helena punched in Aiden's code and stood back, allowing me to open the locker fully. 'Would you like privacy?'

'No,' I murmured, riddled with embarrassment. What was I thinking, acting like a ridiculous mother who didn't trust her son? I should leave.

No, Mags. That isn't true. You're acting like a concerned parent. Of an adult, I heard Aiden argue.

Of an adult who is incommunicado, I countered.

The locker, though deep, didn't have much in it. A personalized leather artist's roll fitted with twenty pockets that Josh had given Aiden. Each pocket held pens, pencils, or brushes. There was also a sketchpad and a paint-splattered plaid shirt.

I withdrew the sketchpad and flipped through it. There were pencil drawings of torsos, faces, arms, and hands, as well as numerous depictions of tombs including the pyramid-shaped one at St Louis Cemetery No. 1 and another at Metairie Cemetery – not the showier one with the sphinx guarding the portal; the newer one for the Pinnell family. I'd seen it when it was under construction.

'Nice work,' Helena said, gazing over my shoulder. 'His shading is excellent.'

A ragged-edged slip of paper fell from the pad. I picked it up and gagged as I read:

> YOU TOTAL NO-TALENT LOSER,
> DIE. SOON. NO LOOKING BACK, DIE.

My hands started to shake.

Helena gasped. 'Did Aiden write that?'

'No. He scrawls everything. The artist in him enjoyed learning cursive. This is printed.' Saying that gave me pause. Maybe he hadn't written the words *Get a bead* on the map of the cemetery. It didn't matter. The clue had proven fruitless. But the note I was holding with its capitalized block letters reminded me of the ones I'd found in his copy of *Lord of the Flies*. Had the same person written this? Was it old or new?

'No students have access to other students' lockers,' Helena said.

'How can you be sure? A cursory glance over Aiden's shoulder is all it would have taken to get the code.'

She frowned, my contention making her uncertain.

I reread the note. Would a handwriting expert be able to determine who had written it? It looked generic. 'I—' I swiveled. 'I found something this morning at Aiden's.' I didn't tell her my search had been clandestine. I wanted her to be able to deny knowledge of it, should Celine press her. 'Other notes. Horrible ones, like this. Also printed in capitalized block letters. I think a person or persons are threatening him.' I pulled my cell phone from my tote and tapped on the pictures I'd taken. I displayed them to her, swiping one after another.

Helena pressed a hand at the hollow of her neck. 'But this note' – she gestured with her free hand to the one I was holding – 'reads like a suicide note.'

'No it doesn't. Not in the least. It's a taunt.'

'Maggie, you as a dean know that students can be under quite a lot of stress. Sometimes they don't feel like they have any other way out.'

I gasped. 'In this case, you're wrong.'

She screwed up her mouth as if she was stifling a response.

'Look, I'm sorry for being so curt. Yes, I know a lot about how students handle stress,' I continued. 'My brother committed suicide in high school. Like Aiden, he was sensitive. The target of bullies. But Aiden knew this. We talked about it. Those chats steeled him against attacks about his creativity. He was strong . . . *is* strong,' I revised. My vocal chords jammed. I swallowed hard.

Helena slipped the sketchpad from my hands. 'We need to show this to the police.'

A charcoal sketch escaped from the pad and fluttered to the floor. We both stared at it as if a nest of asps was slithering by our feet. Cautiously, I lifted the sketch and marveled at the artistry. Aiden had captured Celine's face perfectly. Her blue eyes were demanding and regal. Her cheeks flushed with passion. Her ice-white hair adorned with dozens of silver hearts. There was a second drawing of Aiden and Celine, their cheeks pressed together, as if the two had posed in front of a mirror so he could draw the self-portrait. Both looked hopelessly in love. Why would he abandon her? Had he really left of his own accord? No, I didn't believe it. With the few pieces of new evidence I'd amassed, plus the possibly forged signature at the hostel, would Filuzzi take me more seriously now?

'Maggie' – Helena closed the locker and gripped my elbow –

'let's go back to my office, and you can tell me what's really going on.'

I sat in the chair facing her desk. Balancing a cup of tea on my lap, I told her about the text messages. About Josh being injured. About my theory that someone with a beef against Josh or me might have caused our son harm. 'Celine's anxious now, too, because, as I told you, Aiden has stopped texting her.'

'Text him one more time,' Helena advised. 'Tell him about the note we discovered. Ask him if he wrote it.'

I did as she ordered, doing my best to sound chatty and unflustered.

> Me: *Hey, kiddo, I'm sitting in Dr Hebert's office. She says hello.*

I saw three texting bubbles and held my breath. Was he responding? Was he all right? Was all my stewing for naught?

> Aiden: *Mom, give it up! Back off. I don't need you checking on me. I will be in touch when I'm damned good and ready. Cut me some slack, will you? I've had about all I can take of you pressuring me to be the perfect son. Let it go!*

Whoa! My heart snagged. My pulse started to race. Was this really Aiden responding? If so, he sounded brittle and ready to snap.

'Did he reply?' Helena asked.

'Yes.' I typed.

> Me: *I'll back off, but please call your father. Please.*
> Aiden: *Yeah, fine. Soon.*

Something gnawed at me as I studied the first text in the thread. There were so many words. Aiden didn't write treatises. He was a one- or two-sentence texter at most. And usually he dropped the use of the word *I* and would start with the verb. Plus, he typically used lots of text shorthand. *TTYL, BTW, FYI.* There were none in this tirade.

'And no XO,' I grumbled.

'No what?'

'XO. Usually he ends a text with XO. A kiss and a hug.' I felt
tears forming in my eyes. I refused to let them leak out. 'Even when
he's aggravated with me, he signs off with XO.'

Except lately, I revised silently. He hadn't written *XO* lately.

'At least he answered.' Helena smiled. 'He's fine.'

I gawked at her. Was she too naïve for words? Or was I truly a
histrionic mother battling my own inner demons?

TWENTY

The precinct on Broad Street was showing all the signs of
what could be a busy spring break week in New Orleans.
Three drunken boys in their late teens. A pair of girls in
skimpy bikinis swearing like fishwives. A violinist ranting that a
vagrant had broken his instrument.

Filuzzi motioned me to his desk. 'You're back.' In chocolate-
brown slacks, white shirt, and brown blazer with patches on the
elbows, he gave the impression that he was easy-going. What a
crock. 'With good news, I hope?'

'No. My son is still missing. I left you a message.' I motioned
with my hand. 'You didn't call me back.'

'I didn't get a message.'

That explained his non-response.

He cleared files off a chair and set them on his cluttered desk. 'Sit.'

I plopped into the chair and folded my arms.

'You look guilty of something,' he said with a wry glint in his
gaze.

How could he tell? Josh had never been able to figure out when
I'd done something clandestine.

'What did you do?' Filuzzi held out his hand, palm up, and
crooked a finger. 'C'mon, Maggie. I don't have all day. As you can
see, we're nearing capacity. Spill.'

'I found something in my son's duplex. I took pictures.' I opened
the photo app on my cell phone and swiped to the first shot,
explaining as I went.

'Altars,' he said. 'Lots of people have them in NOLA. Both my
kids do. So does my sister. Next.'

I opened the picture I'd taken of the contents in the bathroom cupboard.

'I'm looking at a prescription bottle,' Filuzzi stated.

'Aiden doesn't take medicine.'

'He didn't used to. Now, apparently, he does. What else?'

I swiped to the next photograph. 'This is a picture of his former girlfriend Keira.'

'The one who died in the accident.'

'Correct. See what Aiden wrote on the reverse? *She knew*. Knew what?'

'Knew he'd screwed around.'

I frowned. 'Get serious. Aiden was the most devoted boy in the world. I overheard Keira and him planning out five decades of life together. Also I found letters in a book he'd hidden. Vile letters.' I displayed the first and then the second.

Filuzzi took the phone from me and, using two fingers, zoomed in on the photo. 'People can be cruel. This doesn't prove he's met with trouble.'

'There was another note stuffed into his sketch book in his personal locker at the art department at Tulane.' I produced the sheet of paper I'd convinced Helena Hebert to let me take. I waved it in front of his face while giving details.

'Maggie, he could have written this himself. As a way to kick himself in the butt. To get his act together.'

'No, Frank! You're wrong. Someone else wrote this. Other students could have had access to his locker.' I hated the way he was looking at me, judging me. 'Did I mention that I've been receiving hang-up calls? From a three-four-six area code. Carl Underhill lived in Houston until he relocated to New Orleans.'

'Again with Underhill? Maggie, c'mon.'

'He holds a grudge against my ex-husband.'

'And he's exacting revenge now? Years later? I think you're barking up the wrong tree. Underhill would be an idiot to attempt a revenge kidnapping.' Filuzzi closed the photo app and started to hand the cell phone to me, but stopped when he saw my text messages. 'Hold on a sec. What's this?' He read Aiden's last text aloud. 'Sounds to me like your kid wants nothing to do with you. Were you going to mention this?'

'I'm pretty sure he didn't write that.' I laid out my reasoning, the length of the text as well as the missing shortcuts using initials.

'C'mon, Frank, can't you do something? Put out an APB?' I sounded high-strung. Irrational. If I was him, I'd dismiss me, too, but I needed him to think I was sane. Steady. On the right track. I tried a softer voice. 'My son could be hurt.'

'You haven't proven that he's injured. And this text—'

'He didn't write it, dammit! And he didn't stay at that hostel!' I leaped off the chair. So much for proving I was sane.

Filuzzi rose and made a *T* with his hands. 'Time out. What hostel?'

I enlightened him about the one-night stay, the register, the phony signature. 'C'mon, Frank. Help me.'

'Maggie, look, the signature thing is iffy. It's not enough to go on. If it'll appease you, I'll tell a few of my buddies to be on the lookout for a missing twenty-one-year-old. But between you and me?' He scrubbed his chin. 'I think Aiden and the missus had a spat. Realizing the hostel was a stupid idea, he probably checked out and holed up at a friend's house. He'll come back after he's cooled down. That's what I'd do.'

'His professor hasn't seen him in days.' I spread my hands in protest. 'Aiden hasn't shown up in person at work. And now he isn't replying to his wife's text messages. Plus I told you, he didn't take his bicycle. He wouldn't have—'

'Filuzzi!' a woman yelled from across the room. 'Line one.'

Filuzzi twirled a finger, signaling he'd answer. 'Look, Maggie, why don't you have the wife reach out to me?' He handed me a business card. 'These are my new contacts. If she's as worried as you, we'll take steps.'

TWENTY-ONE

Air hissed through my teeth as I stomped out of the precinct. Back at my desk sorting through the last minutiae that needed to be handled before spring break, thoughts kept ricocheting around in my mind about Aiden. Was I wrong? Was he missing or not? Had he sent the rage-filled text message? Had he written the vile note to kickstart his creativity? Was my opinion of my son completely off base? Had he changed into a self-centered

human being who didn't care about hurting his wife or his family?
Was there nothing more I could do? Should I give up?

No, I couldn't believe any of that. None of it. Aiden was in
trouble. I could feel it in my bones.

At six p.m. I trudged to the parking lot pushing self-doubt to the
edges of my mind. The sun had set. The air had turned dank. I
switched on the Prius but before putting the car in gear, I sent
another text to Aiden hoping, if it was him responding, that this
response would be more tempered.

Crickets.

Irritated, I dialed Celine. I wanted to see her in person. Ask more
questions. Prayed there was something she'd forgotten to tell me
that might enlighten my search. She answered after one ring and
apologized again for having to cancel lunch. I forgave her and told
her I'd discovered new information. She asked what it was. I held
back and invited her to dinner. My treat. Lightly, I added that I
wouldn't take no for an answer. I could hear the hesitation in her
voice, but ultimately she agreed.

We planned to meet in a half hour at Brennan's on Royal Street,
the original home of bananas Foster – possibly my favorite dessert.
A former student of mine was managing the place now, making it
easy to book the reservation. I had no place to be, so I headed
straight there and checked in at the hostess's station. I asked about
my student. She wasn't around; she had the night off. I moved into
the Roost Bar to nurse a glass of chardonnay. Celine arrived an
hour later.

'Maggie,' she said, but didn't move in for a kiss on the cheek.
Why would she? We hadn't exchanged more than two in the time
we'd known each other. In her ensemble of soft green pencil skirt
and floral silk blouse, she fit right in with the restaurant's garden-
like décor.

'Sorry I'm late. Last-minute meeting,' she said vaguely.

The lame excuse didn't bug me. I'd expected it. In truth, she'd
been crying. The skin around her eyes was dry and in dire need of
moisture. A maternal instinct to hug her tugged on my heartstrings,
but I kept my emotions in check. They were already reeling. I
couldn't afford to be distracted by hers.

'It's OK. I've been people-watching,' I said. 'Thanks for coming.'
I paid cash for the wine, picked up my glass, and returned with her
to the hostess's station.

'Follow me,' the hostess said.

She seated us at a table next to the window that provided a view of the restaurant's patio garden. A baby shower was in progress. Packages with blue ribbon were stacked high on a vacant table. A dozen cheerful twenty-something females were tasting champagne and toasting the mother-to-be, who wasn't imbibing but appeared blissful.

'We're short staffed at the moment,' the hostess said. 'I'll be glad to bring you beverages.' She handed us each a menu.

'Chardonnay,' Celine said, opening her menu.

'I'm good,' I said. I'd only drunk half of the one I'd ordered at the bar.

The hostess sauntered away.

'I've been thinking about the hostel,' Celine said. 'Aiden could have mucked up his signature on purpose. You know, to make us think something was wrong. To make us stew. Don't you think that's a possibility?'

I didn't, but I kept mum.

She lowered her gaze to study the menu. 'What did you discover?' She didn't look up, her words peppered with angst. 'Give me a hint.'

'When you make eye contact.'

'Sorry.' She closed her menu and set it on the table. 'It's a bad habit. I can be micro-focused. It's good for business, not for personal interactions. So tell me.'

'I reached out via text again to Aiden.'

'And?'

'He was not happy about it.'

'He responded? Oh, Maggie, he's alive.' She reached for my hand and squeezed. 'That means he's alive.'

'I'm not sure he sent the message.' I explained my reasoning, the length of the text.

'Multiple sentences don't prove anything,' she countered, her eyes brimming with tears. 'He's written me long texts.'

'You, yes. Me? No. Also I've been receiving hang ups from a three-four-six area code.'

'They're probably robocallers. I get them all the time, don't you? Please tell me more about the text. Did he say he missed me?'

'Celine,' I began, loath to destroy her optimism.

'He didn't, did he?' She looked crestfallen.

The waitress, a leggy brunette, appeared with Celine's wine. I told her we weren't ready to order, and she moved along.

Celine sipped her chardonnay and set it down.

I said, 'What if the calls from the three-four-six area code are Aiden calling?'

'Using a new phone?'

'Maybe.' I wasn't ready to tell her about Carl Underhill yet.

'Where is three-four-six?'

'Houston.'

'It's not Aiden then,' she said. 'He hates Texas. Too muggy.'

Like Louisiana wasn't? 'He wouldn't necessarily be in Texas,' I said. 'You know cell phones. People travel all over the country with them. Just because it says three-four-six doesn't mean the caller is physically in Houston.'

'But if Aiden purchased a new phone, he would have bought it here. We're in the five-oh-four area code.'

'Yes, unless he obtained the phone from someone who'd come from Texas. Or—'

'We don't know anyone from Houston.'

'Or if he hitchhiked and was using that person's—'

'He wouldn't hitchhike. He said only fools did.'

'Or . . .' I sipped the wine. I was so tense I could barely taste it. I held my breath for the count of three before going on. 'Or if someone has taken him.'

'You mean kidnapped? Not possible.' Her hand flew to her mouth. The once hopeful tears in her eyes slipped down her cheeks. 'No, no, no,' she mumbled between splayed fingers. 'Please, no. Why would someone do that?'

'Ransom money is the typical reason.' Or leverage, I thought, but didn't utter. 'No one has asked me for money.'

'Me, either. Not that they would. We don't have any.'

I felt the sting of her words.

'I'm sorry. That came out wrong. I didn't meant to . . .' Celine folded her hands on the tabletop, clenching them so hard her knuckles turned white.

'It's OK. I know you didn't.' I leaned forward, mirroring her body language but with less tension. 'Are you sure he doesn't have friends who might have come from Texas? Other art students? Or bicycle riders? Maybe he's crashing on someone's couch.'

She shook her head. 'None that I know of.'

I pictured the luscious Rosalie at LGP and wondered whether the area code for her cell phone was 346.

The waitress reappeared.

'Not now!' Celine held up a hand to stop her.

The poor woman balked and shuffled away.

'Celine' – I patted her wrist – 'we'll figure this out.'

Listen to you. Sounding like the voice of reason when you're literally vibrating with angst.

'Yes. You're right.' Celine blinked back more tears. 'I have to remain calm. He texted you. He's OK. He's alive.'

'I contacted the police again since receiving the text. Because of it, they think he's all right. They'll keep on the lookout for him, but they won't search for him saying there's no evidence of foul play.'

'Because there is none!' Celine spanked the table. Our glasses jiggled. She steadied hers.

I understood her not wanting to think the worst. She was on tenterhooks. She wanted to remain positive, which couldn't be easy seeing as whenever she met with me I was in a constant state of worry. My stewing and fretting had to be raising alarm bells.

In a tiny voice she said, 'Who is the detective you talked to?'

'Frank Filuzzi. He said if you want to talk to him—'

'No.' She wagged her head. 'I don't. I can't. I . . .' She ran her lower lip between her teeth. 'Besides, what could I tell him that you haven't? But maybe I should. Should I?' Fresh tears pooled in her eyes. She dabbed them with her napkin and then wadded the napkin in her fist.

How I wanted to embrace her. Steady her. But I was feeling just as vulnerable and was afraid if I rose to comfort her, I might crack.

'You wanted to talk to me about something else you discovered,' Celine said. 'Not the three-four-six call or the text. What was it?'

I opted not to mention the disturbing note Helena and I found in Aiden's locker. Celine seemed too fragile to deal with it. Truthfully? I was, too. 'I was thinking about Aiden's journal again.'

'I told you he didn't keep one.'

'But what if he did and hid it?'

She squinted at me and waited for me to continue. I wasn't prepared to tell her I entered her house earlier and found a picture of Keira. That revelation might push her over the edge. Besides, I didn't know what Aiden meant when he'd written the words *She knew.*

'Zach wondered if Aiden might have written about a favorite

hiding spot or hangout in his journal,' I said, embellishing on Zach's theory.

'Like a coffee shop or something?'

'Or a place he liked to paint privately,' I said. 'Maybe a loft or artists' commune.'

She leaned forward. 'He painted at school.'

'And sometimes at Audubon Park.'

'Yes, there, too, and, well, all over town.' Her tears abated. 'We needed to meet for dinner to discuss that?'

'No. I wanted to see you.' I smiled gently. 'To make sure you were OK. Are you?'

'Maggie . . .' Her voice wobbled.

'I don't mean to press you. Truly I don't. You don't need a mother. But I thought we could be friends. A support system,' I added. 'As we figure this out.'

'Thank you. I appreciate that. More than you can imagine.' She ran a finger along the stem of her wineglass. 'You know, maybe he did write in a journal.'

I brightened.

'But if he did, I didn't know about it. He's been drawing inward the last couple of weeks. I think it had to do with more than just the grant for school. It had to do with his prospects at LGP. He seemed nervous they wouldn't hire him after all this time.'

Nerves might make him retreat into an emotional cave, I reasoned, but it didn't explain him running off and ceasing communication.

'I tried to get him to talk to me about it, but he wouldn't.' She lifted her gaze to meet mine. 'Sometimes he can be stubborn.'

'Like his father.'

'Like his mother, too,' Celine said teasingly.

'All too true.' I heard her stomach grumble. 'Know what you want to eat?'

'Scallops.'

I beckoned our waitress and ordered the roasted jumbo shrimp for me and smoked scallops for Celine. For the remainder of the meal, we talked about her work. The constituents. The constant flurry of complaints. We pushed food around, acting as if everything was normal. Neither of us finished our meals.

When Celine and I parted, she seemed on stronger footing. Me? I was as shaky as all get-out because I couldn't prevent ghastly images of Aiden in trouble from churning through my brain.

TWENTY-TWO

After dinner, I drove home with the windows open. Drank in the fresh air. Willed the tension in my shoulders to release. I parked in the driveway, jogged the stairs to the porch, and froze. A package illuminated by porchlight was sitting by the door. Not your typical Amazon delivered-in-an-oversized-brown-box package. It was a white gift box wrapped with white ribbon. Who had left it? When? Why? I inspected it without touching it. No card. No label providing my address. Had it been left by mistake?

I reached for the box and recoiled. Fear slicked the back of my throat. What if someone had put a bomb in it? Like Underhill or Watley or Coach Tuttle? He'd threatened me, saying *This isn't over.*

Feeling like someone had eyes on me, I swung around. I didn't see anyone across the street. No one was down the road staring in my direction. A BMW pulled into the house next to mine. The driver doused the lights. I recognized my neighbor as he exited the car, head lowered, shoulders hunched. The car had to be new; he used to drive a Lexus. I waved, but he didn't acknowledge me.

Seconds later, a car without headlights rounded the corner. Stopped. Idled. It was dark-colored and boxy. An SUV. Something ignited inside. A cigarette? Was the driver watching to see what I'd do with the gift? Suddenly, the lights switched on, and the SUV drove away. The timing seemed suspicious, but I was admittedly mistrustful at this point.

Calm down, Mags. A bomb? A stalker? Get real. If Underhill was after me, he'd most likely hire someone to shoot me like he'd shot Josh. *If* he'd shot Josh. And *if* he wanted me dead. But if he'd kidnapped Aiden—

No. I couldn't think like that. Aiden was fine. No one had taken him. He'd texted. He was alive. Unless, as I said to Celine, his captor had sent the messages on his behalf and that was why this unnerving, motherly-intuition dread continued to swirl inside me. How I wished I could erase the feeling, but I couldn't, no matter how hard I tried.

I nudged the box with my toe. It was light. A bomb would weigh more, wouldn't it? I bent and untied the bow. The ribbon fell to the ground. Again using my toe, I prodded the lid of the box. Up. Up. Until it slid to one side. I peered inside. A voodoo doll with blond hair and cross-stitched eyes lay on a bed of straw. Blond like me. Like Aiden. Like Celine. What was more disturbing was that whoever had left the doll had pierced the doll's heart with a toy sword and embellished the doll's torso with fake blood.

Hands shaking, I removed Filuzzi's business card from my tote – I'd forgotten to give it to Celine at dinner – and tapped in his cell phone number. The call went to voicemail. 'Frank, it's Maggie.'

Would he listen this time, or would he pat my pretty little head and tell me this was a neighborhood prank? Could the police lab techs find fingerprints or DNA on the box? I'd read somewhere that pulling DNA off ribbon and similar slick surfaces was nearly impossible.

'Someone left a suspicious box on my porch,' I said, voice trembling. 'I opened it. Carefully.' He would have told me not to tamper with it all. 'What's inside is disturbing. Please call me back.' I left my information and would let him come to his own conclusions. Had I received a head, a hand, or a finger? For all he knew, I'd received a picture of my son holding a newspaper with today's date, confirming he'd been abducted.

I tucked the box beneath the two-seater swing on the porch, loath to touch it or have its bad luck enter my home. Then I stepped inside, bolted the door, and switched on the lights. No *pop, fizzle*. I shrugged out of my coat and strode to the kitchen. Inside the doorway, I drew to a halt. Someone had been inside. A broad-blade knife lay on the counter. I hadn't left it there. And the drawer below the cubby where I stowed my tote bag and house keys was ajar.

Pulse juddering, I clasped the knife and stole upstairs. I peered into Aiden's old room, the one I'd redecorated in bland beige a week after I'd learned he'd eloped. Talk about passive-aggressive. The bed was rumpled, as if someone had perched on it. Everything else looked intact. There were no lingering scents other than the vanilla I smelled on a daily basis.

A shiver coursed through me when I entered my bedroom and noticed the topmost drawer of my bureau was open an inch. I wasn't imagining things. Someone had broken into my house. Was the intruder still here?

I dashed to my closet. Bent down. Opened a hidden compartment in the floor that I'd obscured with a shoe box. I unlocked the combination safe. I set the knife aside and retrieved my father's service revolver from the safe. A Beretta 9mm. I'd become adept with guns during my brief stint at the academy. I disengaged the gun's safety and crept through the house, weapon aimed.

No one was in the bathroom. The guest room. The hall. The bathroom off the hall.

I tiptoed downstairs and scanned the living room. No one was crouching behind the sofa. I went to the foyer, opened the door leading to the ground floor, and flipped the light switch. The stench of dampness assaulted my nostrils. Fans were still whirring to dry out the area. I listened. Hard. No footsteps. No one scurrying for a hiding place. I tiptoed downward, one stair at a time, without making a creak. When I reached the bottom, I pivoted. There was no one. I was alone.

Bending at the waist, I tried to catch my breath. Was someone gaslighting me? Had Aiden brought the gift and stolen into the house to mess with my head?

No. He wouldn't do that. He wouldn't.

So who had? When? Why? Was it the same person who'd put the box on my porch? Of course it was. What a ridiculous coincidence if it wasn't.

Why hadn't Filuzzi responded yet? Did I need to call 911? Would they do anything? Robberies happened all the time. Often, because they were minor offenses, the police didn't investigate. And if I couldn't prove I had been robbed, what then?

I made a tour of the house, checking all the doors and windows. I discovered the side door into the kitchen was unlocked – it was a door I rarely used – and I cursed at the top of my lungs. Had I been the one to leave it that way? If I hadn't, how had the intruder entered without ruining the lock? Unlike Aiden, I didn't keep a key hidden in a pot or under the mat. Josh had warned me off that bad habit years ago.

My cell phone jangled.

TWENTY-THREE

jerked and scanned the display. *Josh.* Had thinking about him conjured his call? Maybe it was Tess. I hoped not. I didn't have the energy to talk to her. I answered.

'Hey, I'm on my way home from the hospital.' Josh sounded strong, vital. 'Thought you'd like to know.'

'That's great.'

'I won't be running any marathons for a month or so,' he joked. He'd never participated in a marathon. He, like Aiden, preferred riding a bike. 'I got your message about the hostel. Sorry I didn't respond. I've been out of it. The signature thing sounds iffy.'

'That's what the police think, too, but they won't act on what I found.'

'I haven't heard from our son, yet. You?'

'Not really.'

'That's cryptic. What do you mean *not really*?'

I swallowed hard and told him about the angry text message. 'Josh, I don't think he wrote it.' I explained how I'd been in Helena Hebert's office at Tulane when I'd received it. I also told him about the note we'd discovered in Aiden's locker.

'What kind of note?'

'A threat,' I mumbled.

'A threat?'

'Stop repeating everything I say,' I snapped, and pressed on. 'Yes, a threat. It was like the other notes I saw at Aiden's duplex. But worse. Whoever wrote it was goading him. It said, "You total no-talent loser, die. Soon. No looking back, die."' I brought him up to speed about my clandestine break-in and the fact that I was keeping my discoveries from Celine. To protect her. 'She's so vulnerable right now. I don't think—'

'Maggie—'

'No. Don't judge me. I took pictures and showed the police, but they won't do anything.'

'Because our son is an adult.'

'Bingo!' I grunted.

'Mags,' he said gently, 'is it possible you're blowing this out of proportion?'

'No! What if he's been kidnapped?'

'Again with the kidnapping?' Josh sniffed.

'Yes.' My voice skated upward. I sounded hysterical. I needed to get a grip. I took a deep breath and began again. 'What if the note in his locker is the kidnapper's way of toying with me? With us?'

'I told you already. Kidnapping is a leap.'

'You were shot, Josh. What if Carl Underhill—'

'One of Nicky Bilko's crew shot me.'

'Bilko, the money launderer?'

'The same. He's one of the guys I've been trying to take down.'

Bilko, a scrawny, scruffy redhead with a soul patch, wasn't your ordinary money launderer. And he sure as hell wasn't on the same level as Underhill – not in class, mentality, or the scope of his depravity. But he was wily. He swapped legitimate works of art for dirty cash, cash that might have been obtained in drug trafficking. By and large, art for cash was an upscale way of money laundering. Buyers didn't know where the art was coming from and didn't want to know. Sellers were equally opaque. Nothing required paperwork. I'd met Bilko once at a gallery opening. He'd taken my hand to introduce himself, and I'd instantly felt the need to shower.

'FYI, Bilko's behind bars until the trial in October.' Josh inhaled and exhaled. He was smoking, probably. His one-cigarette-a-day habit. I wouldn't fault him after his ordeal.

'But he's calling the shots.'

'Yeah, probably.'

'What if he orchestrated the kidnapping?'

'Mags, stop with the—'

'Someone broke into my house!' I couldn't temper the hysteria. 'Whoever it was left a present on my doorstep.' I described the voodoo doll. 'And there was a knife on my kitchen counter. I did *not* put it there.'

'Why didn't you lead with that? I'm on my way over.'

'No. I'm fine. You don't need to—'

'Don't argue.'

Josh arrived in less than thirty minutes. Despite his arm being in a sling, he looked good. And he seemed remarkably rested, although the concern in his eyes was palpable.

I let him in and bolted the door. 'Do you want something to drink?'

'Have you got iced tea?'

'Sure.'

He trailed me into the kitchen and sat on a stool by the granite island. I filled a highball glass with ice, added tea and a teaspoon of sugar, and handed it to him. I poured myself a glass of chardonnay. I'd been waiting for him to arrive before I drank anything harder than water. I wanted a clear head knowing how my ex-husband would grill me. The effects of the glass of wine I'd drunk at Brennan's had worn off.

I caught Josh eyeing my father's Beretta. I'd set it on the counter near the butcher's block. 'After finding the gift and then seeing the knife out of place, I got nervous.'

'Let me read the note from Aiden's locker.'

I retrieved it from my tote and handed it to him.

He flicked the paper. 'Do you think this is the same handwriting as on the others?'

'Maybe. I don't know. I'm not an expert.' I opened my cell phone app and showed him the photographs of the notes I found tucked into the hidden copy of *Lord of the Flies*. 'I'm wondering if this could have anything to do with Keira's death. The police said it was a hit-and-run, but what if it wasn't? What if whatever she knew put her in danger? What if whoever killed her has Aiden?' I would not add *has hurt* Aiden. I couldn't go there.

'Two years later? That seems unlikely.'

'Yeah, I agree. But . . .' I let the notion fade. 'By the way, I'm not proud of myself for breaking into their duplex.'

'You didn't break in if you used a key. Cut yourself some slack.' He compared the images.

'They're all done in block letters,' I said. 'I'm pretty sure my block letters would look like yours.'

He handed back the note and sipped his iced tea. 'Show me the gift.'

I fetched the box I'd stowed beneath the swing on the front porch, re-bolted the door, and returned to the kitchen. I set the box on the counter and removed the lid.

Josh's nostrils flared. 'Have you touched the doll?'

'No, but the blood's fake.'

'How do you know?'

'I can tell. And, for your information, yes, I contacted the police.'

'Why aren't they here yet?'

'I didn't dial nine-one-one. I . . .' I stared at my cell phone sitting idle on the counter. 'I reached out to Frank Filuzzi.'

'Filuzzi,' Josh repeated with a bite. He knew our history.

'Yes. He's married now. Two teenagers. He's working homicide.' I told him where. 'I contacted him about Aiden. That's why I . . .' I didn't finish. Didn't need to. I sipped my wine and set it aside. 'Do you think one of Bilko's guys left this for me, knowing I'd reach out to you?'

'Maybe. I could see him doing something childish like this.'

'Crap.' I wrapped an arm across my body.

'You know, I've always admired your pluck, Mags. You keep your wits about you.'

'I'm shaken up this time,' I said, instantly regretting how needy I sounded. Adrenaline was pinballing inside me. Soon I would tilt. 'I suppose I am my father's daughter.' And I knew what he, in a sober state, would have said. *Solve this yourself, Maggie girl. The police are good, but they can't crack every case. Use that brain of yours.* I spun my cell phone on the counter and let it spin. When it stopped, I said, 'Do you want to sit on the back porch? I could use some fresh air.'

'Sure.'

I took my cell phone and wineglass. He carried his iced tea. The night air was cool and unmoving. Mosquitoes were roaming, as they often did, but nocturnal creatures hadn't kicked into high gear. I lit the citronella candle. The flame played across Josh's face.

'Nice,' he said, setting his tea on the wrought iron table. 'Peaceful.'

'If only Aiden—'

'Shh.' He wrapped his good arm around my shoulders and guided me into a chair. 'You've been going nonstop with this thing about him.'

This *thing*? Was it a *thing*? Was I totally off base?

'It didn't help that I got shot,' Josh said.

I sat down and extended my arms on the table, keeping my wineglass at a distance. Josh sat and cupped my right elbow with his left hand. The connection was tender. Warm. Reassuring.

'But, Mags, I don't think they're related.'

'You don't know that for sure.' I withdrew my arm from his grasp and fingered the stem of the wineglass. 'Tell me about Bilko.'

'Good old Nicky,' Josh said. 'I guess his ex-wife really hated him.' His mouth turned up on one side. The dimple that I'd often traced my finger along appeared.

The first time I did that, he clasped my finger and whispered *I love you.*

Oh, to be transported back in time.

'She ratted him out to my source,' Josh continued, 'the one who gave me the scoop for my story. They came across over fifteen big-ticket pieces of stolen art ready to go to buyers.'

'How'd the police figure out it was Bilko's guy?'

'Like I said, his ex really hated him. When her gal pal told her that Nicky sent one of his men to take me down – the gal pal is married to Nicky's second-in-command – his ex alerted the cops. If only all my investigations went this smoothly.' He hoisted his glass for a toast.

I raised mine and clinked the rim with his. The tap brought back a flurry of memories. The two of us on the porch. Celebrating Aiden's accomplishments. Celebrating Josh's stories. Celebrating my rise in the ranks at the English department at Tulane and then my appointment as dean at Pelican. All good remembrances, yet sad because we would never make new ones. If I was honest with myself, I missed him, warts and all. Missed the friendship. Missed the discussions. Missed his tender kisses.

'Mags, I'm sorry I screwed up.'

'What are you talking about?'

'The marriage. Us. You didn't deserve what I dished out.'

'Sure, I did. I didn't pay enough attention to you. I took you for granted. I thought you'd always be there. I thought you'd think I was so special that you'd accept half of me.' I swiped a tear off my cheek and took a gulp of wine. And then another. 'When Benjie died, I lost a huge hunk of myself and was determined to become the most in control person I could be. Nothing was going to surprise me. Ever.' I was spewing Gina's friendly diagnosis, but I didn't disagree with her assessment. 'When my mother checked out—' My voice cracked. I started over. 'When Mom mentally shut down, I needed to be even more in control. For a long time, I was able to channel that kind of focus into our family. Into my career. But when my father died, I fell down a rabbit hole. I shut off my emotions.'

'I knew why you did it.'

'Not good enough. This falls on me. I needed to stay in the light for you and for Aiden. And I didn't. It's why I've suffocated him. I was scared. Scared that . . . Scared that he might—'

There. My chest released its stranglehold on my lungs. Finally, I let the truth surface. Ever since kids started bullying Aiden, no matter what I'd told him, I'd been afraid he wouldn't be strong enough to ride the storm.

'*Shh.* He won't. He hasn't.' Josh withdrew the wineglass from my hand, pushed it to one side, and wrapped his hand around mine. 'And for the record? You were plenty for me. Even half of you was plenty. I . . .' His thumb caressed the inside of my wrist. 'I let my guard down. I sought someone who would stroke my ego. And then some.'

'Ha-ha.' I whacked his good arm. Until our marriage dissolved, he'd always known how to make me laugh.

'Men are pigs,' he joked.

'Yes, you've told me that for years.' I lifted my gaze to meet his, and without warning, the dam broke. Tears streamed down my cheeks. 'These aren't for you,' I murmured. 'They're for Aiden. I wish I had a crystal ball.'

'I hate fortunetellers,' he said drily.

I gazed at him. Drank in the warmth of his eyes.

His lips parted. 'Do you . . .' He halted briefly. 'Do you think if we'd gone to therapy, we could've . . .' He let the question hang in the air.

We could've what? Talked through our problems? Found forgiveness in our hearts? Made our marriage work?

My cell phone jangled. I flinched at the sound and scanned the display.

'Is it Aiden?' he asked.

'Filuzzi.' I stabbed Answer. 'Hi, Detective.'

'An officer is on the way over to retrieve the package. ETA, ten minutes,' he stated. No preamble. 'But I gotta say, Maggie, opening a box with no gift card was stupid on your part.'

I nodded, not verbally owning up to my foolhardiness, happy that he was taking the threat seriously.

'Based on this twist,' he said, 'I'll put out an official APB for your son. If he left this for you—'

'He didn't.'

'So you say. But if he did, trust me, there will be hell to pay.

You don't pull a stunt like this on your mother. That crosses a line for me. Understood?'

'Understood. Thank you.'

I ended the call and regarded Josh. His lips were pressed firmly together. His gaze had hardened. The moment of connection that the two of us had experienced was gone. He and I were not going to reunite. We weren't dewy-eyed teens who could forget the bad stuff and move on. Plus he was marrying Tess.

'Good news,' I said. 'The police will look for Aiden. Finally.'

Josh tattooed the tabletop and rose to a stand. Iced tea glass in hand, he headed into the house. Over his shoulder, he said, 'Whatever you need, I'm on board.'

While moving into the kitchen, my cell phone dinged again. Not Filuzzi. I said to Josh, 'It's Celine.'

'Answer.'

I did. 'What's up?'

'Can't sleep.' Her voice was hoarse, as if she'd been crying. 'I had a thought.'

'I'm listening.'

'Aiden . . .' She bit back a sob. 'I told you Aiden has been distracted. It might have been another woman he's been hot for. His muse, he called her.' She let out a bitter laugh. 'As if he needed a muse. He was so talented all on his own.'

I hated that she was using the past tense. 'Is,' I corrected. 'He *is* so talented.'

'What if he moved in with her?'

'Without telling you? Without ending things with you? That doesn't make sense,' I said. 'Aiden isn't like that. He wouldn't. He's honorable.' He wasn't like his father, who had shacked up with his first lover two weeks before I'd gotten wise. Stupid me. I'd thought he was on a long stakeout. 'Who is this woman? Do you know her name?'

'No, but I followed him one time. I know her address.'

TWENTY-FOUR

J osh stayed with me until the police came. Two seasoned officers, a male and female. They made a perimeter search and didn't find anything out of the ordinary. No footprints. No broken windows. No telltale cigarette butts. I confessed to finding the side door into the kitchen unlocked. Josh said he still had a key to the house and asked if Aiden did. I said no. A year ago, he lost it, as he'd mislaid so many things. The officers questioned me further and filled out a digital report form. As expected, they offered to process the gift box but wouldn't promise results. Unless the intruder's fingerprints were in the system – if they could even lift fingerprints from the box or the doll – they had nothing more to go on. On her way out, the female officer recommended that I install a video doorbell system. Maybe I should even contemplate installing security cameras on the four upper corners of the house, she added. Yeah, like I could afford that.

When they left, Josh followed me around the house and helped me inspect all the locks and windows again, double-checking to make sure the side door was secure.

Mission accomplished, he said, 'Want me to stay?'

'You can't defend me with that clipped wing,' I kidded. Sure, I was feeling queasy about being in the house alone, but I didn't want him to stay. Didn't want the temptation of looking at his mouth again. Remembering the way he used to kiss me.

'Bells,' he said. 'Let's hang bells on all the doors. You have dozens in the Christmas decoration boxes.'

I did. I loved the merry jingling during the holidays. 'No,' I said firmly. 'I'll be fine. I have a gun. And I'm good at sleeping with one eye open.'

Josh shrugged, knowing how stubborn I could be. Knowing I wouldn't change my mind. He said, 'In the morning, I'll go with you to find this muse.' Celine had texted the address. 'But you'll have to drive. I'm almost out of gas.'

Lacking the strength to quash the offer and knowing company on the next leg of this journey would be welcome, I thanked him.

Before heading to bed, I called Gina and brought her up to speed about the voodoo doll, Josh, the police. When I finished, she lit into me, upset that I hadn't reached out earlier, saying the moment I'd seen what was inside the gift box I should have phoned her. When I convinced her that contacting the police was the smarter move, she calmed down. We spoke for an hour. Before signing off, I promised I would touch base with more news tomorrow.

I slept fitfully. Dreaming of voodoo dolls. And Celine with cross-stitched eyes. And Josh lying in a pool of blood. And Gina screaming at me. And Nicky Bilko laughing like a hyena while firing off twenty rounds. And Aiden . . . running into the kitchen.

'Mom, Mom!' Aiden was ten years old with blond curls past his ears, one curl dangling down his forehead giving him a goofy appeal. He threw his arms around my waist. 'You won't believe what I learned to do on the computer today. It's so cool.' He handed me a piece of paper.

Using a birthday photo of himself at the age of three, he'd created a digital portrait. I marveled at his ingenuity. 'I remember this photograph,' I said. Happy tears pressed at the corners of my eyes. 'It took a week to get the stain of blue icing off your skin.'

'I did it through Adobe Illustrator. It's all about layering and tracing and getting the skin tone right.' He gave me a gap-toothed smile. 'Isn't it rad? Like really, really rad?'

I awoke in a pool of sweat with the words *Really, really rad* clanging in my ears. How I missed my son. Where was he? I needed to find him. Solve things. If necessary, make amends for my behavior.

Desperate to shake off the mental cobwebs, I threw off the covers, slipped into running clothes, and did three fast miles. After showering, I threw on a crisp white shirt, jeans, and flats, and fetched a leather jacket, then went to the kitchen. Two cups of coffee later, I felt like I could face the world. One step at a time.

At seven thirty, I messaged Yvonne not to expect me until later in the day, and I picked Josh up at his place. I waved to Tess who was standing by the upstairs window looking down. Then I handed him the address, which was near the New Orleans Museum of Art. Josh, Aiden, and I had visited NOMA on numerous occasions. It was situated on property that used to be owned by sugar and molasses merchant Isaac Delgado. He gave the property to the city as a gift.

'There it is.' Josh pointed to a pale-gray, one-story home with orange trim and an adobe roof.

I parked my Prius in front and climbed out. Sheer drapes covered the windows. Two palms and Gulf Stream nandina decorated the tiny garden.

'Do you think this muse will be home?' Josh asked as we climbed the stairs to the porch.

'Here's hoping.'

I heard music playing inside the house, a good sign that she was around, unless that was her way of warding off salesmen and burglars. I pressed the doorbell. The sound of high heels clacked the floor. The peephole opened. The woman peering out gasped.

A moment later, the door opened. Rosalie glowered at me. 'What are you doing here?'

I faltered. She was the muse? She was dressed for work in a chartreuse sheath, bulky gold chain, dangly earrings, and high heels, although she hadn't yet put on make-up. On closer inspection, I could tell her red hair wasn't her natural color. Blond roots were showing.

I raised my palms. 'We didn't mean to scare you.'

'I'm not scared,' she drawled. 'Where did you get my address? Did you follow me from work?'

'No. Ce—' I stopped, not wanting to reveal that Celine had tailed Aiden to Rosalie's place. 'We're looking for Aiden. Is he here?'

'No. Why would he be?' She propped a fist on one hip.

'May we come in?' I gestured to Josh. 'This is my ex-husband. Aiden's father.' I explained to him that Rosalie worked at Le Gran Palais as I tried to peer past her.

She gripped the door tightly, not allowing a better view inside. 'I'm on my way to work. I'm late.'

I stood on tiptoe. 'Aiden! If you're in there, please show yourself. Dad is with me.'

'I told you, he's not here,' Rosalie said curtly. 'He has a wife. A home. This isn't it.'

'His wife said you're Aiden's muse.'

'Aha.' Rosalie barked out a laugh. 'Celine's the one who gave you the address, isn't she? I thought I saw her drive past the other day. She needn't be jealous. Yes, I've fallen for Aiden, but he hasn't got a lick of interest in me other than my opinion about his art. He's madly in love with his wife.'

'Why did he seek your opinion?' I regarded her steadily. 'Are you an artist?'

'No, but I have a good eye, and I'm a mighty good critic. After getting my master of fine arts degree, I wanted to be a curator at a museum. Sadly, that dream fell through. Not enough museums to go around, you know?' She didn't look old enough to have graduated college, let alone to have earned an advanced degree. 'I've been able to steer some artists in the right direction. Many from Tulane, like Aiden. I was scouting there when we met. I'm the one who got him the gig at LGP.'

Josh said, 'I know a couple of museum bigwigs. I might be able to help you out.'

'As some kind of bribe?' Rosalie appeared unconvinced.

'Out of the goodness of my heart.'

'Yeah, right.' Rosalie swept her hair over her shoulders and defiantly folded her arms across her chest. 'What do you want from me?'

'We want to find Aiden,' I said.

'Check. Got that. I'm not deaf.' Her crusty exterior was off-putting, but I suppose I'd have felt the same if a colleague's anxious parents had come calling. 'But like I said, he isn't here, and I don't have a clue where he is. Y'see, all of a sudden, he's ghosting me and Stan like he is you. Ever since you came to LGP asking about him.'

Had Aiden been watching me and tracking my movements? No, that didn't make sense. It had to be a coincidence. 'Did you tell him I stopped in?'

'Neither of us did because, like I said, he stopped communicating. Timing, as my daddy says, is everything.' She forced a tight smile. 'If that's all.'

Something about her glibness bothered me. 'I really need to see inside your place,' I said. 'It'll take less than five minutes.'

'You don't believe me.'

'No, actually I don't.'

'Get a warrant.'

'Look' – I opened my hands, palms up – 'if you're not lying, then you should be fine with my request.'

'I'm not lying.'

'Let me in. I'm his mother, not a monster. I won't hurt you. We' – I waved a finger between Josh and me – 'won't hurt you. Please. We need to check off every box. He's missing, Rosalie. Don't you get that? He could be in danger. We're worried sick.'

Rosalie's expression was unreadable. Why was she being so stubborn? She'd just admitted she had feelings for him. Was it possible that he'd rejected her, so she'd taken him captive, vowing he would remain her prisoner until he proclaimed his love for her? Crazier things had happened. In my freshman year of high school, Benjie and I watched *Fatal Attraction* together. By the final scene, both of us were freaking out.

'Fine,' she finally said. 'Come in. But he truly isn't here.' Her iWatch *pinged*. She glimpsed it and ignored it. 'You've got five minutes.' She sidled to a bright red console table in the entry, pulled a mascara wand from a makeup kit that was resting on it, and started to apply mascara in front of the blue oval mirror.

Her place was Bohemian chic. Floral chairs and sofa. Multicolored pouf ottoman. Numerous apothecary chests, their drawers painted bold blues, oranges, and yellows. The sole contemporary piece of furniture was a black lacquer cabinet holding a sleek television. An array of DVDs lined the cabinet's open shelves as well as a single black-and-white photograph of Rosalie and an older woman I presumed was her mother. Delicate Seurat-style paintings adorned one wall. Hitchcock and classic horror movie posters decorated another.

I eyed the pointillist art and noticed two were signed *Rosalie*. 'You lied,' I said.

'No, I—'

'You are an artist. You're good.'

'I dabble, but I'm not marketable. Bedroom's to the left. Kitchen's straight ahead.' Her iWatch *pinged* again. When she read the alert, a hiss escaped her lips. Was Aiden writing her, telling her to get rid of us?

Stop, Maggie. Her boss was probably messaging her.

Josh and I explored the master bedroom first. The closets were neatly arranged but sparse – Rosalie wasn't a clotheshorse – and a person couldn't hide beneath the low-profile platform bed. Next we inspected the kitchen. Then the bathroom. Both empty.

When four minutes had passed, Josh nabbed my elbow. 'He's not here. Let's go.' He guided me to the front door.

'Sorry to intrude,' I said to Rosalie, who was applying hot-pink lipstick.

'You didn't.'

'Yes, we did.' My cheeks reddened knowing she was probably thinking, *Helicopter mama*. She had every right.

'Yeah, you did, but . . .' She set the lipstick aside and pivoted. Her eyes were moist. Had I finally penetrated her tough exterior? Was she fighting tears? Was she as worried about Aiden as Josh and I were?

'But?' I coaxed.

'But I'm glad you did because now you trust me, right? And I've gotta admit I'm concerned, too. I mean, he and I were texting regularly until . . .' She waved a hand and quickly captured it with her other as if to anchor herself. 'If he's in trouble, I want to help.'

I looked at Josh and back at Rosalie. She wasn't putting on an act. We'd convinced her something was wrong. 'How well do you know him? If you were him—'

'I know he likes to sketch. He drinks his coffee black. He loves to bike ride.' A soft smile graced her lips. 'And he reads some of the weirdest books. None I'd ever read in school.'

'Like *Lord of the Flies*?'

'That and *Dune* and *Animal Farm*.'

Aiden was well read and enjoyed reading across genre.

'He could talk about them for hours,' she added.

I flashed on the taunting notes he'd received. 'Did Aiden ever talk to you about . . .' I swallowed hard. 'Did he ever mention that he was being bullied or threatened?'

'No. Why on earth . . .' She sputtered. 'He's not in kindergarten.'

'People are harassed all the time,' I said, 'well into adulthood.'

'He never mentioned anything like that.'

'Did he ever talk about wanting—' I balked. I hated that I was likening him to my brother, but the comparison kept rearing its ugly head. 'About wanting to hurt himself?'

'No. Never. Not once.' She was adamant. 'Why would you think he would? He was strong. Talented. *Is*,' she corrected quickly. 'Is strong and talented.'

'Why did he visit you here?' I asked, taking one more look around without leaving the room.

'I told you. To get my opinion of his work.' Her iWatch *pinged* a third time. She placed her hand over the face, as if trying to suffocate a pesky gnat. 'We would discuss technique, focusing primarily on his sketches.'

Josh jumped on that. 'Sketches of what?'

'Torsos and hands,' I stated.

'No,' Rosalie said. 'Tombs.'

'Tombs?' Josh threw me a worried look.

Rosalie added hurriedly, 'He wasn't morbid. Aiden was never that. He was . . . *is* fascinated by the artistry of the tombs. His work is quite impressionistic.'

I recalled seeing a few of those when I'd searched his locker with Helena Hebert.

Rosalie went on, 'He particularly likes sneaking into Metairie Cemetery to sketch. He says the tombs call to him.' She painted the air with a hand. 'As if the tombs are alive and breathing and filled with stories and history. He loves the way the light plays across the marble, too.'

He'd said the same to me when he was younger.

'If I may be direct, I don't think Celine . . .' Rosalie chewed on her lower lip. 'I don't think Celine encourages him to sketch. She prefers his digital art.'

I nodded, now understanding why he considered Rosalie his muse. He needed support for his creative endeavors, in whatever form. Keira used to fill that role. Was Celine's lack of encouragement one of the reasons he needed to clear his head? Was it possible this was just a temporary absence? No. The voodoo doll on my porch suggested something dark was at play.

'Listen' – she folded her hands primly in front of her – 'maybe you should check out the cemetery. Sometimes, he likes to steal in and sketch at night and stay there until morning. It sounds creepy, I know, but he is into it. He feels spirits are guiding him. He probably wouldn't insult the ghosts by using his cell phone there, you know.'

With over nine thousand souls buried at Metairie Cemetery, there were plenty of spirits to go around, and locals as well as tourists were intrigued by the idea. The abundance of ghost tours in New Orleans was astounding.

I thanked her, nudged Josh, and turned to leave.

'If you find him . . .' Rosalie faltered. 'I mean *when* you find him' – she clutched her neck with her hand – 'will you have him text me and tell me he's all right?'

TWENTY-FIVE

B ack in the Prius, I reached for the ignition but hesitated. Sunlight gleamed off the white hood. The flash made me flinch. At the same time, the door to Rosalie's apartment opened.

'Start the car,' Josh said.

'In a sec.'

Rosalie stepped outside and locked the door while talking into her iWatch. Her gaze hardened. She shook her head firmly. *No, no, no,* she was saying. She ended the call and dashed to a nearby Toyota Celica. She leaped inside, pulled away from the curb, and made a U-turn. Not in the direction she should have been going if she was heading to work.

'What are you staring at?' Josh asked.

'Rosalie isn't driving toward LGP.'

'Maybe she's doing an errand first.'

'She looks nervous. Panicky.'

'You're reading into things.'

He was right. I was amped up and seeing ghosts where there were none.

'Let's go,' he prompted.

I switched on the engine and pulled on to the road. 'I should tell you about Aiden's altar. He and Celine both made one.'

'I've seen them.'

Of course he had. He'd been invited to their place on numerous occasions. Only I, the mother-in-law, had been given boundaries.

Stop, Mags. Not fair.

'There was a cemetery map on Aiden's, folded into a triangle,' I said.

'For Metairie Cemetery?'

'No, for St Louis number one. What if there was another map of Metairie Cemetery? Or what if the one I found was intended to signify Metairie? It was folded into a triangle, like a pyramid, and there are two pseudo-Egyptian pyramids at Metairie.'

'One.'

'Two. The Pinnell tomb was installed last year.' I glanced at him and back at the road. 'On the map, Aiden had drawn doodles and written digits and stuff around the edge. I thought the scribbles might mean something, so I went to St Louis number one with Gina to search.'

Josh wrinkled his nose. He didn't like Gina. *Cancel that.* He didn't like therapists. He'd consulted one a few times after his mother passed away. He and his mother, like Aiden and me, had been close. Her battle with cancer had torn Josh to shreds. The therapist had encouraged him to come weekly, but Josh demurred. He'd confided to me that the doctor mainly offered placebos, and talking to the guy had made him feel weak. *Men,* I'd chided, pounding my chest like an ape and warbling like Tarzan. That had made him smile. But he never went back.

I said, 'Thinking he might have been urging whoever consulted the map to go on a scavenger hunt' – I told him about the directive near the image of Marie Laveau's headstone to *get a bead* – 'I went there but learned nothing.'

Josh had instigated the first hunt Aiden had ever gone on. The two of them had been so eager, they'd reminded me of kids hyped-up on Halloween candy. Chatting nonstop, punching each other in the arm, tripping each other on purpose. More than once, I'd had to tell them to cool their jets. They were going to get us kicked out. My scolding only made them act out worse. It had taken all my resolve not to join their antics.

'What if . . .' I paused.

'What if *what*?' He twirled a finger. 'Keep talking. I like when you think like an investigator.'

Even though my crime beat career was brief, I'd learned a lot and had served as a good sounding board for his deep dives. 'What if he did go to Metairie Cemetery like Rosalie suggested?' I asked. 'What if he's been camping out there these past few days?'

'Camping out?'

'Remember when he was twelve, and he was angry at us for not letting him do a sleepover with his friends, so he sneaked out? You were frightened out of your wits.'

'Me?' He pointed. 'You were frantic.'

He was right. I'd feared the worst. He'd forced me to drink a vodka to calm my nerves. To this day, I hated vodka.

'Until I found the sketch he'd drawn,' I said. 'The one with clues.'

'Remember where we stumbled upon him? He'd scaled the fence at the cemetery and had hidden himself beneath a blanket at the base of a tomb.' I drew to a halt at a stoplight. 'We can't ask Celine to go through the items on his altar or she'll know I was snooping and all the goodwill between us will be blown. Let's give this a shot.'

'Fine. Turn left at the next light.'

'I know the way.'

Metairie Cemetery, situated in a shady, parklike setting on Pontchartrain Boulevard, was built on a site that had once been a horse racing track. Its gray-and-white marble mausoleums were a study in extravagance, some the size of small houses, some with stairs leading up to stained glass doors.

A female tour guide was standing outside the entrance checking her watch. Josh and I approached and inquired whether she was available. She wasn't. She was waiting for a group of tourists. I asked if she'd mind, when they arrived, if we followed her in, adding that we purely wanted to see the two pyramid-shaped tombs and leave. We were Egyptologists, I added, winging it. Two twenty-dollar bills warmed her to the plan.

A half-hour later, the tour guide led her charges inside and veered left. Josh and I went right. As we neared the Brunswig crypt, a pseudo-pyramid with a mythical sphinx guarding it, a person in black jacket and jeans darted out of sight.

'It's him,' Josh yelled, and took off.

'Josh, wait!'

'It's him. It's Aiden.' He tore around the tomb.

I raced after him. 'Josh! Call his name. Tell him to halt.' If it was Aiden, he would stop, wouldn't he? When Josh didn't bark out the command, I did. 'Aiden! It's me and your dad. Aiden, please. Talk to us. We—'

Josh hurled himself at the fleeing person. Knocked him to the ground. Tore at the hood of the jacket.

I clasped his good shoulder to pull him off. He hauled back with an elbow. Nailed me in the thigh.

'Josh, stop! It isn't Aiden. See the red hair? The beard?'

'Get off me, man!' the victim said. He slammed his fist into Josh's ear and then into his shoulder.

Josh groaned. Reeled.

The victim cursed as he scrambled to a stand and tore away. I saw blood pooling in Josh's shirt. A lot of blood. His stitches had probably opened.

'Josh, I'm calling nine-one-one. You need to go back to the hospital.'

'Don't. They'll involve the cops. They'll arrest us for being here. You drive me.'

Josh and I, with me as his crutch, hightailed it out of the cemetery.

At University Medical Center, the ER team treated Josh with care. One doctor who'd attended to him when he'd been admitted with the gunshot wound chided Josh for even being out of bed. Josh, slightly groggy with meds, didn't argue. When I explained why Josh had risked it, the doctor cut him some slack.

'Maggie!' Tess hurried into the room. Straight to Josh. Her pony-tail swished. Her hot-pink yoga outfit accentuated her curves. I'd texted her the moment we got to the hospital. She kissed his cheek. 'Sweetheart, I'm here.' She eyed me. 'What in the name of—'

'We were following a lead on Aiden,' I said. 'Josh thought he saw him. Chased him. Turned out he was wrong, and the other guy laid into him.'

'You haven't found Aiden yet?'

'No.'

'I'm sorry.' Her porcelain skin was ashen, her downturned eyes heavily outlined with black eyeliner to make them appear upturned.

'Josh,' I murmured. The back of my mouth tasted like dirty pennies. I needed to leave the hospital. Leave him to his fiancée. But I tamped down my urge to flee and outlined what had gone down and the extent of his injuries to Tess. 'He'll be fine.'

'Thank you,' she said.

'If you're OK without me—'

'Yes. Go. Find Aiden.' Tess petted Josh's arm, avoiding the tube feeding fluids into his body. 'I love you so much.'

On my way out, my cell phone buzzed. It was Celine. I answered. She said, 'I have to see you. Now!'

TWENTY-SIX

Celine wasn't at her office. She'd gone home because she'd received a text from Aiden to *meet her*. Her words crackled through the phone's speaker. She said when she got to the duplex, she saw a letter taped to the door. She needed to show it to me.

The moment I arrived, she answered with Spirit pressed to her chest like a security blanket. She pulled me inside, closed the door, and locked it. 'Look.' She pulled a letter from the pocket of her royal-blue dress and thrust it at me. It was an eight-by-eleven sized sheet of paper folded in thirds. 'It's a ransom note.'

Spirit squirmed. She released him. He bounded to his pillow on the sofa.

I unfurled the note. The author had pasted letters cut from magazines:

> *Tell my mother to put $50K in a bag, drop it in the trashcan near the café at Carrollton and Dumaine, and walk away. Tell her not to attempt to find me, or I don't know what I'll do.*

'It's from Aiden,' she said numbly.

'No way!' I said. 'It's generic. Anybody could have pieced it together.'

'But—'

'He did not write this. It's totally out of character.'

I reviewed the message. The intersection of Carrollton and Dumaine was near NOMA. Near Rosalie's house. Had she written it?

'I can't believe he's taking this tack,' Celine said, chewing on the thumbnail of one hand. She wrapped her other arm across her midriff. 'It's lunacy. Why is he doing this to us?'

I jolted. She'd said *us*. Together. We were a team in this. And we were. Of one mind. One purpose. It was my duty to keep her grounded. Focused.

'Celine, stop. Aiden did not write this. It's a ploy. To rattle us.'

She covered her mouth with the back of her hand.

I petted her shoulder to calm her and studied the words on the note again. Where had the writer of the note come up with an amount of fifty thousand? Aiden knew I wasn't good for it. But a kidnapper wouldn't know that. On the other hand, wouldn't a kidnapper want more than fifty thousand? Why not a million? Something seemed off.

'Celine, did you call the police about this?'

'Not yet. I thought you would know what to do.' She twirled a hand and grimaced. 'This makes it sound like he's . . . like he's . . .' She gulped in air.

'I repeat, he did not write this! Breathe.' I explained why I was so certain.

She took the letter from my hands and examined it as I had. She shook it. Hard. 'If he did write this, he's not the man I knew.'

Man? He was hardly a man, I thought, and caught myself. Yes, he was a man – a *young* man, but still a man. A married man. No longer my little boy. 'We have to call the police.' I pulled my cell phone from my crossbody tote.

'No. Wait! They . . . We—' Celine coughed. Recovered. 'We have to have a plan first. A real plan.' She crossed to her altar, set the letter at the base of a white tapered candle inserted into a crystal holder, withdrew a book of matches from the drawer beneath the altar, and lit the candle. She closed her eyes and in sweeping motions coaxed the flame toward her. When she completed whatever she was doing – a prayer for cleansing chakras, I presumed – she strode to the kitchen.

'Fifty thousand dollars,' she muttered. Spirit trailed her. 'You're right, Maggie. That seems too low a number. Why fifty?' She put a pot of water on to the stove to boil. 'Do you want tea while we figure out what to do?'

'Sure.' I couldn't rush her. She needed to process this as much as I did.

'I have herbal.'

'Fine.'

She opened cupboards and began to assemble white porcelain cups rimmed with cobalt blue.

While she was distracted, I edged closer to Aiden's altar and searched for another clue, anything that might lead me to him. I spotted matching ticket stubs on his and Celine's altars – a ticket stub to a ghost walk and another to a sightseeing tour of the Garden

District. I flashed on Josh's and my failed foray into Metairie Cemetery.

'What're you looking at, Maggie?' Celine was staring at me.

'Your altars. They aren't the same, but there are so many items that are, like the ghost walk ticket stubs.'

'Remember when we went on that?' she asked, her demeanor brightening.

Following our dinner at Emeril's, I told Aiden I wanted to get to know Celine better. He suggested the ghost walk, saying she was a big believer in past lives. To humor him, I agreed, hopeful that Celine and I might bond more than we had upon our first meeting. *Baby steps,* I'd told myself. *Make her trust you. Make her realize you aren't going to infringe on their marriage.*

'It was so much fun,' she said. 'Remember that ghost at the old church? The nurse?'

After the tour, Celine claimed she'd seen one of the ghosts. Aiden had been enthralled by her account. I'd been skeptical but only because I hadn't seen it. Hadn't felt it. Though I had been cold throughout the tour.

'She had the most beatific smile, and she'd radiated calm,' Celine said. 'If only she would visit me now. I'd ask her to scour the earth for Aiden.'

A shiver coursed through me. Over the years I'd begged to have an encounter with my brother. A number of times I'd felt a presence. On those few occasions, I'd yelled into the void and told Benjie what he'd done was selfish. Hurting Mom and Dad like that. Leaving me with two worthless, emotionally shattered parents. Forcing me to have to grow up too soon. Whenever I'd ranted, the air had turned chilly.

The teapot whistled.

'Are you OK?' Celine added teabags and hot water to the cups. She set them on a navy-blue tray along with a sugar bowl, spoons, and napkins, and carried the tray into the living room. Spirit dodged her and leaped on to the sofa. Celine set one cup on a napkin and pushed it closer to where she wanted me to sit. 'Here you go.'

My gaze was drawn to a photograph on Celine's altar of a woman with salt-and-pepper hair. She was wearing a nurse's uniform and cat-eye glasses. 'Who's this? Not the ghost nurse, certainly.'

A tentative smile graced Celine's mouth. 'No. That would be weird. I'm not obsessed with ghosts. It's my mother, Lily.'

'Aiden told me she died. I'm sorry for your loss.'

'Thank you.'

'And your father? Aiden didn't mention him.'

'He left when I was two.' Celine's mouth hardened. 'We never heard from him again.' She gestured to the tea.

I moved toward the sofa, picked up my cup, and inhaled the aroma of lemon and ginger, but I didn't sip or sit. I was too antsy.

'Where will we find fifty thousand dollars, Maggie? I don't have it.'

'Neither do I.'

'Could you get a second mortgage on your house?'

'No, I told you I'm maxed out with the flood and the cost of my mother's assisted living. And let's be honest, if we pay fifty, the kidnapper will want more.' Teacup in hand, I roamed the room, studying the art on the walls, searching for an answer. There were plenty of Aiden's drawings of human body parts. I didn't see any impressionistic sketches of tombs.

I paused in front of a photograph of Celine, Aiden, and Keira wearing sombreros at a Mardi Gras parade. Aiden had texted me the photo minutes after they'd taken it. The Three Amigos, they'd dubbed themselves. Keira was staring boldly at the camera, unbridled delight in her gaze. I flashed on the photo of her in Aiden's copy of *Lord of the Flies*. Why had he written the words *She knew* on the back?

Celine drew near and ran her finger along the frame's edge. 'Keira was so special. Oh, the chats we had about politics.' She laughed softly. 'She was fervent.'

'Yes, she was. Women's rights mattered to her.' Aiden said Keira could wax rhapsodic about her plan for the future and the causes she would champion. 'Celine, do you know if anyone threatened Keira? Was it possible someone intentionally struck her in the crosswalk?'

'Please, Maggie, I can't talk about her.' Celine choked back a sob. 'Not now. Not with Aiden . . .'

'Celine, it's important.'

She gripped her own shoulder to settle herself. 'Keira's death was tragic. It broke my heart. But, no, I don't think there was any malicious intent, if that's what you're implying. She never mentioned any threats. No one was after her.'

I let the notion go. If Keira had a known enemy, she would have confided in Celine.

'You know, I've got to wonder . . .' Celine's voice trailed off. She went to the sofa and settled onto it, her motions sluggish. She petted the cat idly.

I waited for her to continue.

'After Keira died, Aiden started seeing a therapist. To work through his sadness.'

He hadn't mentioned it to me, but I was thrilled to hear he had.

'I've got to wonder if he started having dark thoughts' – she tapped her heart – 'because the doctor relocated to San Francisco.'

'When?'

'A month ago. To take care of her aging mother.' Celine stirred sugar into her tea and set the cat in her lap. 'The move was so sudden. Aiden felt betrayed. Truthfully' – her forehead creased with concentration – 'he was disappointed with the therapy, so I'm not sure why he felt betrayed. You know how that is, right? Being disappointed that therapy didn't help?'

I gawked at her. Was she referring to my spotty history with shrinks? After Benjie died, I saw someone who allegedly was good with teens. She wasn't. She let me cry. And cry. But she didn't give me tools to heal myself. I broke down so often that I finally couldn't stand it any longer and quit. With Mom taking leave of her senses and Dad drinking heavily, neither seemed to notice. I didn't seek therapy again, not even when Josh walked out. How could Celine know about that? I'd never shared that history with Aiden. It was a guess, I decided. Celine knew about Benjie. She presumed I'd sought help.

'I wished I'd been enough for Aiden,' Celine said, 'but he was never good at opening up with me.'

'He told me he shared everything with you.'

'Almost everything, but you know men.' She pulled a long face.

I joined her on the sofa and put my teacup on the coffee table.

She twisted in her seat. Spirit didn't take kindly to the move. He sprang to the floor and fled to the bedroom. 'What if that's why Aiden wants money? So he can fly to San Francisco and find her?'

'Celine, how can I make you see that Aiden did not write the ransom note? He did not. Do you hear me?'

'Let's call her.' Celine rose to a stand, ignoring me. 'Maybe he's contacted her.' She sucked in a quick breath. 'Oh, we can't. I don't know her name.'

That astonished me. I'd known all of Josh's doctors' names. But

Celine didn't know the full names of the muse or lender or marijuana
dealer, either. I revisited a notion I'd considered before. What might
have caused Aiden's sudden change of behavior? Did he owe more
money than Celine intimated? Had he borrowed from people other
than the one friend and LeBlanc? Did whomever he owed money
to take him hostage and send the ransom demand?

My cell phone buzzed in my pocket. I whipped it out. The person
with the 346 area code was calling again. I answered. 'Hello?'

Static. Then silence. I stabbed End, jumped to my feet, and
wrapped my arms around myself. Adrenaline caromed inside my
body.

'Who was it?' Celine brushed my arm, her touch causing an
electric shock. 'Was it Aiden?' Her eyes were bright. Wired. She
was breathing high in her chest.

'It was the three-four-six area code number.'

'Maybe he sent the ransom note.' She whipped around and stared
at the door. 'Maybe he's watching me to see what I'll do.'

Or watching *me*, I thought.

'He didn't speak,' I said. 'I only heard static.' The amount of
fifty thousand still gnawed at me. Why ask for such a measly
number? Was it just a down payment? Would there be more
demands?

'Have you tried calling back?' she asked. 'Click on your phone
app.'

I opened Recent Calls and stabbed the last one. It rang through.
The ringing stopped, as if someone had answered. I heard more
static. 'Stupid connection!'

Celine raced to her altar. She blew out the candle and picked up
the ransom note. 'We've got to do something, Maggie. We've got
to get the money. Drop it in the trashcan. And then—'

'Wait.'

'No, we don't wait. We walk away.'

'No, I mean wait, as in slow down.' I held up a hand. 'If we
deposit the money without knowing who's demanding it, it's gone.'

'OK. We'll stake out the area. It's near NOMA. We'll—'

'We can't stake it out. There's no deadline to deliver the money.
We don't know when whoever sent the demand expects to be paid.
Celine, we have to let Detective Filuzzi handle this now.'

'If Aiden didn't write this, as you believe, and he really has been
kidnapped, what if whoever took him will kill him if they don't get

the money? What if there's more than one kidnapper?' She was speaking so fast her words collided. 'Like two or three? Or more? What if they start taking off his fingers, one by one, and then his limbs?'

'Celine! Stop!' I gripped her by the arms. '*Shh*. You're going to drive yourself crazy. C'mon. Calm down.'

She stared slack-jawed at me at first, and then she sank into me. I enfolded her with my arms and let her weep.

TWENTY-SEVEN

I invited Celine to go with me to the police. She declined. She was too shaken. Too nervous. I suggested she go to work. Be around people. Keep busy. She agreed. Before I drove off, she made me vow to contact her the moment I knew something.

The precinct was hopping when I entered. Filuzzi wasn't in. I was referred to a pencil-thin lieutenant named Denton, about my age with an eraser-shaped cropping of tawny hair. I explained what I could in a matter of minutes. He nodded throughout.

'Frank brought me up to speed.' A whistle escaped through the gap in the lieutenant's teeth as he spoke. 'By the way, we didn't get any prints off that box you received. Or the voodoo doll.'

A dead end. Swell. I offered him the ransom note.

Pulling on latex gloves, Denton inspected it, turning it over and back. 'It'll take a while to examine. The magazine clippings look generic. Could be *People* or *Vanity Fair* or even *AARP*.' He chuckled at the last and tried to stifle his awkward response. 'Sorry, this isn't a laughing matter, but all magazines have ads. A perp can cut letters from anywhere.'

'Would you be able to get evidence from the glue that was used?'

'No, ma'am. Glue's as generic as this piece of paper.' He reread the note. 'I got to say fifty K seems like a low demand. Any ransomer worth his salt would've demanded a half million or million to start.'

That was what I'd figured.

'And what's the deadline? There's no deadline.'

Yeah, the whole thing was weird. 'Would you have Filuzzi take a look and weigh in?'

'Sure thing,' Denton said. 'He'll come up with the same findings, though. And if this is from your son—'

'It's not. It can't be.'

'But if it is, we won't go looking for him.'

'But last night, Frank said—'

'Sorry, ma'am. As I was saying, if this is from your son, he's being pretty absurd about communicating with you. There isn't any cause for a kid to treat a parent this shamelessly, you ask me.'

I bit back a response, realizing I wasn't going to be able to convince him otherwise. I knew my son. He might have changed after getting married, but his core principles, the essence of who he was, was intact. On the other hand, I hadn't known he was borrowing money. I hadn't known he used marijuana. Were there more secrets? Was I a foolish mother who, like an ostrich, wouldn't pull her head out of the sand long enough to orient herself to the situation?

Filuzzi emerged through a doorway and made a beeline for us. 'Maggie, what a surprise.'

'What are you doing here, Frank?' the lieutenant asked. 'It's your day off.'

'Mother-in-law's in town. Needed a moment to myself.' Filuzzi winked.

Denton offered a quick recap.

Filuzzi put on latex gloves and perused the letter. 'Your son is messing with you, Maggie. It's an idle threat.'

'That's what I told her,' Denton said. 'Like the voodoo doll.'

'He's not behind this,' I countered, bristling at how defensive I sounded. 'Aiden didn't write it. And he didn't put a voodoo doll on my porch.'

Filuzzi seared Denton with a look. The lieutenant got the message and sauntered away.

'Frank,' I said, ready to pursue a thread even if it put me in hot water. 'Aiden borrowed money from a guy, a lender named Leonard LeBlanc. He's dead. Murdered.'

His gaze turned steely. 'How do you know about that?'

'I was in the building when someone shot him.'

'Maggie, what the heck? You sat on this for two days?' Filuzzi clasped my elbow and guided me into an interrogation room. He pointed at a chair. 'Sit. Talk.' He tossed the ransom note on the table.

I told him how I'd traced LeBlanc to his place of business with the help of Aiden's friend, adding both had borrowed from LeBlanc. 'I entered and heard a gunshot. It was more of a spit. A silencer, I think. The shooter – tall, broad-shouldered – dashed out the rear door. I saw him because of the layout.'

'Got it. It was shotgun style. Go on.'

'I didn't see his face. He was wearing a hoodie. But the killer was not my son.'

'How can you be sure?'

'The shooter was a good head taller. The top of his head almost grazed the door's upper frame.'

'Why leave you as a witness?' Filuzzi removed the latex gloves and raked his hair with his fingers, his frustration with me palpable.

'I doubt he knew I'd entered. I didn't say a word. After he left, when I heard someone moan, I was afraid it might be Aiden, so I sneaked to the far end. It was LeBlanc. His face matched the photos on the wall. Desperate to clear Aiden's name in case . . .' I hesitated.

'In case?' he echoed.

'In case you suspected him of the murder because of his connection to LeBlanc, I searched the cabinets. I didn't leave fingerprints. I was careful. I . . . I located his file. His and his friend's.'

'What's the friend's name?'

'Zach Iles. His father owns a funeral and cemetery service. Zach and Aiden have known each other since high school. Zach is shorter than Aiden, so the shooter wasn't him, either. Both of their debts were marked *Paid*, meaning there was no reason for Aiden – for either of them – to kill LeBlanc. I left the documents in the filing cabinet.'

'And then you fled.'

I nodded. 'I was scared.'

'Not scared enough to get out of Dodge when you heard gunfire.'

'I told you, someone moaned. I thought it might be Aiden. But when I saw LeBlanc . . .' I pressed a hand to my chest. 'It must have been his last gasp. I called it in, Frank. Your guys showed up right away. That's got to earn me a little mercy.'

'Why are you just now mentioning this?' Filuzzi's voice was rough, uncompromising.

'Because Aiden's wife said he'd borrowed before, from a friend, and it dawned on me that if Aiden is desperate for money, maybe he borrowed from someone else, and' – I splayed my hands – 'what if that person is holding Aiden hostage until we come up with fifty K?'

'Why didn't the note spell that out?' Filuzzi pointed to it.

'Because . . . Because . . .' I swayed. My insides felt as if they'd been hotwired with acid. A headache was building behind my eyes.

'Stay here.' Filuzzi left the room and came back with two cups of water. He set one in front of me. 'Let's go through this again. From the beginning.'

An hour later – I never deviated from my story – he released me, repeating that I'd really screwed up this time and said he might need me to come in for a lineup. I assured him I couldn't ID the killer, but he didn't give a crap. *Size,* he wisecracked, *mattered.*

My parting request was that he have one of his people watch the trashcan where the drop was expected to be made. He said he'd see what he could do, which I knew meant *nothing.*

TWENTY-EIGHT

I headed back to the hospital to report to Josh about my meeting with Filuzzi. I was annoyed; Josh would be infuriated. The drive took forever. Disgruntled hotel workers were staging a march throughout the city. Their signs suggested they wanted better pay. Snidely, I mused that they should send their employers ransom notes. That would grab their attention.

Needing caffeine and thinking Josh might like a break from hospital food, I took a detour to his and my favorite café, one that we'd gone to on numerous occasions, known for its cinnamon rolls. We both had a weakness for them. How many Sundays before Aiden was born had we made a run for them and returned home to eat them in bed while doing the crossword puzzle, shoulder to shoulder?

While I waited for my order of hot lattes and sweets, I spotted two women I often saw on my morning run. They waved, and I waved back, once again struck by how small and intimate New Orleans was.

The line moved slowly so I texted Celine, telling her that I'd learned nothing at the precinct. She responded with a sad-faced emoji. I asked if she could remember the name of the friend Aiden had borrowed from.

Celine: *No.*

Time to pull off the Band-aid, I thought.

Me: *LeBlanc is dead.*
Celine: *WTF?*
Me: *Aiden's debt is paid, though. I saw the receipt. Maybe he owes 50K to someone else???*
Celine: *No. Not possible. IDK.*
I knew the translation for IDK: *I don't know.*
Celine: *This is torture.*
Me: *Hang tough.*
Celine: *We have to pay the ransom.*
Me: *I'm going to try to scrape together the cash.*

I couldn't figure out how I would but thought a ray of hope might bolster her.

Celine: *What about putting a package of fake money in the trashcan? To stall.*
Me: *There's no deadline. We've got time.*
Celine: *Does Aiden?*

Her question sent a shiver down my spine. Did he? If his captor didn't get the money soon, would he kill him? Why hadn't the ransomer set a deadline? Was it a simple screw-up?

With a drink tray and pastry bag in hand, I headed back to the Prius. Jittery and unsure, I pulled up short when I caught sight of two men at the corner – Nicky Bilko and Carl Underhill – arguing. Hadn't Josh said Bilko was in jail? How had he gotten out? On bail? I retreated to the wall of the building to hide behind pedestrians and watched, wondering how the two men knew one another, my mind racing with theories.

Bilko, scrawny in jeans and an oversized sweatshirt, was cursing Underhill. In his sleek tailored suit, Underhill looked ready for an important meeting. Bilko stabbed Underhill's chest with a finger. Underhill swatted it away. Bilko snarled. Underhill offered a smug smile. Bilko threw a punch. Underhill caught Bilko's wrist before his fist made contact and twisted. Hard. Bilko yelped. Underhill shoved him. Bilko stumbled backward then leaped at Underhill again. Underhill, who outweighed Bilko by a good thirty pounds, drove the heel of his palm, karate-style, into Bilko's jaw. Bilko reeled and rubbed his soul patch.

Underhill said something I couldn't pick up and then shouted loudly enough for people a city block away to hear, 'Keep your nose clean!'

Bilko looked daggers at him, pivoted, and lumbered away.

I speculated that, given their respective businesses, their meeting could have been transactional. Josh had often told me that corruption created strange bedfellows. Perhaps Bilko had promised to launder some of Underhill's drug money. Maybe that was why Underhill had hollered *Keep your nose clean!* It was code to remind Bilko, who possibly had a cocaine habit, not to dip into the profits.

Underhill squared the knot of his tie and entered the office doors behind him. It wasn't until then that I realized where I was. In front of New Orleans Exchange Center, the building that housed Gregory Watley's offices. Was Underhill on his way to meet him? I recalled seeing a photo of Underhill among Watley's self-aggrandizing gallery of photographs. They'd both attended Harvard Business School. Were they more than acquaintances? Perhaps they were partners in a drug scheme. Maybe Underhill was funneling money through Watley's business. And then my mind made a huge leap in reasoning. Had the two men conspired to take Aiden in order to control me as well as Josh?

Someone touched my shoulder. I wheeled around, nearly dropping the tray of coffees.

Bilko grinned at me, teeth bared. 'Well, well, Mrs Lawson,' he said, his voice as oily as I remembered. 'Long time, no see.'

'Mr Bilko.' I was vibrating with fear, but I forced a smile. 'We met at an art gallery opening, didn't we?'

'We did.' A muscle twitched in his cheek. 'Are you following me?'

'Why would I want or need to?'

'Your husband Josh has been investigating me.'

Which got him shot, I thought acidly. 'Ex-husband.'

'You couldn't hold on to him, huh?' Bilko's malicious grin broadened.

I didn't dignify that with a response.

'Why are you here, right where I happen to be?' he asked.

I raised the bag of sweets. My hand started to shake. Quickly, I lowered the bag. 'This café is one of my favorite places. I will always go out of my way for one of its cinnamon buns.'

He inhaled, as if giving my alibi a sniff test. 'Why were you staring at me back there?' He hooked his thumb.

'I wasn't the only one gawking. Two men fight in public, people pay attention.'

He gripped my arm. Hard. His breath smelled like a noxious mix of Pepto-Bismol and tobacco. 'Listen up. Your husband—'

'Ex.'

'Doesn't know when to back off. I don't take kindly to that. Tell him to steer clear, or else you and your family . . .' He let the sentence hang and flicked my chin with a finger. 'Steer. Clear.' He flicked me one more time for good measure before releasing me and strutting away.

I was shivering, but his threat cemented my resolve.

TWENTY-NINE

When I strode toward Josh's hospital room, I heard scuffling. Miffed that he might be up and about and not resting like he should, I strode in. 'Josh, you have to—'

A dark-haired man was in the room. Trying to smother Josh with a pillow. Josh's good arm was flailing.

I dropped the to-go bag and coffees, yelled for security, and threw myself at the man. I attempted a full Nelson. The guy was too big. Too strong. He elbowed me in the ear. I reeled.

The man swung around. Slugged my jaw. Pain shot through me.

The move caused a wire leading from a monitor to Josh's body to dislodge. A high-pitched beep emanated from the machine.

Lowering his chin, the attacker plowed me toward the exit and into the door jamb. My spine hit first. My head jerked backward. More pain. The man charged out of the room.

Seconds later, a nurse rushed in. 'Ma'am?' She touched my shoulder. 'Are you all right?'

'Help him.' I pointed at Josh, who was coughing and groping for the plastic tumbler on the swivel table to his left.

She hurried to Josh, and I cleaned up the mess on the floor. The coffees had spilled. The bottom of the to-go bag was soaked through. Each move I made was sharp, super-charged. Adrenaline was zipping through my veins at warp speed.

An orderly raced in. The nurse directed him to reattach the wire to the monitor. She righted the straw on the plastic tumbler and handed it to Josh.

'I'm OK,' Josh said between swigs of water. 'Mags.' He motioned for me to come closer.

The nurse gasped. 'Ma'am, the back of your head is bleeding.'

I reached around. Felt the goo. The jagged energy surging through me was masking the throbbing. 'I'll survive.'

'And your ear—'

I could hear. Good enough for now. 'I'm fine.'

'I'll get you a compress.' She left the room.

I dumped the coffees and to-go bag in the trash and moved to the hospital bed. I nudged the swivel table aside. 'I bought you cinnamon rolls. They're ruined.'

'Not hungry.' His hair was mussed, his hospital gown rumpled. 'How are—'

'I'm fine.' I'd once run a ten-K on a twisted ankle. I had a high threshold for pain. 'Who was that, Josh? Did you recognize him?'

'Jango. He works for Nicky Bilko.'

'Bilko? Dammit! You told me he was in prison.'

'Yeah, he's—'

'Wrong. He's out. I just saw him near the café by the Exchange Center. He was sparring with Carl Underhill, and then he . . .' I could barely breathe. 'And then he caught sight of me, and—' I clapped a hand to my chest. 'Ohmigod, did seeing me make him sic this Jango guy on you? Is he the one that shot you?'

'No one works that fast, Mags. Get real. Jango's attack had nothing to do with you. He was probably just trying to finish the job his buddy messed up. But talk to me about Nicky. He's out? Did he hurt you?' Josh started to cough.

I handed him the water glass. He drank while I recapped the encounter with Bilko. I could still feel the sting of him flicking my face with his fingernail.

The nurse returned with a prepackaged cold pack. She cracked it to instigate the cooling process and handed it and a sterile wipe to me. 'Do you want to see a doctor, ma'am?'

'No. I want to—'

'What's going on?' A lanky guard with thinning hair raced in. 'What's the ruckus?'

'You're a day late and a dollar short,' I said.

Josh petted my arm to calm me, then explained to the guy what had transpired.

'Wow, sorry,' the guard said. 'I was downstairs getting the skinny on a teenager who swiped some meds.'

Josh spelled Jango's name and asked the guard to report the incident to the police.

'Will do,' the man said.

'You need a police detail, Josh,' I said.

'No, I don't.' He eyed the guard and nurse. 'If you don't mind, we'd like some privacy.'

They backed out of the room but left the door ajar. I daubed my wound with the wipe, and then applied the icepack to the back of my head.

'You should have someone look at that,' Josh said.

'I'll be OK.' I inspected the wipe. Not too much blood. I tossed it into the trashcan where I'd disposed of the spoiled café treats and returned to Josh's side. I replayed the scenario between Bilko and Underhill. The two men fighting like sworn enemies. 'And get this. After Underhill sent Bilko packing, he entered the New Orleans Exchange where Gregory Watley's company is located.'

'Watley, as in the donor who's giving you grief?'

'The same. He and Underhill both attended Harvard Business School.'

'Interesting.'

'Also . . .' I told Josh about the ransom note and the police's response. 'Has anyone sent you a letter?'

He shook his head. 'Tess hasn't mentioned anything, either.'

'Why single out me to pay it?' I hated the pathetic whine that had seeped into my voice. I was stronger than this. Tougher.

Josh brushed my arm with his fingertips. 'Because you're Super Mom.'

'You mean Helicopter Mom. Smothering Mom. The Mom from Hell.'

'Don't edit me. I said Super Mom, and I meant it. You get things done for your son. Unlike your own mother, who let you flounder. And unlike me, who lets things slide. Face it, Mags, no one comes to me with a timetable. I am not the person people seek when they want a problem solved.'

'You meet deadlines.'

'My deadlines. It's all about me.' He attempted a smile.

I removed the icepack and felt for blood. None. The bleeding had stopped. I would survive. I tossed the pack into the trashcan. Then I swiped my cell phone screen and showed Josh a photograph of the ransom note. 'What's your first impression?'

'I agree with you. It doesn't read like Aiden. On the other hand, if he's behind it—'

'No. He wouldn't do this. Yes, he's miffed at me. Got that. But this isn't like him.' I paced to the foot of the bed. 'What if Watley sent it? Or Underhill? Or Bilko?' I couldn't erase the queasiness I'd felt when that creep gripped my arm. 'Or what if they're working together? To coerce me.' I shot out a hand. 'To coerce you.'

'To do what? My investigation into Underhill is long over. He served his time. He's gone legit.' Josh mimed quotation marks. 'Plastics all the way, baby,' he said sarcastically. 'And, for the record, I think you can dismiss Watley. You said he threatened you with a lawsuit. That seems more his style, right?'

'Yes.'

'As for Bilko, he's a two-bit jerk. He doesn't have the brains to do anything long-term, other than prison.'

'But ransom doesn't take brains. It takes gall.'

'C'mon, Maggie.' Josh clasped my hand. 'You said it yourself. Underhill and Watley went to Harvard Business School. Maybe they're friends. An unlikely pair, true, but I'm friends with some shady characters, too. Doesn't make me a bad guy.'

I gave him a wry look.

'As for the ransom note,' Josh went on, 'it doesn't sound like a big-time criminal wrote it. No deadline? Amateur.'

'Which makes me think Bilko did this. A two-bit criminal with chutzpah.'

Josh released his hold. 'Listen, scrounge up the money. Borrow it from your pal Gina if she's got it and put it in the garbage can. I've got a guy who can stake it out. See what happens.'

I shifted feet. 'Celine suggested we put fake money in the bag.'

'Not a bad idea. Whoever is doing this will want more anyhow.'

I flashed on Celine's fear that an angry captor might hurt Aiden by cutting off his fingers and limbs, and I shuddered.

'How's she doing?' Josh asked.

'Near breaking point.' In the length of time I'd known her, she had never seemed as vulnerable as she did now. 'She loves Aiden.'

'And he's happy with her,' Josh said. 'Isn't that what we want for him? Happiness?'

Yes, of course I wanted him to be happy. I'd thought he'd found his happily-ever-after with Keira.

Out of the blue, a memory of Aiden and her sitting on the couch in our living room flickered in my mind. I'd caught them in the reflection of the foyer mirror. They'd received their acceptance letters from Tulane. Both had goofy smiles on their faces while toasting with non-alcoholic sparkling wine poured into crystal flutes.

'I'll always be there for you,' he said to her, raising his glass. 'And I'll always tell you what I'm feeling. No holding back.'

'Ditto,' she said.

'Ditto?' He knuckled her arm fondly. 'Wow, that's romantic.'

She giggled and clinked her glass to his. 'I love you.'

'And I love you. More than life itself.' He set his glass aside and lifted her hair. He kissed the back of her neck. Her cheek. Her lips. 'Think! In four years, right after we graduate, we'll announce our engagement. In five years, we'll be saying 'I do.' And in six years . . .'

My cell phone buzzed. I scanned the display. *Missed call.* It was the 346 area code.

Josh said, 'Why the frown?'

'I'm receiving hang-up calls from a three-four-six area code. That's Texas. I've tried calling back, but no one answers. What if Underhill—'

'Stop with Underhill.' Josh struggled to sit taller in the bed. 'Have you done an Internet search to crosscheck the number?'

I mentally palm-slapped my forehead. 'No. What an idiot.'

Josh retrieved his cell phone from the swivel table and opened the Internet app. 'Read the number to me.'

As I recited, he typed it into his cell phone. After a minute, he smirked at me.

'What?' I asked testily. I hated when he acted smug.

'It's a telemarketer for condos in Texas. You know the kind. They invite you to come down for a weekend. Listen to the spiel. Get two nights free.'

'Why the repeated hang-ups?'

'Bad connections. Weak signals. Who knows? Probably not inten-
tional. We get such spotty reception around here.' Josh brushed my
arm with his hand. 'It's not Underhill or one of his people taunting
you.'

I perched on the visitor's chair and slumped forward. Every fiber
of my being ached with fatigue, but I couldn't stop searching for
my son. 'Celine said Aiden was seeing a therapist, but the doctor
ended the practice and moved to San Francisco a month ago to help
her aging mother, which made Aiden feel betrayed.'

'No, she didn't.'

'Yes, she did. She also said the therapist hadn't solved his
problems.'

Josh fanned the air. 'Does any therapist solve a patient's problems?
Get real.'

'What if I'm the root of all of Aiden's problems? What if Aiden
did something rash, like borrow money because I cut him off, and
that's what got him into this trouble? What if—'

'Mags, this is not on you.'

'Isn't it?' I placed an arm across my chest. Braced myself to
keep my emotions in check. 'I wasn't as supportive of his marriage
as I should've been.' I grimaced, knowing I needed to fix me if I
ever hoped to have a relationship with my son again. Was it time
for me to bite the bullet and seek therapy? Should I—

'Wait,' I blurted, recalling what Josh said moments ago. 'How
do you know about Aiden's therapist?'

'Last time we talked, he'd come from a session with her. He
seemed buoyed by it.'

'When was this?'

His gaze wandered upward as he thought. 'Two weeks ago.'

'He'd come from the session, as in, he'd seen her in person? Not
via Zoom?'

'That's what he said.'

'I can't imagine why Celine would lie about the doctor going to
San Francisco.'

'Maybe she didn't. Maybe Aiden did.'

When did Aiden resort to lying? That wasn't in his DNA. Neither
was keeping a secret, I thought, but apparently he had plenty of
those.

'Maybe he didn't want her to think he still *needed* therapy,' Josh went on. 'Men aren't good at showing weakness. I'm a prime example.' He held up his good arm and flexed. 'Strong like bull.'

I batted his forearm.

'As a matter of fact, Aiden and I have an appointment to go to a father-son session next week,' Josh added.

My mouth fell open. 'You and him?' I crossed two fingers. 'Together?'

'Don't suck in flies,' he joked. 'I figured since I was getting remarried, he might want to talk about it. Clear the air. What better place than with a shrink? If anyone has betrayed him, it's me. I promised we'd be a family forever. I blew it.'

I sighed. 'Do you happen to know the doctor's name?'

THIRTY

Yet again I touched base with Yvonne and asked her to field my calls. I didn't have time to explain. For her trouble, I promised her a box of her favorite chocolates.

Dr Quianna Swinton's office was in a townhome that had seen better days. The exterior desperately needed paint. The foyer smelled of mildew. However, the moment I entered the office, my opinion changed. The reception area was clean, sleek, and bright with sunlight. White walls, white furniture, white orchids. No one occupied the reception desk. I figured it was there for show. Gina had the same kind of set-up. For anonymity, she scheduled patients with fifteen minutes on either side of arrival and departure. No patient ever met another patient.

The door leading to a room beyond opened, and Quianna Swinton, a tall mid-thirties woman with bronzed skin, piercing eyes, and lean physique, traipsed into view. She was dressed all in white, matching her surroundings. Her Cleopatra-style black hair hung evenly on her shoulders.

'Mrs Lawson, please come in.' Her voice was rich and warm. I imagined her singing in a gospel choir.

'Thank you for seeing me on short notice.' I'd pleaded with her to meet me. Told her Aiden was missing. She'd jumped at the chance, saying she had been concerned about Aiden, too. He'd missed an appointment and wasn't returning her messages.

She led me into her office, which had the same vibe as the reception area. White walls, white desk, white settee and armchairs. White buffet server outfitted with water, coffee, and tea. White mugs. Crystal tumblers. Books on the built-in bookcases and two framed photographs of New Orleans in a raging storm provided the only color in the room.

I regarded the photographs, thinking how much they captured the way I was feeling. My confusion. My turmoil.

She gestured to the settee and offered me water. I accepted. After she placed two tumblers on the coffee table, she took a seat in the armchair to my left. She crossed her legs elegantly, as if she'd practiced the move.

'Doctor—'

'Please, call me Quianna.'

'Quianna,' I said. 'It's a lovely name. Call me Maggie.'

'Down to business. Aiden is missing.' She placed her elbows on the arms of the chair, hands folded in her lap. 'How long?'

'He hasn't answered text messages or telephone calls from me since . . .' I did the calculation but started over when I remembered the text he'd sent when I was with Helena Hebert – if he'd sent it. 'Officially, since Wednesday. But before then, many days passed without hearing from him.'

I launched into the backstory, hoping I didn't sound like a hysterical mother. Knowing I probably did. 'We've always been open in our communication, especially via text, until . . .'

'Until?' She waited.

'Until he married Celine.' I recapped my feelings about how hasty the marriage had been. I told her how I'd had to cut off his funds because of the flood. I summarized his last text telling me to back off. 'It all sounds like something out of a soap opera,' I joked, though I couldn't have laughed if I tried. My throat grew parched. I sipped the water. 'His silence. It's like I've been canceled.'

'For being a toxic parent?'

'A what?'

'Instagram it. You'll find thousands of posts from young adults who've cut ties with their families.'

I shot a hand in her direction. 'Even if he is upset with me, he should've reached out to his father by now.' Unless he deemed Josh a toxic parent, too. 'At the very least he should come to you for guidance.'

'Aiden told me about the money issue,' Quianna said. 'He didn't say he was upset. That isn't the word he used.'

'What word then?'

She pressed her lips together.

'Please,' I said, 'I understand you might be breaking doctor–patient confidentiality to tell me, but I'm worried about him. If he's in trouble and I'm to blame—' I folded my hands. Studied my nails.

After a long moment, she said, 'He felt deflated.'

That made sense. Celine said he was embarrassed about not being able to offer more to their marriage financially. By cutting him off, I'd taken the wind out of his sails. In essence, I'd emasculated him.

'Certainly, some situations call for estranging one's parents,' Quianna went on. 'Even if it comes at a psychological cost to the parent as well as the child. I often see power dynamics inverted rather than negotiated, ending with no winners.'

That summed up our situation in a nutshell. 'Celine said Aiden came to talk to you about Keira. Her death.'

'Mm-hm.'

'Can you share anything about that?'

She stroked her long, narrow fingers in a calming, meditative way. 'Why don't you share instead?'

I understood her reluctance. I'd forced her to cross a line a moment ago. 'When he lost Keira, he blamed himself because he got distracted that day. The sun or the reflection of some other light pierced him like a laser. Someone nearby dragged him to the ground. Aiden reached for Keira but couldn't grab hold. A car with an out-of-state license plate hit her. When he got to his knees, the car was nowhere to be seen. He couldn't get all of the license number. And Keira was dead.' He had told me every horrid detail. 'The investigation provided no suspects, no witnesses, no leads,' I went on.

Quianna tilted her head inquisitively.

'No one paid for the crime. For a full year, Aiden replayed the moment in his head. His thoughts grew bleak. He was drowning. To protect himself, he buried himself in school and in his work. I suggested he seek a therapist.' I gestured with both of my hands. Even though I'd had no luck with therapy, that didn't mean Aiden wouldn't benefit. 'He found you.'

She smiled softly. 'And he found Celine, who he calls his guardian angel. She has pulled him back to the surface. He is no longer drowning.' She looked poised to stand, ready to dismiss me.

'Wait!' I motioned for her to stay seated. 'If that's the case, why isn't he communicating with her? I mean, he was, but now he's not. She said he left her. That' – I slapped one hand against the other – 'is what I can't accept. He loves her. *Loves*. That is why I think something has happened to him. And then there's the ransom note.'

Quianna sat taller. 'You didn't mention a ransom note.'

Hadn't I? Not intentionally. I was off my game. My sentences were truncated. Choppy. I filled her in. 'I don't think he sent it,' I reiterated. 'He couldn't have. It's completely out of character, don't you agree?'

She didn't respond.

'The police won't take his disappearance seriously.'

Quianna tented her fingertips.

'What if Aiden owes somebody money?' I asked. 'What if this is the lender's way of reaping what is due?' I filled her in about LeBlanc, the marijuana dealer, and the note we'd discovered in Aiden's locker.

After a long moment, she said, 'I should tell you that I've consulted a seer – a psychic – about Aiden. I hope this doesn't bother you. I believe sometimes we need the help of the otherworldly to guide us to the truth.' Quianna smiled with a serenity I wished I possessed. 'Do you believe that those from beyond can help us, Maggie?'

Did I? I wanted to. Nearly everyone I knew in New Orleans did. After Benjie killed himself, my mother reached out to a Louisiana psychic over the telephone. Sadly, the woman hadn't been able to contact Benjie, which further cemented my mother's descent into grief.

'My mother was a psychic,' Quianna went on when I didn't answer. 'And my grandmother and great-grandmother, too. They're not my guides, but I know they're involved whenever I speak with a psychic.' She leaned forward, elbows propped on her thighs. 'The woman I consulted said Aiden is in a dark place.'

I shuddered. Those were the words Mirlande had used. Had she been the person who'd recommended this therapist to Aiden? 'He's not considering suicide,' I said like a broken record unable to slide past the scratched groove.

'It's true that darkness can be a state of mind,' she continued, 'but I don't think that is correct in this instance. The psychic believes he is physically in darkness.'

'As in he's hiding? As in he might have escaped from his captor?'

I tried to picture a place Aiden might hole up, and an idea came to me. I sat taller.

'What did you remember, Maggie?'

'Once, when Aiden was doing a project about archaic civilizations . . .' How curious he'd always been. How he'd loved learning. *Loves*, I revised, switching to the more hopeful present tense. *Loves learning.* I caught the doctor staring at me. 'He was in the eighth grade. Josh and I took him to Wolf Rock Cave in Vernon Parish. Near Pitkin.'

'I've heard of it.'

'When Aiden learned the caves might have been inhabited around 2500 BC, he was hooked. He had to see them repeatedly. Six months of cavemen drawings ensued.'

'Mom! Dad! Look. They're not stick figures. They've got form. Shape.'

We agreed.

'Man, they were ugly,' Aiden joked. 'Guess bathing wasn't invented yet.'

Josh kissed my cheek and whispered, 'Boy, can he be intense. He gets that from you.'

How furiously Aiden had drawn. Day in and day out. Jokingly, I'd warned him not to bite off his tongue, the way he would wedge it between his teeth when concentrating.

'Could he be hiding in a cave?' I asked.

'The psychic didn't say where. She gave no specifics.'

'Please, you've got to talk to the police. Tell them what you've learned. Mention the cave. It's a long shot, but maybe they'll take a lead from you more seriously than if it comes from me.'

'I'll do what I can.' Gracefully, she rose and strolled to the exit door.

I left the office feeling elated, even if the emotion wasn't warranted. Whether or not I believed in the supernatural, hearing the words that Aiden was alive gave me hope.

My cell phone buzzed. It was the caller with the 346 area code. I answered. There was no static this time. It connected. As Josh had predicted, it was a telemarketer for the Windsor Palace Condominiums in Houston, Texas. Did I want to *come on down* for a weekend stay? All it would require . . .

Through tight teeth, I told the saleswoman to take me off her list and ended the call. Then I drew in a long, soothing breath and viewed my cell phone. I'd missed a slew of messages from Gina, each more earnest than the previous.

Gina: *How are you?*
Gina: *Where are you?*
Gina: *I can't believe you haven't touched base. You promised.*
Gina: *Do I need to file a missing person's report?*

I dialed her and said, 'I'm fine.'
'About time.'
I told her that we'd received a ransom note. 'Not *we*,' I revised. 'Celine. It was taped to her front door. She phoned me because the note specifically said I was the one who needed to put fifty thousand dollars into a trashcan near NOMA and walk away. The note was written as if Aiden was making the demand, but I'm sure he didn't write it.'
'How is Celine holding up?'
'She's pretty shaken. We batted around theories, and then I dropped her at her office, and I took the note to the police. Who dismissed me.'
Gina cursed.
'When I came up with a theory that Aiden might have owed a lender other than LeBlanc fifty thousand—'
'Another one? Egads. Drinks. Now.'
'Can't,' I said. 'I've got to go home and shower. I smell like a sewer rat.'
'I'm coming over.'

THIRTY-ONE

C autiously, I made my way through my home. Checking all the doors and windows. Looking for unwarranted surprises on countertops. Making sure my father's gun was where I'd placed it, in the drawer to the right of my bed.
Confident I was alone, I trudged to the bathroom, stripped down, and stepped into the shower, praying the hot water would absolve

me of my worry and fatigue. It didn't. I was a taut mess. After drying off and applying lotion to my parched skin, I put on a nubby sweater and jeans, finger-combed my hair and, while applying a dab of rouge – my face was pale and haggard – I thought of Aiden.

The ransom note stumped me. Why would the kidnapper set the price that low, with no deadline? On the off-chance the police would believe Aiden was behind the hoax and wouldn't search for him? I grumbled. Something wasn't making sense.

I moved into the kitchen and poured myself a glass of wine. I stared at it and pushed it away. I opened my cell phone and went through the updates Yvonne had sent me. The attorney for the prosecution wanted to meet again, the Monday after spring break. The person who handled Title IX issues, the federal law that ensures that male and female students and employees in educational settings are treated equally, had returned my call. Southington had a candidate for Professor of History and Associate Chair of Asian Studies he'd like me to consider. Not the normal stuff, but all of which I could handle later.

My cell phone buzzed. *Celine.* I answered.

'Maggie!' She sounded frantic, out of breath. 'You won't believe it. I came home and . . . and . . .' She mewled.

'Celine, what happened?' My heart began hammering my ribcage.

'He . . . My . . .' She slurped in air.

'Celine! Breathe! Talk to me.'

'My shower curtain. Was shredded. To pieces.' Her voice was shrill.

'I'll—'

'No. I'm not there. I left. With Spirit. We're going to a friend's house.'

I heard the whoosh of traffic. The faint thrum of music coming from her car stereo. 'Tell me slowly what happened.'

'I came home. From work. The television was blaring. I thought that was strange, but maybe Spirit . . .' She sucked in air. 'I went to wash my face. That's when I saw the shower curtain. All cut up. Like in a horror movie. I. Freaked. Out. And I ran. Why would someone do this to me?'

Had Bilko, Watley, or Underhill done it to scare her – to scare *me* – into depositing the ransom money in the mailbox? I flashed on the posters on Rosalie's walls that included the Hitchcock classics as well as *A Nightmare on Elm Street*, *Carrie*, and *The Texas Chainsaw Massacre*. For an artist who focused on pointillism, her sensibilities ran to the macabre. She deduced when Josh and I visited her that Celine had steered us in her direction. To retaliate, did she break into Celine's duplex and destroy her shower curtain?

'Was there a note, Celine? Any explanation?'

'No.'

'Books misplaced? Drawers opened? Your altars tossed?'

'Uh-uh.'

'Was anything stolen?'

'No. I don't think so. I don't know. Everything seemed to be in the right place. But I didn't stick around. I didn't search. I—'

'Was the front door unlocked?' I asked. 'Or did somebody jimmy it?'

'Unlocked. I think.' She hiccupped. 'I can't remember.'

'OK. Here's what I want you to do. When you get to your friend's house, call the police.'

'Why? They won't do anything.'

'Do it. Have them check it out.'

'I can't go back.' She keened.

'You have to,' I said, understanding her reluctance. She felt as violated as I had after receiving the voodoo doll. If Josh hadn't come over . . . 'Have your friend go with you. After you talk to the police, call me back.'

'Maggie,' she said softly, 'do you think Aiden did this because we didn't give him the money?'

'No, no, and no. Celine . . .' I sighed, exasperated, depleted. How I ached for her. She sounded so brittle. 'Aiden did not do this. He's in trouble.' I assured her that I would get to the bottom of this and ended the call.

Nerves frazzled, I strode across my bedroom, stepped into the hallway, and screamed.

Gina shrieked, too.

'What the heck?' I threw my arms wide. 'How did you get in?'

'I knocked. You didn't answer. I used the key you gave me.'

Of course. I'd given it to her when I'd gone away for the weekend in case the water remediation company had needed to be let in.

'You're hyperventilating,' she said. 'What's going on?'

In one quick burst, I told her about Celine coming home to find her shower curtain shredded and about my theory that Aiden's muse, Rosalie, might have been the culprit.

'Let's go. My place.' Gina gripped my elbow.

'It didn't happen here.'

'After the voodoo doll and the ransom note? You're not staying.'

I didn't appreciate being managed so I wrenched myself free. 'Gina, c'mon.'

'Look, this is insane.' She faced me, hands on hips. Dressed in black sweater, jeans, and boots, she looked formidable. 'You need to sleep somewhere else. At least for tonight. We'll make a game plan tomorrow. I'll cook you a gourmet meal.' She batted her eyelashes, lightening the mood.

I frowned at her. 'I need to pack.'

'Forget it. You don't need a toothbrush. I've got plenty. And you don't need clothes. You can borrow mine. Tomorrow is Saturday. You can—' She jammed her lips together.

'You were going to say relax, weren't you? Gina, my son is missing. His wife is beside herself with fear. And someone is demanding ransom.' I couldn't temper the terror in my voice. 'I cannot and will not relax.'

'Grab your things.'

Muttering, I nabbed my tote. Inserted my father's weapon. Slung the bag across my body. And then fetched my black jacket and a bottle of Sterling cabernet. If Gina was forcing me to stay at her house, I would drink decent wine.

Brix Market was my favorite grocery, the one I passed every time I ran through my neighborhood. It was small but had a terrific selection of cheeses, salamis, and salads. I asked Gina to pick out a sharp cheddar, and I went in search of crackers and other salty snacks. I rounded the end cap to aisle eight and stopped in my tracks. Coach Tuttle was standing beside a handsome man with chestnut-brown skin. Both men were facing the potato chips. Both were clad in workout clothes as if they'd come from the gym next door. Seeing them in a place I frequented didn't surprise me. Seeing them holding hands did. I'd never met Tuttle's wife, but I'd heard they had a loving marriage.

Hastily, I scurried out of sight and plunged into Gina.

'What the blazes?' she yelped.

'The coach I told you about,' I said sotto voce, and pointed. 'The one who's under suspicion for improper behavior with coeds. He's down that aisle with what I have to assume is his boyfriend.'

She peeked and ducked back. 'OK.'

'He's married.'

Her forehead creased. 'Your point?'

'This proves he probably didn't make advances on those girls.'

'No, it doesn't.' She flapped a hand. 'Maybe he's bisexual.'

I explained how upset he'd been at Pelican the other day. Nearly threatening me. 'Since then, I've wondered whether he, as angry as he was with me, might have done something to Aiden, but now—'

Someone bumped into me. I turned, ready to apologize, as was my nature.

'Coach Tuttle,' I said.

He glanced up from his cell phone. 'Dean Lawson.' He looked surprised. Embarrassed, in fact. In his handheld grocery basket were items similar to what Gina and I had collected as well as a six-pack of pale ale.

I stood taller. 'What a surprise to see you here.'

His friend edged beside him. The prominent muscles of his neck flexed like a football player's. His bulging biceps were impressive. 'Introduce me, Vaughn.' He dropped a bag of vinegar-flavored chips into the basket.

Tuttle swallowed hard. 'Dean Lawson, my friend Axel.'

'Nice to meet you.' What else could I say? 'This is my friend Gina.'

Coach Tuttle nodded to her and handed Axel the basket. 'I'll meet you at the checkout.' He pressed him at the small of his back.

Axel dutifully shuffled away.

Coach Tuttle cleared his throat. 'What this is . . .' He gestured to Axel and to himself.

'You don't need to explain to us,' I said.

'But I want to. You see, what this is, is exactly what it looks like,' he said. 'I'm in a relationship with Axel, but I can't admit it to the world because my family is . . .' He weighed his next words. 'They're very religious.'

'What you're trying to say is you've never been interested in women.'

'Correct.'

'And you want me to believe you when you claim you've done nothing unethical in regard to the students who have accused you of wrongdoing.'

'Yes, ma'am. When I was a teen, my folks sent me for conversion therapy. It didn't work. Be that as it may, I hid the truth and started dating my best friend on the gymnastics team. Years later, she agreed to become my wife. She knows everything and has accepted me for who I am.'

I rested a hand on his arm. 'I wish you'd told me sooner. Let's talk to the attorney for the prosecution together this week. I'm sure whatever testimony you provide will be kept confidential.'

'Ma'am.' He scratched an ear. 'What I can't understand is why those girls would accuse me of such a horrible thing simply because I benched them.'

I glanced at Gina for the answer.

She smiled softly. 'It's a sad fact of human behavior, Coach Tuttle, that some people don't mind destroying somebody else's life. It makes them feel bigger. Tragically, many, like you, suffer the consequences of false testimony.'

I hooked a thumb at her. 'My friend the therapist, who at one time contemplated becoming a lawyer.'

'Thank you,' Tuttle said, and proceeded to the checkout counter.

'Well, one problem solved.' Gina grinned. 'May they all be that simple.'

My gut soured. Nothing was that simple.

THIRTY-TWO

Gina, having abandoned her plan to cook me a gourmet meal, placed our makeshift dinner of cheese and crackers on a tray and guided me to the porch behind her house. She lived a few blocks from me in the home she'd grown up in, a green-and-white Victorian with scalloped flourishes above every window and steep gabled roofs. Her yard was overflowing with white azaleas. The focal point, however, was an artificial turf putting green. Her father had been a golf aficionado and had relished watching the Masters Tournament every year. On his death bed, he'd made Gina promise that she would maintain his little Amen Corner forevermore. She didn't play golf, but over the years, she'd become an ace putter.

She placed the tray on the white wicker table. 'Sit. Take a load off.' She motioned to a chair.

'Can't.' I was walking from one end of the porch to the other, cell phone in hand. 'Need to pace. There's so much going on in my head.'

'Breathe.'

'I'm a horrible mother.'

'No, you're not. Stop beating yourself up.' She petted my shoulder. 'Heck, if we were as mean to our friends as we are to ourselves, we wouldn't have any friends. Now, breathe. That's an order.'

I obeyed, drinking in the scent of flowers that wafted on the air. Night creatures started to click and scratch, their noises sounding much merrier than I felt.

'Have you heard from Celine yet?' she asked.

I shook my head.

While she poured the wine I'd brought into crystal glasses, I dialed Celine. She didn't answer, but texted immediately.

> Celine: *Talked to police. They sent officer. No prints.*
> *Said nothing they can do. Told you so. [Angry-faced*
> *emoji.]*

Her words caught me off guard. One of Benjie's favorite taunts had been *told you so*. So infantile yet so funny the way he'd mock me by flapping his fingers by his ears. I'd laughed every time. Now, I wasn't laughing. My stomach was in knots. I wrote Celine a response to *be brave* and stared at what I'd written, wondering if I should add something warm and fuzzy. Better yet, something inspirational. I decided against it. I wouldn't mother her. She was resilient. She could weather this. On the other hand, I was troubled by the lackluster tone of her text. So I added that I was doing my best to think outside the box. I promised I'd come up with answers.

> Celine: *FYI, my neighbor texted me. She saw a woman*
> *with red hair enter earlier.*

Rosalie? I wondered again.

> Me: *Did she describe the woman to the police?*
> Celine: *She wasn't home when they showed up.*
> Me: *I'll be in touch.*

I dialed Filuzzi and reached his voicemail. 'It's Maggie. I'm sorry to bother you this late, but please call me. It's important.'

'Here.' Gina handed me a glass of wine.

I accepted it and took a sip.

'What does Josh think about all this?' Gina settled on to one of the chairs. She placed a piece of Edam on a rosemary cracker and bit into it.

I took another sip of wine. 'Josh and I can't come to an agreement.'

'OK, that coach is off your list. Let's go through your other suspects.' Gina popped the rest of her appetizer into her mouth.

'They're the same as I told you in the car.'

On the drive, I'd filled her in on the attack at the cemetery, the proof that one of Bilko's men attempted to kill Josh, Underhill's grudge against Josh, and Watley's deep disgust with me. Saying Watley's name, I had to admit that kidnapping Aiden to ensure his grandson got good grades did seem like a feeble excuse. Plus asking for such a meager ransom demand was not something I could see him doing. He was a spiteful man. He'd want to gouge me.

'Josh doesn't think Bilko's smart enough to have pulled off a kidnapping,' I said.

'It takes brains?' Gina clucked her tongue. 'Tell me more about him.' She downed a slice of salami. 'He's a money launderer. Ransom is about money. Trading art is about money. If—'

'The NFTs!' I stopped pacing.

'The what?'

'NFTs. Non-fungible tokens.' I flashed on the conversation at Le Gran Palais with Rosalie and Stan Studebaker. 'Have you heard of cryptocurrency?'

'It's always in the news, but I don't get it. It's not money.'

'It is money, but it's not paper money, and therefore, it's not regulated.'

'Like Bitcoin.'

'Exactly. They work like casino chips. You use them to trade for something else.'

'Without taxation.'

'No, there are taxes involved, but not everyone reports the transactions properly.'

Gina waved a hand over her head. 'Way above my paygrade. Go on.'

'Non-fungible tokens, or NFTs, are tracked on blockchains. An artist, like Aiden, can sell images of his work for NFTs while protecting his copyright. When I went to LGP, I questioned them about NFTs. Both Aiden's boss and Rosalie knew about them. Rosalie said that in several cases there are values in the millions floating around for artists' works.'

'Rosalie.' Gina pushed the plate of cheese out of reach. 'She's the redhead who might have shredded Celine's shower curtain?'

'Yes. Something's up with her but I can't put my finger on it.'

'What if she realized Aiden and his work, or his future work, could be a goldmine?'

'So she kidnapped him, planning to keep him hostage while he churned out art?'

Gina stifled a laugh. 'You're right. It sounds absurd.'

'What if Rosalie is working with Bilko?' I theorized. 'He swaps legitimate works of art for dirty cash. What if he reached out to her, knowing Aiden had a future at LGP? NFTs would be excellent exchange-wise.'

'Interesting theory.'

'Rosalie was dodgy when Josh and I went to her place earlier. She cares about Aiden, of that I'm positive, and she seemed concerned that he was missing, but she was getting messages the whole time we were there. And then, as she was getting into her car, she got a phone call. She didn't look pleased and made a U-turn, veering in the direction *away* from work. Josh figured she needed to do a last-minute errand, but what if the call came from Bilko? What if he kidnapped Aiden and was demanding a meeting? Hold on.' I pressed my palms together. 'Why would Rosalie torment Celine if she or her partner in crime abducted Aiden?'

'A parting comment. "I've got him. You don't."' Gina said it with attitude.

'Maybe, but . . .' I tapped my toe on the patio. 'Aiden's therapist's psychic thinks Aiden is in a dark place. We discussed that he might be hiding, like in a cave.' I explained. 'And Mirlande, I told you about her—'

'The marijuana dealer.'

'Yes. She's a psychic and also said Aiden is hiding, but he's scared. If he was hiding on purpose, he wouldn't be scared, right? So what if these people – these psychics – are picking up on Aiden being held somewhere against his will?'

'Where is this dark place? If not a cave, how about a cellar?'

'A garage?'

'The trunk of a car?'

My cell phone chimed. *Filuzzi*. I answered. 'Frank, thanks for calling me back. Did you hear what happened to my daughter-in-law?'

'No.'

I forgot to ask Celine which precinct she'd contacted. It didn't matter. 'Someone broke into her duplex and shredded her shower curtain.'

Filuzzi whistled. 'Was she hurt?'

'No.'

'Anything else destroyed? Anything stolen?'

'She said the place seemed intact. She didn't stick around. She grabbed her cat and fled to a friend's house. A few minutes ago, she texted me that her duplex neighbor saw a redhead enter. I know a woman with red hair who might have it in for Celine. She's in love with my son, though she says he doesn't return the feelings. Her name's Rosalie. I don't know her last name. She works at LGP.'

'LGP?'

'Le Gran Palais, a digital design company in the Quarter where Aiden is interning. And she lives at . . .' I recited the address. 'Josh and I went there to chat with her, thinking she was Aiden's muse.'

'Muse?'

I explained how Rosalie regarded herself a critic and had inserted herself into Aiden's life after scouting him at Tulane. 'Fast forward to . . .' I rotated a hand. 'Not important. Anyway, she has all sorts of movie posters on her walls including slasher movies as well as Hitchcock's *Psycho.*'

'Got it. Shower. *Psycho*. I'll check it out.' Filuzzi cleared his throat. 'By the way, I'll admit I was curious about that ransom demand, so I dropped a bag of fake money in the trashcan and staked it out for a few hours.'

'You did?' My heart swelled with gratitude. He'd dismissed me. Made fun of me to my face. Now he was on my side?

'Like I told you yesterday, my mother-in-law is in town. I needed something to do. FYI, nobody showed up.'

Had the ransomer made Filuzzi and kept out of sight? With no deadline to aim for, the ransomer could have decided to wait a day or so before checking the drop site. 'OK, in the spirit of full disclosure, you should know that I met with my son's shrink, Quianna Swinton.'

Off to one side, Gina grumbled. She hated the term *shrink*.

'Did Dr Swinton call you?' I asked Filuzzi.

'I saw a message. I haven't had time to call her back.'

'Aiden missed an appointment with her. She was concerned and consulted a psychic.' I knew Filuzzi wouldn't chide me. His family, like many in New Orleans, had a long history with psychics and the supernatural. Back when we were dating, he'd even admitted to me that he'd had an encounter with a ghost, a young girl who'd died in her house and to this day bounced a ball at the top of the stairs.

'Go on,' he said.

I told him how the psychic had envisioned Aiden in a dark place and how that matched with what Mirlande said. 'He's hiding and scared, Frank. Dr Swinton and I batted around theories, wondering if Aiden, afraid of whoever might be after him, ran away and holed up in a cave. In particular, Wolf Rock Cave.'

'I know the spot.'

'But if that's the case, he shouldn't be scared, right? He'd be in control. He'd have the power. However, if he's been kidnapped and his captor has hidden him somewhere . . .'

'Message received,' Filuzzi said. 'I'm taking this seriously now.'

'You are?'

He chuckled softly. 'If I don't, you'll hound me.'

'Wolf Rock Cave,' I repeated.

'Got it. I'm sending a team to investigate.'

'Thank you.'

THIRTY-THREE

At half past ten, Gina forced me to stop pacing and go to bed. I agreed. I'd be no good to anyone if I was sleep-deprived. I slogged to her guest room and dreamed of Benjie dangling from a rope. My father swimming in a sea of booze. My mother aiming a knitting needle at my face. Bilko and Underhill fighting. Jango smothering Josh. Rosalie maniacally shredding a shower curtain with Edward Scissorhands-style precision. In the middle of a nightmare starring Gregory Watley, who was thrashing me with a pair of *We're #1* foam finger souvenirs, I woke up.

The sun hadn't risen. The room was gray and gloomy. I scrambled out of bed, sweat drenching the T-shirt Gina had lent me.

'Maggie?' She rushed in with a golf putter in hand. She flicked on the light. 'You OK? You shrieked.'

'I'm fine. Bad dream.'

She set the putter against the doorjamb and clenched me in a hug. 'Take a shower. I'll bring you some fresh clothes. After that, you're eating a good breakfast.'

'Yes, Mom. By the way, love your jammies.'

She did a quick pirouette. They were purple fleece with white sheep on them. 'My twelve-dollar steal on eBay. Vintage.' She shooed me to get a move on and left the room.

Gina's grandmother had taught her how to make the perfect Belgian waffle. Her coffee, home ground and potent, was extraordinary, too. Her ex-boyfriend never appreciated her culinary skills. I did.

Clad in Gina's white poplin buttoned-down shirt and too-tight chinos – she liked her trousers to fit snugly – I sat on a stool by the white granite island in the kitchen and devoured two scrambled eggs. Next I drizzled syrup on a waffle, took a bite, and hummed my approval. Craving more sweets, I lifted the syrup pitcher and tipped it. Watching the liquid fill the waffle's nooks and crannies, I thought of Aiden, and fresh tears surfaced. How he'd enjoyed pouring syrup with abandon and licking it off the tip of his finger. I recalled the day I'd taught him to bake. He was seven and so eager. Baking, I told him, was all about precise measurements, like chemistry. *Follow the recipe, and you cannot fail.* He loved that analogy and told me I was the smartest mother in the world. *Smarter than smart*, he'd added, giggling.

If I was so smart, why hadn't I found him yet? Grumbling, I set the syrup bottle down, pushed the plate aside, and drank a big gulp of coffee.

'Not hungry?' Gina was washing dishes. She didn't eat breakfast. Ever. She believed intermittent fasting was good for her body. On more than one occasion, I'd begged to disagree, but she couldn't be swayed.

'I'm full.'

'Liar. You love breakfast. You crave breakfast. You think it's the most important meal of the day.'

'Can I use your computer? I want to do a web search.'

'For?'

'Gregory Watley.' I described my series of nightmares. 'I discounted him yesterday because his motive doesn't seem strong enough, but what if my subconscious is trying to tell me he's at the core of this? I mean, he was thrashing me.'

'With very big fake hands,' Gina joked.

'He has friends in high places. And money to spare. And a grandkid that he's been like a father to—'

'A kid he'd do anything for,' Gina cut in, aligning with my thinking. 'Like you.' She booted up her MacBook Air and set it in front of me. 'Here you go. Do a deep dive.'

I opened the web browser and typed in *Gregory Watley* and added *Watley Holding Corporation*. A slew of websites cropped up. There were articles about Watley's success. Articles about his generous donations to political bigwigs. About his involvement with some of New Orleans' neediest organizations. But there were also articles about a vast array of lawsuits. In one, he'd muscled his competition into bankruptcy. In another, he'd sued a woman for accidentally hitting his grandson while he was riding his racing bicycle. The kid, sans helmet, had been pedaling in the car lane, not the bike lane. But that hadn't stopped Watley from pressing charges. According to him, his grandson's injuries had put his athletic future in jeopardy.

Reading on, I tried to get a fix on Watley. Was he capable of kidnapping? Would he have kept quiet about it? The man patently believed intimidation was the way to control people. Lording his power over the defenseless was his *modus operandi*. On the other hand, maybe the loss of his wife last year had driven him to the brink. And if he was collaborating with Underhill, his modus operandi might change.

'I need to talk to Watley again,' I said, rising from the stool and closing the laptop.

'That's not smart,' Gina said, drying my breakfast dishes. 'You said Filuzzi was following up.'

'On Rosalie and Celine's neighbor. Not on Watley. Or Bilko. Or . . .' I grabbed my tote bag. 'Give me your car keys.'

'You don't know where he lives.'

'Yes, I do.'

In recent years, Watley and his wife had hosted professors and staff at his home. When his wife passed away, the parties ended. His Craftsman was in Carrollton a few blocks from Audubon Park. Years ago, he had modernized it by having the siding painted white and the balconies and window frames painted black. Most of the parties had convened in the backyard, an oasis with a saltwater pool, palm trees, and skyline views. The front yard was no slouch, either. Year-round color had been his wife's dream.

As we arrived – Gina had refused to let me go alone – the front door opened. Watley, formally attired in suit and tie, hustled out and rushed to his black Audi. In seconds, he pulled out of the driveway.

'There goes your opportunity,' Gina said.

'Follow him.'

'What? No way.'

'What if he's going to check on my son? Please. Stay back so he doesn't see you,' I cautioned.

Obeying, she made a U-turn. Her dark blue Honda Civic was nondescript. There were loads of others like it driving around New Orleans. Watley, doing five miles over the speed limit, veered left and then right. Gina mirrored the maneuvers.

Ten minutes later, Watley pulled to a stop at *Royal Casino*, a riverboat on the Mississippi. A valet accepted his car and Watley jog-walked inside.

'He's certainly in a hurry,' I said.

I hopped out of the Honda and suggested Gina idle nearby. She protested, wanting to go inside with me. I told her going in alone was wiser. One woman could blend in. Two might stand out. Besides, I was incognito in her sunglasses, the New Orleans Saints baseball cap I'd scored from the back seat of her car, and the black jacket I'd thrown into my tote bag last night.

The interior of the casino, with its black-and-gold décor, looked small, almost cave-like. It featured slot machines, a couple of bars, and a dining room. All were busy. At the far end, there was a games section equipped with blackjack and poker tables. Watley lumbered to a table set apart by a gold velvet rope hooked into a pair of ball-topped stanchions. A broad-chested guard in black uniform allowed him to pass. He reattached the rope to its stanchion and folded his arms.

Watley settled into a chair at the table. Also seated were four men and one woman. Each was wearing sunglasses. Two of the men wore baseball caps backward. Watley pulled out his wallet and handed a single bill to the dealer. The man inspected it. Convinced of its validity, he gave Watley a substantial tray of chips. A couple of the other players sat up and took notice.

Watley was a whale, I reasoned. A high roller. In Las Vegas, he would have been treated to comped rooms, private jet transportation, and a personal limousine. *Royal Casino* didn't provide such luxuries.

I purchased a bottle of water at one of the bars, texted Gina what I'd observed, and told her to leave. I was in for the long haul. When I left, I would catch an Uber. Minutes later, however, I felt a tap on my shoulder. Gina had given her car to the valet. Now she wanted to eat.

A windowed partition between the dining room and games section made it easy to view the private games, which was clearly the casino's intention. It wanted all eyes on the prize. As Gina downed an overpriced sandwich, I watched Watley.

He lost the first hand. And the second. And the third. Over the course of an hour and a half – we had to order dessert and coffee to hold the table – his chips dwindled and frittered to nothing. He beckoned the casino's floor manager. They spoke for a moment, after which the manager shook his head and hooked his thumb, signaling Watley should leave. Watley pulled a paper and pen from his pocket. He jotted something and handed the paper to the manager. Again, the manager shook his head. I wondered how many times before Watley might have requested an IOU. Was he addicted to gambling? Was he in debt up to his eyeballs?

Gina paid for her meal and our desserts and nicked my elbow. 'Time to go. Show's over. Watley's a loser. Aiden isn't here.'

Back in her car, I thought again of Aiden and his secrets. Like the book he kept between the mattresses. And the photograph of Keira. And the note in his art department locker. And the journal that Celine knew nothing about – if there was a journal. And the fact that his therapist hadn't actually gone to San Francisco as he'd told his wife she had. Maybe I didn't know my son as well as I thought. Maybe, with Keira's harrowing death, life had thrown him such an impossible curveball that it had knocked him off course. What if he, like Watley, was in debt up to his eyeballs? Did he craft the ransom note that I was so adamantly denying he'd sent so he could pay off that debt?

An idea came to me. Zach Iles' cell phone number was still in my Recent Calls queue. I selected it.

'What's up, Mrs L?' he answered groggily, as if I'd awakened him from a deep sleep. 'Any word from Aiden?'

'No.'

'Geez.' He whistled. 'That sucks big time. He hasn't texted me, if that's why you're calling.'

'It's not.'

'Are the police, like, involved?'

'To some degree.' I didn't go into detail.

'He's really blowing it if he doesn't finish his last semester, you know? I mean, he won't get his degree, and LGP cares about the degree. Aiden told me so.' Zach coughed. 'Did you talk to his school advisor?'

'I did.'

'How about Mirlande? Was she able to help you?'

'Not really. Zach, did you hear what happened to Leonard LeBlanc?'

He was silent, indicating he had.

'Did you and Aiden consult other lenders?'

More silence.

'Who did you go to?' I demanded. 'Please. It's really important.' I told him about the ransom note and its oddly modest request.

Zach puffed out air. 'Aiden and I met a guy in the Quarter at a sports bar a few weeks ago. He was sort of a creep but a really good pool player. Pool is my thing, not Aiden's.'

'Go on.'

'The guy had cash on him. He was flush. I asked if I could borrow a couple of bills. He agreed.' Zach was talking at a clip, clearly nervous. 'Two weeks later, I paid him back every cent with interest.'

'Did Aiden borrow money from him, too?'

'I'm not sure. Maybe. He needed repairs on his bike.'

'What was the guy's name?'

'Bilko. Nicky Bilko.'

THIRTY-FOUR

juddered. Bilko. I swiveled in the passenger seat to face Gina. 'Did you hear all that?'

She nodded.

'What're the odds Bilko was on hand the very night Aiden needed a loan?'

'Got me,' she said. 'I don't know a thing about odds.'

'Upward of a thousand to one.'

'If you say so. But, face it, New Orleans is a small town. Their business arrangement could be happenstance.'

I folded my arms across my chest and gazed at the oncoming traffic. No. I didn't buy it. Bilko had purposefully tracked down my son. My cell phone thrummed, its hum working down my thigh. I pulled the phone from my trouser pocket. *Filuzzi*. I answered. 'What've you got? Did you interview Celine's neighbor?'

'I did. She didn't see anyone.'

'No redhead?'

'Nope. Didn't even look outside that night. She did hear something, though. She thought your daughter-in-law was watching a noisy TV show and texted her to turn it down, but your daughter-in-law didn't respond.'

'Maybe she didn't see the text.' Celine hadn't mentioned it to me, but that could have been an oversight. 'She said when she came home and found the curtain, the television was blaring.' I mulled over the neighbor's account for a moment. 'I suppose Celine might have made up the thing about the redhead and attributed it to the neighbor because Celine has a hard-on for Aiden's muse. She even tailed Aiden to the woman's place.'

'She stalked her husband?' Filuzzi asked.

'*Stalked* is a harsh word.'

'If the shoe fits.'

'When do you plan to question Rosalie?'

'Don't need to if she's not a factor.'

'What about the cave?'

'Nothing there,' he said curtly, and ended the call.

I growled.

Gina eyeballed me. 'Why didn't you tell him about Bilko lending money to Aiden?'

'Because Zach wasn't sure he did.'

'You could have at least mentioned Bilko's connection to Rosalie regarding the NFTs. Call him back.'

'We're guessing about that, too.'

'Call him.'

I reached Filuzzi's voicemail. I left a message and then said to Gina, 'I'm contacting Celine.'

Celine didn't answer, either, so I texted.

> Me: *Hi. I talked to the police. Detective Filuzzi. He interviewed your neighbor. She said she didn't see a woman with red hair. In fact, she said she didn't see anyone, but she heard someone in your place. Thinking you had your TV on too loud, she texted you.*

Long pause. Three texting bubbles emerged, meaning she was typing something. Finally, her message came through.

> Celine: *Oh, wow, I'm looking at it again. I totally misread it. I must be way too tired. I read redhead when she wrote reheard. Does that ever happen to you when your eyes fill in the missing words or letters?*

All the time, I thought.

> Me: *Want to come to dinner at my place? Let's talk.*
> Celine: *Too scared. Staying with friend.*
> Me: *OK. Be safe. Hey, meant to tell you, Filuzzi put money into the trashcan and staked it out. Nobody came.*

Three bubbles appeared again.

> Celine: *[Red-faced emoji] I should have told you. I wrote Aiden and said no money was coming. I know. You don't believe he sent the ransom note. But I thought if he did and he didn't get the money, he'd give up this stupid game and come home.*

Three more bubbles.

> Celine: *I screwed up, didn't I?*
> Me: *No.*

If the kidnapper had Aiden's phone and saw her message, he could have abandoned the ruse.

> Me: *We'll figure this out.*
> Celine: *[heart emoji and thumbs-up emoji]*

I set the cell phone face-up on my thigh, aching for Celine. What she must be going through. She and Aiden hadn't been married long. The doubts cycling through her mind had to be excruciating.

'Well?' Gina asked.

'She misread the neighbor's text.' As I said the words, I mentally tried to rearrange the word *reheard*. There were so many options if you added or subtracted a letter.

Gina threw me a skeptical look. 'You told Filuzzi that Celine might have been setting Rosalie up.'

'I did, yes, but don't go there.' – I glimpsed Celine's texts – 'doesn't mean Rosalie *didn't* do it.'

Gina chortled. 'If only the world had a Big Brother security system so all bad actors could be caught.'

'Uh-uh, we do not want that. I've seen *Minority Report* and *Enemy of the State*.' I'd watched both with Josh and Aiden. Family movie nights had been a common occurrence before Josh moved out. 'Both movies scared me to my bones.'

I asked Gina to take me home. She didn't argue. We drove in silence, my thoughts reeling. Where was Aiden hiding? Was he scared, like Mirlande claimed, or was that a load of bull? The sun hung low in the sky. Wispy gray clouds were doing their best to obliterate the light.

Gina pulled into my driveway, parked, and rested her hands on the steering wheel. 'What are you going to do?'

'Touch base with Josh about Bilko.'

Gina let out a scornful wheeze. 'What can your ex do from a hospital bed?'

'Give me Bilko's address.'

'And you'll, what, go to his house now? At dusk? And ask if he snatched your son? Maggie, c'mon. Use your brain. That isn't wise.'

'It's proactive.'

'Not today. Tomorrow,' she coaxed.

'But—'

'Tomorrow with a police escort.'

Reluctantly, I agreed to wait and entered the house. She traipsed after me, refusing to leave until she'd helped me inspect all the rooms.

Satisfied I was safe, she said, 'Want me to stay over?'

'I'm good.' I patted my crossbody tote. I intended to keep my father's gun close at hand until I tracked down Aiden. 'Want something to drink before you leave?'

'I have clients bright and early tomorrow. I'd better maintain a clear head. One has the nose of a bloodhound and has left three previous doctors because they'd imbibed before a session.'

'And you want this patient why?' I mocked.

'I bow to the Almighty Dollar.' She winked and kissed my cheek. 'If you get spooked, don't be too proud to come knocking on my door at two a.m. And tomorrow, if I were you, I'd call the water remediation company. That mildew smell is sick. They've got to do better.'

She left, and I stood at the door listening to the drone of the fans on the ground floor. How much longer would they be in my life? I pushed the thought aside. In the big scheme of things, I didn't care.

For dinner, I ate a frozen veggie-tofu meal. I wasn't hungry, but I knew I needed fuel. An hour later, I crawled into bed.

Yet again, I slept fitfully. And dreamed. But this time, my dreams weren't about my family or Watley or the boy who'd killed himself. I dreamed of a team of soaring superheroes fighting a gigantic monolith populated with extraterrestrials bent on abducting humans and taking over the world. I woke up exhausted, as if I'd had to perform every superhero task by myself. I didn't watch sci-fi movies. I didn't read science fiction, either. So why had I conjured up aliens? It was a no-brainer. Because I truly believed Aiden had been kidnapped.

When I clambered out of bed at six a.m. Sunday morning, I lifted my cell phone, ready to call Josh. I noticed a voice message from Tess and listened. She was breaking Joshua out of the hospital – her words – and taking him to her mother's house. She'd secured a round-the-clock detail to watch him until he healed. He was exhausted and sleeping. She added that she hoped he would give up his career. I wished her luck. Josh was a die-hard investigative reporter. He'd never retire.

Given his weakened state, I opted not to question him about Bilko's possible hangouts. Somehow I'd locate Bilko's ex-wife and pin it down.

To work off tension, I threw on spandex leggings, matching hoodie, and training shoes and ran four miles. On the run, I reviewed the incidents of the last few days: a ransom note, an impaled voodoo doll, an attack on Josh, a map with a possible clue, a hidden copy of *Lord of the Flies*, a picture of Keira with the words *She knew*. Knew what? Mirlande the Haitian believed Aiden was hiding and scared, and Dr Swinton's psychic envisioned him in a dark place. Then there was the murder of LeBlanc as well as Celine's shredded shower curtain.

Was any or all of it linked? I did not believe Aiden was behind the madness. I couldn't. It didn't synch with the boy I'd raised or the talented, artistic man he'd become.

After I returned home, while I was scrambling up some eggs, my cell phone pinged. Gina was texting.

> Gina: *Did you make it through the night without doing something stupid?*
> Me: *Barely. I ran this a.m. Eating now.*
> Gina: *Good girl.*
> Me: *I'll be in touch.*

My cell phone jangled. I startled and scanned the screen. Helena Hebert was calling. I tapped Answer. 'Helena? Good morning. Why are you calling? Have you heard from Aiden? Did he—'

'No, Dean Lawson.'

'Maggie,' I snapped, instantly regretting my tone. 'Sorry. Please call me Maggie. Go on.'

'Maggie, something disturbing has occurred.'

THIRTY-FIVE

I raced to Tulane. Helena Hebert was facing her mahogany book-shelves, slotting books into empty spaces.

'Helena.' I stepped through the doorway. 'Why are you working on a Sunday?'

She turned and her pinched expression told me everything. She was agitated. Despite her unease, she looked stunning. I could never carry off the orange-toned, Russian-inspired caftan she had on. 'Maggie,' she murmured.

'You said something disturbing happened.'

'Come. Have a look.' She gestured to the remnants of paper lying in a blue blown-glass bowl on her desk. 'Remember that sketch of Celine and Aiden we saw when you searched the contents of his locker?' Helena's voice was low. Tentative. 'Someone shoved it beneath my office door. Ripped to pieces. I haven't phoned the police because, well, what could I tell them? I don't have a clue who did this. We don't have security cameras in the hall. The CCTV cameras on the campus are erratic. I could tell this was Aiden's work because of the eyes,' she added. 'I remembered thinking Celine's eyes were rather distinctive.'

She was right. It was Aiden's sketch of the two of them. I shivered.

Helena cupped her neck with her hand. 'What do you think? Who did this? Is it possible Aiden sneaked in after hours?'

'No way. He wouldn't rip up his own work. He treasured all of his art, even his mistakes.' And this had been no mistake. It was a beautiful depiction of them, created with love. The pieces were jagged. Definitely torn. Who would have done this? What could Aiden or Celine possibly have done to warrant such a visceral display of anger? 'Have you inspected his locker?'

'Please accompany me.' She motioned to the door.

I followed her down the hall. Using the keypad, she unlocked the door and switched on the light. The room was empty. No students were lingering, as they had been on my previous visit. We strode to locker two-twenty on the back wall. Referring to a file on her cell phone, she punched in the code and stepped away. I opened the locker and peered inside.

It smelled of acrylics and oil paint, the same as it had the other day. The personalized leather artist's roll was there, as was the paint-splattered plaid shirt. The sketchpad, too. I withdrew it and flipped through. The image of Aiden and Celine was gone. I pictured the destroyed sketch in Dr Hebert's office and thought of Celine's shredded shower curtain. Had jealousy spurred the two attacks?

'Helena, a young woman comes to Tulane to scout for artists. Her first name is Rosalie. Do you—'

'Rosalie Hunt.' Helena fingered one of her hoop earrings. 'She works at Le Gran Palais where Aiden has his internship.'

'That's her. Have you seen her on campus recently?'

Helena shook her head.

'Did she have access to this room of lockers?'

'There would have been no reason.'

'Perhaps she accompanied a student.'

'I suppose she could have. Why?'

'She has feelings for Aiden.'

We returned to Helena's office, and I settled into the chair facing her desk. I told her about the shower curtain and the theory that Rosalie had destroyed it to taunt Celine.

'Do you think she might've torn up this sketch?' Helena gestured to it.

'Yes.'

Her mouth curved downward. 'I should call the police. Perhaps they can find a fingerprint on the sketchpad or locker, proving your theory. It would be easier to lift prints off them than off these shreds of paper, don't you think?'

I nodded, though I doubted the police would find anything concrete. Whoever had done this most likely had worn gloves. But if it was Rosalie, I wasn't willing to let her get away with it. I wanted answers. Did she know where Aiden was? Was she holding him hostage? The thought sent a frisson of fear down my spine.

I sped to her house, car windows down, desperately in need of oxygen. When I pulled up to the curb, through the sheer drapes I saw movement inside. She was home. For a long moment, I deliberated getting out of the Prius. I'd come over half-cocked. If I hurled questions at her, she'd clam up.

Suddenly, the front door whipped open. Rosalie in a belted sheath, cardigan, and heels hurried to her Toyota Celica, which was parked three houses down. She leaped inside and ground it into gear. Where was she headed?

I followed, keeping a respectable distance.

She made a few turns before veering east on Tulane Avenue. Traffic was heavy. Was it always this thick on Sundays? She drove past Pontchartrain Expressway, past Dogtopia of New Orleans, past the Metairie Country Club. At a McDonald's, she made a right and pulled into the empty parking lot of a grungy brick warehouse. Nearby was a millwork, cross-fit business, and automotive repair shop. Rosalie climbed out of her car, charged to the entrance of the warehouse, whipped the door open, and darted inside.

My pulse was galloping as I pulled into the lot. I rounded the side of the building, jammed the car into Park, and raced to the garbage bin at the corner to get my bearings. The stench of garbage assaulted my nostrils. The squall of a crow made me shudder.

Was Aiden in the building? Was he OK?

I withdrew my father's Beretta from my tote bag, knowing I could use it if I had to. With two hands on the grip, I crept around the corner to the warehouse entrance and listened for voices. Electricity hissed in the crisscrossing power lines. A semitruck downshifted with a squeal on the main road. Someone honked a horn.

Then a woman screamed. A blood-curdling scream.

Rosalie burst from the warehouse. She stopped by a wall, bent over, and retched. 'Ohmigod, ohmigod.' She started wiping the toe of one shoe with the other. She must have vomited on it.

What had she seen? Was Aiden dead? Unnerved, but not lowering the weapon, I rushed to her. 'Where is he?'

'You!' She registered my face.

'Where is he?'

'Inside!' She pointed. 'He's . . . he's . . . Ohmigod.' She hurled again.

Steeling myself, I kicked open the front door and charged into the warehouse, gun aimed. I flicked a switch with my elbow to turn on the overhead fluorescents. Nothing happened. The single source of light illuminating the place was coming from the sunlight filtering through the grimy windows. 'Aiden!' The word echoed in the emptiness. 'Aiden!'

The warehouse was cold. Hollow.

I trudged deeper into the darkness and caught a whiff of what Rosalie must have smelled. Death. Bile crawled up my esophagus.

I tamped it down and edged forward. Then I saw it. Sixty feet away. The source of the foul odor. A man. Bound to a chair, head lolling to one side.

'Please no,' I mewled, but pressed onward.

From twenty feet away, I made out the dead man's features and breathed easier. It wasn't Aiden. The deceased was older. Scruffier. With a soul patch.

THIRTY-SIX

B lood seeped from a bullet wound in Bilko's temple. I swung around, gun ready. Glimpsed right and left as I'd been trained at the academy. When nobody fired at me, I strode to Bilko and felt his neck. No pulse. Skin clammy.

Why had Rosalie rushed here? Had she and Bilko been working the NFT angle as Gina and I had theorized? Did she kill him? She hadn't exited with a gun in hand. Her teensy purse couldn't have held more than a pocket pistol. Telling by the circumference of Bilko's wound, the shooter would've needed to use a weapon the size of mine. I didn't see one cast aside.

I sprinted outside, expecting to find Rosalie gone. She was still there. Slumped against the building. Crying jaggedly.

'Hey.' I lowered the gun.

'I didn't kill him,' she said, followed by more sobs.

'I'm calling nine-one-one.'

'No, please!' She grabbed my arm. Her fingers cut into me.

I unpeeled them. 'I've got to. There's a dead man inside.'

'His name's Nicky Bilko.'

So she did know him. 'Why did you come here?' I asked.

'He . . . He told me to meet him. Today. At noon. He said if I was late, he'd . . . he'd . . .' She slurped in huge gulps of air.

'Why here?'

'I. Don't. Know.'

'You couldn't have saved him.'

'I wouldn't have wanted to. He . . .' She jutted a hand at the front door.

'He what?'

Rosalie plucked at the buckle of her narrow belt. 'He threatened me.'

'Why?'

She didn't answer.

I pulled my cell phone from my tote and, with gun in hand, using my pinky, selected the telephone app. I hovered over it, ready to press. 'Tell me or I call nine-one-one.' I stepped toward her as my father would have. Intimidation was all about how you carried yourself, he'd told me. If only he hadn't thrown his life away after Benjie ended his. I could have used him right now. His sage advice. His comforting hugs.

'I stole something,' she said.

'What?'

'A Miró. Six months ago. Before I got the job at LGP. I was out of money. I didn't want to tell my parents I'd failed. Nicky brokered the deal, and when he figured out where I worked, he threatened to turn me into the police unless I helped him.'

'Do what?'

'He—' Rosalie hiccupped. 'He wanted access to Le Gran Palais artists' NFTs.'

So I'd guessed right.

'Do you know where my son is? Did Bilko do something to him to make you fall in line?'

'What? No! I wouldn't have! I—'

I slapped her. She winced. Rubbed her cheek.

'If he knew how much you cared for Aiden,' I said, 'with Aiden in tow, he could coerce you to do his bidding.'

'But I'd already agreed. I didn't want to go to jail. Nicky never said anything about Aiden. Ever. He . . . No . . .' Rosalie shook her head adamantly. 'No, it doesn't make sense. He couldn't force Aiden to paint or create digital content. Unless . . .' Her upper lip curled into a snarl. 'Unless Bilko threatened to hurt Celine.'

'You really don't like her.'

'She doesn't value Aiden.'

I observed her for a long moment. What was truth and what was a lie? Was I too gullible for words? 'Did you break into Aiden and Celine's duplex and shred their shower curtain?'

'What? No! Someone really did that? Why would you think I . . .' Rosalie scowled at me. 'Are you accusing me because of the posters on my walls?'

'*Psycho* was a vicious movie.'

'And fiction.' She hitched the strap of her purse higher on her shoulder. 'I didn't break into their duplex. I don't even know where they live.'

'It's time to call the police.' I raised my cell phone to dial 911.

She clasped my arm. 'Wait. I've got to get out of here. Please. Don't tell the police about me. I didn't kill Nicky. I'm innocent. Please.'

'What else aren't you telling me?'

'I might have stolen some other things.'

'Might have.'

'Years ago. I was sixteen. I got off with a warning. This is the only thing I've swiped since then. Cross my heart.' She mimed the gesture. 'Look, I'll leave Aiden alone. Promise. I'll even leave town if you want me to. Please. Let me go.'

I deliberated. Believing that she hadn't killed Bilko and that he was premium slime, I said, 'One last question. Did you go to the Tulane Art department and steal something from Aiden's locker?'

'No. What was taken?'

I studied her. She looked genuinely curious. I decided not to tell her about the destroyed art. If the police wanted to talk to her at some point, the less she knew meant the less she'd be able to fabricate credible answers. 'Go. Get out of here.'

Rosalie couldn't scram fast enough.

Opting to keep her secret unless it became necessary to reveal everything, I dumped the Beretta into my tote and dialed 911.

Ten minutes passed before an emergency medical team showed up. Soon after that, Filuzzi arrived in a black sedan followed by two patrol cars. After I explained that Nicky Bilko was dead inside the warehouse, the EMTs entered. The patrolmen trailed them, guns raised.

Filuzzi stayed with me and narrowed his gaze. 'You invite trouble, Maggie.'

'I don't mean to, Frank.'

'Why were you here?'

'I'm an innocent bystander.' I sounded steady. Trustworthy.

'That's not an answer.'

'I heard a rumor that Nicky Bilko was in the area. I wanted to ask him something in person.'

'Fine, I'll bite.' Filuzzi worked his tongue inside his cheek. 'Heard a rumor from whom?'

'My source.'

'You're not a reporter. Reveal your source.'

'Sorry, I can't do that.'

'Why not?'

'I can't tell you that, either.'

Filuzzi grunted. 'You're trying my nerves.'

'At least your nerves are intact. Mine are frayed. My son is missing, and my ex-husband was assaulted in the hospital by one of Nicky Bilko's people.'

'Yeah, I heard. Jango Jenkins. He's in custody, if that's any consolation.'

'Glad to hear it.'

'Maggie,' Filuzzi said, 'tell me again why you would risk coming to a deserted warehouse to meet a known criminal. Did you follow him?'

'No.'

'Your source told you he was here.'

'Yes.'

'Did your source think he'd kidnapped your son and hidden him in the warehouse?'

'Yes.' The lie had the ring of truth. 'But he didn't. And I swear Bilko was dead when I got here.' I patted my tote bag. 'I'm carrying a weapon. But it hasn't been fired. Want to check it out?'

'I believe you.' He pulled a notebook and pen from his back pocket and jutted a hip. 'Why would Bilko nab Aiden?'

The tension in my chest eased up. At least he was now referring to my son by name. 'To force Josh to refute his investigation. Bilko's case is scheduled to go to trial in October.'

'But Josh was shot Monday morning.'

'Yes.'

'If your theory is correct, your son went missing before that.'

I worked through the timeline in my head. Filuzzi was right. There were inconsistencies. Which came first, the—

'Maggie!' Filuzzi said sharply.

I startled. 'Yes?'

'Focus! Bilko tried to off Josh. He was a cocky SOB. Don't you think in order to leverage him, rather than send one of his goons to rough him up or kill him, he would've stolen into the hospital and personally bragged to him that he'd taken Aiden as a warning to let the case go or else?'

I hated that he made sense. I said, 'Josh has been on pain meds. He's not very coherent. Maybe Bilko did come in, but Josh told him to take a flying leap.'

Filuzzi jutted his chin toward the warehouse entrance. 'Did you see anyone suspicious leaving the area when you got here?'

'No.' I justified my answer as truthful because the word *suspicious* would not have applied to Rosalie. She'd looked downright frightened. Was I wrong to keep her identity out of things? I'd bought her story about being an art thief. Was that a lie? In truth, I couldn't imagine her hiding Aiden somewhere. How would she keep him there? Lock him in a closet? Chain him to a radiator? A jagged laugh threatened to erupt from my mouth. I pressed my lips together.

Filuzzi rotated the hand that was holding the pen. 'You're sitting on something. Talk to me.'

'I happened to see Nicky Bilko and Carl Underhill going at it in front of the Exchange Center on Friday. Also I heard Bilko's ex-wife hated him. She's the one who talked to Josh's source, giving him the lead for his story. Maybe she did this. You should look into their divorce settlement.'

'Don't tell me how to do my job,' he groused, and shifted feet. 'Did you hear what Bilko and Underhill were arguing about?'

'No, but Underhill told Bilko to keep his nose clean. And . . .' I hesitated.

'And?'

'Minutes later, Bilko confronted me. He warned me to steer clear.'

'You could've led with that.'

'I didn't kill—'

'I know. Got it.' Filuzzi pocketed his notebook. 'By the way, I'm putting one of my guys on Rosalie Hunt after all.'

'You know her last name?'

'As a matter of fact I do, because we received a call from Dr Hebert at Tulane after you met with her earlier. You should've told me about that, too.'

I swallowed hard.

'Apparently,' Filuzzi said, 'Miss Hunt scouted for artists on the campus. That's how she met your son. Dr Hebert said a piece of Aiden's art was shredded and shoved under the door of her office earlier. But you know all this.' He gave me a side eye. 'In fact, you suggested that Miss Hunt might have done it. So not only does she shred curtains, but she destroys portraits.'

How could I tell him that Rosalie denied the accusation without eliciting more questions about her, like when I'd last seen her? A breeze kicked up. I wrapped my arms around my body, wishing I'd thought to grab a jacket on the way out of the house.

Filuzzi studied my face. 'Is it possible Aiden ripped it up?'

'No! Dammit. He's missing, Frank. He's not skulking around the campus—'

'Or skulking around his duplex destroying things?' He arched an eyebrow. 'He sounds like he might have anger issues.'

'He doesn't.'

'He's mad at you.'

'He's not mad. He's . . .' *Upset* wasn't going to cut it. I drew in a deep breath and let it out. 'He's not behind all this.'

THIRTY-SEVEN

When Filuzzi released me, I drove home, took two aspirin, and slipped into bed. I needed a power nap. To my surprise, I awoke Monday morning to the chirping of birds and a blade of sunlight cutting through the window. I'd slept sixteen hours without stirring. Not even one nightmare. The notion distressed me. Was it a premonition? Did it mean Aiden was dead?

'No, Maggie, stop!' I bolted to my feet. 'That's madness. He's hiding. He's scared. He's not dead.'

My stomach was sour. I didn't run. Didn't drink coffee. Instead, I showered and put on a pair of khakis, red scoop-necked sweater, blue blazer, and flats. Then I downed a protein shake to coat my stomach and give me an energy boost, and drove to work.

When I walked into my office, Yvonne greeted me. 'Hey, boss. You look rested. Anything new on Aiden?'

'No.' I dropped my tote bag beside my desk and slung my blazer over the back of the chair.

'What about the ransom angle?'

'It was a bust. Nobody's claimed responsibility.'

'I'm sorry. Have you, you know, considered hiring a private detective?' She lifted a Post-it and handed it to me. 'My mother-in-law used this guy to do a background check on a contractor, and he dug up all sorts of dirt. Maybe he'd be able to track down leads that you can't. You know, search places Aiden frequents, that kind of thing.'

'I'll keep it in mind.' I perused the Post-it, dubious a PI could do more than I already had unless he could lift DNA from a ransom note, though I highly doubted the police would relinquish the note to my care now that they were in possession of it.

'By the way,' Yvonne went on, 'Coach Tuttle dropped by a short while ago wondering if he could meet with you. I told him—'

'Yes. I will.'

Her eyes widened. 'Really?'

'He and I ran into each other Friday night and briefly discussed his situation,' I said cryptically. 'Let's see when the attorney for the prosecution is available. I'd like us all to meet.'

'Here?'

'Yes, here.'

'It's spring break.'

'I'll bet she's not taking any time off before the trial.'

'Good point.'

I sat at my desk and viewed my text messages. Nothing from Aiden. Or Celine.

An hour later, Yvonne escorted Coach Tuttle and his wife into our conference room. His wife, a petite nursery-school teacher, was as gentle in nature as I'd expected her to be. When she smiled, her eyes beamed with respect for her husband. Tuttle thanked me for arranging the meeting. Yvonne exited and returned with a tray filled with glasses of ice water. She set it on the buffet to the left.

Out of the blue, Provost Southington appeared, his bowtie matching the blooming anger in his cheeks. He crooked a finger at me. I met him in the hall. Yvonne slipped past me, giving me an *Everything OK?* look. I smiled.

'What's this meeting about?' Southington sliced the air with his palm.

'I suggested a discussion between Coach Tuttle, his attorney, and the attorney for the prosecution.'

'On college property? Unacceptable.'

'The gathering requires some discretion. School is out. I thought—'

'I don't care what you thought. End it.'

I bridled. 'Sir' – I squared my shoulders – 'I happen to have inside information. Holding this get-together out of earshot of the plaintiffs is the wisest solution.'

Southington primped the lapels of his suit. 'Make it fast.'

'It'll take as long as it takes,' I said defiantly.

He inhaled and released his breath slowly, as if trying to compose himself. 'By the way, I heard you received a ransom note.'

I glanced over my shoulder toward Yvonne's office. Shoot. She must have let that information slip to Southington's assistant. I couldn't chastise her. Water-cooler talk often turned gossipy. I turned back to the provost. 'Yes. The police are following up.' As was I, but he didn't need to know that.

'If there's anything I can do . . .' He didn't mean it. The concern didn't reach his eyes, but it was the polite thing to say.

'Thank you, sir.' I strode into the conference room.

Yvonne guided Tuttle's lawyer inside. He moved with the grace of a tiger and had the feral gaze to match. Quickly Tuttle advised the man to let him tell the story, beginning to end. Tuttle didn't want him to interrupt. Begrudgingly, the attorney agreed.

Moments later, Yvonne ushered in the attorney for the prosecution. Miss Pelletier, severe in a pinstriped skirt suit, her wheat-toned hair pulled back so tautly it had to hurt, greeted all with a brisk *hello*. She set her boxy briefcase on an empty chair, unbuttoned the single button on her jacket, and took a seat.

For the next hour, the coach told his story. His wife held his hand throughout. Tears slipped from her eyes when Tuttle said he'd never had a better friend than his wife.

'So you see' – I gestured to Pelletier – 'Coach Tuttle had absolutely no reason to have harassed those students.'

'It's his word against theirs,' she said crisply.

'Yes, ma'am, it is, but I believe him. I met his partner, Axel, this weekend by sheer coincidence. You know how small New Orleans is. Like me, you probably run into people you know all the time. Brix is my market. It turns out the gym he goes to is right next door.'

Pelletier wrinkled her nose.

I glanced at my cell phone on the table. I'd turned it face down so I wouldn't be distracted. 'Ma'am, the two men are clearly in love.'

Tuttle's wife folded her hands primly. 'Axel is a wonderful man. We're all friends.'

'As for you?' Pelletier directed her words at the wife. 'What do you get from this marriage of convenience?'

'A good friend and a marriage that made my mother stop asking when I would tie the knot. I was never into dating.'

'Are you a lesbian?' Pelletier asked bluntly.

'No. I'm neutral, I suppose.' Tuttle's wife looked between her husband and the attorney. 'When Vaughn and I were on the gymnastics team, I could talk to him about anything. He listened, as I know he listens to the young women he coaches, with the same dedication. If he says the girls are suing him because he benched them, then that is exactly what happened.' She released her husband's hand and leaned forward on both elbows, hands folded, to drive home her point. 'He has no interest in women. He would never make a move on one. We married to stop our parents from pressuring us. It was a win-win for both of us. Until now.'

'Until now,' Tuttle echoed.

Pelletier observed Tuttle and his wife and Tuttle's attorney, who had kept mercifully silent throughout.

After a long moment, Pelletier rose to her feet. She smoothed the wrinkles from her skirt. 'You make a good character witness, Mrs Tuttle. I believe you, and I believe a jury would believe you, as well. I'll have a chat with the claimants and their families and resolve this. Coach Tuttle, I apologize for any embarrassment or anguish this might have caused you.'

Tuttle's attorney said, 'We will countersue—'

'No we won't.' Tuttle gripped the man's wrist. 'Thank you, Miss Pelletier.' He faced me, his eyelashes moist. 'Dean Lawson, I don't know how to . . .'

I smiled and nodded.

Back at my desk, I wished that by settling one situation amicably I might have earned a goodwill token from the Universe – a token that would reveal the whereabouts of my son – but it was not to be. There was a single text on my cell phone. From Gina. Encouraging me to be brave.

Brave? What did that even mean? Was she fearing the worst, as I had upon waking? No. I couldn't think like that. I wouldn't.

Instead, for the next hour, I focused on work. I reviewed applications for professorships. Two of the history professors were retiring. I sorted through mail. I responded to a parent's plea for a meeting about her daughter's choice of major.

When I finished, I paced my office, thinking about the ripped-up artwork. The shredded shower curtain. Was Rosalie to blame? Why had I promised her I wouldn't tell the police about her being at the scene of the crime? If Filuzzi's techs discovered Rosalie's DNA in the warehouse, or if someone in the nearby buildings saw her car in the vicinity – and she did kill Bilko – I'd be dubbed an accessory. I picked up my cell phone to call Filuzzi and come clean.

'Knock-knock.' Yvonne stepped into the office with a fresh cup of coffee. 'You look like you could use a mid-afternoon pick-me-up.'

'Thanks.'

'And a power bar.' She placed them and a napkin on the desk. 'You didn't eat lunch, did you?'

'You know me too well.' I set the phone down. Face up.

'Did you solve the world's problems?' She eyed the track I'd made in the carpet.

'No.'

'Called the PI yet?'

'Uh-uh.'

'Think about it.' She returned to her desk.

I resumed pacing. Filuzzi was wrong. No way Aiden was causing this craziness. He would not have killed Bilko to get out of debt. Even if he was struggling financially, he would never resort to murder. I debated calling Josh to bring him up to speed and decided against it. He needed his rest. How I wished I could turn back the clock, and we could bat around theories like we—

No, Mags. I smacked the back of my chair. Hard. I had no right to wish Josh back in my life.

I stared at my cell phone. I contemplated calling Celine to ask if she'd heard from Aiden, but pushed the idea aside. She would've written me a text.

Unless she wouldn't, a voice said in my head.

Unless she wouldn't because she and Aiden were in this together. Hoping I'd throw money at the problem. Money I didn't have. Money I couldn't get. I pictured the two of them shredding the shower curtain and destroying the portrait, all the while laughing at me.

'Stop it!' I said aloud to curb the horrific thoughts. That wasn't Aiden. It wasn't Celine, either. Not the Celine I was getting to know. Money was not what was driving her. Love was.

Yvonne raced in and scanned the room. 'Who are you shouting at?'

'Myself.'

'Need a riding crop or a whip?'

I willed my shoulders to relax. Flicked a hand. 'No. Go. I'm fine.' I sat in my chair, cupped the coffee mug, and leaned back. I needed a moment to regroup. To think things through. The instant my eyes closed, my thoughts rocketed back five years.

'Mom, Mom!' Aiden raced into my office, gawky at sixteen, all arms and legs and no meat on his bones. 'Mom, I won!' He waved his Scholastic Art and Writing award. It was the nation's most prestigious acknowledgement of creative teens.

'Oh, Aiden, I'm so proud of you.' I leapt to my feet, embraced him, and stepped away. His hair was tousled, his face flushed with joy. 'I'm sorry I couldn't make it to the ceremony.'

'It's OK.' He'd been upset earlier when I'd said I had important meetings to attend to. Now, he didn't seem to mind. Winning had made all the difference.

I chucked his cheek. 'This will look great—'

'On my college application. I know.' He grinned, looking so like Benjie it made my heart ache. 'Tell me you're proud of me.'

'I'm so proud.'

My cell phone buzzed. I startled. Coffee spilled over the rim of the mug and splattered down my sweater and chinos. I set the mug on the desk, blotted the mess with the napkin, and viewed the cell phone screen. Josh was calling via FaceTime. I answered.

'I've been thinking,' he said, without greeting me. 'We need to track all the places Aiden might be hiding. All his favorite haunts.' His jaw was ticking with tension, the way it did when he was on the hunt for a story. He tugged on the collar of his white Henley shirt to center it. 'Where have you searched so far?'

'I've been to the cemetery and to the art department at Tulane. The police checked out Wolf Rock Cave.'

'He loved wandering through NOMA.'

'He's not hiding in the art museum,' I chided, though I was warming to the idea of acting like a PI.

'How about Audubon Park?' Josh asked. 'You know how much he likes going there. Plenty of places to camp and hide out.'

Audubon Park was named in honor of the ornithologist and naturalist John James Audubon, a New Orleans resident who became known for his extensive paintings of birds. Around the age of twelve,

Aiden, thanks to Audubon's *Birds of America*, had taken up sketching birds. He'd been particularly proud of getting the faces right.

'Or Audubon Aquarium,' I said, remembering how Aiden would skip with delight as he went through the tunnel beneath the Great Mayan Reef. 'Though I can't figure out how he could hide there. Security guards must sweep the place religiously.'

'What about Mardi Gras World?' Josh suggested.

'Good idea.' At the gigantic facility, guests could see floats up close and learn how they were made.

'Remember when Aiden was eight and he put on the King Neptune costume? He had to stand on a ladder. He . . .' Josh's voice cracked. 'Mags, we've got to find him.'

'*I*,' I stressed. '*I've* got to find him.'

'I can help.'

In the background, I heard Tess say, 'No, you can't. You've got to stay in bed.'

Josh turned his head to the right. 'He's my son.'

'Josh,' I said.

He swiveled back, his eyes sorrowful. He was no longer a skeptic. He, too, believed Aiden was missing.

'Tess is right,' I said, letting him off the hook. 'You rest. I'll do this. In the meantime, I've got to tell you something else. Nicky Bilko is dead.'

'Dead!'

Tess shrieked in the background. 'He's dead?'

'Bilko,' Josh said to her. 'Nicky Bilko is dead. *Shh, babe.* Let me find out what happened.'

Babe. It used to be his term of endearment for me. I sighed. *Let it go, Maggie.*

'Go on, Mags.' Josh hitched his chin. 'Talk to me.'

I replayed the incident but left out any mention of Rosalie.

'And Filuzzi didn't run you in?'

'He knows I didn't do it. Listen, do you know who might've killed Bilko?'

'Like someone would loop me in? Ha!' He grimaced. 'Not a chance.'

'Filuzzi said the police arrested Jango.'

'Good to know. What else you got?'

'Zach Iles,' I said. 'Aiden's buddy. He says Aiden might have owed Bilko money.' I replayed how they'd met him.

'Uh-uh. Don't go there, Mags,' Josh said. 'Our son did not kill Nicky Bilko. Remember Aiden and guns? He never wanted to see one, let alone touch one. You can rule that out.' He sliced the air with a hand.

Tears welled in the corners of my eyes. I pressed a palm to one eye and then the other to stem them.

'Hey, you saw Bilko arguing with Underhill,' Josh said. 'Maybe Carl killed him.'

'I mentioned that to Filuzzi.'

'Of course you did.'

'One more thing.' I told him about Helena Hebert finding the shredded remnants of the picture of Aiden and Celine. 'I thought Rosalie did it, so I went to talk to her, but she was hustling into her car, which is why I followed her—' I halted, realizing I'd slipped up.

'Followed her where? To the warehouse? She was there?'

'Yeah.' Quickly I explained about her past, the art thefts, and how Bilko had threatened to expose her if she didn't help him. 'She denied killing the slimeball,' I said, adding that she also swore she didn't shred the portrait or the shower curtain. 'I believed her. Should I have turned her in?'

'Trust your instincts. They're rarely wrong.'

The compliment imbued me with confidence.

'Ferret out Aiden,' Josh said. 'When you find him—'

'If. *If* I find him.'

Josh's face sagged. 'Mags, if Bilko's people have him, they're on their own now with no captain steering the ship. That means they're even more dangerous than—'

'I know.'

'Be proactive. Be hopeful.'

THIRTY-EIGHT

Needing a moment to reflect, I swiveled in my chair and stared out the office window at Serenity Lake, the man-made body of water beyond Pelican Plaza where students and teachers could sit on benches and drink in the calm. Today, there was little activity. No students. No tours. A gentle breeze was blowing leaves across the water. A snowy egret was parading in front of a string of baby chicks along the edge. She bickered at them to stay in line.

A pair of men in suits came into view. Provost Southington and Gregory Watley were walking toward one of the benches. Watley was punching the air with his pudgy fists. Was he complaining about me? Had he caught me spying on him at the casino? Would Southington fire me if I didn't put up a defense?

Intent on being my own advocate, I shrugged into my blue blazer and rushed outside. 'Provost Southington,' I said as he dusted off the bench with his handkerchief and sat. 'Isn't it lovely out today?' I nodded to Gregory Watley. 'Nice to see you, sir.'

Watley remained standing. His tiny eyes narrowed. 'Are you stalking me?'

'No, sir. I'm out for a bit of fresh air like you.' I offered a pleasant smile.

Watley's lip curled up on one side. 'You were seen loitering outside my office Friday.'

I felt my cheeks warm. 'Merely by accident. I was fetching coffee at a nearby café to take to a friend in the hospital when I stopped to observe an altercation between Carl Underhill and another man.'

Watley shared a look with Southington, who was watching the two of us like a chair umpire at a tennis match.

'What was that about anyway?' I asked, even more curious now that Bilko was dead. 'Mr Underhill entered your building right afterward. You know him, right?'

Watley straightened his tie. 'Carl told me Mr Bilko was hitting him up for money.'

Aha! So he knew Bilko's name. Interesting. I said, 'Running low on funds must be an epidemic right now.'

'What's that supposed to mean?' He arched his eyebrow.

'As I told you, a pipe broke in my house. At the same time my insurance lapsed. I'm literally under water.' I spread my hands. 'Go on about Mr Bilko. Why was he dunning Mr Underhill for money?'

Southington shot me a withering look.

'I ask, sir,' I went on, steeling my resolve, 'because Underhill's son is applying to the university. We should know the source of any and all of his assets. Especially if he's being funded by illegal drug transactions or money laundering.'

'That's slanderous!' Watley exclaimed. 'Carl is no longer in the drug business. He's gone straight. He served his time.'

Josh had said the same. Filuzzi, too. I wasn't sure I believed any of them.

'Mr Bilko,' Watley continued, 'claimed Carl owed him a great deal of cash. Carl assured me he'd paid off the debt years ago. He's got the paperwork to prove it.'

I said, 'I had no idea Nicky Bilko was a lender.'

'He's not officially.' Watley had used the present tense. He didn't know Bilko was dead.

'Yet Mr Underhill borrowed from him,' I went on, 'and not you.'

'It was a casual deal, granted when Carl was heading to jail and selling off some art.'

'And Mr Underhill has paperwork to prove it,' I reiterated.

'Yes. It was a short-term loan to help his eldest son invest in a company, which is now thriving.'

'What kind of company? Plastics?'

'Don't be snide.' Watley folded his arms.

'I'm not being snide, sir. That was Underhill's previous business before he went to jail, wasn't it?'

He grunted. 'His son owns a premier plumbing company.'

The breeze blew a stray hair into my face. I brushed it away. 'Do you speak often to Mr Underhill about his finances, sir?'

'Of course. That's what a true lender does.' Watley puffed up his chest. 'We advise clients.'

'Hold on.' I fanned the air. 'So now you're the one lending Carl Underhill money?'

Southington scoffed. 'Please, Dean Lawson, that's none of the university's business. Leave us be.'

'I beg to differ, sir. As I said before, Mr Underhill is considering sending his child to Pelican.'

Watley glowered at me. 'Carl recently secured a construction loan through my holding company so he can build high-end condominiums in the Warehouse District.'

'How, exactly, will you be able to lend money to him?' I asked.

'That's what Watley Holdings does. There. Now you know everything.' Pompously, he sat beside Southington and folded his arms across his chest in an attempt to end our conversation.

'Yes, I know, but . . .' I looked between him and Southington, knowing I shouldn't bring up Watley's gambling situation. I decided to allude to it and smiled ever so slightly. 'Did you enjoy your walk by the river Saturday?'

Watley's neck and ears reddened. His gaze lasered into mine. He knew I knew.

'Mr Watley, sir, you're one of Pelican's largest donors. You've poured money into the university.'

'Indeed I have.'

'We care about our donors. It would be a shame if your company was struggling.'

He bounded to his feet. The flaps of his jacket flew open. 'My business is in fine stead, I'll have you know.'

'I certainly hope so, sir, because if you're in need of money—'

'Are you accusing me of sending you a ransom note?'

'Dean Lawson, what the hell?' Southington shot to his feet. He must have been the one who'd clued Watley in. 'Don't be absurd. Fifty thousand dollars wouldn't solve Gregory's issue.'

'So you know about his *issue*' – I added air quotations to the word – 'as to why he's in need of money?'

Southington snorted.

'How much are you in debt, sir?' I pressed Watley again.

'One million,' he blurted. 'What's it to you?'

'OK, Dean Lawson, that's enough. I'm . . .' Southington stopped and stared at Watley. 'Is that true, Gregory? A million?'

Watley's face blazed with shame. 'When Harriet got sick, we didn't have proper insurance. I borrowed against our house.'

'From Nicky Bilko?' I asked.

'Hell, no,' Watley said. 'A friend has been gracious enough to help me out, but I'd like to pay him off sooner rather than later. I know gambling isn't the way to handle it, but I was desperate to get the debt off my books.'

Southington patted Watley's back. 'Come to my office. Let me pour you a glass of whiskey. I might have a solution. As for you, Dean Lawson, I'm putting you on notice.'

The two men strode away.

For a long while I watched ripples move west to east on the lake, appalled by the way I'd steamrollered Watley, but I'd had to. I'd needed answers. Now, after the fact, I admitted his personal situation sounded legit; however, learning how in debt he was, his explanation about funding Carl Underhill's new venture left a bitter taste in my mouth.

Back at my desk, I did a quick Internet search and drummed up
a listing for Underhill Building Ltd. on Veterans Memorial Boulevard
in Metairie. I wasn't a map guru, but that sounded suspiciously
close to the abandoned building where I'd stumbled upon Nicky
Bilko and nowhere near the Warehouse District. I fetched my tote
bag and was ready to head out when the office phone jangled.

Yvonne said through the intercom, 'Gina Rousseau is on the line.'

Anxiety shot through me. Gina rarely telephoned me. She texted.
I answered. 'Hey, everything all right?'

'I need you,' she said, her voice quaking.

'What's wrong? Are you hurt? Where are you?'

'At my office. I'm between patients. I . . .' She blew out a stream
of air. 'I didn't want to tell you, but my mother is sick. Cancer. I
just learned it's terminal.'

'Oh, Gina.'

'Needless to say, my brother' – her mother had relocated to
Arizona to be near Gina's brother – 'is a hopeless wreck. I should
fly out, but Mom told me not to. She's fine, she said.' Gina huffed.
'Who invented that stupid word anyway? *Fine.*'

'Cancel your next patient,' I ordered. 'I'm coming to take you
out. You can cry on my shoulder.'

I drove Gina to Bobby Sox, and we sat at a table by the window.
Although the sky was a dusky gray, revelers were out in droves. A
few waved to us. Someone inside the restaurant queued the jukebox
to play a Rick Springfield tune, 'Mother Can You Carry Me.' Gina
hitched her chin in that direction and rolled her eyes at the irony.

A waitress arrived at the table, pink-and-blue-covered iPad in hand.
I ordered each of us a glass of chardonnay and two sides of fries.
Neither of us had an appetite, but we would need something fatty and
salty to absorb the alcohol if we wanted to indulge in a second glass.

For an hour, Gina summed up her on-again-off-again relationship
with her mother. Unlike my mother, her mother's mental faculties
were in good shape. And despite being a therapist who was expected
to modulate her behavior, her mother could be downright vicious.
She hated that Gina hadn't followed her to Arizona. She loathed
that Gina hadn't produced any grandchildren.

'I know this isn't fair of me to unload on you' – Gina sipped her
wine – 'given your situation.'

'You can unload anything you want to. Heck, I've been unloading
about Aiden for the past few days.'

She attempted a smile, but it barely made it to her upper lip, which was quivering.

I clasped her hand. 'Look, you're the one who said any time we hear bad news we need to process it. It's time for you to process this.'

'I failed her as a daughter.'

'You did not.' I swatted her forearm. 'You made your life what you wanted it to be, which is what any parent should wish for their child.' I flashed on Aiden and felt imaginary fingers grip my heart. I did want him to be happy. If that meant a future with Celine, so be it. I liked her now. She trusted me. We would grow fonder in years to come.

'I never married,' Gina said.

'I did, and it didn't work out. There are no guarantees.'

Gina ate a couple of fries and followed that with more wine. 'Enough about me. Catch me up on Aiden. Anything?'

I told her about the shredded sketch, Rosalie, and Bilko.

'You saw another dead guy?'

I shuddered. Two dead men. In a matter of days. An image of Aiden lying dead in a ditch popped into my mind. I forced it away. 'Josh thinks I should check out Aiden's favorite haunts.'

'You've already visited two cemeteries. Where else?'

I spouted off the list.

'Do what you have to do. That's what a good mother does.' The words brought tears to her eyes. Angrily, she swiped them off her cheeks. 'But fair warning, it could take weeks to physically search all those places.'

'I've got to start somewhere. He could be hurt. He could be—'

No, I would not utter the word *dead*.

My cell phone *pinged*. I'd received a text.

> Celine: *It's quiet without Aiden here. He's gone, isn't he? Gone forever.*

Her despair unnerved me. I responded instantly.

> Me: *Don't think like that. Want me to come over?*
> Celine: *No. I'm fine. Just sad. Ansel Adams said something about being content with silence. That's where I have to be for now.*

For Aiden's sixteenth birthday, I'd given him copies of Adams'
Basic Techniques as well as *400 Photographs.* He was so ecstatic
you'd have thought I'd given him the world. He showed every photo
to Keira while explaining the nuances. He must have done the same
with Celine, hence the abridged quote.

Celine: *Silence is unbearable. [sad-faced emoji]*

I couldn't let our conversation end like that, so I wrote what Josh
had said to me.

Me: *Be hopeful.*

THIRTY-NINE

When I arrived home, I switched on the foyer light and
gasped. Someone had broken in again. The picture of
my family had been swapped out with a photograph of
Aiden as a boy, one that typically hung in my bedroom. I pulled
my father's gun from my tote and edged to the door leading to the
kitchen. I peeked in. Everything appeared normal. But it wasn't. I
smelled coffee. Brewed coffee. I flipped on the light. A mug of
coffee sat beside the sink. I touched it. Lukewarm.

I turned in a circle. The invasion reeked of cageyness. Did the
person who'd gifted me the voodoo doll sneak in? Bilko was out
of the picture, but one of his crew might have done so to mess with
me. Watley was no longer on my suspect list. What about Underhill?
I couldn't rule out Rosalie, either. What if she'd hoodwinked me at
the warehouse and was now menacing me?

Something *creaked*. I remained where I was. Listened.

Something *clacked* and then *clacked* again.

I raced to the arch leading to the living room and peeked around
the corner. The porch door was open and striking the ladderback
chair to the right. A strong gust was casting loose leaves into the
house. I crouched. Peered beneath the furniture. I didn't see anyone's
lower limbs. Nobody was lying down, ready to get the jump on me.

Quickly I closed the door. Inspected the latch. Wobbly at best. I needed to get a handyman over soon – jobs Josh would've done in a pinch.

I peered out the window at the yard, on hyper alert. Moonlight created shadows in and around the trees and bushes. I couldn't detect movement. And yet I felt that sense that someone was watching me. That gnawing in my gut. Sure, I was overwrought, but Josh had been attacked and my home had been broken into a second time. I was certain of it.

A car revved to life. I dashed to the front door and whipped it open. A sedan was in the driveway next door. A BMW. My neighbor's. Headlights flicked on. The car backed on to the street and drove away.

The wind blew the door open, I told myself as I returned to my living room.

But the wind hadn't rearranged the picture frames or made the coffee, I reminded myself. Would the police believe me if I contacted them and said someone had been in my house again?

I wasn't waiting around to find out. I stuffed my laptop computer and a change of clothes into my tote bag and raced down the front stairs. Climbed into the Prius. Pulled on to the street. From the car, I dialed the Residence Inn in the French Quarter, the place I'd been ready to secure if I hadn't been able to return home due to remediation. I couldn't burden Gina, not after the news about her mother. The inn had a room available. On the way, I checked the rearview mirror for a tail. I didn't spot one. When I arrived at the inn, I registered and went immediately to my room. The clerk was surprised I didn't have more luggage. I didn't explain.

Sleep didn't come easily. When it did, I didn't dream.

In the morning, although I was bleary-eyed, I decided to follow Josh's plan. After a strong cup of coffee, I slipped into jeans, sweater, and tennis shoes, and informed Yvonne that I wouldn't be coming in.

Audubon Park, situated in historic uptown New Orleans across the street from Tulane, was a popular place for picnickers, joggers, and people enjoying the playgrounds. In addition, there were tennis courts, riding stables, and soccer fields. I walked once around the jogging path, taking in the various areas looking for places my son might hide. His favorite spot to visit at the park was Ochsner Island, more familiarly dubbed Bird Island. It was situated in the

center of a lagoon and boasted one of the most prominent rookeries
in the southeast. Species on the island included egrets, a variety
of herons, and the double-crested cormorant – Aiden's favorite
bird. Typically a stocky black bird with a long neck, it gained a
small double black-and-white crest during mating season, which
intrigued him.

After two hours of searching, I felt overwhelmed by the sheer
size of the park. No way in hell was I going to figure out where
my son might be camped out on my own. Dr Swinton said her
psychic thought Aiden might be in a dark place. There were no
caves at the park and no shadowy places other than beneath the
bridge and under trees.

Frustrated, I decided to try my luck at the aquarium. Positioned
on the Mississippi River next to the French Quarter, it was a huge
tourist draw. Visitors could view the underwater world of the
Caribbean and transport themselves to the Amazon rainforest. As a
young boy, Aiden had enjoyed stopping by the African penguins
exhibit. They'd been given the nickname jackass because they brayed
like donkeys. He would *hee-haw* and egg them on whenever we
saw them.

When I arrived, visitors were circled around a jazz quartet playing
a rousing rendition of 'Memories of You.' Josh, who could barely
carry a tune, had sung that song repeatedly to Aiden as an infant.
The recollection tore at my heartstrings. I stemmed tears and hurried
inside.

Navigating the first floor, I inspected the restrooms and gift shop,
but there were no places to hide. I climbed the stairs instead of
taking the elevator to the second floor, thinking Aiden might have
found a pocket where he could disappear from view. No such luck.
I passed through the concessions and dining area. Nothing. He was
nowhere.

After explaining my quest to a security guard, who had three
grown children and understood a son's defiance, he guided me into
the kitchen where I questioned the staff. None of them had seen
Aiden.

Giving up, realizing I wasn't schooled in finding missing persons,
I exited the aquarium and lingered by the entrance. Deciding to give
it one more college try, I pulled my cell phone from my tote and
texted Aiden. Maybe, if he had been kidnapped as I truly believed,
his captor would see the message and respond.

Me: *Hey. It's Mom. I went to Audubon Park and the aquarium, hoping you might be there. I know, stupid. You're not behind this. I just wish . . .*

I stopped typing. Waited. Nothing. The silence was, as Celine had texted, unbearable.

Sun blazed down on me. My stomach grumbled. My head ached. I needed fuel. One of my favorite Japanese BBQ places was in the Warehouse District, a few blocks away. I headed toward Poydras Street, trying to decide between *umakara* pork and spicy pork, when I remembered Watley saying Underhill was building high-end condos in the area. Could I find the place? See if it was legit?

Ever since Hurricane Katrina, construction noise could be heard everywhere in New Orleans. I followed the rumble from one site to another, none of which proved to be Underhill's new venture.

But then I heard the sound of riveters driving nails into wood. The racket was steady and intense. A multilevel condominium complex was going up, the project protected by a mix of chain link fence and orange safety fencing. A tower crane loomed beyond the barriers.

A flashy sign on the chain link fence boasted the name of the construction company – Underhill Builders Ltd. I neared the dusty fencing and peered through a viewing hole. The framing for six stories had already been completed. There were more than two dozen workers milling about. To my surprise, Underhill, in business suit, work boots, and hardhat, was addressing a pair of similarly dressed men. If I approached him and point-blank asked if he'd taken my son, would he confess? He wouldn't attack me with witnesses around, right? On the other hand, he'd fought Nicky Bilko in full view. And Bilko was dead.

Someone bumped me from behind. I did a face plant into the screen. Dust rained on me.

'Sorry,' the person said, and pressed onward.

Brushing the filth off me, I heard a whistle. Underhill was signaling a burly Hispanic to fetch me.

The man reached me in three quick strides. 'Mr Underhill wants to see you.'

Innocently, I glanced over my shoulder and back at him. I pointed to my chest.

'Yeah, you. Inside. Now.' He unhooked a gate and gestured for me to follow him.

Underhill was standing by a food cart, set a safe distance away from the construction. 'Fancy seeing you here, Dean Lawson,' he said as I drew near. 'Coffee? Donut?'

'No thanks.' I would not break bread with the man.

Underhill requested a coffee for himself from the vendor. The man handed him a cup inserted into a corrugated sleeve. Underhill took a sip. 'What brings you to my neck of the woods?'

'Japanese BBQ.' It wasn't a lie.

'Why were you so interested in this particular construction project?'

'Honestly' – I figured that would be the best policy – 'Gregory Watley told me you'd gone into the construction business, and I didn't believe it.'

'Did you think I was still in drug distribution?'

What a quaint phrase, I mused.

He squinted, assessing me.

'I didn't know what to think,' I said.

'Haven't you reviewed my son's college application?'

'No. The Dean of Admissions does that. I only review paperwork when there's a question or an override decision to be made.'

'I've gone straight.'

That's the word of the hour, I thought glibly.

'According to Gregory Watley,' Underhill continued, 'you're worried about the state of my finances.'

'Not the state. The source.'

Underhill cocked his head. 'Ma'am, I did my time. I paid my dues. I'm legit now.'

'Have you spoken to Mr Watley recently?'

Underhill smiled, his best feature. 'Yes.'

Interesting. Had Watley called Underhill the moment he'd returned to his office? To get their stories straight? 'Have you spoken to Nicky Bilko, too?' I asked, studying his reaction.

His smile turned south. 'What does he have to do with anything?'

Like Watley, he'd also used present tense. I said, 'You and he fought. In public. He believed you owed him money.'

'I paid him back. In full.'

'He's dead. Murdered.'

Underhill's gaze turned icy. He inhaled and exhaled, wrestling with what he would say next. 'I'm sorry to hear that, but not my problem.'

'I told the police I saw you and him arguing. They'll want to chat with you.'

His nostrils flared. 'Look, Dean Lawson, back off.'

'Is that a threat?'

'No.' He held up his hands, palms forward. 'No. Let me explain. What I meant to say is try not to judge me without understanding the circumstances. What's past is prologue, correct? You see, I didn't have a good role model growing up. The family business was entrenched before I was knee-high. But I've changed.' He placed an earnest hand on his chest.

I waited for more.

'Two years ago, my wife vowed to divorce me and take the children if I didn't turn my life around. I love my boys. I'd do anything to make them proud of me.'

Aiden saying the words *proud of me* pealed in my head.

'Look at this beauty.' Underhill motioned to the project. 'I've hired the finest architects in New Orleans. The finish work will be done by artisans. It'll be stunning. Me and my boys – and their families – will have something to admire for years to come. You understand this sense of pride. You have a son.'

I felt my breath pitch and snag. 'How did you know I have a son?'

'It's not uncommon for me to know specifics about leaders of companies with whom I might do business. In your case, Pelican University.'

Did his tone have an edge? Was he warning me?

'I asked myself, is this the school I want my son to attend? Is it worthy of him? His older brothers opted to skip college. They're all brawn. They work with their hands.'

'Your oldest is in plumbing, I hear.'

'That's correct. But my youngest's mind is top-notch. He wants to major in English.'

'You said history the other day.'

'Both. He wants to become an author of historical fiction. And he's got his heart set on Pelican. Your son attends Tulane, doesn't he?'

Imaginary fingers gripped my heart. How did he know where Aiden went to school? *Steady, Maggie. Watley could've told him.* 'He does.' My throat went dry. 'He *did*. Right now, he's MIA.'

'What do you mean?' The concern in his eyes looked real. Not forced. If he'd snatched my son, he was a pro at keeping cool.

'I'm afraid he might have been kidnapped. We received a ransom note. I think someone with a grudge against my ex-husband might've taken him.'

Underhill gripped my elbow and guided me out of the construction site to the street. 'Dean Lawson, let's speak frankly. You came to this construction site to grill me, didn't you?'

'Yes, sir. I'd like some answers.'

'Fire away.' He released me.

'Gregory Watley says he's your lender.'

'It's true. I don't have a dime to spare. When I went to prison, I gave up my past life and all the trappings that went with it. The vacation home. The yacht. The private jet.'

The art he'd sold to Bilko.

'My family and I now live frugally. All I have in savings will go to college tuition. But I would never kidnap a child to fund an enterprise or to even a score. Therefore, listen to me and listen good.' He removed the hard hat and brushed his hair with a palm. 'I want . . . no, I *need* this condominium project to succeed. For my future. For my family's future. I won't jeopardize it for anything. For *anything*.' He aimed two fingers at his face. 'Look into my eyes. You'll see I'm not lying.'

FORTY

I skipped Japanese barbecue, returned to Pelican University, and settled into my office. Yvonne brought me a bottle of water and sent me an email listing my messages. Nothing that required immediate attention. I stared at my cell phone, willing the kidnapper to respond.

It chimed, unnerving me. Gina was calling.

'I'm flying to Phoenix,' she said when I answered. 'If you need me—'

'I won't,' I assured her. 'Go. Be with your mom. Don't get distracted.'

'When you hear from Aiden—'

When, not *if*. 'I'll text you. Promise.'

Prompted by Gina's course of action, I headed to Inner Peace

Assisted Living to visit my mother. The facility never wavered on the amount of lights it kept on. It wanted its patients to feel upbeat, not gloomy. Generators made sure of that.

I signed in, and a nurse guided me to the rec room. My mother was yet again seated in a chair by the window. Because I'd phoned ahead, one of the attendees had added a small amount of blush to my mother's cheeks. Per usual, Benjie's afghan was draped over her lap. Her gnarled fingers clutched it like a lifeline.

I sat beside her and gently touched the back of one hand. 'Hi, Mom.'

'Hello.' Her gaze registered me. She smiled.

'It's Maggie.'

'I know who you are. Benjie's sister.'

'Your daughter.'

She nodded perfunctorily. At least we'd solved that issue.

'Have you been eating well, Mom?'

'I don't like vanilla pudding.'

'Me, neither.'

'I like chocolate pudding.'

'And you like chocolate ice cream.'

'My favorite. Benjie's, too.'

I'd always preferred rocky road. Benjie would make fun of me. *That's because you're nuts*, he would taunt.

'Your father took me for ice cream on our first date,' my mother said.

I stared at her, surprised she remembered. How I'd adored hearing the story of the way they'd met. Dad had seen her pumping gas at a gas station. Too slow to ask her out, he followed her to her next destination, a wine store. Clad in his police uniform – he was a beat cop at the time – he followed her inside and flashed his badge, demanding to see her ID immediately. She spun around, flustered, as if she'd been caught doing something wrong. For a moment, he made her sweat bullets. Then he admitted that he was just having a bit of fun. He asked her on a date, and they went out for banana splits. The two of them had been inseparable after that.

For a long time, my mother and I sat in companionable silence.

'I saw Benjie,' she said suddenly. 'In my dream. He was with that boy.'

'What boy?'

'The student that hung himself. They're friends.'

Oka-ay. Gently, I said, 'They're friends?'

'Yes. They tell each other stories that make the other laugh.'

At least they were happy stories.

'When Benjie laughs, his eyes water.' My mother frowned. 'When he's done laughing, he cries.'

'Oh, Mom, I'm sorry.' I petted her hand.

'It's all right. He's crying for the boy because the boy will never laugh out loud again.'

'Benjie isn't crying for himself?'

My mother stared daggers at me. 'He never cries for himself. Never! He is content. I can see it in his eyes. The eyes never lie.'

My mother's words haunted me as I left the facility. Mirlande had said the same thing. She hadn't given me a full psychic reading because she'd been miffed by my attitude. Had she kept something from me? On purpose?

I went back to Marie Laveau's House of Voodoo, but Mirlande wasn't on duty. The saleswoman had no idea where she might be. I reached out to Zach, hoping he might have a clue. He told me to try the Spotted Cat Music Club. He was pretty sure she worked there as a waitress.

The Cat, as it was known by locals, was on Frenchmen Street in the Faubourg Marigny District. It was an intimate bar that presented nightly jazz music. I'd visited on a couple of occasions, but not recently. The queue to get in wasn't too long. I waited twenty minutes to enter.

A four-piece band was playing 'Prodigal Son.' At the microphone stood a brunette in a paisley halter dress, her arms adorned with musical instrument tattoos. She was grinning and dancing in place to the brisk music. When the trumpeter launched into a solo, the brunette whooped in support.

I caught sight of Mirlande dressed in a black spaghetti-strapped T-shirt with the Cat's logo on it. She was wiping away moisture from a recently vacated table for two. I weaved through the room, beating a twosome to the table, and sat down.

Mirlande regarded me warily. 'Have to pay for both seats at a table.'

'Fine.' I set the cover charge in front of me. 'I'll have a Nola Blonde.' One of my favorite beers.

She returned with the order.

Before she could make her escape, I gripped her wrist. 'I need you to do another reading for me.'

'Why?'

'Because you cut the last one short.'

'Did not.'

'Did.'

Mirlande gazed at the crowd and then her watch. 'I got a break in fifteen minutes. Meet you out back.'

'Out back?' No way. That didn't sound safe. 'Out front.'

'OK. But I stay nearby. In case the boss needs me.'

'We'll stand outside the shop next door. For privacy.'

She gave a curt nod.

The music was jaunty. Fun. The crowd was eating it up.

Fifteen minutes later, I left my half-drunk beer on the table and met Mirlande. We skirted the line of customers waiting to enter. We stopped in a semi-quiet spot, and she pulled a pack of cigarettes from her jeans pocket. She offered me one. I declined. She lit up.

'You're a hard worker,' I said. 'A day job and a night job?'

'Gotta pay the bills. I work here Mondays and Tuesdays.' She took a drag on her cigarette and held it shoulder high.

The smoke wafted in my direction. I didn't wince. I handed her a twenty-dollar bill.

'Double at nighttime.'

I forked over another. She tucked them into her cleavage.

'Aiden is still missing,' I said. Uttering the words aloud made my pulse spike. Perspiration bloomed above my lip. 'He—'

'*Shh.*' She tossed her cigarette on the pavement. Ground it with the heel of her espadrille. Seized my hand. The other day she'd held it away from her. Today, she pulled it to her belly. I flinched but didn't wrench free. She lifted her chin and closed her eyes. 'He's in a dark place.'

'You said that before. You also said he was hiding.'

'*Shh.* I was wrong about that. He is hidden. It is different.'

'How can I find him?'

'What do you not understand about *shh*?' she said with a bite, and closed her eyes again. 'He doesn't want to fail, but he feels he might. He is trapped. Struggling to breathe. He cannot escape this . . . this . . .' She rotated her free hand in the air. 'This torment.' Her eyes snapped open. Fear flooded her gaze. I'd never seen anyone look so haunted. She released my hand. Nearly threw it at me. 'Go!'

'But—'

'Go! Find him! Save him!' She couldn't run fast enough to get away from me.

Rivulets of sweat sluiced down my back as her words scudded through my mind. *He cannot escape this torment.*

My cell phone jangled, jarring me. I skimmed the display. *Quianna Swinton.* I answered.

'I hate to be calling so late,' she said, 'but I have to be honest with you.'

'You know where Aiden is?' People on the street stared, I'd spoken so loudly. I tucked my head down and kept walking toward the parking garage.

'No. I'm sorry. I didn't mean to mislead you. I meant I wasn't straightforward with you. Aiden stopped his sessions with me when he learned . . .' She hesitated. I heard the sound of voices behind her, like she was in a bar or restaurant. 'When he learned that I was speaking to a colleague about him.'

'You broke confidentiality?'

'I was concerned about the immensity of his despair because of losing Keira. I'd never had a patient witness a loved one die the way he did. I'm a young therapist. I'm not wet behind the ears, but I'm not a veteran, either. I was out of my depth.' Quianna drew in a breath and exhaled. 'At his last appointment he arrived early and, rather than remain in the anteroom, as all my clients are instructed, he rushed into the office saying he had big news. He found me with my colleague. His file was open on the table between us.'

I was speechless.

'Needless to say, he was shocked. I tried to explain, but he swore at me. He ran out, cursing all the people who'd lied to him.' She choked back a sob. 'He never returned.'

'When was that appointment?'

'Ten days ago.'

I reached my Prius, my mind reeling with thoughts. Who else had lied to him? Keira? He'd written *She knew* on the back of her picture. What had she known? If only I could rewind the clock.

'Thank you for telling me,' I said, climbing into the driver's seat and switching on the ignition.

Quianna hummed softly. 'You haven't heard from him or the kidnapper yet?'

'Not a word.'

'You must be heartbroken.'

You have no idea.

'By the way, how did you learn Aiden was seeing me?' the doctor asked. 'He didn't want you to know.'

I put the car in reverse and started backing out of my spot. 'I was talking to Celine about Keira. She was happy Aiden had chosen therapy to work through his grief.'

'Celine said as much when she came to see me.'

'Wait, she what?' I slammed on the brake. Set the car in Park. 'Celine told me . . .' My breathing grew choppy. 'She told me she didn't know your name. Didn't know your address.'

'Perhaps she was embarrassed to admit she'd consulted a therapist,' she offered.

I supposed it was possible. 'When did she see you?'

'After Aiden's missed appointment. I think it's safe to say that in the session – I mean, I don't believe it's unethical for me to say – that she seemed truly concerned about him. She inquired how she could help smooth things over between him and me.'

'Did you give her tips?'

'I did.'

I told her Celine's theory that Aiden might have sent the ransom note so he could get enough money to fund a trip to San Francisco to search for his therapist – i.e. *her.*

'San Francisco?' the doctor asked. 'Why?'

'Aiden told Celine that you'd gone there to tend to your aging mother. Except my ex-husband refuted that. He said he and Aiden were planning to have a session with you soon.'

'Aiden did set a dual appointment with Joshua. He hasn't cancelled it. I was hopeful he would keep it, and we could work through my betrayal of his trust.'

I drummed the steering wheel, working through the facts. OK, to be fair, Celine had been shaken. Confused, even. Maybe she'd misheard Aiden. 'I can't imagine the abandonment Celine must be feeling,' I murmured, the words of empathy pouring out of my mouth surprising me, but I couldn't help thinking about her last pitiful text. 'With her mother dying and her father walking out, and now believing Aiden has left her.'

'Her mother isn't dead,' Quianna stated.

'I'm sorry. Wh-what?' I sputtered.

'She's not dead. She lives in LaPlace.'

FORTY-ONE

D riving to the Residence Inn, headlights strobing the wind-shield, I replayed the conversation I'd had with Celine in the duplex the day she'd received the ransom note. I'd asked about the woman in the nurse's uniform and cat-eye glasses on her altar. She'd said it was her mother, who was deceased. Why not say her mother lived in LaPlace, a town on the western edge of New Orleans? If she'd lied about that, what else might she have been untruthful about?

Back in my hotel room, I opened my laptop computer, went online, and did a search for *Lily Boudreaux, nurse or caregiver in LaPlace*. Nothing cropped up.

I swiped the photo app on my cell phone and flipped through pictures. I landed on the one I'd taken of Aiden's altar. Using two fingers, I enlarged it. At the edge, I could see approximately an eighth of Celine's mother's figure. A badge was affixed to the pocket of her uniform. I could make out the last four letters of the facility, *NITY*.

Online I typed the word *hospital*, added *NITY*, and hit Enter. Nothing. I wondered if the word might be the ending to *UNITY* and searched again. There was a Mercy Unity in Minnesota, Long Beach Unity in California, and Unity Hospice, also in California. Nothing in New Orleans.

Josh was great at tracking down sources. Much better than I'd ever been. I dialed him. Tess answered. She said Joshua was sleeping.

In the background, I heard him say, 'Who's calling?'

Tess sighed, like an annoyed keeper of the gate. 'Maggie.'

'Give me that.' Josh sounded cranky. A second later, he said into the phone, 'Mags, any word on our son?'

'No. Listen . . .' I told him about Mirlande's frantic second psychic reading and my confrontations with Watley and Underhill. Then I offered the kicker from Dr Swinton, about Celine's mother being alive and the photo of her mother on the altar. 'I can't make out the whole name of the hospital she might work at. It ends in N-I-T-Y. I tried unity and struck out. Any clues?'

'How about humanity? Divinity?'

I jotted those down.

'Eternity. Insanity.' He chuckled at the latter.

'Ha-ha.'

'Fraternity, maternity.'

I tapped my pencil on my chin.

'Opportunity,' he said. 'Impunity.'

'Community!' I typed the word into the search engine. 'Got it! Lake Community Medical Center, LaPlace.' I thanked Josh, wished him a speedy recovery, and ended the call.

Then I dialed the medical center and asked if Lily Boudreaux was an employee. The receptionist said the center didn't employ anyone by that name. However, it did have a nurse on staff named Lily *Bruno*. Maybe the woman had remarried, I reflected.

'May I speak with Nurse Bruno?'

'Not while she's on duty.'

'Oh, my, that's too bad. I've got a prize to bestow,' I said, taking my cue from the 346 area code phone calls I'd received. 'She's been hard to track down. I don't imagine you'd share her home address with me so I could contact her later?'

'No, ma'am.'

'Her phone number?'

'Sorry.'

I hung up and searched online for Lily Bruno in LaPlace. She wasn't listed. Thwarted but not stymied, I headed to the hospital and approached the parking attendant. For twenty dollars, he was willing to tell me that Mrs Bruno ended her shift at six p.m. and she drove a blue sedan. To win the woman's trust, I stopped by a florist and picked up a bouquet of daisies, hoping a peace offering might make her amenable to chatting with me. Then I returned and waited in my car, checking each face that exited the hospital. At a few minutes past six, I caught sight of the woman I'd seen in Celine's photo, though she looked much older, her hair more salt than pepper now and her face more creased. She climbed into an aging Celica, and I followed her to LaPlace Mobile Home Park.

In the dark, the park with its smattering of gnarly oak trees looked eerie. There were forty-plus sites lined up in two rows, all surrounded by a white metal fence. The road was patchy, but, overall, the park looked well-tended. Lights were on in many of the homes. Due to the cool temperature, only a few smokers were sitting outside.

Lily Bruno's mobile home, a prefabricated white-and-gray structure with a scalloped edge and in dire need of paint, was set on a permanent chassis, second to the last on the left.

I waited until she got situated and turned on the interior lights before I knocked on the door.

Mrs Bruno opened it wearing neon blue cat-eye glasses and a pale blue robe, having quickly changed out of her uniform. 'What do you want?' she asked with a slight slur. She was missing a few of her lower teeth. At one time, she'd been attractive. Without the teeth, she looked forlorn.

'Ma'am, I'm Maggie Lawson. May I come in?'

She clutched her robe. 'I'm not buying anything.'

'I'm not selling anything.' I smiled and held up the bouquet. 'For you.'

'What's the catch?'

'I'm your daughter Celine Boudreaux's mother-in-law.'

'Don't have a daughter named Celine. My girl's name is Cici. Haven't seen her in ages.'

Cici? Maybe I was totally off base. 'You're Lily Bruno, aren't you? You're a nurse at Lake Community Medical Center.'

'The same.'

'Celine has a picture of you at her duplex.' Right down to the cat-eye glasses. 'Is Boudreaux a family name?'

'A distant relative.'

I offered the flowers again. 'Please, may I come in and we could talk for a minute? If you're not too busy.'

'Don't see why not. You look harmless.' She took the flowers and opened the door wider.

I stepped inside. The living room held a threadbare couch and armchair. Both were dark blue with a diamond-shaped pattern. The small kitchen was to the right. To the left, three doorways led to other rooms. Two bedrooms and a bath, I figured. I spotted a picture of dark-haired toddlers with pixie-like expressions on the wall. 'Twins?'

Lily followed my gaze. 'Almost. Born ten months apart. Otis came first. Then Cici.' Her smile softened. 'Oh, how those two were joined at the hip. They were best friends forever.'

'Were?'

She tightened the sash of her robe and went to the kitchen. 'Want something to drink? All I can offer is water or tea.'

'Tea, please.' It would take longer to prepare, giving me more time to figure out why Celine had lied. Maybe she'd wanted to distance herself from this woman. Lily didn't look like an abuser, but how would I know?

'Sugar?' she asked.

'Yes, thanks.'

A small dining table was covered with a blue tablecloth. A white pillar candle and book of matches sat on a dish in the center. The sparse kitchen counter held a blue-and-white cookie jar, knife block, and toaster. Celine had decorated predominantly in blue, too, I noted. There were framed pictures of Lily's children everywhere.

'You said Otis and Cici were best friends,' I prompted.

'*Mm-mm*. Otis, sweet thing, had the world ahead of him.' Lily opened a cabinet. The door squeaked. She withdrew a box of Lipton teabags and two blue-rimmed china cups and saucers. She put a bag into each and set a teakettle on to boil. 'He went off to college. To Pelican U. On a scholarship. He was very bright. He dreamed of becoming a history professor, but he couldn't cope with the stress . . . and killed himself.'

My breathing snagged. No. It couldn't be. 'Did he call himself O?'

'At times, why?'

I stared at the woman harder as realization threatened to over-whelm me. She was the mother of O Bruno, the student who'd died under my watch. I didn't recognize her at first because of the graying hair and the eyeglasses and the missing teeth. I recalled the boy's sister, the dark-haired girl with the tattooed neck, storming into my office with her mother, the girl furious that I hadn't done anything to prevent her beloved brother's death. Like O, she'd called herself a letter – *C*. Until now, I'd forgotten their last name.

'Cici had a meltdown after he died, and she ran off,' Lily said, her tone resigned. 'I've phoned and left messages, but she never returns the call. Breaks my heart.'

I pivoted, looking at other photographs on the walls. Cici and Otis, about five or six years old, putting on a puppet show. Cici and Otis, closer to ten and eleven, huddled together on the couch, reading books. Cici and Otis, hanging on each other as teenagers, both clad in *Les Misérables* peasant costumes. Best friends. Forever.

'You can read about my son's death there.' Lily pointed to a framed newspaper article.

It was from *L'Observateur*, LaPlace's local newspaper. April, five years ago. The newspaper headline read: 'College Student Driven to Suicide.' The article didn't mention that I or the college was at fault. It talked about how bullying had gotten out of hand and how doctors, therapists, and teachers needed to pay more attention to warning signs.

I teetered and placed a hand on the wall to steady myself as the memory of meeting C and her mother roared into my mind.

'You!' C stood opposite my desk, arms flailing. 'You did this.'

'No,' I said, adding that I had no knowledge of her brother's situation because the director of athletics hadn't looped me in until it was too late. He thought he could manage it and accepted full responsibility for the tragedy.

'I don't care. I don't care. I don't care.' C waved her fist. She keened. She vowed revenge.

I served her and her mother tea and waited through her tirade. Mrs Bruno was stoic throughout. When the girl finally calmed down, they left, and I folded in on myself.

FORTY-TWO

N*o, no, no* resounded in my head. C – *Cici* – couldn't be Celine. They looked nothing alike. Cici was about as tall as Celine – she'd worn flats; Celine always sported heels – but Cici was slender with a delicate chin. Celine had curves. And blue eyes. Cici's were brown. Celine had poise. Cici had been raw, almost coarse. During her diatribe, she'd inquired about the photograph of Aiden and Keira on my desk. To calm her, I'd told her about them, saying they were both going to Tulane in the fall.

'The last thing Cici said before she walked out' – Lily set napkins on the table – 'was that she would keep her eyes on the prize because she wanted to make Otis proud.'

Her eyes.

Bile rose up my esophagus as I studied the teenaged picture of Cici and Otis in *Les Mis* costumes. *The eyes never lie*, my mother had said. Mirlande had echoed the sentiment. Other than the color,

Cici's eyes were Celine's eyes. Keen yet wary. Filled with spirit. The shape matched, too.

'Are your children in high school in this picture?' I asked.

'Yes,' Lily looked where I was pointing. 'Cici . . .' She chuckled. 'She was a drama queen. A real chameleon. She acted in all the school plays. She was very talented. Otis went along for the ride.'

Could colored contacts conceal eyes as brown as Cici's? I'd seen a case for contacts in the duplex's medicine cabinet.

'She's very pretty,' I said.

'Thank you.'

I studied the picture harder. Cici was flat-chested, but breasts could be enhanced. Chins tweaked. Hair dyed. Tattoos eradicated.

How could Celine have afforded to make such a physical change? Her mother wasn't rich. Had Celine worked two jobs? Put up a *GoFundMe* page? My thoughts raced back to C ranting in my office. When a year passed and neither she nor her mother lashed out at me or the university or the AD, who'd resigned, I stopped fretting about retaliation. The single incident out of the ordinary during that time had been someone breaking into my office and stealing my grandmother's cameo necklace. Was Celine that brazen? Had she swiped the pendant? I flashed on her altar. Was it possible it lay beneath the myriad beads draped on the fertility statue?

What's past is prologue, Underhill had said, quoting Shakespeare in *The Tempest*. History set the framework for the present.

Mentally, I reconstructed the timeline of Cici's transformation. She altered her appearance, changed her identity, and transferred to Tulane. She befriended Keira and then Aiden. When Keira died—

Another thought struck me. I visualized Aiden's handwritten note on Keira's picture: *She knew.* Had Keira figured out who Celine was? Did she confront Celine? Did Celine decide right then and there that she had to die? Yes, it made sense. Because if Keira had lived, Celine wouldn't have been able to wheedle her way into Aiden's life.

I paused. *Don't be ridiculous, Maggie. Keira couldn't have caught on. If she had, she would've told Aiden.*

The teakettle whistled. Lily made the tea and brought me a cup on a saucer.

I accepted it, my hands trembling with alarm.

'Careful there,' Lily said. 'Don't spill. It's hot.'

'Thank you.' I released the breath I'd been holding. 'Tell me more about your children.'

'Otis was the sensitive one.' Lily fetched a cup of tea for herself. 'He was so sweet. So gentle.'

I blew on my tea to cool it.

'When I learned I was pregnant for a second time, I was overjoyed. I wanted two children. My husband did, too. He died a month shy of Cici's birth. Heart failure.'

Celine said her father had run off. Another lie to make Aiden – to make *me* – feel sorry for her.

Lily said, 'Let's sit.' She took her tea to the table. I followed. 'All Cici's life she protected her brother. If he was bullied, she fought for his honor. If a teacher didn't give him a fair grade, she went to bat for him. She was my little warrior princess. They were inseparable.'

After a long moment, I said, 'I'm certain Cici is my daughter-in-law, Celine. I believe she's changed her name and appearance. She's blond now.'

'Blonds have more fun.' Lily smiled and recited a telephone number. 'Is that the number you have for her?'

'Yes.'

'Maybe I'll ring her again. I miss her something awful.'

She rose to her feet and lit the candle in the middle of the table. As the flame flickered, she coaxed the air toward her, as Celine had done, and mumbled a prayer.

I recalled one of Celine's texts to me. *My mother wasn't as supportive as you.* I'd taken it as an olive branch, a way to connect, when in truth it had been manipulative. All of it was starting to make sense now. Cici – Celine – angry at losing her brother. Blaming me and, thereby, targeting Aiden. What was her endgame?

I scrambled to my feet. 'Thank you for your hospitality.'

'What's your son's name?' Lily asked, walking me to the door.

'Aiden.'

'That's a lovely name. I always wished I'd given Otis a nicer name – Otis doesn't roll off the tongue like Aiden – but I named him after my father.'

My gaze tracked to the article in the newspaper and I froze. The date of Otis's death was April fourteenth, the same date of the text that Aiden sent saying he was taking off to get his head on straight. The events were five years apart, of course, but the date gnawed at me. What if Celine authored Aiden's text and chose that date to make a statement, wondering if I'd connect the dots? Had she – my breathing snagged – killed Aiden as retribution for her brother's death?

No. I had to believe he was still alive. I had to keep the faith. She didn't hate *him*. She hated me. According to the psychics, Aiden was scared and finding it hard to breathe. *Present tense.*

Clinging to that scrap of hope, I hurried to my car.

FORTY-THREE

I started the engine and tapped in Celine's cell phone number. She answered after one ring. Keeping my voice as steady as I could manage, I invited her to dinner. She declined, saying she had to work late.

Desperate to learn more about her plot, certain that I was right – she had hidden Aiden – I made a beeline for the duplex. Maybe she'd chronicled her cleverness in the diary she allegedly kept. I parked around the corner and hoofed it to the front porch. Celine hadn't removed the key from its hiding place.

Stupid girl.

While making sure no one was watching me, I slotted the key into the lock and stole inside. I didn't switch on a light. I didn't want to alert her neighbor or anyone else to my presence. The dim light of the streetlamp made everything in the place look like something out of a black-and-white movie.

Their cat Spirit peered at me from his spot on the sofa. His eyes glowed an eerie green. I held my finger to my lips, as if that would help him understand to keep quiet. He lowered his head and fell fast asleep.

I tapped the flashlight app on my cell phone, cupped my hand around it to keep the light as muted as possible, and tiptoed to the altars. Without touching anything, I probed the items draped on the fertility statue. In seconds, as I'd speculated, I discovered my grandmother's cameo necklace buried beneath the trinkets. My blood seethed, but I pushed the emotion aside – anger would blur my judgment. I left the pendant in place and snapped a picture to document its location.

Next, I strode into the bathroom. The shower curtain was gone. Had it even been shredded in the first place? Yes. The police saw it. But who'd shredded it? Celine? I crouched and searched beneath the sink. I withdrew the FreshGo contacts container. Aqua-blue-colored contacts were inside. I opened the make-up kit and feminine product boxes but didn't find a diary. I stood up. Caught sight of a bottle of Dior's vanilla-scented Diorama perfume on the counter. I recalled the scent I'd picked up at my house the night the knife had appeared on my counter, the scent so much like my candles and infusers that I'd dismissed it.

Spurred by confidence that I was on the right track and Celine was the person who'd broken into my house not once but twice, I tiptoed into the bedroom and combed her side of the bed for the diary. I checked the nightstand. Underneath the base of the lamp. Between the mattress and box springs. I rifled through the bureau. Looked for false bottoms in the drawers. I scoured the closets. The shoe boxes. I searched for a safe in the floor like mine but came up empty on all counts.

On impulse, I returned to Aiden's side of the bed and removed his copy of *Lord of the Flies*. Then I delved deeper to see if I'd missed finding his journal on my previous raid. I hadn't.

I pulled the picture of Keira from the book and aimed my flashlight on it. I read the back again. *She knew.* It dawned on me that Aiden might have written the words because he'd figured out Celine's identity, too, and believed Celine killed Keira to protect the secret. How and when Keira figured it out didn't matter. Had Aiden confronted Celine with his theory? Was that what had spurred her into abducting him?

A car door slammed outside. Spirit yowled. My adrenaline skyrocketed. I shoved the book back in place. Sneaked to a window. Peered past the drapes. An elderly woman, not Celine, was exiting a silver Jeep. Spirit brushed against my ankles.

I nudged him gently with my toe. 'Go back to sleep.' I returned to the living room, Spirit traipsing behind me as if now on the alert to my every move. Fine. 'Have at it, cat,' I hissed, and ignored him. I gazed at Celine's altar. I opened the drawer beneath the altar but found only matches and replacement candles. I searched behind the cabinet. No diary.

I swung around and stared at the kitchen. During my previous foray, I hadn't taken time to properly scour it. I strode there. Peeked beneath the sink. Only cleaning products. No diary. I pulled open the trash drawer and rifled between the bag and the container. Zilch.

Probing the cupboards, I spied a tin of poppy seed tea. Again, using my flashlight, I read the claim on the back of the box. Like chamomile, the tea was a natural remedy to treat insomnia. It went on to say that the poppy was the source of opium as well as other narcotics. Could the seeds be used to make a victim docile? Was that how Celine had manipulated Aiden? She couldn't have knocked him out and transported him somewhere. She was tall and strong, but not that strong.

Rummaging through cracker and cereal boxes didn't produce a diary.

Neither did searching in the drawer beneath the oven.

Standing with hands on hips, I spun in a circle. I caught sight of a narrow cabinet I'd overlooked. Beyond the oven. Inside were slots created to hold cutting boards. I pulled the boards out one by one. A basic cedar style. Two antibacterial kinds. When I pulled the paddle-shaped board from its slot, I spied something wrapped in newspaper behind it. I held my breath and reached in. It felt bigger than a diary. I slipped it out and removed the paper.

Inside was not only another of Aiden's sketchpads but also a silver MacBook Air computer with a Le Gran Palais sticker affixed to the lid. Celine said Aiden had taken his laptop with him. Yet another lie. I opened the lid. The computer was switched off. I pressed a button. The screen came to life. A prompt for a password or fingerprint appeared. I sagged, knowing I couldn't provide either.

Unwilling to stick around any longer, fearful Celine might sense my invasion, I inserted the computer and sketchpad into my tote bag alongside my laptop, wadded up the newspaper, and opened the pullout trash can to get rid of it. I paused when I noticed snips of paper beneath the remains of an apple core and a string cheese wrapper. Colorful glossy torn paper. Like you'd find in a magazine or, say, pasted on to a ransom note.

Hurrying to the living room, I lifted a copy of *Elle* off the coffee table and flipped through it. Letters had been cut from it.

Spirit meowed imperiously.

'Yes, I'm snooping. Get over yourself.' I leafed through *The Week*, a political magazine. Letters had been cut from it, as well, confirming Celine had crafted the ransom note herself, right after

I'd mentioned that neither of us had received one. I recalled her frantic phone call.

Drama queen, indeed.

I thought of the shower curtain, shredded to establish that she, Celine, was a victim and to point the finger at Rosalie. I visualized the ripped-up portrait of her and Aiden that Dr Hebert had found shoved beneath her office door and was now convinced that Celine – not Rosalie – had done the damage. Not because Aiden was finished with her, but because she was done with him.

Fury surged within me. 'Where is he, you witch?' I whispered. 'What have you done with my son?'

On my way out, I glimpsed Aiden's altar again. A notion gnawed at the edges of my brain as I homed in on the map of St Louis Cemetery No. 1 folded into a triangle and peeking from beneath the voodoo doll. When I'd first met with Mirlande, she'd said the truth was *buried*. It was an odd expression. I hadn't thought much of it at the time. What if Celine had hidden Aiden in a tomb? A pyramid-shaped tomb?

Not at St Louis Cemetery No. 1 but at Aiden's favorite cemetery – Metairie. Had his origami or his drawings in his sketchpad given Celine the idea? If she had locked him in a crypt, was he able to get enough oxygen?

My lungs seized.

Breathe, Mags. He's scared, and scared means alive.

I rushed to my car, tore from the curb, and dialed Josh. He answered, not Tess.

'What's up?' He sounded rested. Strong.

Words tumbled out of me. Celine. Cici. The boy who committed suicide. The lies and deceit. 'My guess, she took him to Metairie. To the Pinnell tomb.' I doubted Celine would've chosen the Brunswig crypt. It was too public. Too showy.

'How would she have been able to get him inside the grounds?'

'If she drugged and gagged him, he would have been docile enough to muscle into submission.'

'And she forced him over the fence?'

'I don't know, Josh!' I couldn't tamp down the terror in my voice. 'Maybe there's a break in it.'

'OK. I believe you. I'll meet you at the entrance.'

Next I reached out to Frank Filuzzi. He took a bit of convincing, but telling him about the clippings for the fake ransom note cinched the deal. He said, 'On my way.'

Lastly, I phoned Celine. She answered after two rings. 'What?' She sounded hassled. 'I just got home. I told you I can't meet—'

'Stop, Celine! Just stop!' I couldn't hold back any longer. I felt like lightning was flick-popping inside my veins. 'I know what you did. I know!'

'What're you talking about?'

'You have Aiden's cell phone. You sent those texts from him to me.'

'No I didn't. What's gotten into you?'

'You created the ransom note. You've hidden my son.'

'Are you on drugs, Maggie? Have you been drinking?'

'Where is he, dammit?'

'Maggie, calm down. I know you're upset. His disappearance has to be eating at you. Let's meet. Let's talk.'

'If you've harmed him—'

'I'd never hurt him. I love him. I'm sure he'll come home soon. Why won't you believe me?'

Because yesterday you were acting as desolate as a widow. Silence is unbearable. *Bullpuckey!*

'Where is he, Celine, or should I call you Cici?'

There was a long pause. Air whistled from something in the background. Finally, Celine said in a low raspy voice, 'You've lost it, Maggie. Truly gone over the edge.' She ended the call.

As I merged on to Route 61, my phone pinged. I'd received a text message. I risked looking at it.

Aiden: *Mom. Celine touched base. She said you're wigging out. Look, I know I've been silent. Relax. I'm OK. By the way, yes, I sent the ransom note. It was infantile of me. Sorry. I'll be in touch soon.*

I studied the text. No *XO*. No texting shorthand. Aiden hadn't sent it. Celine had. Clearly, she was the one who had gone over the edge. I replied.

Me: *Meet me. Now. Metairie Cemetery. Pinnell tomb. To complete the scavenger hunt you started on the map on your altar. PS saw the note on Keira's picture. I know what she knew.*
Aiden: *Sure. OK. Cool. See you there.*

Sure and *OK* sounded like my son. But he never used the word *cool*. It was passé.

FORTY-FOUR

etairie Cemetery was closed. I couldn't wheedle my way in with a tour group, as Josh and I had done the other day. And though I knew I should wait for him and Filuzzi, I couldn't. I drove around the perimeter searching for an open gate, a break in the exterior fence. Something. Along Fairway Drive, I noticed an abandoned teardown that might provide cover and give me access. I parked on the street, slung my tote across my body, and hustled to the lot. The full moon lit the way. I didn't need a flashlight.

The fence wasn't tall, but I couldn't leap over it, not even with a running start. *Wait for Josh and Filuzzi* cycled through my brain, but could I? What if Aiden only had seconds to live? I felt the way I had on the day he was born, a deep need to get him out. To help him take his first breath. Now!

I backtracked, looking for something I could stack near the fence. I landed upon a discarded crate as well as a half-dozen bricks and a rusty, two-foot stepstool. I was no Lego master, but in a matter of minutes, I was able to create a precarious staircase. I scaled it and dropped to the ground on the other side.

In the shadows, I texted Josh that I was stealing in and would see him at the tomb, and then I waited a moment to make sure a guard hadn't spotted me.

Assured I was undetected, I weaved between bushes, keeping to the shadows. I reached the Brunswig crypt and paused. After turning in a circle to get my bearings, I set off toward Pontchartrain Boulevard.

The Pinnell tomb was half the size of the Brunswig one. At the entrance, in the glow of the moonlight, the iron sculpture of a bare-chested man in loincloth gleamed. He was holding a lantern and looked steely-eyed. Wary. The tomb's iron portal was inscribed with symbols that reminded me of the digits and shapes I'd seen on the St Louis No. 1 map on Aiden's altar.

I peered through the gate but couldn't get a fix on the interior. 'Aiden?' I called.

Silence.

Switching on my cell phone's flashlight, I aimed the beam inside while questioning the absurdity of my theory. Surely if Celine had forced Aiden into a crypt, he'd have yelled out, hoping a passerby would hear him. Unless, as I'd suggested to Josh, she'd gagged him and sedated him.

I counted eight crypts on the left. Four rows of two. A narrow altar table holding two tooled candlesticks stood against the right-most wall. A pair of tapers and a book of matches lay to one side. A religious painting in a gold frame adorned the wall above the altar.

'Aiden!' I called. Rage swelled inside me. I pounded on the portal. 'Aiden.'

No answer.

I tugged on the handle. The door didn't budge. It required a key. 'Aiden, I'm here.' Desperation leaked into my voice. 'I'm here, sweetheart.'

'Looking for this?' a woman said from behind.

I whirled around.

Celine, in a dark shirt, pants, hiking boots, gloves, and camo backpack, was dangling a long skeleton key on her index finger. I dove for her.

'Uh-uh.' She raised the butcher knife that glinted in her other hand. 'Back up.'

I obeyed and stumbled into the bare-chested statue. The iron was hard. Unyielding. 'I spoke to your mother, who, to my surprise, is alive.'

'I know you did. She contacted me.'

'You haven't answered her calls for years.'

'This time I did. Call it daughter's intuition,' she said with a snarl. 'She's exactly like you. Worthless. But this time, at least she had valuable information.' She handed me the key. 'Open the lock. Go inside.'

I did as ordered. The air was musty. Dust filtered through the portal. I searched for a way to get control of the situation but didn't see any. Talk, I decided. Get the whole story. 'You're Cici Bruno,' I said. 'Sister of Otis Bruno. You're the girl who called herself C that stormed into my office and blamed me for her brother's suicide.'

She grunted.

'You changed your appearance. Your body, your hair, your chin. Your eye color is different, too, but the shape of your eyes is the same. The eyes never lie,' I intoned like Mirlande. 'When you caught a glimpse of a picture of Aiden and Keira in my office, you set your course. To punish me, you worked your way into my son's life. Now you're putting him through hell.'

'You put *me* through hell, Maggie. Through. Hell.' She shot out a hand. 'Toss your tote in the corner.'

I shrugged it off, placed it on the floor, and shoved it with my toe. It bumped into the altar. The candlesticks wobbled. One clattered to the floor.

'Phone, too.'

I set it on the floor and kicked it. It spun until it hit the tote bag. 'Which crypt is Aiden in?'

'He's not.'

'Sure he is. Otherwise, you wouldn't have come.'

She cocked her head.

'I know he's here, Celine,' I said. 'I feel it. I sense it. Plus I consulted a psychic. She said he was hidden and scared. He'd only be scared if he didn't come here of his own accord. She said he was trapped. This has to be the place.'

'You think you're so smart.'

'Which one?' I demanded, nearly shrieking. If Filuzzi and Josh were nearby, they should be able to hear me. 'I understand why you want to punish me, but why are you punishing him? What did he ever do to deserve this? He loved you.'

She didn't respond.

'Have you been feeding him? Providing water?'

Her implacable gaze was maddening.

'Aiden!' I yelled.

Silence. Had he stopped breathing? No, I couldn't believe that. I wouldn't. *Aiden, please be alive. I'll save you.*

'When I searched your place, Celine, I found his computer. Behind the cutting boards. You lied about him taking it with him, but then you lied about a lot of things.'

She sniggered.

'I came across scraps of letters cut from magazines in your trash, too,' I went on. 'And I saw my grandmother's cameo necklace – the one you stole from my office – buried beneath strands of beads on your fertility statue. You are vile.'

She brandished the knife.

I shrank back but continued. 'I looked for Aiden's journal, but I didn't find it. Did you destroy it like you destroyed the portrait of the two of you?'

'I didn't—'

'Yes, you did. You ripped up the sketch, and you shredded the shower curtain. You probably even wrote the horrible notes to Aiden telling him to end his life.'

Her mouth turned up on one side. 'Yes, those were brilliant, weren't they? You should have seen his face when he received the first one.'

Her smug expression turned my stomach. 'Did you get rid of his journal because he'd written the truth about you in it?'

Celine scowled. 'Him and his precious journal.'

So she *had* seen the journal. Was it an entry that had spurred her to action?

'You texted me that Aiden charged a room at the hostel to throw me off the scent,' I said. 'You're a master of disguise. I'm guessing you dressed as him, in a blond wig, sunglasses, and peacoat. But you messed up. You signed for him.'

She shrugged one shoulder.

Something else occurred to me, something I hadn't picked up on at the time. 'In your office, when I made you send a text to Aiden and he didn't respond, you acted as if all was lost.' I whistled softly. 'Wow! That was good. Your performance was spot on. Dumb me. I'd heard a muted buzz within seconds of you sending the message, but three of your coworkers scanned their phones, so I'd presumed it was one of theirs. Since you'd said they weren't supposed to use them during office hours, I didn't think anything of it. I should've figured out then that you had Aiden's cell phone. That you were writing all the texts.'

Celine tucked a stray hair behind one ear. 'Yes, that was sloppy, Maggie.'

'I was definitely off my game.'

Were Josh and Filuzzi on theirs? Had Josh received my text saying I was inside the cemetery? Would he partner up with Filuzzi? My heart was jackhammering my chest. My hands were coated with sweat. I had to find Aiden. If only I could disarm Celine.

'You know, you were sloppy, too,' I said. 'If you'd hidden Aiden's bicycle, I might not have searched for him. That would've given you more lead time.'

'I've had plenty of time. Ple-e-enty.' She leered at me.

'Do you know how I figured out what you were doing?' It was my turn to smirk. 'Dr Swinton told me you met with her. She's how I learned about your mother.'

'So much for confidentiality.'

'I recognized you in the photos at your mother's trailer.'

'It's a *house*,' she hissed.

'Yes, of course.' I tempered my tone, using a soothing voice I might use on a child. Celine was brittle. Pushed too hard, she would attack. I needed to keep her engaged. 'It's a very nice house. You and your mother have a similar fondness for blue.'

Celine sniffed.

'Because of what she shared with me,' I said, 'I concluded you were the one who'd kidnapped Aiden because you wanted to punish me. So I went back to your duplex and searched for your diary, hoping you'd documented your plan.'

'You didn't find one.'

'No, I didn't.'

'That's because I carry it with me.' She blinked.

I noticed tattoos on her eyelids. I'd probably missed seeing the ink before because she'd worn heavy make-up. 'Those math symbols on your eyelids.'

'What about them?'

'You removed all the other tattoos from your neck and arms, but you kept those. Why?'

Her mouth curved up on one side.

I thought for a moment. 'Hold on. I get it. An equal symbol with a tilde above stands for congruence.'

'Ooh, very good,' she said enthusiastically, like I'd answered a final *Jeopardy* question.

'As a reminder of your brother. You were very close.'

'We were like this.' She crossed her fingers. 'Equal in every way.'

'Except you weren't.' I flashed on Benjie. Giving up. Not fighting. My equal, yet not. 'Otis was weak; you were strong.'

'No!' She lunged at me with the knife. Stopped short.

I recoiled and hated myself for the knee-jerk reaction.

'Chicken.' She cackled.

'No I'm not. I'd just like to live long enough to save my son. Where is he? Please tell me, Celine. You're not a mean person. I know you aren't.' As the dean of a college, I was usually good at making people do what I wanted them to do. Not Watley, of course, but most. It was a skill I'd learned as a mother. Not a suffocating, overly protective mother. Just a good mother. A loving mother. 'If he's alive—' I bit off the word. He was. He had to be. 'There can't be much air in those drawers. How long has he been in there?' The possibility terrified me. Had she imprisoned him ever since he'd gone off the grid a week ago? Or had she kept him holed up some-place else – another hostel or motel – and moved him recently? Mirlande said he was afraid of failing. Failing to breathe? 'Please, Celine. He'll suffocate.'

'Like my brother did. A fitting end.'

'Not for Aiden. He's not the guilty party. Neither am I.'

'Yes, you are! It was your fault! My brother died on your watch. You did nothing to save him. There was no counseling on campus.' Her nose flared as if she'd smelt a foul odor. 'No one for him to turn to. He was bullied, but you didn't care. No one gave a rat's ass. The students that ridiculed him? They all got off scot-free. They're living happy productive lives. But Otis? He's dead! He didn't deserve to die.'

'No, he didn't, and I'm sorry he killed himself.'

'You're sorry!' she shrieked. 'Save it for someone who cares how you feel.'

Josh. Frank. Please show up. What's taking so damned long?

Out of the corner of my eye, I spied my tote bag on the floor by the altar. If I could grab it and use it as a cudgel, with Aiden's and my computers tucked inside, it would land a hefty blow. I inched discreetly sideways. 'You're the one who sneaked into my house.'

'Good guess.'

'You removed a knife from the knife block and put it on the counter. You sat on the bed in Aiden's room. You left the voodoo doll on my porch. You swapped out the picture of my family with Aiden's. The lingering scent of vanilla remained after you left.' If only I'd associ-ated the scent with her at the time. 'What I don't understand is how you were able to coerce Aiden to come to this place.'

'I drugged him with Zolpidem and convinced him to walk along-side me.'

Zolpidem. Of course. Not poppyseed tea.

'He's always been easy to manipulate,' she added.

'How did you steal on to the grounds?' I asked, edging farther. 'If you drugged him, he wouldn't have been able to climb over the fence.'

'It's amazing how many security guards need extra cash.' She swung the skeleton key, as if flaunting yet another item the guard had been able to provide.

I peeked to the right. A few more inches to my tote bag. 'Which burial chamber is he in, Celine?'

She kept mum.

I studied the bank of crypts opposite me. Three lacked plaques. Two high and one low. Without a ladder, Celine couldn't have hoisted Aiden into either of the upper drawers. He had to be stowed in the lower one.

'Your mother told me something interesting,' I said.

'My mother.' She grunted.

'She said you were her little warrior princess. You fought all of your brother's battles.'

'Shut. Up. I'm warning you.' She thrust the knife at me. Stopped short again.

How long would she play cat and mouse? Claws out. Retract. Claws out.

I glanced to my left. At the portal. Where were Josh and Filuzzi? Had Celine paid a guard to stop them from entering? No, Filuzzi wouldn't have stood for that. Were he and Josh together? Were they close?

'Aiden was the same as Otis,' Celine said. 'Always expecting me to fight his battles.'

Was. Past tense. No, no, no.

'I didn't mind doing it for my brother. He was so vulnerable,' she went on. 'But for a grown man? A mama's boy?'

'My son is an artist. He's sensitive.' The words popped out of me. 'He's not a fighter. He never has been.' I hoped I sounded conciliatory as I inched closer to the tote bag.

'Stop. Don't move. I see what you're doing. Do not reach for your purse.' She waggled the knife.

I froze. 'Your mother said—'

'My mother!' she erupted. 'After coming to your office, my mother made me back off. She said suing the university wouldn't solve anything. She said it was nobody's fault. It couldn't have been helped. He was weak.' She snarled like a caged animal. 'He wasn't weak. He just wasn't . . . He just wasn't strong.' Her voice cracked. 'I blame her for not giving him the tools.'

'That's why you haven't spoken with her.'

'Yes. I hate her. Despise her. She could've helped him. Could've gotten him therapy. But she said therapy was for wimps.' She growled. 'I loved him. And you, Maggie? You. Let. Him. Die.'

Something went *thud*. And *thud* again. And then I heard *clawing*. In the lower rightmost crypt.

FORTY-FIVE

'A iden!' The straps holding my emotions in place broke. 'Let him out. Please. The police are on their way.'

Celine craned an ear. 'I don't hear sirens.'

'My husband is coming, too. I told him about you. About this.'

'Bull. Joshua, your *ex*' – she stressed the word – 'doesn't listen to you. He hates you as much as Aiden does.'

No, he didn't, but it wasn't the time to argue.

'Let Aiden go free, Celine, and kill me. Please. Let him live. Me for him,' I pleaded. 'That's your dream come true.'

She weighed my offer and brandished the knife. 'OK.'

I hurried to the crypt and pulled it open. The stench of urine fumed out, but also a gust of air. There had to be some kind of vent. Aiden was in sweats and hoodie, lying on his side, curled in a ball. He'd soiled himself. His ankles were tied. His hands were bound behind his back. His fingernails were bleeding. His knuckles, too. He must have been trying to claw his way to freedom. My stomach wrenched at the desperation he must have experienced.

'Aiden,' I said. 'It's Mom. I'm here.'

His mouth was gagged and looked painfully cracked, but his lips clung to the straw of the hydroflask above his head, a flask similar to the one he used when bicycling long distances. Celine had provided water. She wasn't a complete monster.

Or maybe she was. Maybe she'd wanted him to live longer to heighten his fear.

'Aiden, sweetheart, can you hear me?' I asked.

He tried to open his eyes but squeezed them shut, the moonlight obviously too much for him to handle. I reached to pet his hair.

'Don't, Maggie!' Celine barked.

I stepped back, hands raised.

After a long moment, she said, 'Slowly help him out of the drawer.'

Shakily, I hoisted him into a sitting position. Next, I lifted out his feet, then braced his back and helped him to the floor of the tomb. I placed him on his side, facing me. Beyond him, I glimpsed the drain at the center of the drawer, the reason he hadn't been lying in a pool of his urine. I also spied a black book with a busted spine. His journal. Beneath it were soggy pages of paper. Why had Celine buried it with him?

'Tie him up, ankles to wrists.' Celine produced a rope from her backpack.

A memory of me and Aiden, age six, making a macramé wall hanging flickered in my mind. Oh, how he'd struggled with the double half hitches.

Risking Celine's wrath, before tying him as she'd instructed, I undid the gag at the back of his head. Aiden coughed as he gulped in air.

'Tie him up, Maggie,' she repeated. 'Now.'

I bent Aiden's legs at the knees and did as she bade, ankles to wrists.

When I finished, she said, 'Your turn, Maggie. Lie down on your side over there.' She pointed to the opposite wall. 'Hands behind your back.' I did as commanded, facing Aiden. After she tied my wrists and ankles and linked them with another rope, she pulled a noose from her backpack and dangled it in front of my face. 'Made just for you.' She slipped it over my neck. 'A perfect fit,' she cooed, and attached the tail end to the rope around my ankles. She touched the tip of the knife to my face. I flinched and the noose tightened.

'How does it feel knowing you're strangling yourself?' she asked.

My eyes stung. My throat was parched with fear. 'Please . . .' I couldn't die yet. I needed to save my son. Where the hell were Josh and Filuzzi? 'Celine, please . . .'

'This is all your fault.' She clipped off her words. 'You were in charge. You didn't take your position seriously enough. You weren't present for your students. You failed.'

'I didn't know. I relive that nightmare every day of my life. If I could have saved Otis—'

'You had the power.'

'If I'd known, maybe. But I was in the dark.'

'That's a load of bull! You were the dean. The dean! You owed your students to be present. To be on top of things. My mother was stupid, but you were smart enough to know better. *You* should have known better.'

She grazed my nose with the tip of the knife.

The sting focused me. A drop of blood dripped on to my upper lip. Celine moved to the crypt. Peered in. Grunted with disgust. 'Aiden, you made a mess.'

While she was distracted and my hands were out of her line of sight, with minimal movements I loosened the knot around my ankles. I could feel some give. The slackening helped lessen the pull of the noose but didn't free me.

Aiden moaned. Opened his eyes. Registered my face. 'Mom . . .'

Thank heavens. He was coming around. Hearing his voice bolstered my resolve. 'Yes, sweetheart. I'm here.'

C'mon, Josh. Frank. Where are you?

Celine stood up, soggy pages of the journal in her gloved hands. 'Do you know what your son wrote about me?' She whirled around.

I stopped working the knot. Paid attention.

'He wrote that I'm nuts. That I'm a control freak.' She dropped the pages on the floor of the tomb, stomped on them, and strode to Aiden, giving me another unwatched moment. 'You shouldn't have written in your journal, Aiden. You . . .' She dragged the knife along my son's jaw.

He shuddered. But her taunting seemed to rouse him. To focus him. 'You . . .' He licked his lips and tried again. 'You killed . . .'

'Spit it out, Aiden. Cat got your tongue?'

'Celine, there's something I need to clear up,' I cut in, forsaking the knot, more concerned about preventing Aiden from suffering another ounce of pain. 'Keira figured out you'd changed your identity, didn't she?'

Taking the bait, she glanced over her shoulder but didn't really see me, and returned her gaze to Aiden.

'She planned to tell Aiden,' I went on, 'but you stopped her before she could, didn't you? I'm guessing you rented a car. Out-of-state. You knew her routine. You picked the perfect moment and ran her down in the crosswalk.' I could see the whole scenario play out like a scene from a movie. 'When I tell the police what to look for, they'll track down the rental agency you used. The car will have been damaged. The agency will have records, even if you paid in cash.'

Celine spun around. I froze. Her eyes sparked with venom. Had she seen that I'd loosened the knot? I waited. After a long moment, she pivoted and refocused her attention on my son.

'Keira,' Aiden whispered.

'Keira figured it out, didn't she, Celine?' I resumed my work on the knots. 'And you . . .' I recalled the words *She knew.* 'Aiden, how did you learn the truth about Celine? If you'd discovered it before Keira died, you would've turned to me or your father for help. Or at the very least the police. But if you didn't know the truth until after Keira died . . .' It came to me in a flash. 'Oh, my God, Keira left you proof, didn't she?'

'She . . . wrote it.'

'Where? In a journal? A letter?'

'Code.'

'A code. Of course.'

A smile tugged at the corners of Aiden's sore mouth. When he was a kid, Josh had taught him how to create ciphers. Enthralled by them, Aiden had taught Keira, using three hyphenated numbers like 125-25-5. The first would represent the page of the book, the next for a line on that page, and the last for a word in that line.

'What did the code translate to?' I asked.

'Don't . . .' He moistened his lips again. 'Trust Celine. Not . . . who she says she is. Her brother. Suicide. Seeking revenge.'

'Where did she hide the code so you could find it?'

'On my altar.'

I mentally smacked my forehead. What an idiot I was to have missed that. Aiden hadn't doodled the digits and drawings on the edges of the map for St Louis Cemetery No.1; Keira had. Too distracted by seeing the command to *Get a bead*, I hadn't paid attention to the pattern of the numbers. Each set of hyphenated digits must have corresponded to the page, line, or word of a book.

'I didn't realize . . . until two weeks ago,' Aiden said haltingly. 'Was rearranging . . . my altar.'

'Why didn't Keira tell you flat out?' I asked. 'Why hide it in a cipher?'

'Because I threatened her.' Celine coughed out a laugh and faced me, knife shimmering in the light. I stopped loosening the knot and let my hands go limp. 'I warned her if she told Aiden about me, I'd kill him.'

'How did Keira find out?' I asked.

'Like you, she saw the contact lenses and wondered what was up. Then one day she saw my cell phone light up when I'd stepped away from it. My mother's name appeared. Stupid me, I'd labeled the contact Mama. Like you, she thought my mother was dead. Realizing I'd lied and figuring I'd wormed my way into hers and Aiden's lives for a reason, she tracked down Mama at the hospital, pretended to be a reporter, and learned what happened to Otis. Digging further, she found out you were the dean at the time he killed himself. She put two and two together and confronted me.'

'Didn't Keira let on to you, Celine, that she'd created a cipher?' I asked.

'No, she was clever, I'll give her that. Aiden didn't tell me, either. I had to stumble upon it in his journal.'

'The code referred to which book, Aiden?' I asked. 'No, don't tell me. *Lord of the Flies*. Keira knew it was your favorite book.' Unwilling to part with a treasured story that had bonded him to her, he'd hidden it between the mattress and box springs to keep Celine from finding it.

Celine squatted beside Aiden, her face close to his. 'She loved you so much, dear husband, that she believed once she'd revealed to me what she'd figured out, I would back off. She even offered to pay me money to leave you and her alone, but I couldn't do that because—'

'Aiden wasn't your target,' I cut in. 'I was.'

Celine bounded to her feet and grinned at me, her teeth bared. 'Ding, ding, ding! Give the lady a prize!'

'After you killed Keira and got rid of the car you'd used as a weapon, you flew as fast as you could to the hospital to be by my son's side. To be the person he turned to in his grief. That had always been your plan. Win his love and make him turn against me. You knew cutting me off from my son would destroy me. But we were close. Too close. Even when I had to dial back the finances, he didn't hate me. And that vexed you.'

'When that plan didn't work,' Celine said, 'I knew I needed to do something worse. Not merely make him loathe you. Not simply kidnap and hide him.'

My insides went cold with panic as I realized what she was saying. What she planned to do. Her endgame. 'You're going to kill him here, in front of me, so my heart will break the way yours did when you lost your brother.'

'One cut at a time. But first—' Celine pounced and plunged the knife into my arm.

I shrieked. The noose constricted. I could barely breathe.

'Don't . . . hurt . . . her,' Aiden ordered, sounding stronger than he looked. Fury to avenge Keira, fueled by adrenaline, had to be aiding his recovery.

Celine took a step toward him. 'Your turn, baby boy.' She nicked his ear.

He whimpered.

She slashed his chin. He howled.

Was anyone close enough to hear? Josh? Filuzzi? For heaven's sake, a night watchman that Celine hadn't bribed?

Despite the throbbing in my arm and the lack of oxygen, I wriggled both of my feet. Thankfully, I'd loosened the rope enough that my ankle knot came free. The stranglehold of the noose eased a tad, but my hands were still bound behind me.

Out of the corner of my eye, I saw Aiden studying me. He realized what I was up to. He winked and then growled at Celine to hold her attention.

She cut his other ear.

His cries wracked me to my core. Using my shoulder for support, I scrambled to a stand, and started to stretch my arms backward as far as they would go so I could wedge my ass beneath the rope, but I didn't get the chance.

Celine whirled around. Shrieking, she charged me. I twisted and slammed her body with my shoulder, using one of the underhanded wrestling moves Benjie and his friends had taught me. She coughed and jabbed the knife into my side.

I reeled backward, the knife going with me. Hot searing pain shot through me. I stumbled and plowed into the gold-framed painting. Celine ran at me to retrieve the knife. I knee popped her, knocking her arm wide. Still on my feet, I shoulder-slammed her again and followed the blow with my other knee. It caught her in the solar plexus.

But Celine wouldn't give up. She grabbed the knife with both hands and yanked. It came free. I howled.

A gunshot resounded. The bullet careened off the ceiling of the tomb. Struck the wall near me. I ducked, expecting to see Filuzzi. I was wrong.

'Don't move, Celine!' Aiden rasped.

He'd untied his bonds – I'd purposely made his knots loose – and was sitting beside my tote bag, my father's service weapon in hand. Aiden, who'd never wanted to touch a gun. With all the evidence I'd collected and shoved into the bag, I'd forgotten about the Beretta.

'Drop the knife, or I'll shoot,' he said.

'Stop!' a woman screamed. Lily Bruno pushed open the gate and charged inside. She'd changed into jeans and a heavy sweater. Her hair was a ratty mess. She took in Celine. Me. Aiden.

'Mama!' Celine's mouth fell open. 'How did you—'

'You said you were coming here. I didn't understand why. But now I see.' Lily's voice was sharp. Accusatory. 'You want to kill this woman.'

'She killed Otis.'

'No,' I wailed. 'He took his own life. And you' – I jutted my chin toward Celine – 'buried my son alive in that crypt.'

Lily glowered at Celine. 'You did what?'

'I did it for Otis, Mama. For O. I needed to settle the score. You didn't follow through. You gave up. I couldn't. Don't you see? I had to fight. For him. For his honor. Don't you see? An eye for an eye. A boy for a boy.' Celine started to sob.

Lily squalled like a savage cat.

Aiden looked torn, trying to decide who to take out. He swung the gun toward Celine and then her mother and then back at his wife. 'Drop the knife, Celine.'

Celine screeched and rushed him.

He fired, but the bullet went wide, whizzing past Celine and piercing her mother. Lily fell to the floor.

Celine juddered and spun around. She raced to her mother. 'Mama!' She dropped the knife and grabbed Lily in her arms. 'Mama, don't die. Please. Don't die! I'm sorry, Mama. I'm so sorry.'

I hurried to the knife and kicked it toward the portal. 'Celine, I know how it feels to lose a brother.'

'Shut up.'

'I know how much courage it takes to put yourself back together. To go forward. To cope with the loss. The frustrating feeling of futility.'

'Mama,' Celine said, stroking her mother's hair.

As much as I despised this young woman, I understood her pain and wanted to help. 'You are strong, Celine. You did it. You graduated college. You forged a great career. You could have had a beautiful future and made your brother proud.' I hoped that was what Benjie would think if he could see me now. 'Unfortunately, you let the rage eat you from the inside. I understand . . .'

'Stop, Maggie.' Tears sluiced down Celine's cheeks.

A siren pierced the night air. Red lights flashed outside the crypt. Finally!

Doors slammed. Footsteps slapped pavement outside the crypt. Filuzzi raced in, a Colt .45 aimed at Celine. 'Police! Hands up!'

Seconds later, Josh pushed through the portal, his relief palpable.

FORTY-SIX

Three months later

I sat on the porch of my home, a glass of chardonnay in hand, the jazzy strains of an instrumental 'Amazing Grace' playing through my Bluetooth boombox speaker. I gazed at the yard. The impatiens, begonias, and zinnias were lush. A trio of hummingbirds were divebombing each other by the handblown glass feeder. A pair of squirrels skittered noisily as they chased each other up and down the sycamore. It was warm out, but the standing fan was keeping me cool enough. I preferred sitting outside as I wrote. The sounds and aromas of dusk made me feel more creative. The protagonist in my novel, which was a work in progress and nowhere near done, was no longer living on an island. She was a teacher in New Orleans bracing for the impending hurricane.

Write what you know, I taught my students. Yes, I'd gone back to teaching English Lit. Being the dean of Pelican or any university had lost its charm. Provost Southington had approached me a few times about reconsidering my decision. He had yet to find a suitable replacement. He assured me that Gregory Watley would no longer be requesting a change in the sports program. Watley's grandson had switched gears and was now a hurdler instead of an aspiring basketball guard, plus he didn't need someone to pad his grades; he had no intention of attending Harvard Business School. Every time Southington and I spoke, I told him that I was doing the right thing for me. For my family. On my desk in the English department, I'd set a plaque that Aiden had given me: *Listen. Discuss. Don't smother.* I treasured it. It made me focus on becoming the best teacher and mother I could be.

After the showdown with Celine, Aiden was taken to the hospital; he'd needed sedation and fluids. Lily Bruno had a tricky time of it for a month but ultimately made a full recovery. She didn't press charges against Aiden. A few days after I brought him home, he surprised me by asking to see my mother. How she'd enjoyed that visit. She'd called him Benjie and offered him the afghan for warmth. He'd blossomed under her fawning attention. Too traumatized to complete his education, he dropped out of Tulane. I hoped he would find the courage to go back.

For the time being, he was living with me and painting. Not tombs. No more torsos, hands, and feet. Only birds. In particular, jackass penguins. Dr Swinton assured him that he would feel closure after Cici's trial. Celine had reverted to her given name. Her attorney had filed a motion to have her evaluated for competency following the arrest. She pleaded not guilty by reason of insanity. Dr Swinton also assured Aiden that after Cici was sentenced, he would once again be able to focus on his digital design work and studies. I prayed that would be the case.

Rosalie Hunt had relocated to California. Occasionally, a postcard arrived in the mail for Aiden with the initial *R* hidden somewhere on the front of the card. I'd told him the truth about her. He threw each of the cards away. Lies, he'd said, didn't sit well with him.

One of Nicky Bilko's crew was convicted of killing Bilko. He'd wanted to take over Bilko's turf and was now serving a long prison sentence for murder. Underhill's condominium project was halfway to completion. He was all over the news touting how extraordinary it was going to be. Coach Tuttle was still the gymnastics coach. His wife attended every event. Axel, too, though all of them continued to keep their arrangement a secret.

Josh and Tess got married, as planned, but after Aiden's latest visit to see them, he'd hinted that there was already trouble in paradise. Tess wanted Josh to give up his career. Josh was resisting, as I'd predicted. Whenever Aiden visited his father, he got an earful about pursuing one's dream no matter what roadblocks stood in the way. He got the same earful from me, so in that regard, Josh and I were providing consistent parenting. Occasionally, Josh and I met for coffee. We agreed that our chance had come and gone. I wasn't dating anyone, but I didn't feel the need to. I enjoyed my own company and the company of the imaginary friends I was writing about.

As for Frank Filuzzi, he'd extended a couple of invitations for me to come to a barbecue and meet his family. I'd declined each time. I didn't want to relive the agony I'd experienced while searching for my missing son, and seeing Filuzzi would have dredged up those feelings. Plus I was pretty sure he hoped to introduce me to one of his friends. Dating a cop again was not in my future. Ever.

My cell phone rang. It was Inner Peace Assisted Living calling. I answered.

A nurse said, 'Your mother would like to say hello.'

I smiled. On most occasions, my mother wasn't grasping who I was, but the staff had warmed to me because I was now visiting her weekly. They would initiate these calls. When I visited, I would read her excerpts from my novel. I wasn't sure she understood that I was the person writing them, but like the excellent English teacher she'd been, she always had comments about how to give the story more depth. I relished every one of them.

The day after the ordeal in the tomb, Gina had touched base, saying she intended to stay with her mother until she passed. She'd suggested, for perhaps the umpteenth time, that I find a therapist. So I'd taken her advice. I wanted to be a better mother. I wanted to mend my relationship with Aiden. I regretted having lost Josh. The therapist pointed out that my anger at losing my brother, and subsequently, losing my father and mother to grief, was at the core of my problem. True, not having them in my life had made me self-sufficient and strong-willed, but it had also made me bitter. To be a better mother – a better woman – I needed to engage with people. Not always be the boss or the reliable one. I listened to the therapist and I processed. I agreed with almost everything she said. Almost.